fast sofa

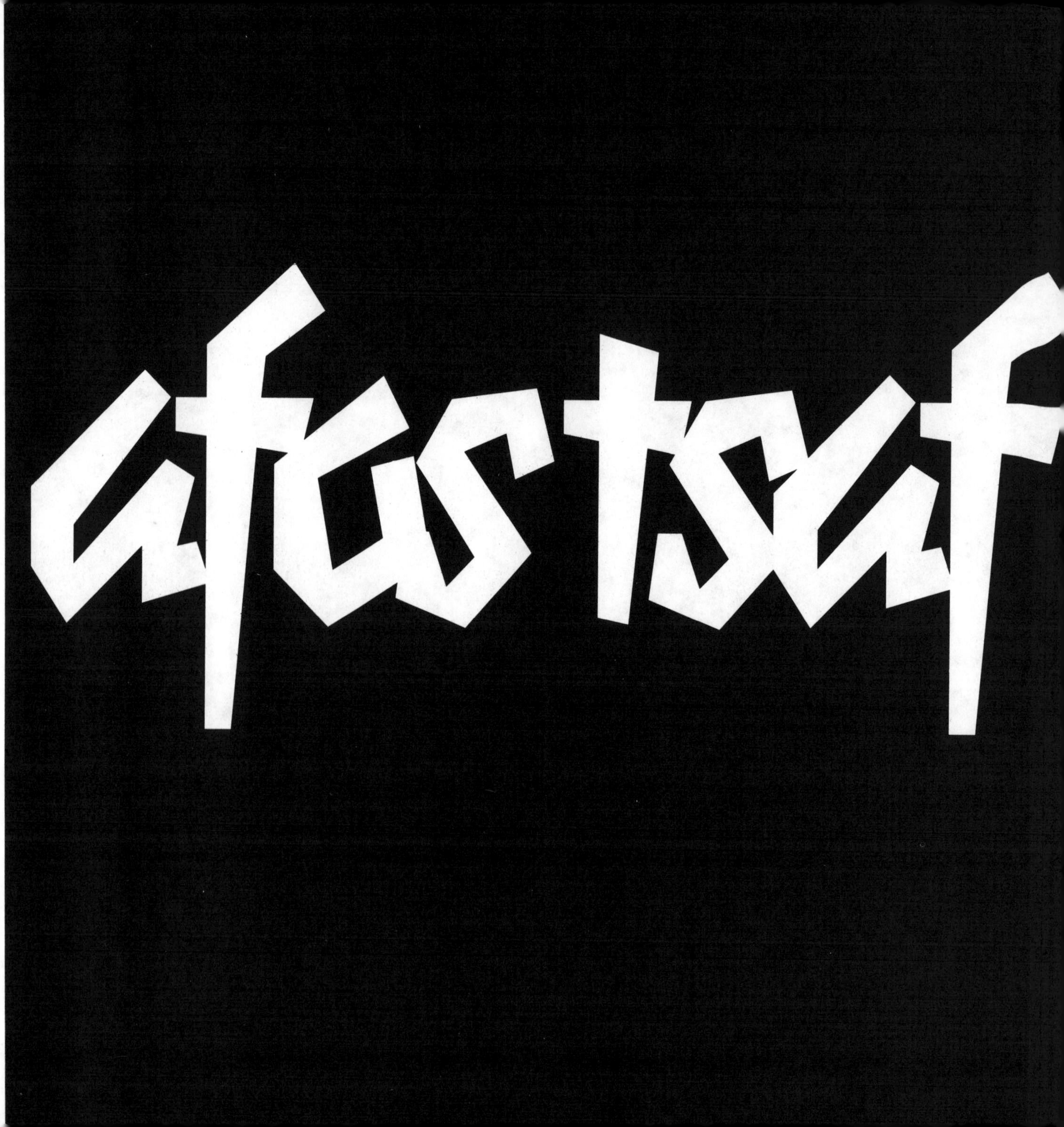

Bruce Craven

fast sofa

illustrations by mike louth

New York • Inc. • Morrow • William • Quill

It is the policy of William Morrow and Company, Inc., and its imprints and affiliates, recognizing the importance of preserving what has been written, to print the books we publish on acid-free paper, and we exert our best efforts to that end.

Library of Congress Cataloging-in-Publication Data

Craven, Bruce, 1960- Fast Sofa / Bruce Craven.
p.   cm.   ISBN   0-688-12336-8
I.   Title.   PS3553.R2745F37   1993
813'.54—dc20   92-20167
                                            CIP

Book design by Michael I. Mendelsohn and Veronica Ahn of M 'N O Production Services, Inc.

Printed in the United States of America

First Quill Edition

1   2   3   4   5   6   7   8   9   10

Grateful acknowledgment is made to the following:

"Dragstrip Riot" by Chris D. and Wayne James. Copyright © 1992 by Shakeytown Music (BMI). Administered by Bug. All rights reserved. Used by permission.

Stanza from "The Walls Do Not Fall," from H. D.: Collected Poems, 1912–1944. Copyright © 1982 by the Estate of Hilda Doolittle. Reprinted by permission of New Directions Publishing Corp.

Lines from Duino Elegies and The Sonnets to Orpheus by Rainer Maria Rilke, traslated by A. Poulin, Jr. Copyright © 1975, 1976, 1977 by A. Poulin, Jr. Reprinted by permission of Houghton Mifflin Company. All rights reserved.

"Killed by Death" by Ian Kilmister, Philip Campbell, Michael Burston, and Peter Gil. Copyright © 1984 by EMI Music Publishing Ltd. Rights for the U.S. and Canada controlled and administered by EMI Intertrax Music Inc. All rights reserved. International copyright secured. Used by permission.

For Tim Dwight

&

#32

FAST

Gods, goddesses
wear the winged head dress

of horns, as the butterfly
antennae,

or the erect king-cobra crest
to show how the worm turns.

—H.D.
"The Walls Do Not Fall," *Trilogy*

Every angel's terrifying. Almost deadly birds
of my soul, I know what you are, but, oh,
I still sing to you!

—Rainer Maria Rilke
"Second Elegy,"
Duino Elegies

If you squeeze my lizard
I'll put my snake on you
I'm a romantic adventure
And you're a reptile, too.

—Ian "Lemmy" Kilmister, Motörhead
"Killed by Death," *No Remorse*

Craven

So let's put our pedal to the metal
before they devise our demise,
gonna rip it up, tear it down,
drive around and around . . .

—**Chris D., The Flesh Eaters**
"Dragstrip Riot," Dragstrip Riot

Part One

Napping With Angels

Something clicked midway through Pleasure Quest. Something clicked and Rick paused, Ginger Quail's engorged labia lowering upon the question mark of the nurse's tongue. Rick paused, Ginger's pleasure a tight-lipped grimace—a puppy yelp. Rick's hips drifting as Tamara's fingers scratch his thighs. Their bodies lit from the pageantry of the Magnavox. Ginger tumbling onto the steel examination table. Tamara's eyes snapped shut. Darts of pleasure piercing Rick's neck. Ginger's smooth skin buffed to a high gloss, honeyed with attention; her hair a bleached fan. The image on the TV sick with shadow, drawing back to reveal a complex net of gently restraining arms. Ginger in the hospital bed, surrounded by nurses. Tamara, wiggling across the wild prairie of mattress. One slick kiss on the tip of Rick's finger.

An old whitewashed picket fence, a red silo, a rusted truck. Ginger Quail out for a drive. Flat tire. Trapped by the baddest female farmhands in the West. Faded overalls. Big work boots. Bales of hay. A pitchfork.

Swallows banking, pillowed beyond the oaks in a thousand black points of light. The TV a kaleidoscopic cavern. Ginger turning, hungry for the glow of the strap-on; hungry for the grin of dusk, her captors adjusting the coarse woolen blanket. A big heavy car shines in the moonlight.

Ginger sighing. Closing her eyes in the firelight.

1 ◄ ◄ ◄

A crackle of curtains and Tamara, one hand gripped the shade cord, the other patted the curve of her naked hip. The window streaked clean with Windex. Afternoon. Lavender blossoms of hibiscus against the white of the neighboring apartment building. Hollywood. Traffic outside nasty with persistence.

"Let's go, Rick . . . I can't afford to be late again."

Rick pressed his head against his arm, his body trembled. Magnified genitals flashed, a ghost-white heat lightning, an afterimage: *the flickering of indistinct bodies slapping; threads of indigo swept from the awkward shudder, the arched back, the silver of breasts. The firelight.* An aftertaste of TV static. "Okay, I'm moving. . ." he grunted. "Just relax."

Tamara nodded, padded off, a Winston trailed smoke behind the long angle of her. She turned at the bathroom door and looked back. Rick groaned himself upright. Tamara's down comforter trimmed his waist. He stared around and looked confused. "I've got to be there by one-thirty," she added.

Rick traced the spine of his teeth with his tongue, unraveled from the comforter, and scratched at the wad of hair between his legs. Pinched his penis and wiggled it, then limped over to his boots, his Levi's and white T-shirt and flannel shirt. The boots were emerald leather, flat-heeled. The salesman called them *ropers.*

The shower started behind the bathroom door. Rick tapped on the VCR, pushed Rewind. Tapped on the Magnavox, pushed Play, leaned back and pulled on his Levi's. Ginger Quail flashed on the TV. Rick yawned as she stumbled through a brief patch of dialogue. Helpless, her voice reminded him of the sound of stacking plates. Clacky. Fragile. Eyes turquoise, Ginger's nervous fingers clasped and unclasped her wrists.

Rick whistled. Man, was she *dumb*. The video spliced abruptly, a pair of male hands on her hips. "Of course, you can," she begged with porcelain assent, "only *harder!*"

Rick watched, Ginger fucked. A vein visible along her neck. Her moans grinding through the air.

He liked the way her bleached hair tickled her shoulders. He liked the way her hands opened and closed, flickering pink, against the mattress.

But she was *way* stupid. Nice house, no one home.

►　►　►　**2**

"This has to be the lamest machine I've ever seen. You call this a car?"

"Yeah, I call it a car. It's an *American* car," Rick said. "Remember them? Big, fast? Buick Skylark GS. Automatic transmission, oil leak . . . but we'll deal. Now you getting in or what?"

Jack pulled the door but it failed to latch. He shook his head with disdain and looked at Rick. Jack's face was sunburned from riding his motorcycle. His eyes strangely lunar. What Tamara had once called *sensitive.* Jaw obtrusive. His body muscular from the weight room, but soft at the edges from too much beer. Girls had called him pretty when he was in high school.

Jack thought of high school too much.

Oakdale High in Burbank, California. Burbank. A wing tip of the San Fernando Valley caught smooth between the pressure of the Hollywood hills and the Verdugo hills. Concrete. Mediterranean flora. Strip malls marked with Western wear outlets, appliance stores, coffee shops. Promiscuous oak trees and their shrub relatives fenced back against the concrete channel of the Los Angeles River or pushed up into the foothills, where the really rich people lived. The hot stomach grid with its square lawns, white sidewalks, freeway greenbelts. Then sometimes it would rain. Leave the brown sky blue. Chains of tight, well-kept houses. Algebraic apartment complexes, stairwells stacked up around fat, jungle plants. The movie studios. The TV studios. The shiny corporate aeries.

Jack and Rick had been friends since that fourth grade recess when Jack had put his red Jansport daypack down on the concrete and punched two fifth graders who had shoved Rick against a fence. That was a different time. A different Los Angeles. Shooting caroms. *Johnny Appleseed* flickering in an air-conditioned grade school auditorium. Weird music blasting out of some big kid's house down the street. Throwing rocks at cars. The best of times, the worst of times. But when it was time to ride your Schwinn Sting-Ray bicycle home, you still couldn't make it all the way without lying down in the ivy to gasp. Your lungs like pink sea anemones. The air like water you'd never want to drink.

Yeah, things hadn't changed that much.

And it had not been the last time Jack had helped Rick around violence.

"Tamara's car's in the shop. Like permanently," Rick explained, peering over his green Ray•Bans. He handed Jack the free end of a bungee cord. "Hook it in there." He pointed to the lattice of shredded vinyl and soldered steel that was the passenger door.

Jack stared. "You've got to be kidding?"

Rick reached into the pocket of his flannel shirt. "Got you a present last night." He pulled out a pair of inexpensive aviator-style sunglasses with metallic purple lenses. DISCO was printed upon each glittering ellipse. "Tamara and I went to Magic Mountain last night to ride the roller coasters." Rick pointed out the window at the white sky. "Figured you can always use extra protection. The sun-god is cool, but he *kills.*"

Jack nodded, slipped the sunglasses on, and opened the glove compartment. "No smokables?" He was wearing a blue, wrinkled button-collar shirt and a tie with frayed edges and thin blue and yellow stripes. Underneath, his dark blue T-shirt was visible. Jack yanked the tie loose and struggled out of both the tie and the wrinkled shirt.

"Too bad," said Rick. "You looked real nice."

"No *ganja?*" Jack scrunched the shirt and tie into the seat crevice.

"Nope. Not with. Tamara's been giving me a hard time about it. You know, *adulthood.* But back at the ranch . . ." Rick grinned.

Jack removed a transparent plastic folder from the glove compartment. Flipped through it. The folder was filled with math tests. Xeroxed math tests with scribbles, doodles, and different names. Scores inked in with red felt-tip. "I'm really burnt. I *need* to get baked." His blue T-shirt fluttered as the '71 Buick Skylark rolled down Sunset Boulevard. The under-inflated tires sucked at the cement. The door rattled. "Can you dig it? First lunch with my dad and then the Suzuki gacks." Jack shook his head. "I'm too old for this grief."

Rick nodded. "How's work going?"

The twin DISCOs were tinged with a patina of gold. "More misery, more grief. Nothing but assholes. Drunk business types. The scene is a *serious* stress."

"We need gas."

Jack shrugged. "*We?*"

"*You.* Unless you're into walking." Rick loved this Buick. "Like what's the evil dad doing in Hollywood anyway?"

"Nothing." Jack looked out the window.

"What do you mean, *nothing?*"

"He wanted me and Jennifer to meet the mystery siblings this time. The *stepfamily.* Like what am I going to say to them, right? A bunch of fucking ugly people I've never met in the past fourteen years. Like what am I going to say to my *stepbrother?* Hey, dude, nice face, looks like mine. But no, Dad said it was *time.* Time to talk. Time to clear the air. Time to make amends. Major error. *Dad* drives a DeLorean now. Got a *deal* on it. Can you believe it? A *DeLorean?*"

Rick was silent.

"Mom hated sports cars."

"Good eats?"

Jack shook his head, looked down, and flexed his forearm. "All right . . . I guess, but it was like art food. Three scallops, a spear of asparagus, and a little thing that looked like a root."

"Yum. What'd you talk about? The last fourteen years?"

Jack grinned flatly. "We talked about *him.* And the price of his favorite champagne. We talked about anything he wanted to talk about. Just like when he invited Jennifer and me at Christmas, only this time Jennifer figured it out. Jen won't even deal with him. So I got to *entertain* the *family."* He reached over and turned on the radio. The speakers implanted in the dash emitted a solitary whine. "It's a short," Rick said over the noise. "A wire gig."

Jack thinking about his father and his weird disappearance fourteen years ago. The stepbrother only a few years younger. This bad scene his mother never had to face. For fourteen years, Jack and his sister, Jennifer, used to play a guessing game. Take turns. Their father was a CIA double agent. No, their father was a successful gun runner. Their father was on the lam. Maybe he was wanted for political reasons. Maybe he was a criminal. But their father would be saved. Rescued someday, maybe even by them.

They never guessed that he was on the run from Burbank. On the run *from* them. From Jack Weiss. From Jennifer Weiss. From their mother.

They never guessed that he would just pop up a year ago on Easter and invite Jack out for a round of golf. He had joined some new church. The church of assholes, thought Jack. Let's have lunch. He said it was the first he had heard about their mother's death. Yeah, they never guessed their father was just living in Thousand Oaks. Living at the other tip of the San Fernando Valley, making his loot in software.

Rick watched the Hollywood Bowl drift past on the left. The whine increased as he accelerated. "Yeah, definitely some wires crossed," he explained professionally. "It's a three-fifty," he added, "Power central."

Jack swept his hand through the air. "They made four fifty-fives . . . where'd you get this piece of shit anyway?"

Rick turned the radio off. "It was a gift. Sort of. Kind of a *deal.*"

"Yeah?"

"Yeah. Remember Estelle Maddox? *Mrs. Maddox?*"

Jack shook his head as the Buick window filled with slopes of manicured lawn and the flapping pennants of a condominium complex.

"Sure you do. Taught geometry at Oakdale. I saw this Xeroxed ad tacked up at Kmart and gave her a call, you know . . . just to remind her of all the good times we'd had and clue her in to how good I was doing these days thanks to her teaching. Before I knew it we were talking about her car and I had myself a deal." Rick smiled. "She said she'd rather give me the brother-digit 'cause I was cool, you know, *meant something to her.* Like I wasn't just some Cal Worthington used-car dealer dude."

"Did you write her a check?"

Rick looked from the tangle of approaching intersection and turned up the corner of his lip.

"And she signed the pink slip?"

"It's not my fault. If she really knew how to *teach* I'd probably be some big finance wizard or fat-cat computer lord like your dad . . . besides, her doctor was tense about her driving 'cause of her eyesight."

"How much?" Jack turned the radio back on.

"A hundred bucks, plus change. I figure I can make it in the next week and then I can square things. The problem was wheels. That was *crucial.*"

Jack shrugged. This was Rick. Things were always *crucial.*

"Besides," added Rick. "It's like survival of the fittest. The old and weak are weeded out by the young and strong. It's all part of the evolutionary process. Darwin full-on. I'm just the wolf doing the weeding . . . getting blind ancient cunts off the road." He cackled · and looked up in the rearview, showing his straight teeth. His eyes glistened behind the sunglasses, the bridge of his nose like a finger pointed straight at your face.

He guided the Buick toward the red stripes of a minimart service station. Then a Highway Patrol car edged up. Fat, black, white. Predatory.

Rick checked the speedometer. He hated this scene. Cops with monster engines going twenty-seven miles per hour in the fast lane.

"Fuckers," he whispered. Nursed the Skylark to the right and crept past the mirrored gaze of the officers. *Robo-squids.* He knew they did this just for kicks. Just daring you . . .

Rick stepped on the gas and passed the black-and-white with a rush, tires bouncing over the curb of the service station entrance. The back fender scraped.

The Highway Patrol car glittered away into the sunlight.

Jack stared at the gas pumps. Oblivous.

"Fuck the police," Rick said.

"What?"

"I said, fuck the police. They're fascists. Nazis with a license."

Jack nodded. Stared out the window.

"Forget your dad, man. Just get over it. He's a loser. A squid. He's not your fault . . ."

Jack's eyes were heavy in his face. That Jesus Christ look. But what was really starting to get on Rick's nerves was the sad grin Jack cultivated. A grin that crawled out and said everything was over. A grin that said *I give up.*

And it was just 'cause Jack couldn't get laid. Like the night the two of them blew out to Santa Monica on Jack's Suzuki to catch the Red Hot Chili Peppers. Dancing with these girls with chopped hair, pointy hipbones, and red lips. Smoking some bomber joint in the parking lot. Rick finally turning up his eyes into the stained morning, checking out the stuffed animals and posters of the Cure in some strange bedroom. Jack back in Burbank, passed out. Drunk, sweat-soaked, alone.

"I said I'm broke," Rick added.

Jack had put in extra hours in the gym. It showed in his arms as he shifted. "Yeah?"

"*Yeah,*" Rick explained.

Jack dug into the pocket of his Levi's and handed Rick eight dollars. "I think you're just scared."

"What?"

A man in tennis shorts fumbled with the gas nozzle.

"Cops. They're tough and they don't take shit and that ticks you off. You don't like that someone can tell you what to do. You don't like that people can stand for something."

Rick made an *oh wow, perceptive* face. "Is this bartender philosophy or *what?* Shit, I'm not scared of shit. I just don't like people who get *off* on messing with my life. Nazi clerks. They're losers. They're a waste of taxpayer cash. The only reason to have cops is 'cause of those real-life TV cop shows. Like great, so they're cheaper than *actors.* Big deal. But like are you safe 'cause they're *around?* No. The whole city's rolling with all these *sets.* Tool down to catch a Laker game and next thing you're buzzing up to a stoplight and looking at a lot of pissed-off gangbangers in a cherried-out Pontiac filled with semiautomatic ugliness. Just out taking a break from all that bliss of subsidized housing and unemployment. Yeah, cool. AK-47s, Uzis, Mausers, Brownings, Glocks. Ordnance Central. Just the Krenshaw Mafia Bloods or the Ghost Town Crips out *frontin'.* Good thing the police have been stick-whipping people for speeding. Look at someone wrong . . . and *later. Smoke.* And forget all these fucking *cholo* dudes. Or the Koreans. The Chinese. The Vietnamese. Am I forgetting anyone?" Rick looked up at the torn ceiling upholstery. "Oh yeah, *the white people.* We're the best. We just drive around in Japanese sedans with stupid-ass computer-babble names like *Sentra* and *Integra.*

The white people? Forget it. Just hiding up in the hills or at the beach." Rick reached into the ashtray and pulled out a stubbed Tiparillo. He hit the cigarette lighter with the heel of his hand. What the fuck was he talking about? Oh yeah. "And the police? *Fuck the police.* Jesus, this city is a hardware store. One big raging Western hardware store. The only difference is you've got *these* Nazis tooling around and messing with your fun. And I don't care what color a cop is, they're all Nazis. They all speak the same language. They all speak the language of Handcuff, Nightstick, Stungun, Bullet. And I hate that language. I like driving. I like the wind at one hundred miles an hour. I like it fast. I like it loud. Fuck those squids telling *me* what to do!"

Jack shrugged. "Yeah, a real *outlaw.*"

Rick got out of the car, strolled in to prepay, then filled the tank, digging behind the license plate for the nozzle aperture. Got the air hose and pumped the tires up. The tire gauge on the pump was busted. He filled them good. Better gas mileage, better handling. Ran his fingers down the smears of steel belt that showed through the tread. Wiped the excess gasoline on his Levi's. Thinking, strangely enough, of that old TV show *Kung Fu.* Something about this Buick Skylark made him think of *Kung Fu.* Maybe it was the flayed '71 gold paint, maybe the used-car scent of metal and defeated leathery vinylish upholstery. Something about this car reminded him of the desert and being a kid in Los Angeles. Kwai Chang Caine walking under the hot yellow sky. Leaving no mark on the rice paper. One lone dude hiking across the desert. Or how about the episode where he gets shot by the assassin? Arrow buried in his back. Yeah, that'd been one of TV's *crucial* episodes. Sonic wildness. *Adventure.* Mano a mano. Or like the time Caine was a prisoner with this young dude with greasy hair, real predisco, post-Woodstock hair, and they were in this corrugated miner's shack, left to die of dehydration. Except Caine had taught the young dude how to dream of rivers. To dream of fields of snow. Their bodies cooling, surviving in a fiction of cold waters. The bad guys outside spitting plug juice. Waiting.

Rick pulled the Buick into the Jack in the Box parking section across the street from the liver-colored Disney Studio building. He found a space next to a white AMC Matador with a bumper sticker that went MY KID BEAT UP YOUR HONOR STUDENT. Jack and Rick walked in and each ordered a couple of Super Tacos. Rick took Dr Pepper and onion rings. Jack took skim milk. No onion rings. No fries. He paid. "Ugh," said Rick. "Can't get over that white stuff, huh? That'll kill you, Logan." Logan was one of the aliases of Jack's favorite Marvel Comics character. Wolverine. A member of the good mutants, The Uncanny X-Men. *Logan* and *Patch*. Patch was the recent alias Wolverine was working under in doing whatever it was comic heroes did all day long. *Logan* and *Patch*. Rick liked to interchange them.

Jack nodded, "Can't work out on sugar." He squinched his stomach. "Got to lose a few."

"So where are we these days, Logan? Where are the bad guys, the foes of freedom and righteousness? In the Canadian Rockies? Japan? Fresno? Or that other place . . . where the dinosaurs hang . . . what is it called . . . the Savage Land? Where goeth the fierce Wolverine? Supertough hombre of the mighty mutant team of X?"

Jack took a mouthful of taco. "Stith en Mattlesore."

"What?"

"Madripoor. Still there. Low Town. We've bought an interest in the Princess Bar. It's a crime-infested island where Tyger Tiger, alias Jessan Hoan, lives, remember?"

Rick nodded professorially. "Yeah. I forgot my notes. What about that other nectar, what's her name, the Japanese wayhone?"

Wayhone was Rick's supreme term for an attractive woman, although he would rely on *nectar* and *scruff* for punchiness. For rhythm. Wayhone was Rick's creation, a combination of the Hawaiian *wahine*, with *very honed*, i.e., in shape and aesthetically pleasing. *Hone* was also an intransitive verb meaning to whine, moan, and yearn for. Rick had looked it up once in *The American Heritage Dictionary*. *Way*, of course, was also just *way*, critical modifier to Rick's vocabulary.

"Mariko." Jack explained. "She's our love. We are her champion. She is a woman of culture and breeding. We are a superhero and outlaw. A mutant with the power to heal our body. We are both loner and psychotic. A guardian of society, yet an outsider. Beast and man. Problem is after being forced to kill her father, Shingen, who brought shame to Clan Yashida and who was being a real pain in the ass, we were given the honor sword but Mariko left us at the altar while under the spell of Mastermind. Called us *gaijin*. Which means sort of like *hessian. Mondo-valley.* Foreigner. This was cold and we took it hard. It was right after we'd joined the X-Men and dusted these characters Silver Samarai and Viper . . . saving Mariko's life. Thus, the betrayal was particularly harsh."

"And?" Rick licked his fingers.

"Anyway, we're in Madripoor. It's our kind of place. Lots of action. We use our adamantium claws, our keen wolverine sense of smell, and our mutant healing factor whenever necessary. We like the tradition and ritual of the East."

"You like the submissive wayhones," said Rick. "Like Mariko."

Jack finished his milk. Mariko. Proud, strong, beautiful Mariko. And Rick dared call her *submissive?* "Duty holds her back. The time is just not right. We respect that . . ."

"I don't get it."

Jack looked at Rick. "We're sort of into this idea of mastering the vicious part of us . . . the animal thing that makes us such an awesome X-Man. We are a natural killer. We go into *berserker* rages. We can defend the common good. But this is not enough. We are tormented by inner suffering. Mariko offers us something different."

Rick looked out the window at the neon sign for the Pago-Pago Bar. He looked back at Jack and shrugged toward the doorway. "In Burbank, *we* go to the Pago-Pago. It's like the Princess Bar 'cept you don't have to fly to distant Madripoor. Burbank's cool that way."

As they were walking out the door, Jack thought,

The garden has been wrecked, its pattern broken. Order turned to chaos. The story of my life.

The tradition and ritual of the East . . .

Like Wolverine, Jack was burnt on the West. Burnt on wilderness.

They each had a shot of something in front of them, ice cubes melting. "Mötley Crüe? You must be kidding?" Jack was incredulous. "Waste of umlauts."

"No, man. They're cool. At least that one album *Girls, Girls, Girls*."

Rick was drinking tequila. Jack, whiskey.

Jack was offended. "If they're so good. How come you never play them on that piece of shit you call a *stereo* . . . that turntable? I've never even *heard* you play *Girls, Girls, Girls*."

Rick shrugged. "I'm just saying it's a good *album*."

"You mean those strippers on the record sleeve? Wake up, Rick. Substance counts. Go down to the Tropicana if you want to see blondes with fake tits. Now take The Flesh Eaters—"

"*Jesus!*" Rick spat. "They're dead, aren't they? That's like earliest Eighties. If we're going back ten years, might as well roll into the Seventies. Might as well crank up Hawkwind. Or go with some fierce Lynyrd Skynyrd."

"Aren't you leaving someone out?" Jack gave him a hard look.

Rick sipped his tequila. "Oh, you mean what's their face?"

"Nazareth," Jack said. "Their name is Nazareth."

"Right," said Rick. "Right, right."

"You know, Rick . . . those dudes *mattered*. That album *Hair of the Dog* was *very* cool.

Cool for the Seventies. Cool for the Eighties. Cool now. Cool forever. 'Hair of the Dog.' 'Miss Misery.' 'Love Hurts.' 'Whiskey Drinkin' Woman.' 'Please Don't Judas Me.' That purple wolverine creature on the front." Jack looked off toward an empty pool table. "The Seventies were all right thanks to Nazareth."

"Logan, *dude.* I *understand* the Seventies. We grew up on common soil. Nazareth. Hawkwind. Skynyrd. Zeppelin. Aerosmith. All cool here, hombre. But let's remember that Skynyrd are . . . *were* . . . the only *Americans.* Those other dudes are like English or German or *Scottish.* And"—Rick was feeling a fierce theoretical *urge*—"let us not take this thing too far. You deal *me* grief over Mötley Crüe and then you present me no more *recent* choice than the Flesh Eaters or Nazareth? Are those even wolverines? They look like deformed owls. Or some really pissed-off prehistoric poodle creatures with yellow eyes. Shit." Rick finished his tequila. "Who even knows what a wolverine looks like? But I'll back off on the Crüe. It's shaky soil. But since we're talking late Eighties. Give me G N' R."

"Okay." Jack was thinking of his father, his *stepfamily.* The air smelled of fancy cologne. Champagne bubbled in fluted glass. Reflections sat in white china plates and watched the ceiling. Jack couldn't figure out the forks. The knife was a strange shape and wouldn't cut. "But first of all Aerosmith *is* American. And I'll give you G N' R. But not *Appetite for Destruction.* You know, Slash called that their Motörhead album? Sacrilegious."

"Look, Patch. Aerosmith is from *Boston.* That's not America. That's like a theme park *in* America. Like let's go to Bostonland and see where they threw tea in the water about a million years ago. Yeah . . . maybe we can go down to the Boston Garden and watch the Celtics get *dusted* by the Lakers."

"Rick . . . if Boston isn't America, then there *isn't* any America. You can't get more American than *Boston.* You ever been there?"

"Have you?" Rick finished his tequila. " 'Cause if you go, you might want to pop over to Scotland and visit Nazareth. Scotland, Bostonland. They're practically neighbors."

Jack finished his whiskey. "You're not only an *outlaw,* you're kind of a geography *wizard.* No wonder the girls like you."

"They like me 'cause I don't mope around all day doing stupid shit like *work* and *lift weights.*" Rick motioned his empty glass at Jack. "But speaking of Guns N' Roses . . . since we *were* talking about America, like *real* America, and since they *are* American . . . I disagree on *Appetite for Destruction.* That was an *unhinged* piece of work. Fundamental to everything that followed . . . and will follow. The whole Bay-City-Rollers-on-junk attitude. This is solid footing, dude. G N' R. Straight up, no chaser. White-trash lyrics. Robert Williams's rape-machine dust jacket. Naked wayhone liner notes. W.Axl Rose hip wiggle. Grinning skulls on a cross. Tattoos. Punchy guitar. This is *crucial.*"

"Take your pick, Rick . . . but don't walk away from *tradition.* And don't slam Nazareth. *Or* the Flesh Eaters." Jack was not going to let all this slide. "G N' R is your call. But *remember* Motörhead." Jack let *that* one sink in for a moment. They had this argument often. No, Rick was *not* going to argue with Motörhead. Jack put his palms flat on the table. "Nazareth was the wood. The Flesh Eaters were the nails. And Motörhead *was* the hammer."

Rick thought about getting a beer. He hated sitting in a bar without a drink. And Jack's argument was weak. "That doesn't even make sense, Logan. If anything, Ted Nugent was the wood. X *were* the nails. And the Butthole Surfers *are* the hammer. Maybe Motörhead can be some kind of hyperfine wood finish . . ."

"Motörhead, Rick. I'm just saying." And Jack watched Rick, feeling deep in his guts that this was not academic. "That Nazareth *was* the wood. The Flesh Eaters *were* the nails. And Motörhead *was the hammer.* Now, if you want to tell me that Metallica is the vise grip and Barry Manilow is the circular saw, okay . . . but what I'm talking about is Nazareth, The Flesh Eaters, and Motörhead. It spreads *across* decades. Across national boundaries. Louder and faster than your pretty boys, G N' R. Don't *even* try to argue with Motörhead . . ."

Rick realized they had a problem. Because even Jack for all of his sense of *tradition* couldn't be completely serious. Sure, he had to concede Motörhead. And the others were cool. But were they really that *fast?* Were they fast *enough?* In all seriousness, he would have gone Metallica/X, (w/Billy Zoom) / Megadeth, *or* maybe some hyperspeed creation like Slayer/ Angry Samoans/Anthrax. Some sandwich of late-Eighties speed with a tasty slice of early-Eighties attitude. But that was Rick. He was always looking *forward.* He could hardly expect even his best friend to have the same excellent *sense* of what was crucial on the horizon. Jack was not out there on the *frontier.* Jack was back in the cabin. Jack was into CDs, sure, but he only had about five or six, 'cause he was saving money. He had Nazareth's *Hair of the Dog* and Motörhead's two recent offerings. Black Flag's *Who's Got the 10 1/2?* And some new regrouped Flesh Eaters gig that he had found in the loser dump down at some music barn. Like can't sell it, dude. Take it for a nickel. An SST gig. Which was cool. SST was crucial. Nice shiny, smelly records . . .

Yeah. Jack had lost all of his albums in an electrical fire in his apartment last summer. S.O.L. First his mom dies, then his dad creeps back, then his house burns down. Heinous. No wonder he was bumming fierce. Everything he owned reduced to a black mattress, black carpet, black aquarium filled with steamed fish, and a black turd of melted record goo. So Jack went CD . . . a high-tech urge. Now Jack was saving money for something. Some big airplane road trip somewhere. Some figure-out-your-life kind of gig. Probably off to Wolverine Land. Japanland. He was crashing at his sister's place up the road, near the airport, watching her TV and hanging out. Doing his bartender scene at this yuppie fern bar. Saving. Saving. Plus, Jack had always stuck to his bands. Nazareth was a good example. I mean, *who* listened to Nazareth anymore? Maybe Jack *did* have a CD player, but Jack wasn't really into change. And that was cool. Jack had a good sense of *history.*

Jack had something solid. A little insane and angry, but solid. Way down where it counted.

They both stared at the bar TV, watching a list of sentences. "Look, dude." Rick pointed. It was a survey of the workplace. This list, ascending. *During This Fiscal Year, Two Americans Have Been Killed at the Workplace Due to Robotics.* "It could have been us, Patch. Killed by robots."

Jack looked around the bar. Rick could tell he was tense. Ready to start punching something. Rick watched him. What were they doing in a bar with no wayhone? And what about hoops? No Laker game? Not even a Clipper game? At least they were close to the apartment. Close to tuneage. Close to the fridge. "C'mon, Patch . . . let's go crank up some noise."

Jack ripped his cocktail napkin in half, then quarters, then delicate eighths. "Yeah, let's get out of here." His barstool scraped. He threw back his whiskey. The ice tapped against his teeth.

Rick's apartment was only a few blocks away. Jack thumbed through the phone bill, then shook his head. "None of these are mine." He tossed the bill to the carpet. Rick was in his burgundy recliner. A game show on the box. Imagine three six-foot game show hostesses dressed in shredded safari costumes, arms all cobralike above a pile of household appliances. Fake banana trees shine. Plastic coconuts piled in a cairn beside an ebony refrigerator. One of the hostesses is blonde. One brunette. One a redhead. The blonde motions toward a pirate-style treasure chest that brims with cutlery. A brigade of twelve-speed blenders and chromium toasters advance in formation from behind a distant curtain.

Rick put down the bong. "Check out the nectar. Those are serious breasts."

Store-bought, thought Jack. The blonde. Cosmetically modified. Necklace of boar's teeth rising. Jack helped himself to more marijuana, the fragrance drifted toward Rick. Twin cans of Schlitz malt liquor dangled from their fingers in the apartment air. The blue bull on the silver cylinder.

The camera panned to the contestants: a young graduate student from Cal-Poly Pomona, a high school teacher from up north in Fremont, and an accountant from Indianapolis, Indiana. The camera paused, caressing the accountant's blank face. The accountant reminded Rick of a traffic victim lost in that last second before impact.

The accountant waved and began to share with the audience about his wife, about how she'd had a *boudoir* photograph taken for his thirty-sixth birthday.

Shithead, thought Rick. Boudoir photographer. Republican.

He could just imagine their little kids grubbing around at the base of their sorry secondhand fridge. Yeah ... what a life they must have back in Indiana, Indianapolis. Wherever the fuck that was. Dad with his blank death stare. Watch him lift a glass of instant lemonade crystals. Or how about the *boudoir* cunt stacking Triscuits in her cellulite. And the kids. Definitely oversized maggots. Skin riddled with subterranean channels and passageways. Teeth cankerous spikes, a spittle of cheese and human flesh tucked up under the gums ...

Yeah, malt liquor. There was nothing like it for getting you fucked up.

"Need one?"

Rick nodded. The blonde TV hostess waved, eyes round, slick. Rick motioned toward Jack, "Why don't you put on something fast and turn down the tube. I could use a break ..."

Jack handed him a silver can.

Rick popped the Schlitz and held it up in the curtained sunset glow of the apartment. To Tamara, went his silent toast.

But last night was gone forever and with Tamara you never had too much fun without a nice long stretch of worry. Tenseness. Talking and talking about *commitment* and *responsibility*. The phone against your ear. Horniness like something in your eye.

Jack bent over the turntable, a purple silhouette against the curtains. Outside an ambulance hurried. The siren discord merging with the strains of Motörhead's *No Remorse*.

"You're right, Logan. These dudes are *crucial*. Very *unhinged*."

Jack nodded, and began to flip through the *TV Guide*. "When are you going to break into the present and get something compact-disclike?"

Rick watched a commercial for the New Feelings Alcohol Treatment Center. It was curious that his favorite shows were the target of every substance abuse center, populist attorney, and posturepedic furniture outlet in the Los Angeles basin. "Records are *crucial*. CDs are for losers. Slaves. Technosquids. I bet they buy a lot of CDs in Japan. Maybe you can bring me back some. They probably only cost about a hundred bucks each over there." Rick waved his Schlitz. "See anything?"

"What?" Jack looked up.

Rick pointed to the TV. The commercials had ended and a young black man sat on a sofa watching three small video screens superimposed above him. In each one a black woman smiled, frozen midframe. The black man was wearing a jacket that glimmered like cellophane. He had a comfortable manner and spoke without moving his hands. The host was intent, punctuating the man's pauses with a smile or a wink. They were surrounded by lavender arrows and red hearts. "TV," said Rick. "Anything on?"

Jack held the *TV Guide* sideways, sort of just staring off. "*Cupid's Arrow,* you know, the love game . . . which I dig fiercely." He dropped the magazine in his lap and took a long draw from his Schlitz.

Rick laughed. "That's serious herb, huh?"

Jack nodded and leaned back. Intoxication skewed his expression. He appeared calm.

Rick watched Jack, thinking about the time in high school when they'd taken this station wagon filled with gear up in the San Gabriels. Chowed some acid and gone bombing around in the middle of the night, climbing rocks and howling at the moon. They had made a big fire and thrown all this stuff on it, watching it burn and melt. The weirdest had been this typewriter, melting all over the gooey remains of a hollow metal skeleton ghost of a webbed lawn chair. A million shades. That's when Rick had turned to Jack and said that he,

Rick, was Satan. Lucifer himself incarnated in the body of a Burbank thrasher. The two of them standing on a promontory that overlooked the sprawling foothills and starlit quilt of the San Fernando Valley.

"*Six sixty-six,*" Rick whispered. "It's carved on my skull. And I've been here forever. Waiting to take your soul."

Jack had got spooked and walked off into the black pines. Yelling for Rick to stay away, stay away from me!

Rick would always remember the look on Jack's face. "Hey, man, what about the time I told you I was Satan?"

Jack finished his beer and crushed the can. "No," he answered evenly.

"Aw, c'mon! No *what?* That was *too* hilarious. You were seriously freaked."

"I don't remember." Jack stared at the television. "Must've been someone else."

"*Dude,* you know it was you! Fully. I remember 'cause you started going to those Christian youth meetings . . ."

"You're stoned. I've never even done LSD."

"Who said anything about that?" prodded Rick with a grin. "Yeah, you were one spooked critter. Our hero, the uncanny Wolverine, melts in the face of superior psychic powers. A battle rages. The fierce mutant. Alias Logan, alias Patch. Can't deal with the mental strength of that other-dimensional entity . . . *The Evil Rick!*" Rick laughed and reached for the bong.

Jack went into the kitchenette and returned with tortilla chips and a jar of El Paso salsa.

The young black contestant with the cellophane jacket selected his date. This was the object of the show. You didn't win money. You went on a date. Later, you and your partner would share your feelings about the event with the cameras, the crowd, and the syndicated audience. The person who did the selecting was then requested to decide whether he or she wanted to ask the selectee out again. This made for lots of dramatic tension. The selectee had the option of refusing the date, of rejecting the potential suitor on national television. Love was high-risk. Syndicated humiliation the price.

Rick watched as the host talked to the young man. "Look. This dude in the Saran Wrap's in heaven. Did you see that wayhone he picked?"

"I can't handle this show right now..." Jack walked over and turned the channel knob, pausing at a rerun of *Black Sheep Squadron*. Behind him bowers of luminous green shimmered, hooded luminaire streetlights white behind the curtains.

"Whatever," said Rick, sipping at his malt liquor. He watched the swooping Corsairs. The bronzed rawboned jaw of the major shone in the jeweled South Pacific sunlight as he stepped from the door of a Quonset hut.

Jack lifted his beer to his lips. "So what about Tamara?"

"What?"

"Well..." Jack stared forward. "Like what gives?"

Two servicemen began to throw punches at each other. Their crisp uniforms flashed in the tropic glare.

"Fuck, I don't know... I'm into her and everything, but it seems like there's a load of unnecessary grief. It's burnt." Rick's voice faded, mesmerized by its own inarticulation. "She's really cool," he tried. "*Really*. But sometimes I just feel like *whatever*. It's like owning a Jaguar with leather seats and wood paneling and just hankering for an airbrushed van with shag carpet and swivel buckets. I mean, Tam's got that fierce edge. Twenty-four hours a day, seven days a week. Three hundred and sixty-five days a year. Total nectar. Wayhone. But like I'm not even *there* sometimes. *Way* not there. And I don't know why. I think I just want to want her more. But how do you say that?" Rick took some malt liquor into his mouth. "I need room."

This was followed by a series of shattering explosions and the clatter of strafing. Rick exhaled as a jeep slid out through a burst of flaming palmettos. Trying to figure out relationships was a bad move. Rick knew that much. But tough to avoid. Bad habit from his years with Tamara. Years of talk talk, worry worry, suffer suffer. No, that wasn't going to be his style anymore. He'd rather sit alone in his apartment. Do something useful like wack off or hit himself in the head with a brick.

"I wouldn't blow it," Jack said, eyes masked by the twin DISCOs.

Rick lit a match, held it to the bong. There was a red *hush.* The album ended with a dry scrape.

3

Midnight found Tamara at their favorite bar, Teddy Ancient's Lounge. A typical, red-upholstered Hollywood lounge bar. Named after this old crooner who had died in a helicopter crash in the desert outside Las Vegas. Tamara ordered her second kamikaze. She'd been walking all day. Walking in L.A. *Which* took forever. *And* was embarrassing. Then her audition had not gone well and her dinner shift at Deacon's Garden had been a relentless cavalcade of customers. *Poseurs.* It was as if the whole restaurant had been filled with celebrity imposters trying to get into a post-Oscar bash at Spago. Fake Nicholsons. Fake Beattys. Fake Madonnas. Peach blossom voices whipping her into a silent and malicious frenzy. Commands, demands. And those aqua lights! Voices like a jillion tin slippers on the coral tiled floor of the restaurant. From 6:00 to 11:30. Until that final steeple of manicured fingers accepted that final check, the high beams of some creepy Mercedes-Benz scooping at the black boulevard. And from there it should have been as easy as just dividing up the tips and having a salad and a cigarette, except Tamara was expected . . . no, *required* . . . to help her boss close up. Yes, she was ordered to stand around and not look bored while he fumbled with his ring of keys, working overtime to figure out the password to her heart. A password, she'd decided long ago, he'd never know.

All he had to say was *Tamara.* Just pronounce her name, tongue sliming around the last two syllables.

His name was Todd. Todd Mann. And he excused this final imposition on Tamara's time by insisting it wasn't safe for him to be left alone with the Mexican dishwashers. Apparently the Mexican dishwashers were just waiting to slit his throat and empty the register. Their blood lust held at bay by Tamara's presence.

And tonight was the last straw. Not because Todd had managed to outdo his usual sad lechery. No, it was just that after a few cocktails, the world seemed to be a better place. A place with options. The reality of people like Todd Mann and his advances were more difficult to accept. *A racist. A sexist.*

"Another?"

Tamara nodded. Slid the loose bills toward the bartender. *Infected.* She was infected by her proximity to Todd. He was viral.

No, I've got to find another job, she decided, thinking again of the audition, remembering how quietly tense and wonderful she felt as she waited to read. It was only *after* that they told her she was probably too tall.

Always too tall for the part.

Almost as tall as her boyfriend.

Rick the outlaw. The kind of bad boy she always chased. The kind of guy who doesn't let you get bored. Not like this work that killed her with predictability, killed her with going nowhere. Killed her with Todd Mann.

She wanted the pressure of something you could count. When the days added up, they should be exciting.

On her fourth kamikaze. Four was her limit. Five and she'd be collapsing under the bar, grabbing the bartender. Puking. Attractive stuff like that.

Rick. She wanted to ask Rick why *she* was always the one who waited. Always racing around against being late and then waiting for him, for Todd Mann, for some casting lech to tell her she was *too* tall. And here she was again. In a bar. Alone. Waiting. Sharks closing in and no ride home.

And had it ever been any different? She couldn't remember the last time she'd really felt that sharpness. That things-really-matter feeling.

Her body stirred at the memory of the condo in Mammoth the winter she met Rick. The stars spread beyond the frosted window like an upturned city. Until, on the last day, they'd actually made it out of the A-frame as far as clamping the skis onto the rack on top of the Toyota. Engine warming, grunting out black smoke. Burning oil, she remembered. Amazed that while Rick could talk about cars all day, about his *road trips,* he couldn't do much more than change a tire.

While Tamara's dad had taught her about engines, about shooting pool, about black jack and five-card stud . . . about euchre and crazy eights. Rick had taught her how to turn on a TV and shoot a basketball. And maybe a few other fun things.

Tamara's dad was a good family man. Always had a good story about growing up. Wild times in Denver. Wild times as a helicopter pilot in the early days of Vietnam. Wild times in the aerospace industry. Line manager to corporate staff. Tamara's mother was still around, nurturing and a little spaced-out. Sort of a cocktail party goddess who grew up to do community service. Tamara felt okay about both of them. Knew she loved them. But had difficulty reconciling something about their marriage and the way it related to her life. To be honest, her parents' relationship just seemed *incidental.* As a young girl she had always sensed, if not been able to explain, that life had weight. That there was a contract that was noble, behavior that was valid, accountable. That every moment would contribute to the next in a way you could remember and believe in. And then she had discovered that it was all affected by time, capital *T.* As she got older all the relationships and bonds she remembered as strong and necessary suddenly seemed weak and arbitrary.

. . . but the A-frame in Mammoth. That first time she'd borrowed one of Rick's T-shirts and left him asleep in bed. Snow falling against the window. The day drifting away as the flames flapped in the black metal fireplace. No, they hadn't done much skiing, but they *had* had a great time. You could always count on Rick for that, even if he was being a heel lately.

But maybe his *heel*ness was inevitable? Maybe his irresponsibility was the price paid for his charm? Maybe. Or maybe she was just being stood up by a jerk she once thought was her lover.

At first, she hadn't exactly understood her attraction to Rick. Maybe she'd just been thankful for what she could expect: his Levi's on the floor, his obsession with cheering her up. The way he teased her from her binges of sadness, the binges of worrying about her acting career and being too tall for the good roles. The way he would stop some kid on the street and just start talking, as if he was still a kid himself. And it would make her feel good. The way he ran his fingers through her hair or just encouraged her to tell everyone who hassled her to just fuck off. Yes, Rick had qualities that made her eager to get on with things, to make things happen in life. Which was ironic, since he didn't do anything.

Tamara lit a Winston and slid back on the edge of the barstool, realigned her long legs. She smoked too much. It was definitely time to quit. She had promised herself that she would stop after five years. But then, that was back when five years was forever.

Fishing a quarter from her purse, she decided it was time to call a cab. Could you believe it? *A cab in Los Angeles?* This was the last time she'd wait for him. The very last. She, Tamara Jenson, had no intention of putting up with this treatment. Unless he had a great excuse, a really unequivocal excuse. Like maybe jail. Or *death.*

She tipped the bartender and tried to smile, then headed toward the pay phone. Her black flats wove beneath her across the hardwood floor.

She breathed Rick's name to herself three times.

4 ◄ ◄ ◄

Tamara was in the shower the next morning. The loofah gasped with suds. It was a prehistoric thing. It probed the sides of her breasts. She pressed with her finger. Nope, nothing bad. No lumps.

God, the rustle of hot water reminded her how good it usually felt to get up in the morning. Mornings not like this one. Mornings when she would slip into her kimono and whisper secrets to Mr. Coffee, snap the rubber band off the *Los Angeles Times,* reprimand herself for forgetting a cantaloupe to go with her yogurt, a chain of smoke crinkling up from her first cigarette.

Mornings when she was not ill from liquor.

Yes, she thought, leaning back and holding her hand against her forehead—the glamorous movie star pose—mornings *definitely* not like this one.

The maintenance man placed the chaises around the edge of the swimming pool. In white overalls, he crept through his duties. A weathered Angels cap bobbed on his head as he worked. Behind him a young woman lay stretched out on a towel, her pale skin damp with baby oil. Black bars of shadow sliced in diagonals across the freshly hosed cement.

The scene reminded Tamara of the days when she'd been ready to tan at the pop of a Tab or diet Pepsi. Back before melanoma and sunscreens and premature skin damage. Maybe like that first year after high school, driving the Toyota all night from Arizona State back to her parents' house in Redondo Beach. A box of clove cigarettes in her lap as she hove through dawn at the outskirts of Los Angeles. Bare shoulders shimmering against the straps of her cotton dress, her raven hair stained with a purple wash, her black boots tapped the car floor in time to the Replacements. But the face in the rearview surprised her. It was her face, but a younger face subdued in adolescent softness, her whole body plump, brown from the desert sun. It seemed like a long time ago.

And Tamara would never forget how that year had turned. Her only year at ASU focusing into a telescopic pinprick of bright pain. The realization she was pregnant. Pregnant and not prepared for the dark smile of her dream. So there was only one resolution. Her boyfriend steered through the back streets of Tempe, fingers brushing down the back of his neck, one hand on the wheel. Tamara pulled tight against the passenger door. Taste of almonds in the dry wind that came through the open window. Claret desert penciled black at the horizon, rows of pastel houses disappearing behind a red-and-white Kentucky Fried Chicken.

Tamara curled up on her creaking dormitory bed. *It's over.* Unable to do anything except concentrate on the pillows of Nembutal slipped beneath her. A blank wall of sky through her window. Tired beyond sleeping. Forced to face herself. Alone with her body's hunger. Alone with her own empty words.

She hadn't expected it, but as she held onto her knees, the exhaustion and anxiety glazed over, so that Tamara, half-awake, understood that she was much stronger than she would ever have imagined. Much. And would get better. Her girl friends' voices outside in the hallway. Ole-anders brushed by the wind. Tamara awake the following morning. Intuitively, she *knew* he wouldn't be there to comfort her, would stay at the pool, working his shift like a young prince up on that lifeguard ladder, a treadmill of capped and goggled swimmers churning the numbered lanes. Yes, and she was sure he would smile at a couple of the regulars, watch them watch him with thick glances while they tugged at their Lycra swimsuits.

But let them, she decided.

Even though she cared, which bothered her. In fact, this was probably the first time she had ever admitted just how much she wanted and needed someone, someone real.

That summer Tamara had moved back to Los Angeles and fallen into a relationship with a carpenter ten years older. She had first wanted him for his beautiful hands. Calloused, large, beautiful. Had moved in with him in Venice Beach, where they spent the evenings drinking red wine and listening to the ocean. He stopped seeing other girls. He would write poems to her. He would compare her body to the crash of the surf and the taste of red wine.

It was the carpenter who first suggested Tamara try an acting class. He even bought her Shakespeare's plays and read them to her when they lay in bed in the evening. Her fa-vorite was *The Taming of the Shrew.* Kate of Padua was a tall girl, at least Tamara read it that way. Passionate behind her bitchiness. Waiting for a partnership that could overtake her. Wanting room to be a strong woman and still be loved. But wanting someone strong enough to give herself to. Kate didn't want to just be some wedded *thing.* It had to be a partnership. At least, that's how Tamara read the play. At least that's what Tamara told the carpenter. He treated her nicely. They agreed on everything. Except marriage. He wanted it. She didn't.

Tamara got tired of him.

He was older. He had lived his twenties. Acted like a parent sometimes . . . or an older brother. Like a mentor. Which *could* have been okay. But she got tired of him, though not of

Shakespeare. She signed up for two acting classes at Cal-State L.A. and moved back toward that part of town and then into the Hollywood hills, where she took classes privately. That's when she began to waitress at Deacon's Garden. She was on her third agent. This one seemed convinced she would get Tamara work. But then so had the other two.

She'd always dated, but it was two years later, when she was sitting at a molded plastic table at the *panadería* on the corner of Pico and Union, looking at photographs she had commissioned for her portfolio, that Rick walked up and offered her a bite of his *pan dulce*. "Your what?" "My sweet bread," he said with a smile. "Do you want a bite of my sweet bread? *Pan dulce*. It's like Mexican for donut."

"Oh," she answered.

That had been almost three years ago.

All that time spent waitressing and driving to auditions. Without much luck. Except for two student films she had acted in for friends at USC and one small speaking part that was left on the cutting room floor . . . well, there wasn't much you could call a career. There *was* a music video which she didn't count and had accepted against her better judgment. There were some small parts in local theater productions. But Tamara just didn't see any direction. She couldn't find a part she really cared about . . . her auditions were all for tall, gawky introverted types. She wanted to do something that had some passion.

Almost three years of waitressing and auditions. Almost three years of too many cigarettes, dividing her time between Rick and Deacon's Garden.

Tamara watched Rick materialize, making his way past the sunbather, stepping over the chaise lounge. He offered her a wave through the window. She put down her cigarette. Her head throbbed. She was angry. She hated the way she wanted to go to him.

Rick had on that black T-shirt she had bought for him the first weekend they'd gone up to San Francisco together. It was the same weekend she had approached him with her apprehensions about their relationship.

Rick had shrugged and looked confused.

. . . their hands together as they stumbled from their motel room in Oakland, Tamara squeezed into her favorite outfit at the time: a fire-engine red sheath of soft leather, cut out along her hips. Tamara doing that thing that was easy for her: looking tomboyish, tall, and fine. Up at a bar on Haight Street, a frayed tuxedo shirt wrapped around Rick's waist, he kissed her, guiding her into the Gold Coast to watch a band called Deth Nell. The lead singer a bloated woman with shellacked white ducktails in an American Eagle jumpsuit zipped down to reveal a sweating pink V. As Deth wailed, Rick's fingers caressed Tamara's thighs. Later, they were in a purple room hazy with bodies under a string of black-light fixtures. Psychedelic posters of naked white women with long blonde hair, black men with Afros. Huge peace signs. Pentagrams. Lizards crawled in a terrarium. And maybe it was because she was high from the liquor, but as Rick led her into a cubicle of blinking votive candles, she realized she was satisfied. "It's Flipper," Rick whispered. "Sex Bomb Baby." Carnage of guitar noise as she placed her palms flat against the wall, Rick's chest against her shoulder blades. A half-lit movie poster went *The Hellstrom Chronicle.* "*Witch,*" whispered Rick. "*My long, tall witch.*"

Thinking about it later, Tamara came to the conclusion that *this* was the problem with Rick. He was great in the darkness, in the flickering votive candles. Under black light. But he got bored too easily. Which is bad. So did she. And they were always entertained with the trouble they could create. So they'd fight and make love, fight and make love. And forget how to just hang around and have fun. With Rick, everything was a burning cup. And you *had* to drink.

But when Rick knocked, Tamara opened the door and ducked into his arms.

She wished she could ignore the vague way he held her. The steady thump in his chest. The fact he existed.

She wanted to forget. Forget all about Rick.

► ► ► 5

Rick caressed the top of Tamara's head with his lips and chin. He didn't know what to say. He'd found himself alone in a coffee shop. Everything clouded from cocaine, liquor, and half of a Percodan he'd found in his shirt pocket. His fingers smelled like pussy. He'd decided to head over to Tamara's and deal. It was either now or later.

The small of her back against his arm as he looked around the room. A cup of coffee steamed beside the newspaper, a cigarette stubbed out in the ashtray. Domestic bliss. Sort of. If kind of not. Maybe she won't care? he thought. 'Cause he really had figured on meeting her and probably would've if Jack hadn't bailed. Jack. That total burnout. Walked out without any excuse. Couldn't deal with partying. While Rick had even remembered to scribble *Ancient's/Tam* on a pack of matches. Jack just bailing when there were still beers in the fridge. *Weak.* I mean it wasn't like the dude had wayhone. He was just tense. And it was getting to be a major drag.

But Jack had shrugged, cauterizing Rick's glare with the *slump* of the door.

Too many bong loads, Rick decided. And now he was stuck alone in his apartment. Spears of condensation glittered on the orange table. Stalagmites of ash littered on a copy of *Sports Illustrated.* Magic at the hoop, radiant Forum-gold uniform rising above the flustered arms of the Boston Celtics. Or was it the Dallas Mavericks? Milwaukee? Someone in green. Yeah, 32. The man who owned the league. Okay, so maybe they didn't win *every* championship. But the Lakers won enough. And the way Magic ran the court? Rick moved his Schlitz can as if handling the seed against tough D. *Pressure on. Some Detroit squarehead in his face. The Magic One double-pumps.* Rick double-pumped the Schlitz can, then went into his best Chick Hearn. *Earvin puts him in the popcorn machine . . . and you can taste the butter all the way back in Detroit, folks! Beautiful shot! Beautiful shot!* Rick missed the wastebasket. Malt liquor leaked on his mattress. Motörhead screamed through the speakers.

A door slammed outside as Rick took another cold can from the refrigerator and punctured the base of the can with a ballpoint pen. He held the puncture up to his mouth and pulled the tab. Suds of cold malt liquor rushed down his throat.

. . . 8 seconds . . . 7 seconds . . . 6 seconds . . . the Magic Man moves . . . 5 seconds . . . He's in the paint. . . . 4 seconds . . . It's a baby-sky! . . . 2 seconds . . . It's good! It's good! It's pandemonium in the Forum. Rick belched and threw the can at the wastebasket. Two points. He took a quick post–Pago Pago inventory: four cans of blue bull, a couple bong hits, and *no* tequila. How fucking sensible could you be? *No tequila* since the Pago Pago. Since that one late-afternoon wake-up shot. At least not yet. He pulled on a black T-shirt and picked his Lee duster up off the floor. Popped another silver can of malt liquor and gulped a mouthful. Bringing him closer to seven than six in the frostie column, depending on whether or not you accounted for the usual spillage . . . but then, the sixteen-ounce cans probably made up for that. Anyway, the *crucial* thing was that there was a number, something you could hang on to when the night got dizzy. When the wayhones got wavy. That's what mattered. Who needed exact calculations? That was for physicists and baseball fans. That was for the Japanese.

Rick stepped into the hall and pulled the door shut behind him. It locked. That's when he remembered his keys on the drain board.

He gripped the joint of the window frame, where the paint had cracked from the rotten wood. Slipped his fingers along the metal overlay and was able to get some purchase. Casements were good this way, he thought, gritting his teeth as the sash whined, handle rotating behind the screen. The window opened. No luck jimmying at the border that fit into the U-clips, so he started punching, bowing the creature. The whole creature a giant silver moth that collapsed upon the dustcover of his turntable.

Rick clambered through headfirst, barely missing the receiver with the toe of his boots.

Not bad, he decided, flicking his hair back and pocketing the keys. The door behind him, screen slipping to the carpet.

Headlights sprayed the stucco hallway.

The Buick Skylark loved to make that left turn onto Cahuenga Boulevard. His ride was angry with love to get out of Burbank and descend into Hollywood. The V-8 purred.

The notebook of math tests rested on the seat. Rick reached over and tossed it out the window. He yanked Jack's tie and collared shirt from where it was still wedged in the seat. He shook his head and let the wad flee into the night air. Detroit-engineered power steering traced his thoughts as he removed a Tiparillo from his duster and popped the lighter in the dash with the heel of his hand. Who needed that little Jap tin box of Tamara's? It was lame driving around in a car like that. Those protectionist swine. Kissing your knees in gratitude for nuking them into the gold halls of the twentieth century. Yeah, he was seriously burnt on the Japanese. A nation of yes-men and closet boozers, and according to Rick's dad, they were buying up every inch of L.A. Yeah, scarfing up the whole city. *His city.* But could you fuck in the backseat of one of their cars? No way. And Rick knew, 'cause he'd blown out the rear window of Tamara's Toyota with his cowboy boots. It'd cost him seventy-five bucks. Yeah, leave Japan to Jack. Wolverine dreams. The City of Angels was cool enough for Rick. Way. Big cars. Hot sun. Noise.

Like this here Buick. It was one fine ride.

Besides, he didn't really plan on ripping ol' Mrs. Maddox off for the whole enchilada. That'd be cold. But he could justify a *temporary* delay of payment. 'Specially now that he'd lost his job and was going to have to rely on a little dealing. How did that saying go? *You had to have money to make money.* Uh-huh. No doubt. And without a car you were *really* hurting. Cars were *crucial.*

Blue cigar smoke swirled around his head. The traffic ebbed as he wheeled a slow left turn.

It was March. Wednesday night. Headlights in his face. *Hump Day.* That's what the disc jockeys called it. *Hump Day.* And then they'd put on another wimpy Seventies tune. Crank some Kansas or Fleetwood Mac or something fierce like that, some fierce elevator music. Yeah, they called it *classic rock.* It was the bane of the L.A. radio waves. *Hump Day* and *classic rock.* And you couldn't blame *that* on the Japanese.

Hump Day. 'Cause once Wednesday was over, you were over the hump and only one day shy of Friday. Big deal. His calendar was like every day was Friday. Friday week. Friday month. Friday year. Friday life. 'Cause he wasn't going to waste his time waiting for some squid to tell him when to party. That's why he'd been forced to lose that job at the pizza parlor. He just couldn't accommodate himself to that nine-to-five tenseness. *Scheduling conflict* was the way he'd put it to Tamara. Nothing to do but look for something more agreeable. Something he could deal with. Like including a little more coin of the realm. 'Cause life'd hose you if you let it. The trick was to stay casual. That was *crucial.* Monster on the partying and just *stay* casual. I mean, he'd done the college thing, sure. Smoking dope, sleeping late. The toughest part had been the hoops, but once he'd bailed on that noise everything'd been cool. 'Cept that he never made it up for Egg McMuffins anymore once those practices were history. *And* he never got to eyeball those female sprinters anymore, working out against the dawn. Jocanda Whatever Her Name Was. Beautiful quads glistening above the blocks. But whatever. The golden arches'd still be there, waiting. And basketball? Whatever again. It was Division III. *Way* over. The cheerleaders would've looked better in a blender. Besides, if he hadn't quit he would never have gone out and drunk himself into that hard one-in-the-afternoon headache, this wild scruff tangled in the ropes of bed sheet, her freckled chest lost in narcotic rhythms, tawny curls pressed against his neck, the scent of lilacs sweet against the back of his tongue.

No, 'cause it was only being pissed-off from hoops that had taken him over that night into Pasadena. Frustration and the desire to forget all the times he stood alone, shooting jumpers in some empty gym. Yeah, the sound of his Converse squeaking on the hardwood, the ball down once for the beat, eyes trained on the back of the rim. Net snapping like dried grass. Until he'd just handed back his uniform and locker key. Later coach. Later Arroyo College Tigers.

'Cause the team was nowhere—o in 4 at the start of league play. But instead of being angry, Rick figured he just didn't care. It was Division III. He'd already failed. The whole thing was a joke.

But he could still remember how he'd sat on the edge of the bed and nudged the ornate silk skirt that lay in a spangle on the floor, his toes burrowing into the field of fleurs-de-lis. Green fleurs-de-lis. Gold silk. Yeah, he could still remember when he lifted the skirt, watching as a mauve camisole slipped to the carpet. The taste of aspirin in his mouth. The girl's body one curved burn on the black sheets, a tunic of dust on the economics textbooks on Rick's desk. Her lips move in preconscious nibbles as he touches her stomach. Her thighs the color of cirrus clouds.

Yeah, a gorgeous rich little deadhead. Angela. Angela from Pasadena. So Rick resigned himself to a brand-new chunk of *crucial* bliss. He could deal with the Dead. Angela was worth it.

And in the beginning it *was* good. Nothing to do but build up a little sweat in the weight room, then walk back to the dorm, grab a Dr Pepper, and kick, staring at the entrails of laundry that spilled from his open closet. T-shirts, white socks, and towels illuminated in the fluorescent hum of the Gro-lite bulb. The green plants. A few copies of *Thrasher* and *Forced Exposure* around in case he felt like reading something that wasn't stupid.

The stillness of 3:00 A.M. finding him in his headphones, Angela asleep in a litter of Sweetheart cups. Red lights of the Nakamichi topping out as Rick punched the air, the blue smoke. Tiparillo a red eye in his teeth.

What a little scruffy unit of wayhone nectarama Angela had been! Her attorney dad inadvertently placing a handful of shiny credit cards right into Rick's paws. The two of them naked in the black dorm hallway, zinging a Moonglow Frisbee. High on mushrooms. The slice of meringue caroming in strange messaline configurations while the Grateful Dead's *Steal Your Face* blared from the JBL speakers they'd dragged into the doorway. Angela's voice disembodied above the rippling guitars; the disc waving in the tunnel of shadows, sailing, her feet patter as she sprints into him, her wet mouth. Crinkles of light glitter behind closed doors. Rick's shoulders against the cold plaster. The carpet raspy.

The thing he didn't want to name, naming itself. Then falling to pieces. Angela's freckled chest bowed before a new teeth-grinding gift. Cherubic hips tight, backwinded with the flutter of starved muscle. Her calves stained with blue flowers.

"But Rick, it's nothing. I just want to lose some weight."

So it'd been Christmas Trees, Black Beauties, and Cross Tops. Angela craning to point at her thighs. "See?" she'd say sadly. "Right there . . . that's fat." Then it simply became a steady diet of cocaine. "Because that other stuff *burns* too much," she'd add with authority, touching her nose with the back of her hand. "And it makes me jittery."

But Rick'd been cool. Speed and coke. Whatever. They both got you wired. They were both a blast. Fuck, fuck, fuck. All day, all night. At first. Then there was never time. Or they'd just lie there, trying to suppress the terrible sound of birds chirping out the window in the ugly morning. Car doors slamming as ugly people headed off into their ugly day. Rick's and Angela's lips sticky from the bottle of NyQuil they kept at the side of the bed.

Until one afternoon when Angela leaned over the bathroom sink and told Rick to get lost. She was seeing someone else. Was into it. *Totally.* Her pale breasts pressed against the porcelain. Tawny hair coiled, damp, pinned above her damp neck. "Get lost," she repeated in a strained voice. "I'm sick of looking at you."

Rick had found a postcard in his mailbox the next year. From Hawaii. Three words. *Sorry . . . love, Angela.* No return address.

Rick spent that night with a bottle of Sauza Gold against the wall of the Alta-Dena drive-thru on Olive Avenue in Burbank. Barfing into a dumpster. It had been beautiful. One of life's peak experiences. Kind of a pain-of-betrayal gig.

Later, he'd decided it was for the best. 'Cause she was spoiled. Tasty but spoiled. And a deadhead. Which was okay 'cause she could handle acid, but it'd have got pretty bleak when that biological clock started ticking big time. Deadheads always ended up broke, begging for concert tickets. Yeah, he could just see himself washing diapers in the kitchen sink while Angela stirred a wooden spoon through a big cast-iron pot of textured vegetable-protein chili and yapped about driving up with the rent money to see Jerry and the boys play their New Year's show in San Francisco.

Sugar magnolias. Blossoms blooming. Heads all empty.

No, thought Rick, I don't care. No love was *that* strong. But now he was caught up all over again with Tamara. The love thing. The game. *Cupid's Arrow* gone haywire. Way. But so what? He was cool. He'd survived Angela and graduated with a degree in sociology. Quit that first job delivering carpets in Hawthorne. Life looked bleak, sure . . . but a few weeks of dining on boxes of macaroni and cans of tuna—a specialty Rick called Tuna Mac—ended when the phone rang and this dude he'd hung with in his sophomore year called from up in Eureka and asked him if he'd be interested in flying up once a week and making some cash bringing some *green* back down to the city. Rick'd said sure. And that'd held him for a spell. Yeah, he'd figured it out okay. Gone solo. That's when he met Tamara. Stumbling into her on a day he was so hungover he could barely grit his teeth, much less smile. But he'd done it. Her voice unguent, lifting him above himself. A pair of sea gulls squawking over a discarded tamale corn skin. So he'd bought her a cup of coffee, which led to a movie that afternoon. Something black-and-white she'd wanted to see. Something about Philadelphia.

But then his buddy up in Eureka stepped on a punji-stick and lost his foot, and Rick found himself scrounging off Tamara. Then six miserable months shoveling tar onto roofs and a year as a hardware salesman at a Builder's Emporium. Then something in an office on Wilshire. This telemarketing gig. Then the pizza parlor. Three months.

Rick angled the Buick into an open parking space. Across the street a yellow neon sign glowed above a crowded doorway. FROLIC ROOM COCKTAILS. It'd been a while since Rick had been here.

It felt good to be back.

Jack held a Styrofoam cup of thin coffee. He was sitting on a metal chair. He was at a Narcotics Anonymous meeting. It was not a great place to be after a couple bong hits, a shot of whiskey, and a few cans of malt liquor. The people around him did not look good. They were speaking together. The Serenity Prayer.

He had been walking home from Rick's apartment. This address in his wallet. Next thing he knew he was in a Methodist church, going down the stairs into this conference room annex. Not a good way to spend your night off. But that lunch with his dad had fucked him up good. Jack could feel it. A young guy in a conservative suit was talking about how much trouble he had getting everything done. That's why he wanted it. Just to lose himself for a while. But it never worked out that way. And people at the office could tell. He was sure that no one really trusted him anymore. People looked at him strangely. He didn't get access to the interesting jobs. Other people got promoted.

Jack thought about his motorcycle. He hoped it wasn't seriously fucked. He'd pushed it down the street to a mechanic. His father asked him why he didn't own a car. Jack said he didn't like cars. Jack thought about money. He needed more money. His sister could use more help with rent. And his savings weren't good enough for his plan to travel through Japan. And now his bike was fucked and he'd be bumming cars and riding the *bus.*

But no way Jack was asking *that* asshole for anything.

Los Angeles hung on his shoulders like a spell. He was a prisoner. Trapped in a bad land.

Trapped by a malicious authority.

On his way to the coffeepot beside the stacks of sugary cookies, he bumped into a man with a face like a dove. Round, smooth head. Long nose. Tiny black eyes. The man had a muscular chest and huge arms. He moved like someone who didn't like to get bumped. His legs were thin. They stood face-to-face. The man looked up as Jack stepped back. The man had dropped a cookie. He watched Jack's eyes. "Still *out,* huh?"

Jack didn't understand. "Just getting some more coffee."

The man smiled. "Maybe you should get it at a *coffee* shop. Maybe you're not ready to be here."

Jack didn't know where it came from, but if it was fear, it felt warm and comfortable. "Maybe you should shut the fuck up and get out of my way."

Dove Man nodded and put down his paper tray of cookies.

Jack knew the language. It moved through him like adamantium. He was a mutant. He was a certified machine of death. He *was* Wolverine.

"Kiss my ass," said Dove Man.

Jack laughed.

Surrounded by silent, alien faces. His eyes went blurry and he forgot how to worry. This was a different world and fate had yet again threatened his all-too-insecure grip on sanity. It was an ugly night in Low Town. He was the baddest mother in Madripoor. *Berserker rage.* It was on him. "I would, if you'd take your finger out of it."

Dove Man swung first and clipped Jack above the eye. Jack went back into the wall.

But Jack was out of himself. He was a government-certified, psycho killing thing. *Bub,*

I'm the best at what I do! Dove Man's face transformed into different faces as it was slammed against the floor. Jack noticed the quiet. The quiet of the strange city, this strange land.

Later, he was standing on the sidewalk and people were screaming at him. The aliens threshing the streetlight with their fists, the guardian of their evil municipality vanquished. Because Jack was chaos and he had taken pleasure in wreaking such unholy destruction, they hated him. Blood spilled down his chest. They watched him smile. They watched him walk slowly into the night.

They listened to him chant, Dad, Dad, Dad.

6 ◄ ◄ ◄

"So what happened?" Tamara believed it was better to get difficult things out of the way. "You understand that I could have gone home and caught up on my sleep, don't you? Or *even* had another date or something? I didn't have to spend my night waiting for *you.*" She spoke with a self-mocking lilt and arched her eyebrow to disguise the hurt. She balled up a handful of Rick's T-shirt and gave it a tug.

He kissed her.

She tasted the liquor. Rick wordless as he slung her up in his arms and walked for the bedroom. Struggling with his long-legged cargo.

Except there hadn't been any answer.

"So really, Rick. What happened last night?"

Rick grimaced, kneed open the bedroom door, and twisted Tamara between the jambs.

The bedroom was still tousled from two nights before, the *Pleasure Quest* VHS cartridge on top of the VCR. Rick noted that Tamara's Robert Frank print was on the carpet, a jagged chipwork of glass stuck to the inside of the frame. He nodded, adjusting his arms to get a better grip. "What happened?"

"It fell," she murmured. "Last night . . . while I was sleeping."

The print was of a naked woman, alone in a rundown room, her right hand on her hip, her abdomen wove beneath the exclamation of black hair that fell to her shoulders. Her skin was blurred, a scrawl of ink across the top and bottom of the print went 4 A.M. Make Love to Me.

Rick let Tamara slip to the mattress and rolled against her. "I guess it's a sign," she added.

Rick snorted and lifted himself to his elbows.

Tamara eyed him. "At least say you're sorry."

"I'm sorry."

"Say it and mean it."

"I'm *really sorry*, Tamara."

His long hair fell about the narrow angles of his face, tickling her nose. Tamara reached up and brushed it to the side. He was wearing the silver ear clasp she'd bought him down on Melrose Avenue. His face the color of the moon rising through smoke. Sort of magical. Rapacious. His eyes bloodshot. Blue.

And shifty with sincerity, she decided as she allowed him to kiss her again. His hand moved to touch her breast. But then she was wriggling. Got to free herself. Stale beer a fist in her throat.

She pivoted into a sitting position and squared her shoulders. "Look . . . I want an answer. I deserve that much and you know it. *You stood me up.*"

Rick's silence was clinical. Tamara understood from experience that he was in control now, judging her outburst. *Keeping* control. And Tamara felt weak for caring what he did and where he was . . . and possibly, who he was with. Sometimes she wanted to be just like him.

In control. She understood why he acted this way, but sympathy was a mistake. Sympathy made her vulnerable.

Rick's measuring look flickered. Then, the gesture of a kiss. He pulled himself to his feet and walked out of the bedroom, fingers snapping against his Levi's.

Tamara restrained herself. She had nothing to offer but forgiveness.

The refrigerator opened. He was probably pouring himself a bowl of Cheerios. Then she heard the *hiss* and understood. He was already into the beer. Fine, let him. They were his . . . he might as well finish them off and disappear. First, he stood her up and now he wouldn't even explain himself. Wouldn't even *talk* with her.

Twelve-fifteen. Tamara looked up from the old Timex wristwatch that her father had given her. The one he used to wear when she was a girl. The one she kept on her nightstand. Her fingers trembled. She leaned back and listened as Rick rustled through the kitchen. Closed her eyes, imagining a blue lake above treeline. *Blue.* That was the color they'd taught her to think about in acting class. Blue when you wanted to calm yourself. Red when—Tamara thought of blue. Blue. Blue. Blue. Concentrated on tightening the muscles in her feet. Counting thirty seconds, then relaxing. She tightened her feet and her calves. Thirty seconds. Relaxing. She moved up her body, clenched her muscles, and relaxed. All the time thinking, blue . . . blue . . . blue.

Blue water . . . ``Blue,'' Calming herself. Alpine lakes in a necklace of evening skies. Hummock of lichen. Sand dunes under a blue sky. The flap of a United States flag. Young girl standing beside rusted Texaco tanks . . . a white camper disappearing down a cone of pavement; wind whispering away beside the feathered blue dunes, magenta gullies; azure in puddles of gasoline, buttes of blue oil traced on the black pavement . . . the smell of angel food cake on a warm blue day, icing fibrous . . . dryer clacking away on the service porch . . . lawn interlaced with *lengths of garden hose and wounds of red earth; a screeching collage of metal against blue metal. The distance laced with fluid white.*

Tamara opened her eyes.

She was thirsty.

She moved from the bed. Her tongue pasty. Walked into the other room. There was an empty Burgie can at the foot of the sofa. Tamara picked it up, went into the kitchen, and drew herself a glass from the tap. She needed to go to the market and get some spring water. Something that was better for her body.

The pale sunbather was still there. Still pale.

She looked over at her digital clock.

Twelve thirty-seven.

Rick was gone.

► ► ► 7

Rick leaned his forehead against his apartment door. Nice and solid. It was a contrast to the action in his brain: a stygian calliope of clicking and reverb, occasionally interrupted by screechy patches of vertigo. A speed-metal solo of pain. Rick scraped the broken remainder of his apartment key against the lock and moaned. *How fucked.* A fragment of the key glinted at him from inside the keyhole. A harsh parallelogram of white soiled the exposed hallway. Rick turned and leaned over the wrought-iron balustrade. Green smegma floated in the kidney-shaped swimming pool. Rick stared down at The Manager's room: 1D. He couldn't believe he had to deal with that asshole when he was this seriously burnt. But then, when else would his key decide to sabotage him? Yeah, it all made perfect sense. Like everything, his relation-ship with his apartment was falling apart. His apartment was mad at him. First Tamara and now his apartment. He was temporarily vulnerable and now every*one* and every*thing* would exact its evil retribution.

Of course, he *could* go through the window again, but he needed a breather first. Otherwise he'd be blowing chunks.

From somewhere in the apartment complex he could hear marching music. A fat wad of jungle leaves had the voice of Jim Morrison. *L'America! L'America! L'America!*

Rick wiped the sweat from his face with his T-shirt and pressed his stomach against the rail. That breakfast beer at Tamara's was seriously *uncrucial.* Heinously *anticrucial.*

His temples rippled. He belched. Imagine an immense screw winding through his skull. Razor-bright edges twist. Bone shavings. Organ music. Screams.

Things were desperate. He thirsted for black darkness, iced liquids. Ibuprofen. The door locked. Window beyond him. He needed to be horizontal. Like right now. Like on this feathery concrete. Uh-huh, rest. Let his eyes nap. Escape through the portals of imagination: last night still wound around his tongue. Absolution spewing in an open faucet of familiar fevers . . . (those thighs!) . . . Rick's head upon his arm . . . (those kisses!) . . . the liquid-red fi-berglass Corvette. The blinking grid of Hollywood slipping from his hands as he gazed off, parked on a turnout; the woman in the driver's seat none other than Ginger Quail, gold miniskirt spray-painted on her hips. The coconutty, dry-ice fragrance. Those same hips Rick remembered hovering above the diligent tongue of the nurse in *Pleasure Quest.* Ginger's backless blouse and that same smooth skin that once shone in firelight beneath the smiles of the female farmhands. Her breasts swayed beneath the loose drapery. Her abdomen lifted to the guitar noise. Guns N' Roses. "Move to the City." Ginger's brow wrinkled as she placed her finger against her nostril and inhaled, reminding Rick of the way Angela had hungered, played the bad girl. Ginger handed him the compact. Like with Angela. Air heavy with mannitol.

Angela. The comparison stirred him. Except it meant nothing. This girl wasn't Angela. Her voice was flat, free from the playful edginess that meant everything to Angela. Working without a net and letting the boys and girls *know* she knew it. That was Angela. All in the voice. Something raw and aware of itself. With Ginger maybe it was more in the eyes. But whatever. It could just be that she was buzzed. Rick took the rolled bill from her fingers and did a line. Ginger smiled. The smile twinkled with a million stars of possibility. Rick yawned. His dick felt like it wanted to get hard. Like was *thinking* of getting hard. His stomach tight when he thought of Tamara alone at Ancient's Lounge.

Ginger took back the compact and turned up the volume on the Blaupunkt. She sipped occasionally from a bottle of Perrier-Jouet. The bottle decorated with white petals. Rick watched her out of the corner of his eye. Took a slug from his pint of Cuervo Gold. Ginger's eyes closed in adrenaline meditation. Yeah, she must look *young* beneath that candy of gloss, eyeliner and mascara. How did that Motörhead tune go? "Jailbait." Yeah. Patch was right, Lemmy said it all. My decision made at lightning speed. Jailbait, baby, c'mon! But the thing was . . . where'd they raise girls like Ginger? Probably out on some bimbo ranch. Force-fed a steady diet of crystal meth, cottage cheese, and Scope.

Yeah, the coke was definitely fucking with him. Exhilaration. Tragedy. The white sisters of guilt and doubt. Ginger like the photograph some vegetarian had shown him once, the one of the calf strapped up in the stall, motionless, milk-fed. Veal.

'Cept it was probably different with Ginger, 'cause she was having fun . . . I mean, she was *fierce.* Cranking tunes and washing it all down with champagne. Not freaked by the fact she was livestock.

Rick looked down the length of her, measuring her up. She strained with health. A lost white-trash kid who probably just snuck away under the streetlights one night. Under the freeway overhang. Probably bailed on some ugly family gig.

And Rick liked it that way. Ginger standing alone out in the West. Rick respected people who couldn't hack the bogus—the 9-to-5. Couldn't hack the weak. 'Cause he couldn't hack it. Take the time he'd told that Persian chick from UCLA *he also* was *enchanted.* Knowing she'd believe him, probably needing a reason to crawl into his bed. Rick almost beginning to believe it all himself. Those afternoons when he was like still a kid in high school. That summer spent drinking Mondavi, naked before the open window of his apartment. Satanic caricatures of Jimmy Carter burning on the TV. The shah's wife wiping the tears from her eyes in the White House gardens. Plasterboards of torture victims sprouting from the sidewalks, the Persian girl lowering her eyelids with a whisper. Soviet automatic rifles and taunting mobs on the nightly news severing her from the orchards of home. Until she'd had to reveal her fear at standing alone in America, asking Rick for marriage. And not just for a green card, but for love.

Sure, said Rick. *Love.* I'll call you. Soon.

But that's how people played in his city. Cowardice was no excuse. And asking for love was chickenshit. *Love.* That word was history.

"You like that stuff?"

Rick watched the pint of tequila in his hand, "Sure, don't you?"

Ginger made a look of disgust. "Yuck. *Not* psyched."

Her face was more pinched than it appeared on the screen, chin tucked like a dimple beneath her lips. He pointed to the bottle between her thighs. "Nice petals."

Ginger looked down. Her blonde hair glinted, teased by the teeth of peroxide. He was glad his own hair hung long. He shook it. Smoothed it back with his hands and looked up and under at her with his blue eyes. Kind of bored, though. She adjusted the rearview and began to give her face a cursory examination. Fingered at her eye shadow. Ginger was about five five without the stilettos. Yet the delicate squareness of her shoulders and the thrust of her sternum carved her body upward, making her seem taller. *Limber.*

She lifted the bottle of champagne and held it in the purple light. "Yeah, they're nice . . ."

The ivory blossoms hummed.

The music stopped, CD discharging with an amped *leet.*

"Want to pick one?" Ginger motioned to a wine-dark case with a metal clasp.

Rick flipped it open. The case was filled with CDs. Some stuff from the early days: Led Zeppelin, Black Sabbath, Aerosmith, Van Halen, Judas Priest, Alice Cooper, AC/DC, Ozzy, Cheap Trick. Okay, Rick could deal. Plus, some late-eighties stuff: Poison, Mötley Crüe, Cinderella, Def Leppard, Scorpions, Warrant, W.A.S.P., Bon Jovi, Slaughter. More Van Halen.

Yawn. The soft underbelly of The Headbanger's Ball.

Rick ran his fingers over the smooth plastic covers. It made perfect sense to him that Ginger listened to these kinds of bands. "No Motörhead, huh?"

Ginger wrinkled her nose. "That's *speed.* Speed's no good. It's got to be *heavy.*"

Rick liked *speed-metal.* Rick liked *hard core.* Rick did not completely approve of what he saw before him in the wine-dark box. He lifted up the Warrant, holding it like a dead mouse. "This is serious *poseur* shit."

Ginger gave him a hard look. "*Is* not. Warrant *rocks.* Pick one or don't. I don't care."

Rick considered the Crüe. Sort of a *diplomatic* urge. However, the Slaughter CD had this fierce wayhone shackled to a carnival knife-thrower's wheel? Could be cool. Difficult to deny the lure of honeage. But then, this was an unhinged gig—parking with Ginger—the moment deserved *perfection.* He went with early AC/DC. Rick punched around and landed on "Highway to Hell." Another sip of tequila as Ginger tapped her fingers on the leather-bound steering wheel. Rick dreamed of 1979. Not his own 1979. Ginger's 1979.

Imagined a tract house lined with bedraggled junipers. Ginger dancing to an older sister's Kiss or Queen. *Psyched. Psyched* to stand around the Orange Julius in the mall. *Psyched* to sit on the hood of a Camaro and smoke her first Marlboro. Seriously *psyched.*

Rick looked into Ginger's eyes. The coke had taken her off a few steps.

She smiled and licked her lips. "Want to fuck?" Ginger didn't wait for an answer. She slipped her shirt from her shoulders, pulling it across her breasts and shaking her hair free. "And since I *know* you do . . . *how* do you want to do it?"

Rick took a mouthful of tequila. This was Ginger Quail. Right out of the video box. She walked. She talked. "I, ah . . . thought I'd use my cock."

"Good idea," she breathed. Her hand snaked toward the business end of Rick's Levi's. His stomach fluttered. *Tamara. AIDS.* He stared at the keys hanging from the ignition. Sighed and turned onto his hip, helping Ginger slip his pants toward his ankles. The music a howl as she began to lick.

Rick reached from behind and caressed her breasts, running his open palms down toward her hips, then back; his fingers along the crest of her arms. Her triceps taut as stretched rope.

Then her mouth forced a sharp lisp from him, the broth of her skin hot on his thighs. He sprang free as her mouth moved. The window steamy. Her fingers searched out his nipples. Tequila crawling, the euphoria of cocaine italicized as Ginger moaned. As Ginger whimpered. As his shirt shucked over the gas pedal. Her breasts suffocated him in the cramped Corvette. His fingers walked the slippery trail. This furled desperate rhythym. Eyes slitted. Following the pattern woven with her hips. Lost beyond the shrubs of reservation. Suburbia, gasoline, fire. *Slowly, slowly.* He placed the tip of his tongue on her navel. Her beautiful tight belly. Car light washing her electric as Ginger sprung the door. Rick's pants wrapped around his ankles. Ginger with one thigh up on the prow of the Corvette, guiding Rick with her free hand. Rick followed Ginger's soft groans with thrusts. Fingers helping herself. Fast, fast. One long nervous question. Rick pinched her narrative into a tight salient answer. Remembering, with the lucidity of a tragic figure, that for all of his good intentions, he was still *unprotected.* Condomless. Evil.

Trying to downshift. Metal vultures flapped in his brain. Shadows lifted on the horizon. Things waited in the trees. Ginger prowled her hips against the tension . . . until with one mad thrust, Rick yanks back, ejaculating. Grasping for her waist, he trips on his pants. Ginger erupts like a stadium of synchronized sprinklers, her body stuck to the Corvette. Rick's legs caught in the clot of his Levi's. His butt smacks on the hard-packed dirt. Eyes still on Ginger Quail in the privacy of her orgasm. Her bare arms hug the streamlined flanks of fiberglass, the small of her back illuminated in moonlight and dust, undulating grid of the city phosphorescent across her skin. Her stiletto heels bite the dirt. Rick touches his penis with a shudder. *A condom?* He was wearing a condom? A sorry teaspoonful of sperm dangles in the end. Weird, he thinks, peeling it off and tossing it into the sage. He dusts at his thighs and pulls up his Levi's. Ginger must have slipped it on.

Ginger, bending toward the upturned wing window of the Corvette.

"Hey," he said.

She turned and looked out from beneath her hair, an easy smile on her face. "You want to keep partying?"

Rick thought about the tequila. Her breasts bobbed as she stretched. He said, "Yeah. Totally."

"Then get in the car," she ordered. She licked her fingers, puckered, and kissed the air. "I always taste best when I come."

"But get in the car," she repeated firmly. "I'm in the mood to drive. *Fast.*"

Rick reached for the open door. He felt beautiful with obedience.

The Corvette whistled through the abalone predawn of the San Fernando Valley, aimed for the heart of Northridge. Rick closed his eyes, blunt night air against his face. Ginger swung the car toward a green exit sign, turned up an empty avenue of clicking yellow streetlights and into a stucco parking garage surrounded by pastel Malibu lamps and deciduous trees, thin trunks rising through the lawn mist.

Rick stepped out, ROBINSON stenciled in white paint on the wall in front of the car. "Hey, is Quail a stage name?"

Ginger looked back. "No, it's real . . . you know, like the birds."

Like the birds.

"Then who's Robinson?"

"My husband."

"Oh," said Rick. But fuck it. If she didn't care, why should he? Why did it matter? Just as long as he didn't get some jealous dude wanting to stick a knife in his back. Yeah, it'd be a serious drag to end up cold meat in some triple-X porn princess's apartment. That'd be bleak. Seriously *uncrucial.*

Ginger gave him an ingenuous look. "Don't worry. He's in the Navy right now . . . in the Philippines."

"Yeah?"

"Uh-huh. He's never around. He just sends me postcards and stuff. He's like on a submarine or something, I think . . ."

"Yeah?"

"He wants me to go out there, but I don't know . . . why should I?" Ginger watched him, her teeth stuck on the narrow love of her lips. "I don't know . . ."

" 'Cause he's your husband?"

Ginger looked at him.

"What's wrong?" he asked.

She smiled and unlocked the door. "Nothing. C'mon in . . ."

"The Philippines, huh?"

Ginger didn't answer. Rick wondered if Robinson knew the scene with his blushing bride. You had to figure he'd see the light at some point. Maybe even dug the whole twisted gig. Strange shit. But sort of out of control in a killer way.

Ginger found the light switch and Rick found himself in an apartment with a teal carpet, a peach leather sofa, a love seat, and a black marble cocktail table that filled the space not otherwise filled by the pantherine wall system and a drop-leaf wet bar with an assortment of liquor bottles and a tray of crystal highball glasses. Bifolding cabinet doors opened up, revealing stereo components piled high in a tomb of gyrating red, green, and yellow monitor gauge lights.

Ginger removed a CD from the shelf and placed it on the retracting tongue of shiny ebony. She handed Rick the case. "A guy I knew gave me this . . . *you'll* probably like it."

Rick looked down at the empty plastic snap box. MEGADETH. The cover showed a skeleton crouched in a decimated cityscape. The skeleton wore shades. His name was Vic Rattlehead; he leans over a FOR SALE sign. The decimated United Nations building is behind him. The caption went PEACE SELLS . . . BUT WHO'S BUYING? "Yeah," said Rick. "I know these guys. They can seriously hurt you. My favorite's that first one where they cover Nancy Sinatra's 'These Boots Are Made for Walking.' Combat Records." The room filled with beautiful noise. The far wall covered with framed photographs. Portrait shots of Ginger decked out in various exotic costumes. *Exotic.* Not pornographic. A glance of bare skin, the hint of breast. A bare shoulder. Rick looked closer. Yes, Ginger had the sweetest belly button.

He removed the pint of tequila and killed it. Ginger in a buckskin Pocahontas bodice, web-work of yellow beads across the cleft of her breasts. Feather earrings dangled beside her bleached pigtails, her face and neck ocher. Her blue eyes sleepy, cheeks pouched with bad light. Lips given the benefit of full red lipstick. Or Ginger as the gangster's moll; her powdered breastbone bare beneath a wide-lapeled pinstripe with padded shoulders, red carnation nailed to the dark fabric, a black bow tie looped around her neck. A fedora balanced on the stacked tendrils of her excruciatingly curled hair, tommy gun cradled in her arms. Or how about Ginger as an Inca princess? Her ivory gown trimmed with gold and offset by a conquistador's helmet that looked like it had been torn out of a plastic-wrapped five-and-dime Halloween costume. War club clenched in her hands.

Rick pointed to the latter. "Who're you doing here?"

Ginger's hands were buried in her purse. "That? I was the daughter of some Mexican king. We shot that one out around Antelope Valley. Like beyond the city limit."

"Yeah, but how come the helmet?"

Ginger squinted at the photo. "I think it's 'cause the king had to trade me . . . so the other guys wouldn't waste the whole town. Something like that."

"What happened?"

"What do you think?" She dumped the guts of her purse onto the marble.

"I'd guess they fucked your lights out?"

"And then?"

Rick thought for a moment. "They wasted the whole town and fucked *everyone's* lights out?"

Ginger clapped, her eyes glowed above the composition of lipstick containers, Kleenex, compact, and keys. "Smart boy! You should be a writer, Rick."

Rick's lips turned up. It was cool to hear her say his name. He shivered from the cocaine, put his hands in his pockets and leaned back. He rubbed the toe of his ropers against the back of his calf. Louvered blinds between the crack in the heavy chintz curtains. The room had a timeless, sealed quality that was hard to ignore. Except for the tulips in the Oriental vase. They were just dead.

"So you like your work?" He motioned toward the photographs. He was glad he'd admitted to recognizing her. It would be fucked, a serious pain, if they had anything to hide. It'd get in the way of all this crucial fun.

Ginger withdrew a Chivas Regal bar mirror from underneath the sofa and spilled out the contents of her bindle, giving the powder a critical appraisal. She reached under the sofa again and pulled out a fuchsia handbag embossed with matching fuchsia lizard skin. She pulled a Ziploc plastic bag out of the purse. Rick looked at the Ziploc and sighed. It was full. He watched Ginger tap delicately at the corner. She dialed out two lines, chopping at the cocaine with a gold Bullock's department store credit card. Her shoulders hunched as she concentrated.

Rick dropped the tequila bottle onto the carpet and kicked it toward the wall. It made a hollow *clunk* when it hit the molding.

Ginger bent to the mirror and began to snuffle with a brass straw. Rick walked over to her CD collection. It was basically more of the same commercial heavy metal, except for Frank Sinatra and a CD of *Herb Alpert & His Tijuana Brass Greatest Hits.* Rick popped out the Megadeth and put on Herb Alpert. The song was "Lonely Bull." Very western in sort of a *Playboy*-magazine-1960s kind of way. It reminded Rick of childhood. Tight shoes. Going to church. Sunlight through the station wagon window. His parents' cocktail parties.

Ginger pointed at the mirror. "You should go look at my refrigerator." She sniffed. "That's where I keep all my full-access passes. You know . . . the stickers they give you so you get backstage. Last month I got to meet Tyler. Steven Tyler from Aerosmith. It was *too* awesome. I gave him a rose, like after pulling out the thorns, right? Then I said *Tyler*! I went right up and gave it to him. He *even* knew who I was! He said we should do a movie, you know, *together.* He's sort of old, but really hot. He's stopped partying. I'd still fuck him though . . ."

Rick's face loomed convex.

He straightened, wiped his nose, thinking of a cold beer. His olfactory nerves crackled. Yeah, then brief as a kiss, he found himself touched by some secret assurance. Some greater thrill that glowed like brake lights through the fog. He held his hand out flat to see if it was shaking. After what seemed like hours, he asked, "Got any beer?"

"In the fridge. And get me some champagne."

Herb Alpert and his Tijuana Brass were playing very loudly. Big swooping trumpet noise. Congas.

Rick stepped around the side of the sofa and patted her on the head. Her smile was pleasant and sexy. Nothing like the hard, jeweled weight in her eyes. "I'm looking for something," she added.

Rick opened the refrigerator and found wire racks stacked with magnums of Perrier-Jouet and bottles of St. Pauli Girl. Rick pulled out a beer and peered around for a church key. He rustled through a few drawers before noticing the magnetized opener stuck to the glistening side panel of the refrigerator.

The first cold throatful was paradise. And the second.

He pulled out a magnum of champagne for Ginger and closed the door. Shiny backstage passes were pasted around a Polaroid of a naked person on a white sand beach. Rick looked closer and saw that it was a man with tan lines like a white bikini. The man's head was covered with an orange bicycle cap. A blur in the foreground appeared to be a fragment of railing. There were also palm trees and a strip of blue. The Philippines, Rick decided. The light still on back in the living room, but Ginger was gone. Rick heard sounds and found the bedroom. Ginger naked again, arms crossed. She was on a circular bed, leaning against a headboard that looked like a giant clamshell. The mirror was on the carpet. The room flickered as Rick grinned and took a hit from his beer. Yeah, things were about as good as they could be at 3:30 on a Thursday morning. He walked over and slipped beside her, opening the champagne. She took it and giggled as it frothed up and spilled down her chin, spreading in a net of diamonds across her sloping breasts.

The TV was a Mitsubishi forty-five-inch rear-projection screen with VCR hookup. Rick recognized his hostess in her Inca princess role. She was chained to a gold wall of cinder blocks, patches of the wall dripped with excess gold paint. A hooded half-man—half-eagle creature covered her body in strokes of red liquid.

"It was supposed to be blood," Ginger said. "They mix red dye with Karo syrup . . . so like to make it thick and dark enough."

Rick sipped and watched as Eagleman, who he figured was a high-ranking priest, began to work Ginger into a sacrificial heat. The princess strained against her manacles, crimson slopping her vagina, breasts, and thighs. Eagleman's fist wielding what looked, in the candlelit air of the temple, like a blood-soaked feather duster. Her smooth skin anointed. Slapping with a *mush mush*

mush as she moaned to the beat of a distant gong. The priest freeing himself from his winged robe and moving closer, penis soft. The princess's eyes rolling back anyway as he stuffs it in. The camera concentrates on the tug-of-war of bloody genitalia. Rick takes another sip, closes his eyes. Slipping into a vague reverie composed of squeals and tiny splashing.

Rick's hand on the neck of the bottle. Hammered. Buzzed bad. Weaving on the ledge of exhaustion. Endless day unraveling as the squeals flash white. *Ginger.*

His eyes open to that same hard, jeweled blue. Ginger's irritated breath mixed with the hum of the vibrator between her hand and the cuspate swell of her pubic bone. Cries of the princess a curtain behind the glow of TV rain. Images on the screen descending upon each other in a roil of flesh. The princess's stomach slick from a syllabic attack of sperm. Fire storm sweeping across a stand of papier-mâché pyramids. Costumed men and women drag each other down into a sea of spotlights, muscle. Two conquistadors sharing a grin as the princess dons one of their helmets, curls back, and opens her mouth against the hum. Groping for Rick, slapping his thigh with her hand. Rick guides the white phallus. The destruction of the Incas behind him. He tastes. Squirms at her sacrifice. Interlocked against the clamshell headboard. Her upturned face is pale. The stereo silent. TV monochromatic, a pearl. The princess in his hands. Her destruction as simple as fantasy.

Rick opened his eyes. Cotton mouth. Ginger's legs wrapped around him, face turned away. Her fingers flitted across the bedspread, body curvy in the necromancy of blue and purple. Rick's belly and chest damp, dactyls of body hair gleamed.

"You like that?" she asked.

"Hmmm?"

"Pulling out."

"Yeah . . . I guess."

The silence begged.

Ginger stretched her arms and yawned. "I can't believe we ran out of condoms. I can't believe we're really *using* condoms. I just did it that first time to be careful. You know, you never know."

Rick grunted. "Never."

"Have we fucked a lot or something, tiger?"

"Or *something*," said Rick. "Something like *more* than a lot."

Ginger let out a muffled laugh and tightened her grip. He shivered. He *knew* this shiver. It wasn't the drugs. He slapped his stomach and yawned. Ginger's skin had the look of industry, reminding him of the bronzed halos at night above the high rises downtown. His knees sparkled from carpet burn. He stood and went to get himself another beer.

"So how come all the fancy stuff?" he asked when he got back. "All those costumes and sets must have cost *beaucoup* cash."

Ginger rolled to her hip. "What?"

Rick pointed at the TV. "That video. That wasn't just like humping in some bogus motel. I mean . . . you know, costumes, etc."

"It *is* sort of new," Ginger mused. "But the market's ready now. You've still got your basic stuff, like just turn on the camera. But also new stuff: mock bondage, new toys, amateur videos . . . big productions. More people're watching *mature* films 'cause everyone's like into VCRs. So now it takes more to make it all interesting . . . to make it believable."

"*Believable?*"

Ginger looked at him.

"Yeah," Rick continued, "*believable.* Way believable. Like a documentary."

"You know what I mean. People wash their feet now. The product's got to keep up with the developing tastes of the consumer. We've got to keep ourselves looking good. Stay healthy."

Her voice reminded him again of someone stacking plates.

" 'Cause now," Ginger continued, "with AIDS, the industry's really starting to think. You know, like companies where people get tested and stuff. And use rubber more . . . like bodysuits and latex gloves. Some studios even use condoms, somewhere, I think. Maybe in San Francisco." She pointed to the TV. "Today's directors and producers need to develop along with the public appetite." Ginger slid to the foot of the bed and stood; her body downshifted through the variegated apartment shadows; her weight on her right foot as she looked back over her shoulder, a ceremony to her movements that reminded him again of Angela. A ceremony very different from the way Tamara would have angled careless and athletic off the bed and pretended to shiver in the warm Los Angeles night, her hair a black scythe against the white of her back. No, Ginger had Angela's sense of anticipation. Angela who would claim that nothing mattered, then lower herself upon her own trembling fingers, watch herself in the mirror and sigh. Wrapped up in sexy despair. Sighs like black orchids. Angela, who would smear baby lotion over Rick's chest while talking about the meaningless of being alive. Every orgasm a last kiss before death. Naked on the sofa. Naked in the kitchen. Naked in the car. Angela, her fragrance sinister. A match for Ginger's little tomboy navel. Or Tamara's lips parting soft as doves off a lawn.

Ginger came back into the room and offered Rick another line.

"Sure," said Rick.

"It's good when the man makes you feel delicate," Ginger said, holding up the mirror. "But if you like it too much, it's hard to concentrate. You know, remember what the director wants."

"How come you've got those photos back in there?"

"I've got a friend. He takes them for me . . . after we shoot. We're going to try and use them so I can . . . you know, get some straight work. As an actress."

"Like not X-rated stuff?"

"Uh-huh. That's my dream, you know, to be a straight actress."

"Do you take any classes for anything or anything? Like other than fucking?"

Ginger gave him a pointed look. "I don't take classes for fucking. I'm a natural. But I'm going to take acting classes *real* soon . . . after I save up some money and stuff."

"Yeah," said Rick.

"*Really.*" She looked past him.

Rick's mouth tasted like soil.

Ginger's blue eyes flattered him. "Don't you think I'd be good?"

"I think you're kind of fooling yourself. I mean, how many porn stars end up in real movies?"

"What about Traci Lords? She's got big parts in two new movies."

"Yeah?"

"Yeah, I think one happens in outer space. Sort of like a comedy. Or what about Linda Lovelace? She wrote a book. Two books really."

"A *book*? So what? No one reads books."

"Or that girl in *Emmanuelle*? Huh? What about her? She's an actress. Crystal. I think her name's Crystal. With a *C* or a *K.*"

"Yeah?"

"For sure, like she's real popular in France and stuff. Or maybe it's her last name? Anyway, I was even going to fly to Europe and audition for the last one. *Emmanuelle 9* or something. There were like a hundred million girls from all over the world. I think they finally picked one from one of those really blond countries like Norway."

"Europeans," explained Rick.

"*And what about Marilyn Monroe?* What about her?"

"I don't get it . . . what *about* her?"

"Oh, Rick, c'mon! Everyone knows about *that!* About back when she was what's her face and made that loop, the one of her playing with herself, and *you know*? I saw the pictures even . . . the stills. She looked kind of fat and gross, but it was her all right."

Rick was incredulous. "*C'mon, you know* yourself. That'd be in the Smithsonian or something. Give me a break."

"I'm not kidding," insisted Ginger. "My friend, he had it in an old *Penthouse.*"

"Jesus!" spat Rick. "Don't tell me you believe *that*? Shit, they probably paid some chick to get her face rebuilt or something heinous like that."

"I saw it," Ginger griped. "They were the *stills.* And she had these ugly stockings and big white thighs . . . but it was *her* face! Back when her name wasn't Marilyn and she had brown hair. Like it was Mary something or something . . ."

"I think it was Norma something," said Rick. "Norma Jean. Elton John did a song about her. I saw the video. He was dressed up like Beethoven. It was kind of lame."

"Weird. Why would he dress up like Beethoven?"

"I don't know, unless he was trying to be someone else."

"He's gay, right?"

"Elton John or Beethoven?"

"Elton John."

"Totally. I think," said Rick. "Maybe he was trying to be Liberace. That'd sort of make sense . . ."

"I'm not going to get that," Ginger blurted.

"Get what?"

"AIDS." Ginger looked down at the mirror and began to scrape out a new line.

"Good," said Rick doubtfully. "That'd be a serious drag."

Ginger took a slug of champagne into her mouth, the liquid sparkled at the corners of her lips. Rick could feel the string of chemicals tighten. God, this girl was dumb. He watched as she ran the base of the bottle across the bedspread. *Dumb.* The word thrilled him. It was the pure *dumb* in her he wanted. The soft childlike *dumb.* The wild adult *dumb.* His spine cranked down. His chest a kiln. Her *dumb* curved body. Her *dumb* blue eyes. Her soft *dumb* breasts.

His chest throbbed.

Rick wiped his hand across his nostrils. "What was that movie about gangsters about?"

"Gangsters."

"And? Like what was it called?"

Ginger lay back and talked to the ceiling. "I think they were going to call it *Restless,* but they ended up calling it *Bunny and Clyde.*"

"And you were Bunny?"

"No way. I was the rich lady in the bank. Bunny and Clyde got to fuck me in the vault. Like I was a hostage."

Rick thought back to *Pleasure Quest.* "You're sort of everyone's toy, huh?"

Ginger laughed. "I get paid to make you *think* that. You know, make it *believable.*"

"And you don't care?"

She smiled, then shook her head. "But I won't do anal," she added. "Never have, never will."

"That's probably a good idea." Rick stood, went over to the TV, and looked at the stack of tapes on the floor. *Back Door Delights, Bunny & Clyde, Pork Sword Widows.* And one called, mysteriously, *Steam Cleaning.* Plus, part two of *Gone with the Wind.* He clicked *Back Door Delights* out of its plastic case and ejected the other, hitting Play without bothering to rewind. Instantly, the room was sprayed with a frantic *yes! yes! yes!* Muzak jazz spilled from the giant TV screen. The room moon-bright. A string of oily plastic pearls emerged from an immense blinking sphincter. A shaved pudenda filled the screen. The camera jiggled, revealed a woman with green hair, fingers gripped onto the pearly string of love beads. Her free hand came down hard on the rump of her prisoner.

Yes! yes! yes! The hand slapped. The women's lips out of sync with the sound of her voice. The pearls like a cap gun. The prisoner? A blonde with blue eyes. Knees bent as the other reaches into a doctor's bag for a candle. Then, on her toes as she stretches to the shelf for a double-headed dildo. Then it was into the closet for a big padded black matte box with a speed-control knob and a vibrating plastic cock that hummed, shook, wiggled, gyrated.

Rick finished his beer, the polished clamshell smooth against his bare back. The room fragrant with the smells of new furniture, sex, and stale liquor. Sounds of traffic leaked from behind the louvered blinds. Rick moved his foot, touching Ginger's ribs. The mirror was empty. Rick's nauseous delivery to the Buick only a couple of hours away. Ginger leaning across the passenger's seat to kiss him, shading her sunglasses with her hand. Rick stuck with a smile that rises to his lips like a blister. His shirt thwaps back in the white-hot spot of sun beside the Buick. The rules of night no longer applicable. Corvette too shiny in the morning.

Gone.

▶ ▶ ▶ **10**

The Manager found Rick still stretched out, his head rested on the lemon WELCOME. The Manager pushed his corduroy slipper up against Rick's unshaven cheek. "Mr. Jeffers? Hey, brother?"

The smell of Pall Malls and Thunderbird was irrefragable. It clung night and day to this petty bureaucrat of rents and leaking sinks.

Rick opened his eyes. "Don't call me brother."

The Manager's bermudas were covered with unsightly orange stains. Rick groaned into a fetal position.

"You living in the hall now, *brother*?"

"Fuck you," Rick mumbled.

"Ah, the white man's burden. Now what's this about?"

"My key."

"Your key?"

"Yeah. Just half of it's stuck in the lock."

The Manager bent over with the master. Huffed. Straightened. The thin key chain recoiled with a snicker to his belt. A squiggle of jagged metal glinted in the lock. The Manager gave a low whistle. "Bad business, this key. I'll have to call a smith and that's going to run you some."

"What?" croaked Rick. "It's *your* fucking door, squid! Management's responsible for this kind of thing. Give me a break . . ."

"No," mused The Manager. He rubbed his cigarette into the stucco. "We're not liable. It's in the rental agreement. The undersigned is responsible for *all* malicious damage to rental units."

"Malicious? I was just trying to get in the door! It probably busted 'cause of negligent lock maintenance. You know, dude, like you have to lube these things more than once a century. I was lucky I wasn't seriously hurt!"

The Manager wiped at his neck. A smile crawled at his face. "No . . . I'm afraid *you're* mistaken, brother. But you're welcome to read the contract."

"You're bogus!" Rick sputtered. "I *know* it's a state law, like that all life-threatening *crucial* mechanisms, like door locks, be checked annually by state agents . . . and, ah, in lack thereof of said approval, the management, repeat *management,* is *always* responsible for coughing up for mishaps that extend from previously stated irresponsible actions that affect the renting party. And that means . . ." But it was no use. Rick briefly closed his eyes against the threshing needles of daylight.

The Manager's smile adjusted into a smirk. He withdrew a pack of Pall Malls from his gold Munsingwear shirt.

"Just call the dude," Rick said. "I don't give a fuck."

"Certainly, Mr. Jeffers. Damage probably won't be *too* bad." He followed this with a stream of smoke.

Then the wide shadow dissolved. The Manager was gone. But so was Ginger. So was the night. And Rick was alone. Yeah, awful morning had *definitely* arrived.

He rolled over and stared down at the smooth concrete below his chin. How long would a locksmith take? Hours? Days? Weeks?

Shakily, he stood and begun to claw at the casement. He managed to wind the window back and crawled through, knocking the receiver to the ground with his boot. He stared at it before rolling over. His hips ruby-throated and soft from the multiplications of Ginger. Her smell painted on his fingers.

He stepped off a cliff when he closed his eyes.

The curtains shut. The room silent. Silence burning above him like a black sun. Everything simple. The sum of beauty and poison.

▶ ▶ ▶ **11**

Tamara was surprised she'd called Jack, but she had and now here they were. The two of them knocking back a few racks of eight ball and sipping at Cokes. Jack with a strip of surgical tape over his right eye.

Jack was terrible at pool. "It's nothing," he said softly, when Tamara asked about the cut.

Tamara had tried to introduce him to a few of the basic bridges, but he just dropped the cue across his knuckle and misstroked. Tamara watched as he scratched on the 7.

"You really should try to hold it the way I suggested," she said. "You keep lifting your hand . . ."

Jack ran his fingers over his sunburned forehead, his thick curls. Tamara noticed the buckshot of blue ink on his right bicep. Rick had told her about that once. Told her about the night in high school when Jack had given himself a tattoo while Rick held a bottle of Wild Turkey and watched. Jack cursing the dull pain. Rick had bet Jack thirty-five dollars and a double chiliburger at Tommy's that Jack, Jewish, would never have the balls to tattoo a cross on his arm. A Christian cross. And sell his ticket to the Jewish burial ground.

But Jack had taken him up on it, poking a needle and cotton and dipped in blue ink into his arm. And when he'd had it surgically removed in his senior year, he'd made the mistake of going to football practice and running a few tackling drills; a McGregor helmet finding the fresh stitches and skin graft, parting them into a beautiful red mouth beneath his gold-and-green meshed practice jersey. The intern in the Emergency Room sewing it all back up so that Jack's cross was resurrected in a finite particle explosion of blue freckles on his arm.

"Here," he said, handing her the cue.

Something in Jack excited her. She was noticing it more and more. Maybe the sad eyes. Maybe the body. But it was more than the muscles. It was something in the way he moved. Athletic. Slow and precise.

She ran the chalk between her thumb and forefinger, just like her father had taught her. Then proceeded to pocket the 9 and the 13. "Maybe we could go to your gym together? I need a personal trainer . . . need to tone up."

Jack nodded in agreement as she completed a two-cushion combo, sinking the 11 and the 15. The 10 was a simple kill, with a little backspin to bring her out; the 14 tucked behind a wall of solids along the footrail. She eyed the cue ball and delicately nudged it off the right rail at an oblique angle, causing it to trail in and caress the 14. But not enough.

Jack sighed. "Yeah, Tam, sure. Anytime."

Tamara looked at him and smiled. "I'm the worst, huh?"

"Pathetic," he agreed, and smacked the cue ball randomly, watching as Tamara's 14 trickled into the left corner pocket.

Tamara took the cue and mercifully sunk the 8. Jack offered to buy her another Coke and she accepted. She watched him walk to the bar. What was it that had kept Jack and Rick so close over the years? It probably had something to do with habits. And a taste for fast, loud music. Jack with his weights, his comics, his marijuana, his fighting. And Rick with his tequila, his laziness, his cowboy *attitude*. This attitude that was going to get him into trouble. And made him such a shitty boyfriend.

"Where was I when you were teaching Rick to shoot pool?"

"We played a lot that one summer. Back when we were house-sitting for my parents. That's when Rick invented Truth-or-Dare pool." Tamara smiled. "You wouldn't believe the shots he could make with the right inspiration." She watched Jack blush. She liked the feeling of being the wild one. It was different than her situation with Rick. Here she wasn't trying to hold on. She could just relax. "We really only played Truth-or-Dare pool once," she admitted. "But it was fun. It was good for your concentration when you knew that missing was going to put you in an embarrassing position. Literally . . ."

Jack laughed, looked down, and began to twirl his red straw in his soda glass.

The smoky poolroom reminded Tamara of the time she and Rick had gone camping up in the Sierra Nevada Range, up around Shaver Lake at a place called Evolution Meadow. Their cheap tent had collapsed in the rain, the two of them strapping everything onto their packs and hiking for twelve hours down trails of mud and sodden manure. Eventually they made it to the Toyota and then into a pine-paneled restaurant with a pool table and a bar. Tamara waiting for her turn at the table, then showing the locals what her dad had taught her back in the rec room downstairs in her adolescence. An orange beanbag chair under a poster of Raquel Welch walking on a beach in bell-bottoms and a wide black belt. Tamara's father's stomach crushed against the edge of the table. Pennies in his loafers. The two of them playing for cans of Fresca. Those rednecks on the outskirts of Fresno forced to suffer down. The one, Tamara remembered, grinning through his whiskers as she cleaned the table, accepting Tamara's skill with beautiful redneck grace. The rain majestic across the flat fields of grapevine.

"So where's Rick?"

Tamara had an ice cube in her mouth.

"Rick? Where's Rick?" Jack repeated.

"I don't know really. I think he needed to sleep."

"But weren't you guys going out last night?"

"*I* thought so. But, well, he didn't show . . ." Tamara's voice dropped off.

"You're kidding?"

She shook her long hair gently. "Nope. 'Fraid not."

"You know, we got kind of stoned last night . . . maybe he just fell asleep?"

"I don't think so, Jack."

"Well, maybe that bogus car he picked up broke down?"

"Broke down?" Tamara echoed. "I'm sure. And every phone in L.A. *broke down,* right?"

"Did you try to call him?"

"This morning he stopped by. I could tell he'd been up all night. But he wouldn't talk to me about it."

"Maybe it's a surprise?" Jack lobbied.

"That's one possibility," said Tamara. "Or maybe he just went out and got laid and isn't responsible enough to admit it."

Jack was silent. He looked down at the pebbles of ice in his glass. Rick messed around some behind Tamara's back, but that was Rick. Jack knew that. And he didn't really know what Tamara did on her own time, but to just leave her sitting somewhere. And *then* not talk about it. That was uncool. That was unfair. The whole thing made him feel lousy. He felt like it was his fault. Which was stupid. She was waiting for Rick.

Rick. Rick would never be able to give Tamara what she deserved. No, 'cause Rick was just Rick. Would always be Rick. The same Rick who'd been sitting with Jack just a couple of weeks before in the brown Burbank heat, nursing a Sidewalk Sundae, when a sleek girl had walked by, her white teeth flashing. You know her? Jack had asked. Yeah, Rick had answered. I met her on the Disney lot while I was delivering a *large* with pineapple and Canadian bacon back in the glorious days of *employment.* She was walking down Mickey Mouse Lane. It ended up being a pretty bitchen afternoon. Sort of like your first ride on the Matterhorn, if you know what I mean.

Then how come she didn't say anything? Jack had asked.

She said something. You just never learned the language, dude. Your ear isn't trained for subtleties.

Fuck you.

See? You're just a little limited when it comes to communication skills . . . but that's cool. It's just 'cause I'm better. I'm the advanced model and you . . . you're just the squid model.

Jack admitted to himself, as he watched Tamara stare off at an empty pool table, that maybe Rick *was* the advanced model. 'Cause nothing ever seemed to hurt him. No one ever seemed to *own* any part of him. Even in high school. Spinning tall tales about his skill on the basketball court, but never learning to play much defense or even trying to rebound. Just shooting sweet jumpers. Yeah, the advanced model.

While Jack was ruminating, Tamara suggested they have a drink. Dump the Cokes.

"Sure. Wild Turkey."

"Seven-Up?"

Jack huffed. "Rocks."

"I should remember. You don't care if I have some Seven-Up, do you? I mean, I *am* a girl and everything."

"And everything," Jack said bravely as she tucked her hair back behind her ear.

She reminded him of his favorite heroine from TV. Mary Ann on *Gilligan's Island*. A stormy real-life tall, 3-D Mary Ann. Her hazel eyes flecked with gold. Jack had a crush on Mary Ann when he was a kid. Rick knew it. A point of contention between them 'cause Rick went for Ginger. In fact, could never make it through an afternoon rerun without starting in on all the evil he'd do to Ginger if only *he* could get stranded on that island.

I'd be like JFK, he said once. You know, like when he was president and kept Marilyn Monroe all drugged up? Yeah, and like I'd let everyone pork her. Gilligan, the Skipper, Mr. Howell, Mrs. Howell. Everyone except The Professor. No. Uh-uh, dude. Sorry. I'd never let that yuppie get near her. 'Cept maybe to watch. Yeah, I'd tie him up and force him to check out Gilligan giving it to her doggie-style. Make Ginger wear one of those sequined dresses. Man, can't you just see The Professor all tied up and drooling? Eyes rolling back in his head. Gilligan swinging his white hat and riding that wayhone like a bronc. The Howells traipsing in. Mrs. Howell flapping her fan. *Yes, lovey. Why don't you join poor Gilligan and give it to that little strumpet? Fuck that tart!* And then, after The Professor had *way* lost it, I'd paint him up in a lot of funky colors and send him off naked into the jungle. Give everyone a pointed stick and have ourselves a big yuppie boar hunt. And when we'd caught that squid we'd roast him slowly over some open coals. Chow time! What hilarious bliss that'd be! Maybe let his bones bleach down by the lagoon as a warning. And I'd chain your love slave Mary Ann down there as punishment for consorting with the dude . . . you did know about their *thing*, didn't you? Their sick hard-core lovefest? You did know about *that*, right?

It was platonic, Jack had argued, lost in fiction.

Platonic! Didn't you ever see the one where Gilligan caught them in the cave while The Professor was bonking her up the Hershey Highway? Now *that* was some ugly TV.

No way! Jack insisted.

You only wish, dude. And she dug it.

Rick, you're losing it. There was *never* a show like that.

Look, Rick said in a measured, reasonable tone, It's not my fault The Professor got to cornhole Mary Ann in some damp island cave. *I* wasn't the one who took her up there. It's the *Professor's* fault. And what's worse is that The Prof made her beg and beg 'cause he said it was a health hazard and he didn't want to do it. Like it's unsanitary. Gross me out, Mary Ann! Icky.

Well, I guess history's proving him right, said Jack.

Sure enough. Let's just hope that one time wasn't the wrong time.

But Jack didn't think that was funny. Poor Mary Ann, he thought.

It's too bad, Rick continued. She was such a sweet little girl. Probably'd just been stuck on farms and islands too long and it all went to her head. The isolation. The bright sun. Just turned her into a rutting little lambchop. But now Ginger! Now there was a fine piece of scruff. Scruff City. Those breasts. Complete pendularity. And that walk. That voice. Can't you imagine slipping the reins on that buff filly? Man, get yourself a handful of that red hair and *ride!* Whew! She was a compete frontal assault. Like total nectar.

Yeah, offered Jack.

Yeah? For sure, full-on *yeah.* Randomly optic. Like as in eye candy. And that name. *Ginger.* Elegant and yet trashy. Wayhone-a-rama. If you know what I mean . . .

It's sure better than Bubbles or Wilma, said Jack.

Can't argue with you on that one, hombre. The name speaks a certain quality. And I'll tell you a secret, Rick continued, voice flecked with conspiracy. It's also the name of my favorite porn star.

Ginger?

Yeah, Ginger Quail.

I didn't know you were part of the raincoat crowd.

No, sometimes Tamara and I just pick up a few videos. You know, like stoke that little frenzied heart into action.

Nice, Jack offered, voice dim. And?

What do you mean, *and*? It kicks! Rick pointed to the frayed Lakers cap on his head.

Porn is like the Lakers?

Sure. Rick laughed. Fast, full-on, agile. *The best.*

And Tamara goes for it?

Yeah, usually. Unless they're too brutal or everyone's ugly or something. But that can be avoided through careful selection.

Well, there you go, Jack said with sarcasm. Rick, it must be *love.*

Besides, continued Rick. *I* go for it.

And everything was tangled. Everything soured by Jack's inability to forget that it was Tamara they were talking about here. Tamara. She was just one of Rick's stories.

On the TV, Gilligan ran helter-skelter through the jungle, then over the white sand. He flapped his arms. They were strapped with fantastic wings made of palm fronds and lianas. Gilligan hopped up and down. Gilligan with his red shirt and white pants and floppy white hat. Hop. Hop. Hop.

Pow, Rick whispered, sighting down an imaginary rifle scope. Pow. Pow. Pow. He made an imaginary bow-and-arrow movement. *Zing,* he whispered. *Zing, zing, zing.*

Tamara handed Jack his drink and looked at him. Touched him softly on the white strip of surgical tape over his right eye.

The window behind the bar burned with afternoon light.

Part Two

Hitching to Arcadia

12 ◄ ◄ ◄

I love that sound, thought Rick, flat on his mattress. The bitchy phone whined from beneath a pile of laundry.

Rick crawled to his feet and answered.

No response. Probably someone trying to mess around. Then it made sense. Tamara. He recognized *that* silence.

Her voice fragrant. "Don't you think you ought to call me and see why I hate you?"

"Uh, sure. Like right now?"

The phone glittered in the filtered light.

"Yes. Like right now." *Click.*

Rick scratched his balls. It sure was morning. Or was it? He pulled the shade cord. Not even. It was that other thing. Night. Thursday night. He tapped Tamara's phone number out on the push button. A series of merry beeps followed the silver rings on his fingers. The phone rang once on the other end.

"Hello?" Tamara asked sweetly.

"Uh, hi."

"Yes, this is Tamara. What may I do for you?"

"The question's what *I* can do for you?" he asked lasciviously.

"Oh, Rick, it's you! How nice of you to call. Are you in town, sweetheart?"

"Uh, yeah . . ." said Rick. "I live here."

"Yes, of course you do . . . how silly of me. It's just that it's been such a long, *long* time. What *have* you been up to? Fucked any new girls lately?"

Yeah, this was going to be tough. "No, not *lately*," he said. "Yesterday."

The phone quietly burned. Went dead.

Rick made the merry beeps. Honesty had been its usual mistake. He decided he should try the buddy approach.

"Hello?"

"Howdy, Tam. Rick here. How're tricks? Everything cool?"

"Oh, *tricks* are fine, Rick. How're your *tricks* doing?"

"Pretty fine," he answered. "'Cept I kinda miss you, pal."

Click.

Rick went to the refrigerator and removed the last can of Hires root beer and a piece of cold pizza wrapped in aluminum foil.

He jumped when the phone rang.

"Yeah?"

"Hey, Rick."

"Oh, Patch. What's up? I thought you were Tamara."

"Sorry. But you ought to call her. She's *teed.*"

"No kidding." Rick stared at the phone. "What makes you say that, Sherlock?"

"Oh, I just spent the day with her. We had a good time and everything, but she's kind of hurt . . . I guess, about last night. Like you blew her off?"

"Like," said Rick.

"Nice. How come?"

"I don't think you'd believe me."

"Try."

"Well, to make a long story short . . . after you bailed, which was sort of lame, by the way, Logan . . . after that, I decided to cruise down to the Frolic Room and kill some tequila, you know, before heading to Ancient's Lounge to meet Tam. Well, I was at the Frolic, kicking back under the colored lamps having a glass of Cuervo on ice and I wanted a burrito, so I went to that place next door, you know? Anyway, *après* I bumped into this serious scruff, this wayhone who was trying to turn off the automatic alarm in her Corvette, this awesome red thing . . ."

"Yeah?"

"Well, I was spewing, talking endless, and one thing led to another and soon we were taking a cruise down Hollywood Boulevard, then up into the hills and . . . like things got out of control, you know?"

"You're telling me you left Tamara alone in a bar all night so you could go mess with some sleazy chick in a Camaro?"

"Corvette."

"Worse. Those fiberglass bodies aren't worth shit."

"I *had* to attempt it," Rick insisted. "I mean, we're talking crucial, hard-core wayhone."

"Yeah?" Jack wondered why he cared.

"Yeah."

"And?"

"There's one other crucial thing here. Another point of interest . . ."

"Yeah?"

"Her name was Ginger."

"Like *Gilligan's Island* Ginger?"

"Sort of."

"Sort of?"

"Well," confessed Rick. "She was more like Ginger-the-Famous-Porn-Star Ginger."

"How much more?"

"Like completely."

"Oh."

Jack was silent.

Next thing he's going to be monstering me with his seriousness, decided Rick. His Laker cap on the carpet. The yellow letters vibrated.

"So are you going to die now or what?"

"What are you talking about?"

"C'mon, Rick. A porn star? Sounds like AIDS city to me."

Rick mulled this over. "I was careful. You know, like *safe*."

"That's comforting. Was it worth betraying your girlfriend?"

Rick slammed the receiver against the wall. "*Way!*"

"Way," mimicked Jack.

"Way," repeated Rick. He stared down at himself, ran his hand over his stomach. "Way."

"And Tamara?"

"I don't know. The whole scene's kind of burnt."

"Yeah," agreed Jack.

"But if I keep pulling lame stunts like . . . you know. I mean, if I keep ditching her . . ."

"Yeah, but that's sort of a very uncool exit strategy."

"Yeah," said Rick. "But why's she so tense, anyway?"

Jack was silent for a moment. "Maybe 'cause you fucked her over? Maybe it's the time of month? Pick your answer."

"Maybe whatever. It's bad doing lame shit. I just keep feeling like a prick."

"Yeah," agreed Jack. "Because you are. But I've got some good news. The reason I called is I wanted to invite you and Tamara over to watch this movie we got on video. My sister got it from this friend who works in home video for Maraschino Entertainment, you know, distribution. It's like a new release. Never made it to the big screen. She said we should check it out. *Generation of the Warlock*."

"Yeah, I've heard of it. Saw something in a magazine. Sounds hilarious. Let me try and deal with Tamara. I'll call you back. Laterish."

Rick dropped the phone in its cradle and finished the pizza. It was Thursday and Tamara would be leaving for work soon. Rick decided to drop by Deacon's Garden and pay her a visit. Yeah, he'd take a shower, splash on some stinkwater and go make the world a better place. Then maybe they could all go check out *Generation of the Warlock* at Jack's sister's. Rick had heard it was a cranking story, complete with lots of hellacious weapons havoc and high-density car thrashing. Major money shots. Major hewing of flesh. Major sunlight patches on the bad dudes. A big-budget gig aimed for last summer's release. It sounded full-on. Someone like a young Dyan Cannon holding up the breast end of things.

Rick stepped out of the shower, swallowed his last three Advils, and toweled himself dry, selecting a clean pair of Levi's and a glossy Indonesian shirt he'd stolen from the Salvation Army Thrift Shop. He pulled on his boots and grabbed his duster off the carpet. Picked up his stereo receiver and put it back on the milk crates. Tried to wind the window shut, but the gears were stripped and the lever rotated in his hand. He pulled at the casement, redrew the curtain, and opened the door, the sliver of key still visible. There was no way of working the lock, so he just left it open. Changed his mind and stepped back inside and slid the bolt shut. Again, going through the painful procedure of climbing out the window, remembering to leave just enough room for his fingers to get it open later.

As he walked down the hallway, he looked at himself in the glass. His teeth fluttered green from the reflection of a neon car wash sign across the street. His eyes red. Red, white, and blue. Yeah, he thought, like the American flag.

He reminded himself to make some calls later that night.

He had *ecstasy* in his closet. Packed away. Hidden. Powder form. He needed to put the powder into gelatin capsules and sell it. He needed to make the ecstasy into cash. Fast.

► ► ► **13**

Tamara was visible through the triangles of glass that made up the entrance to Deacon's Garden. Rick climbed out of the Skylark and ambled across the parking lot, through the walnut doors. The restaurant was empty, except for one table in the far corner. Tamara was serving them. Her hair pulled into a loose braid. She was wearing a backless silk blouse, a skirt that shimmered against her dark stockings. Then there were these emerald pumps Rick had never seen on Tamara's feet.

And a new cashier. She couldn't have been working at Deacon's Garden more than a week and already she'd mastered that look of exquisite boredom. No Todd Mann. This lifted Rick's spirits. Free meals were much easier when that tan squid wasn't standing around showing off his malignant freckles.

The cashier stared at her fingernails. "Dinner for one?"

She was a full-on bitch. That was obvious. Rick was seized with the soft desire to fuck her. He shook his head. "Just visiting."

The cashier looked down at her fingernails and blew on them. They wiggled back like tiny, shiny worms.

Tamara was sloshing water into long-stemmed glasses, tapping the toes of her new shoes absently against the baseboard of the waiters' station.

She returned to the couple with two glasses, then caught Rick with a smile. The man and the woman appeared to have been built specifically to play evil step-parents on soap operas. They had plastic faces and their fingers moved as if on hinges. Their laughing diced the restaurant into cubes.

Tamara poured the wine and turned the bottle over in the ice bucket. The man made his hand move for her, saying something. Tamara nodded and went through the kitchen doors. The man continued to laugh. His hand wouldn't stop. His eyes turned to the ceiling with mirth. Tamara returned with another bottle, opened it, and poured a small amount in the man's glass. She winked at Rick. The elusiveness of her angers always surprised him.

Her hips swished hello as she walked over across the coral tiles.

"Hi, Tam. Still hate me?"

Her hazel eyes sparkled. "Sure. But I'm getting over it. I *assume* you're hungry?"

Rick touched her hip.

"Baconburger? Steak?" she asked.

"Whatever." Rick leaned forward. "Maybe a little *tongue* for dessert?"

Tamara took a step backward. "No, but how about a salad or some fruit? Something healthy."

"How 'bout a milk shake? One of those ones, you know, with the espresso?"

"*Espresso?* Isn't that a little high-brow? Wouldn't you prefer me to just dump some Folgers crystals in it? Or maybe Ovaltine? In fact, on that theme, we could just skip the red meat and I could order out for some Space Food Sticks."

"Space Food Sticks!" Rick smiled. "I'd almost forgot 'bout those things. They were NASA at its best."

Tamara gave him her once-over.

"Yeah," continued Rick. "Space Food Sticks. They were like Tang, only food. Or like Sno-Balls, those cupcakes covered with marshmallow and pink stuff? Remember those babies? Had a shelf life like cesium 90."

Tamara made a face. "You didn't eat those, did you?"

"You kidding?" Rick grew silent, remembering one day on Catalina Island at YMCA summer camp when he was a kid; tropical-print jams steamy from the sun and salt water, green hills in the distance, a paper sack in his hand. His package of Sno-Balls floated in the blue beneath the pier. The plastic wrapping breaking free. Sno-Balls sinking. Two Day-Glo punctuations in velvet.

"And Cactus Cooler was your favorite, right?"

Rick nodded. "Yeah, I always thought the cans were *too* cool. They had cacti all over them and this orange sky. Jack and I used to just hang all day, ride our skateboards, play Ping-Pong, and slam back the Cactus Coolers. Then we'd watch all the killer shows like *The Rat Patrol* and *Gilligan's Island*. Like *Bonanza*, *The Big Valley*, and *The Wild Wild West*. Chow down on cereal. Fruit Loops and Captain Crunch with Crunch Berries, Count Chocula, Krumbles, Lucky Charms, Frosted Mini-Wheats."

Tamara had always been curious about Rick's fascination with the minutia of his childhood. "And what about that other show? *Branded*?"

"That was one of our favorites. Chuck Conners was in it—he used to play pro baseball with the Dodgers. *And* basketball way back whenever. We always kind of dug his, I guess . . . *adaptability* with the TV/sports thing. First guy in the NBA to break a backboard when he dunked. A white dude. Probably the *last* white dude. But whatever. And in *Branded* he's this cavalry hombre who gets busted for being a coward, so they break his saber and send him off packing in the desert. Like *later*. And it had this cool theme song that made you feel like walking out of the fort and, you know, just going for it. 'Course that show's serious history now. These days it's nothing but back-to-back talk. Johnny, Dave, Arsenio, Oprah, Geraldo . . . and that other dude with the gray hair . . . that dude who looks like someone's grandmother. Shit, what a sack of clowns. Talk shows *or* shows about cops busting people." Rick looked piqued. "I mean, what's that *say* about us? Hey," he added, "do you remember how many shots the Rifleman shoots at the beginning?"

Tamara looked back at her one occupied table. "The beginning of what?"

"The beginning of the show . . . the beginning of *The Rifleman*."

Tamara shook her head.

"Twelve. Twelve fucking shots. People never believe he was that fast."

Tamara was getting tired of the subject. "It's only TV, Rick. Worse, it's TV history. Trivia."

"Spring that one on Jack," Rick suggested, ignoring her. "He'll probably want to marry you or something."

Tamara made her voice coy. "Or something?"

"Right," Rick said. "Or something."

Tamara watched him. It was like he just didn't care.

14 ◄ ◄ ◄

Tamara's Timex caught the moonlight upon her ceramic nightstand. She lay curled against Rick. Three years wasted, she thought. Their legs entwined, her eyes on the luminous coin of the watch. Rick breathed quietly.

Tamara pressed herself up against him and concentrated on his slow breathing. They had finally *had* their talk and now he was hers in sleep. Which might have been enough for the moment if he hadn't left her sitting alone in a bar while he chased some blonde whore. And after three years! Just to fuck some poor messed-up girl he'd never see again? It was sad. He had finally admitted the truth. The situation was worse than she had expected. Inexcusable. She told him it was over. Then made love with him anyway, like she knew she would.

Tamara picked up the Timex. The watch felt solid between her fingers. She could just barely make out 3:33.

She stared back across the chasm of bedroom. Bare walls ambivalent in the blue gauze of the dark room. Her emerald pumps from Nordstrom's upended on the carpet.

Tamara thought of Jack. Thought of his desire for her.

There was this dizziness. A familiar anxiety lifted her. Rick murdering her twenty-four hours a day with his behavior. Jack lonely. Everyone just hurting each other all day long. And all night.

Enough. Her decision was final.

But what's he going to do? she thought. Marry that girl and start a cute little drugged family of exhibitionists? What was the attraction? And since there couldn't really be any sincere attraction, why had he risked everything? Just for *sex?*

Her and Rick's privacy invaded as the triple-X porn princess stepped right off the screen with her brown roots and bad acting.

Tamara untangled herself from the sheets and moved to the edge of the bed. The carpet lush beneath her feet.

She stood and tugged the down comforter free. Wrapped it around her shoulders. The sheets a whip of turquoise around Rick's ankles. His body an invective. Blue shadows reminding her of those Jacques Cousteau specials she used to watch as a girl, her parents down in the rec room playing bridge. That same declension of blues. As a girl, Tamara would imagine the parrot fish that nibbled at the window outside, manta hovering in the covelite passage of the hallway. There! A barracuda flashing just past the bathroom door.

Her fingers sad over the swell of her abdomen.

Then she was out of the bedroom, taking the comforter with her. The Frank photo still rested within its cracked frame.

She dropped onto the cold sofa. The business of love her pillow. Her dreams, when they bore themselves, a labyrinth, a winding monologue of knives ripping through muslin sacks of silver and gold fish, her mother screaming from the kitchen.

The armrest left a red scald mark on her cheek. Her neck ached. She opened her eyes. Sunlight blasted the window. Tamara was alone again. Thankfully alone. Rick was gone.

15 ◄ ◄ ◄

The Buick idled before the confetti speaker box. Rick's arm out the window. His fingers tapped against the side of the car.

"Would you like anything to drink with your order, sir?"

"Yeah," repeated Rick irritably. "Dr Pepper. Large."

"I'm afraid we don't carry Dr Pepper, sir."

"Since when? Get off it. *Dr Pepper.* Large."

"I'm sorry, sir. Would you like a Coca-Cola or a Sprite?"

Rick ground his teeth. The speaker box had a voice like grape bubble gum. No Dr Pepper? But he *always* ordered Dr Pepper. Didn't he?

Rick stared venomously at the speaker box. "Look, I don't like Coke. I want Dr Pepper. And maybe you should try getting into *pleasing* your fucking customers!"

The box hissed, then crackled. Again, the same polite query, "Would you like anything to drink with your order, sir?"

"Yeah. Cunt juice. *Large,* please."

"Excuse me, sir?"

"Water," said Rick. "Just give me a glass of water, okay?"

"Three Super Tacos and a large water? Will that be all, sir?"

"Yeah."

The machine hissed. Rick's city was in serious trouble. The angels needed help. No Dr Pepper at the Jack in the Box? What was the world coming to? Capitalism in full-scale retreat.

He slipped the Buick into Drive and allowed the V-8 to drag itself forward under the plaster overhang.

He would kill for a large Dr Pepper on ice.

Staring out the window, Rick wondered what had happened to the way things used to be. Back in the days when everything was wild and everyone wasn't trying to make an excuse for their life. But now? All the fast-food places were selling out and marketing like croissant sandwiches and squid-friendly pasta salads. Before you knew it, it'd be carrot juice. Wheatgrass. Spirulina.

He pulled up to the take-out window and held out his hand. He was in a bad mood. He didn't like seeing Tamara sacked out on the sofa. But then, he'd blown it. And now it was over. He couldn't apologize for something he'd just turn around and do again. Like in a minute.

A teenybopper with rivulets of acne and pins in her yellow hair handed him two white sacks. "Here's your food, sir . . . and your water."

Rick put the first sack in his lap and counted the tacos. Everything was cool. He looked back up at the girl. "I'm sorry I hassled you."

The teenybopper watched him. She was a pink reptile.

"I was just saying, ah . . . that I'm *sorry* I gave you so much grief." Rick explained.

The teenybopper blinked. Primordial.

"Forget it," Rick snapped. "By the way, don't you think it was fairly hurting that you guys blew up the clown? Remember the clown? The Jack in the Box clown? Well, it's sort of a drag that *you* work for a place that'd kill a clown. Like *execute* it just for the sake of a TV commercial. I mean, what's that say about *you*?" Rick was referring to a series of advertisements that heralded the restaurant chain's move to establish itself in the competitive, health-conscious decade past, a marketing series on TV that involved exploding their Jack in the Box logo. "Clown Executed. World Mourns Tragic Loss." Rick showed the girl his teeth.

The teenybopper's face was blank as she fumbled with the microphone implanted in the wall. "I don't think I understand."

Rick watched. It was difficult to believe, but here was a citizen of his country, a fellow American of the wayhone persuasion, and she had absolutely no handle on the past, on the history of sacrifices that made her magical life possible. Just smug, vapid, and butt-ugly in her sliding-glass hutch. "I think you're brilliant and beautiful." Rick smiled at the pink lizard in the glass cage. "Don't worry about the clown. You're right. It doesn't matter. The big thing's that *you* just deal, you know, do *your* job and don't complain. Give of *yourself* and work in the spirit of the Lord."

An uneasy expression stuck to the girl's face. "OooKaay," she sang in a San Fernando Valley lilt. "Whaatevrr you saaay." Then she showed him her high-tech plastic orthodontia.

Rick shuddered. Was it possible that *this* morning was even more horrible than the last?

He drove the final mile home and pulled the Skylark into the apartment lot, opened the door, and headed slowly up the steps. It was an evil thing, this business of life. First, you were bailing on your girlfriend, and then, before you knew it, you were trying to carry an intelligent conversation with a brain-dead Valley scruff in a drive-thru. Wow. And it wasn't even noon.

At the top of the steps, Rick saw the sliver of key still glinting in the lock. The door ajar.

He looked in the window. His stereo was gone and his room was trashed. Yeah, good morning, Rick.

He'd been ripped off.

16 ◄ ◄ ◄

Rick was in the process of scarfing his tacos, when The Manager arrived, humming. The Manager hadn't expected this kind of good luck. He listened with a smile as Rick moved around in the apartment, cursing the little effervescent knock. Out popped Rick's bleary face.

The Manager pushed past him. The mattress was flipped over, the orange plastic table severed of one leg. Levi's, T-shirts, and sliced portions of lounge chairs strewn around the carpet. Everything chopped, diced. The closet door was off the hinges, the clasp and padlock torn away, barbs of laminated veneer hung beside cupulate marks in the plaster. "Lock your closet? *Valuables?*"

Rick nodded. "Yeah," he said carefully. "I had some nice *suits.* And china and a silver tea service, but . . ." He gestured at the clothes on the floor. "Looks like they got everything but my rags." The Manager nodded and lit a cigarette, watching Rick thumb his way through his albums.

Motörhead? Guns N' Roses? Slayer? Megadeth? Metallica? Skid Row? Faster Pussycat? Nuclear Assault? Corrosion of Conformity? Storm Troopers of Death? GWAR? Method of Destruction? Morbid Angel? Even his Mötley Crüe *Girls, Girls, Girls.* Gone. His early metal? His Zep? AC/DC? April Wine? Black Sabbath? Rainbow? U.F.O.? Deep Purple? Hendrix? Kiss? Iron Maiden? Van Halen? Early Motörhead? *The Runaways?* .38 Special? Bad Company? Thin Lizzy? Gone. His hardcore? Angry Samoans? Black Flag? Hüsker Dü? Dirty Rotten Imbeciles? Red Hot Chili Peppers? Sonic Youth? Firehouse? Jane's Addiction? Thelonious Monster? The Didjits? Social Distortion? Suicidal Tendencies? Minor Threat? Flipper? X? Gun Club? Dead Kennedys? Minute Men? Divine Horseman? Flesh Eaters? Circle Jerks? Fear? Butthole Surfers? The newer stuff he could still find in album format. firehose? Jane's Addiction? Thelonious Monster? Present and accounted for. Pretty simple, deduction-wise. This one wouldn't take Detective Columbo. Any squid could read *these* clues. The criminal was a metalhead of the speed-metal school. Appreciative of the early heavy roots of the discipline, yet unable to translate *across* disciplines into the less ritualistic world of post *core.* His critical skills dulled by a bad swim in the Burbank gene pool. A fool, close to Rick's age, probably trapped in a day job unloading crates at a supermarket chain like Lucky's or Ralph's. Perfect breeding stock for that stupid chick back at the Jack in the Box. Two nightmares just waiting to mate in the darkness behind a Foster's Freeze. Shotgun wedding. The *baby* scene. A couple of crates of Pampers disposable diapers, twelve to thirteen years of institutionalized public school and . . .presto! Another serial killer stands in line at the hardware store with a McCollough chain saw, a box of Hefty trash bags, and a twenty-pound sack of lye. And yet, on the positive side . . . Rick had been convinced no one listened to records anymore. And here was some lone agent out *collecting* records, stereos. Interesting. Our criminal had a certain *nostalgic* bent . . . a classicist, who yearned for the days of yore when you could clean your herb on the album cover while the wax spun under your state-of-the-art diamond stylus and something like "Black Dog" echoed over the sidewalks. Yeah, *at least* in his mid-twenties, if not older. A metal-head grocery clerk born in the early- to mid-sixties. Working somewhere around the San Fernando Valley. Rick walked into the kitchenette. Yeah, might as well forget it. Sounded like the personality profile of half of the city. The window screen sliced open. The parking lot below fringed with tall yellow weeds and chaparral. Clueless idiots. They could have used the *front* window. Man, he felt *pillaged.*

The Manager smoked and scrutinized the looted room. "This better not affect getting your rent in . . . *brother.*"

"Look," Rick suggested. "Don't call me brother. And why don't you *leave*? This whole scene is sort of your fault and, I mean . . . why don't you have any security around here? First the fucking death key almost shreds a major artery and now my place gets ripped off. It's sort of too burnt for words . . ."

The Manager grinned. "Jeffers, we have very little crime here . . . at least, none of the *good* residents."

Rick placed his palms flat against the wall. "*Good residents?* In this swine hole? Look," he stressed. "*Whatever.*" Almost talking to himself. "Shit happens." He glared at The Manager, focusing his hatred on The Manager's small breasts of fat. "That stereo was like my favorite thing." Rick stared at the carpet. They took my records! Turntable! Then it hit him. Closet. *Drugs!* The *ecstasy!*

"I bleed for you, Jeffers. Unfortunately, I have to go call the police. House rules."

Rick's eyes moved with disgust to the weasel of fat that squirted above The Manager's slacks. "What?" he asked softly.

"As I said, *brother*. House rules. If we didn't report the *few* crimes we have around here, well, then the police wouldn't know to keep an eye out for us, would they?"

"Yeah. Uh-huh. Just send 'em right up."

The Manager grinned. "I'll do that. I'm sure they'll want to take a look around."

Rick watched The Manager's fat butt. Then stuck his last taco in his mouth and began to rummage through the refuse of ransacked board games, clothes, and hangers at the back of the closet. His red and blue plastic Battleship boards had been crushed, jagged pieces of plastic glittering among cardboard segments of Arkansas Bluff. Oh, the wadded paper play money—Rick's Masterpiece value cards, yellow clips, and playing pieces . . . five-by-three re-productions of the works of Klee, Kandinski, and Pollack scattered on the plastic Twister sheet. The red, green, yellow, and blue Twister circles. That spinning dial. Right-foot-green. But *now* he was in trouble. 'Cause the *Mille Bornes* game box was definitely not there! And not there with it was the Ziploc filled with Methadimethyl amphetamine!

And it would've been *so* easy.

Designer drugs. No frantic coke-addled knocks at 4:00 in the morning. No giant Hefty trash bags of aromatic contraband. Nothing but a pocketful of gelatin capsules and some friendly exchanges. Handshakes. 'Cause everyone could use at least one hit of *X* for a rainy day. Everyone.

Yeah, thought Rick. *Everyone*. Great. Even metalhead grocery clerks. And now he was broke, with no way to make rent. And no girlfriend to protect him with hot plates of grub and freshly laundered bed sheets. No, trying to bum off Tamara would be a severely wimpy move. He thought of Jack. Yeah. *There* was some daylight!

At least they left the phone. He tapped out Jack's number.

"Hello?"

"Yo, dude, *qué pasó*?"

"Not much . . . what about you?"

"Nothing really. Just hanging. Waiting for the cops."

"The *what*?"

"Oh," said Rick calmly. "I got ripped off last night. My stereo. Tube. You name it. They just came in the back and snaked everything. All I got is like this phone . . . and I mean things are *serious* if they're stealing my shit." Rick gave the table a kick. It skidded across the carpet and tapped over the bong that leaned against the wall. "Yeah, I'm pissed. Pissed and beerless."

"Why'do think they picked your place?" Jack paused as something occurred to him. "You weren't holding were you?"

Rick stared around his room.

"Were you?"

"Yeah."

"Green or white?"

"What'do mean, *white*? You know, I stopped that shit with Angela."

"Then it was herb?"

"Well, no. It was actually *ecstasy*. So, I guess, technically . . . *white*."

"Groovy," Jack said flatly. "How'd you end up with that?"

"This guy from the pizza place. We partied one night and he ended up giving me the brother-digit. A killer price. It looked fairly painless."

"How well did you know this character?"

"No . . ." thought Rick aloud. "He wouldn't have been up to it. Too fried. Filled with love for humanity. Your basic acid wreckage."

"Okay. Then who?"

"*Who?* Who fucking cares? It could have been some squid who just got lucky or it could have been some dude who cased the place. He bogarted my metal, but that only limits it to about three million potential suspects. Right? And what's it matter? Basically, I'm hosed. That profit was going to be April rent and payments on that Buick."

"Payments?"

"You know what I mean. Throw a bone to that old bitch for not tormenting me too much when I was in math. I was also planning on treating you, like in special thanks for all the crucial stuff you've done for me in the course of our long and *reliable* friendship. You know, I didn't want to tell you, but I'd sort of planned this road trip to Mexico. Sort of a surprise gig. Endless Pacificos. *Ballenas.* I'd even planned to set you up with a little senorita," he added. "Like with this *serious* unit who's dying to road-trip with you."

Jack listened patiently. Jack always felt Rick really *would* have liked to do all the things he offered . . . that is if his act was even halfway together.

"Yeah," added Rick. "Her name is Ashlyn. She's from Westwood . . ."

"Save it. I can probably spot you a hundred, but that's it. I'm just tapped out right now."

"Yeah? Well, that's cool. That'd be a major save on your part."

"And if you need to crash over here or something, that's okay. Just remember my sister gets kind of stressed."

"Thanks, dude." A hundred bucks and a spare sofa wasn't bad for his first telephone call. But then Jack *was* his best friend. "Seriously," he added. "This *is* cool."

"Yeah, I know. Just don't forget it."

"Later," agreed Rick, hanging up the phone as two Burbank police stepped into the white doorway. Navy blue shirts pressed free of wrinkles. A martial flare to the seam of their pants. PR-24 batons. The whole effect set off nicely by rubber-soled black shoes and Brinkman flashlights the size of baseball bats.

Nazis, thought Rick. But he showed some teeth. "Come in, gentlemen . . ." One of the cops was female. Mexican American. Delgado. The other a male Caucasian. He stood a couple inches over six feet, weighed around 240. His name tag said Wink.

Rick smiled with greater determination. "Welcome. Can I get you guys something cold? A glass of tap water or something?"

Delgado walked into the kitchen. Her holster slapped against her thigh.

"You the occupant?" asked Wink. His complexion implied a diet of red meat and scotch.

"Yeah."

"Name?" Wink prepared to take notes on a leather-bound pad.

"Jeffers," answered Rick. "Rick B. Jeffers."

"B.?" asked Wink without looking up.

"Just B."

"It doesn't stand for anything?"

Rick wanted the cops to leave. Consequently, he wanted to be helpful. "Nope. But my dad and grandad had the same B. It's sort of a family tradition."

Wink gave him an appraising glare.

Delgado returned from the kitchen, shaking her head. She went up to Wink and they began to confer with the prescribed look of terse, cop boredom.

Rick figured the thieves must've also pocketed his Ziploc of marijuana. He spied the bong where it rested beside a stain of resinated bong water.

He slipped over and discretely knocked it back under the raped sofa with the heel of his boot.

Wink turned from his conversation with Delgado.

Rick grinned. Both Wink and Delgado watched him with cold eyes. The grin chewed at itself.

And why? he thought. Just 'cause they're cops? Even though *he* was the victim? Even though *he* was innocent? *Innocent. Innocent. Innocent.* 'Cept . . . they'd find *something.* They always did. 'Cause he was guilty, right? Unemployed. Passing bogus checks. Dealing. Partying endless. Yeah, they'd find him. If not now, then soon. There was no escape . . .'cause the law was not into the kind of liberties he practiced. The law was not into *freedom.* But fuck that!

These cops were here to protect *him.* 'Cause he wasn't the bad dude. No, *he* was the guy who stood alone on the dusty street while the clock ticked. Yeah, *he* was the hero. He was the Gary Cooper dude. The only one with the guts to protect what life was all about in this full-on Western movie. The only one with the courage to stand alone as the bad dudes walked up the dirt street at high noon. Yeah, he was fucking *Gary Cooper. Clint Eastwood. Charles Bronson.* He was Rick B. Jeffers. Our hero. And now someone had trespassed on to his territory. Had fucked with his *house.* Desecrated what he most held dear. His tunes. His property. His livelihood. "I can't believe this!" he snapped aloud. His eyes flashed at Wink and Delgado. "It's just so hurting! I mean, why would someone trash my place?"

There was stillness. Imagine the blue sky. Eventually, Wink said, "What exactly *is* missing? What items were removed from the premises?"

Rick felt the warm adrenaline of anger embrace the exhaustion of all his recent chemical kicks. "I don't know . . . my TV and stereo system, basically. My *hot* collector's item turntable rig. Maybe a couple of shirts . . ."

Wink nodded. "Have you seen anyone unusual hanging around here? Any unfamiliar vans or trucks in the parking lot? Anything out of the ordinary?"

"*Vans?* This is L.A.! This city is Van World, U.S.A."

Then Delgado, her voice like a knife, "Is there any reason you can think of why they might have chosen *this* apartment?"

Rick made a thinking kind of sound, then shook his head. There was a scream, an interminable pause, then a murky *slush* as someone cannonballed into the fungus swimming pool. The *sproing* of the diving board stuck to the air like a cartoon. Rick grimaced at the thought of all that green water.

Wink clapped his notebook shut, his eyes business. "Well, Mr. Jeffers . . . usually these things suggest some forethought on the part of the perpetrator. For example, the need of a ladder, choosing a second-floor apartment, etc. These things usually make me think there was a *reason.* In this specific situation, my guess is that someone got an ear on your stereo and katie bar the door. They thought they ought to get themselves a look."

Rick waited for the logic to draw him into the net of responsibility. *Ecstasy.* The word burned on his forehead. *Ecstasy.* Drug dealer. He could taste the guilt. And he knew from experience that when things looked best, right when it looked like everything was cool . . . that's when you were about to be strip-searched at some holding cell and sent down to County.

He concentrated on the rouge of burst red capillaries that latticed Wink's face. The officer continued, "In this case, I think it was just *that* simple . . . someone got a whiff of that stereo and they took themselves a chance to make some fast money on resale."

Rick nodded. "Yeah," he said with caution.

Delgado continued where Wink had left off. "Did you write down any of the serial numbers?"

"Like from the stereo? The serial numbers?"

Delgado looked at him. "Yes. From the stereo. The serial numbers."

"No."

"Then I'm afraid there's not a whole lot we can do for you."

Lame-ass cops. Dumbshits. It was obvious Wink wanted to bust him. Rick could see it in the dude's eyes. He just didn't want to bust Rick *enough* to think of a reason. Rick shook his head politely. "That's cool. I guess I had it coming to me."

Delgado looked at Wink. Wink shrugged.

After they took down his phone number, Wink pointed to the *Sports Illustrated* on the floor. "Lakers?"

Rick nodded, relaxing at the final clap of the leather-bound notebook. "Crucial."

"I'm a Celtics man."

Rick looked at Delgado and lifted his eyebrows.

"He's from Beantown," she said. "Don't worry. His bark's worse than his bite."

Wink's eyes narrowed. The Celtics were in trouble. He knew it.

"Celtics? Yeah, well, that's a drag . . ." Rick grinned, thinking of his Los Angeles Lakers. "Maybe next year, dude."

Wink twisted his lips.

Then they were gone and Rick was alone. Tuneless. Tubeless. Buzzless. But *freedom* burned in the dingy light. *Free.* He was *free.* No County. No thumbprints. No strip search. No ugly graffiti on holding-cell walls. Yeah, and forty bucks in his checking account! Rick owned the world.

He patted his pockets for the car keys and his wallet, sunglasses in the glove compartment.

No reason to lock the place. The door to the apartment slapped behind him. Silver of key still glittering in the lock.

▶ ▶ ▶ **17**

It was winding into late afternoon when Rick walked out of Grauman's Chinese Theatre. The sun filled the sky white. Red service pagodas shined. The air was cold. Rick thought of summer. That roller coaster of June scored with thick mists, the skies of July bloody, a glottal stop.

The Santana winds in September were a long way off. Rick had forgotten his duster. He rolled down the sleeves of his shirt and headed east on Hollywood Boulevard. Regretted that he had just shelled out part of his last forty dollars to watch a stupid movie about gangbangers shooting each other into threads. It had a cool soundtrack. Rick liked Ice-T. But the movie had been predictable Hollywood torment. *Way* predictable. And the popcorn tasted like shit.

He watched a girl with long black hair walk past him.

He continued east. After a couple of blocks he decided to see how Tamara was handling the end of their relationship. At the cross street he noticed a pay phone down past the awning of a magazine dealership. He imagined Tamara sitting on her couch, wrapped in her comforter; she was smoking cigarettes and drinking herbal tea, probably watching some old movie on Channel 9 or 13.

Rick fished a quarter out of his pocket. She was crying. He never knew what he was supposed to do when she decided to cry. Yeah. Rick paused. Maybe he should save the twenty-five cents. He could just see her tangled hair. Hear her voice bitter with Winston smoke, the TV glimmering. Probably one of those bizarre afternoon kids' specials, a bunch of undernourished German kids kicking around a soccer ball, their voices out of sync. Rick imagined that everyone in Europe had voices that came out about three seconds after their lips moved. It was a weird Europe kind of deal. Rick dropped the coin in the slot and dialed anyway. He had always hated those shows. Flute music and haunted gray walls and cobblestone streets. Everything so weird and dim and brown compared to the white sidewalks, trim grass, and blue skies beyond the cloverleaf. The foothills. The sun burning, watching. Sprinklers revolving. And TRIX commercials. Man, that was normal. Not belching smokestacks and all those dark clothes clipping up and down damp stairwells. All that subterranean light. Shit, no wonder Europeans were always blowing themselves into juice with car bombs. Who wouldn't be tense? And he could only imagine the stuff they ate. Like gruel. Yeah, gruel and porridge. Nothing to do all day but stare at your maggot friends and crawl around in an alley, waiting for that bowl of mush. Serious bummer. There should be a government program started to cart over stuff like Super Tacos, Pop-Tarts, maybe even boogie boards, skateboards, Frisbees. Lawn darts. Slip N' Slides. Did they still make Slip N' Slides? Anyway, you could call it Kool-Aid. Shit, you could *send* Kool-Aid. And maybe some killer herb . . .

The phone machine clicked in. Tamara's prerecorded voice invited Rick to leave a message at the beep.

Rick turned, reflection in the glass of the phone booth, then again, in the glass panel of an adult movie house. He didn't look bad. Maybe threatening and of a violent nature, but that was groovy.

He put the phone in the cradle. Didn't leave a message. A collage of naked women stared back at him, their lips parted in OOOOOs. Rick grinned. The Orpheum Theater.

He walked over to the window and paid the corpse behind the glass. *PLeaSuRE UeST—dIAL "T" fOR TA-TA's—StRANGE WINDowS 10:30 4:00 9:00 on M-F Sat/SUN conseCutive Shows . . . 24hrs. $4.50.* He was in the mood for pornography. It'd be hilarious to watch Ginger on the screen, particularly after Wednesday night.

The carpet was ripped up at the edges of the lobby. Near the entrance, twin pillars of opaque plastic emitted a lavender glow, cords strung out of each base and plugged into an outlet beside an ashtray filled with sand.

Rick stepped into the dark theater, amused to find himself alone, staring at the tablet of blank screen. The darkness flickered as he waited for his eyes to adjust. He made it to the center of the cordovan seats and kicked back. His boots up on the seat crest in front of him. Cordate lamps fixed to the red-textured walls hummed. The black dazed momentarily, then redescended. The screen flashing. Bright credits moved like white ants.

Tamara sat in the padded Cybex pull-over machine. Her arms were above her gripping the bar, her elbows pressed against the elbow pads. She had a padded belt around her waist.

Jack stood next to the machine. He wiped at his arms with a small white towel. He was wearing a faded green T-shirt that stopped halfway down his stomach. The T-shirt went Oakdale Football. Then in a yellow square, the green number 77. He was wearing black Champion shorts and some cross trainers he'd picked up at a discount shoe outlet. Tamara was wearing her gray cotton aerobics outfit, a loose white T-shirt and old aerobics shoes with a bright stripe pattern that sort of embarrassed her now. As she concentrated on exhaling, she pulled down at the elbows, her palms flat against the bar.

Jack watched, noting the trim mouse of black hair under her arms. It flashed as her arms sliced up and then down. He wondered if other men found this kind of thing exciting.

"How's that?" she asked after completing her first set.

Jack was all business. He reached down and unbuckled the belt. "C'mon. Let's make this *aerobic.*"

Then it was the military press and shoulder machine and on and on into the leg press for quads and hamstrings and at the end a very light set on the Smith Press. "That's good for now," Jack said. "We should take it easy your first day out." He smiled. "Why don't you try to do a few dips and then we'll finish with some crunches. Run a few laps to cool down and take a sauna. Hang on for a second, I want to knock out some lat pulls."

The Complex Venus had everything Jack wanted in a workout facility. It was his concession to comfort. Even had a juice bar. And this coed sauna out by the Olympic-size pool. Even had Tamara draped on one of the redwood sauna benches. "I feel good," she said unconvincingly. "Working out is *real* invigorating." In the sauna, Tamara was wearing a blue one-piece swimsuit. She kept pulling at it, letting her skin breathe. The idea of a bathing suit in a sauna bugged her.

"Your body will get used to the punishment." Jack leaned forward and watched the sweat run down his belly. "What happened to you guys last night? I talked to Rick earlier . . . and then this thing about his apartment."

Tamara said nothing. Her gaze drifted to the blue ink freckles on his bicep.

Jack watched the sweat pool against the waistband of his shorts.

"It's not working."

Jack nodded. He didn't know what to say.

Tamara held the bathing suit up and ran her hand against her stomach, sweeping off the sweat.

Jack watched the redwood slats, the black-grilled electric-heat unit. The small wooden ladle and bucket.

Tamara leaned up on her elbows. "What was that about his apartment?"

"He got robbed last night. Called me up. The cops were on their way over."

Tamara shook her head. There was too much to process. "We sort of broke up, Jack. He told me about the other night." She looked Jack straight in the eyes. "I don't want a boyfriend who sleeps around . . . with porn actresses. With *anyone.*"

Jack was done with the sauna. "He's borrowing some cash. I'll probably hear from him today."

Tamara looked at the white strip of surgical tape above Jack's eye. "I should have just hit him with something."

"Lucky he's got nothing to steal." Jack didn't mention the *ecstasy.*

Jack had his sister's Honda Civic. "Want to do me a favor . . . the Suzuki's sitting over in Hollywood costing me money. Maybe we could stop by. You could drive the Honda back?"

Tamara stood. Jack watched her. She was thinking about something. "Jack, did Rick have drugs at his place?"

18 ◄   ◄   ◄

Jack looked over the top of his burrito at Tamara's red eyes. They had picked up the motorcycle and dropped off Jennifer's Honda. They were back in Burbank, having a late lunch. They had been talking about Rick. Tamara had started softly to cry.

Jack ran his hands across his chest. He felt itchy. "Want some salsa?" He held out a ceramic cup caked in brackish sauce. Tamara gazed on, then shook her head. Jack placed the cup back on the red-checked tablecloth and began to tap out a ditty of plastic *clicks* with his disposable spoon. "Sure?" he asked, motioning back to the salsa.

Tamara didn't answer.

Jack looked out on to the busy street. "Don't get so down, Tamara . . ."

"What if I really love him?"

Jack imagined Wolverine-san. Logan. Patch. The vagabond. The loner. The psychotic. The beast. A man with a future as enigmatic as his mutant origins. Mariko. An heir to different rules. *Giri.* Obligation. Duty. Honor. The pain in his mutant's heart. *Compared to this, Logan thought. Death is mercy.*

Tamara was staring at her right arm. She began to pinch the skin.

"Zit?"

Tamara concentrated. Exhaled and looked up. "Ingrown hair. They're the worst." She pursed her lips. "Pretty hot date, huh?"

"Is this a date?" asked Jack, his voice catching.

Tamara smiled. "Sure . . . why not?"

There was an uneasy interval.

"Rick?" Jack suggested.

"Lot of good *he* does me," she said with a small voice.

Jack wondered why he ever bothered to open his mouth. He wasn't Wolverine. He was like some pathetic character on a TV sitcom. He was Richie Cunningham on an old *Happy Days* rerun. Everything reduced to the cheerleader with the fuzzy sweater. They would never kiss. Not at the sock hop. Not at the drive-in. Not in the backseat of the convertible. Never. *Don't worry, Richie . . . we can still be friends.* Jack began to pick at his teeth with the corner of his disposable fork. He realized what he was doing. Stopped. Tamara's fork flitted around her tostada.

"Is it difficult for you . . . that I care for him?"

Jack pointed his fork into a red check. "No, it's just the scene. The unhappiness . . ."

"Really?"

"What are *you* worrying about *me* for? *I'm* supposed to be comforting you."

Tamara smiled and took a tiny bite of her tostada. The indolent smell of refried beans steamed from the kitchen, a perfume of chicken and rice in chafing dishes. A boy in a Pee Wee Herman T-shirt was drinking a bottle of Jarritos. "Do you want to go for a ride . . . up in the mountains?" Jack asked. "We could take the Suzuki."

Tamara smiled. "Do you have an extra coat or something?" She motioned down at her loose dress and her worn Levi's jacket.

"No problem. How about that red leather one?"

"Good." Tamara stood up and stretched.

Shading her eyes in the parking lot, turning back to Jack.

Jack: the glass door closing behind him as he points across the street in the direction of the Music Plus.

It wouldn't be the first time Tamara had joined him for a ride on his motorcycle, yet he shivered as her arms wrapped around him. He slipped on the DISCO sunglasses and stepped on the kick start. Her hands moved to his hips.

The traffic was a vein of dry, cool air and telescopic afternoon Los Angeles horizon.

15 ◀ ◀ ◀

History. History, thought Rick. That nectar is history!

A siege of pink filled the screen. Rick watched as the woman quivered. A line of pasty men in leather chaps watched. They were in some heavy-duty industrial site.

This went on for some time.

"Okay, okay," snapped Rick. "Enough."

The figures uninspired, mechanical; their meshing skin indeterminate. If it hadn't been for *Pleasure Quest* . . .

Then, a jump cut and *Strange Windows* transformed into a Western motif in a blue-leather upholstered Streamliner trailer. Four women. Three were wearing cowboy hats. One was wearing an Indian feather headdress. She was very blonde.

"Whoa." Rick clapped his hands. A redhead with a cowboy hat lifted the blonde's loincloth to reveal a trim dusting of black pubic hair. "Fake!" Rick laughed. "Dye-job city!"

But the woman was beyond the reach of Rick's cosmetic criticism. Braced against the stainless-steel two-burner stove, legs spread, she waited as the cowboys threaded a brace of some soft material between her thighs. Another very blonde cowboy gave her a delicate shove. The woman with the feather headdress rhythmic as the brass arm of a metronome.

The theater empty, soundless except for an occasional squealing from the blonde Indian. The women handed each other their hands and groaned.

Rick thought of pulling out the wand and giving it a tug. He remembered a recent headline in the paper, a headline about a guy sentenced to a prison term for getting caught wacking off in a bathroom in Orange County. Yeah, it was bleak but the criminals of the new West were a *weak* crowd. Drive-by gunmen, screw-driver artists, business scum rapists of all sorts. Even some desperate dude squirting his load against a public john. Not to mention shitty small-time metalhead record thieves. Life was getting seriously heinous in the old urban desert. No doubt about it.

Rick watched as the Indian turned around and began to kiss the redheaded cowboy.

He smiled. How had that Doors song gone? Something to do with the West? Yeah, that was it! Something about the West being the best.

Uh-huh, thought Rick. It was simple. The West *was* the best. Why? 'Cause it was further. More.

West.

 **20**

Jack downshifted and hugged the Suzuki in against the swaying mountain road. Manzanita ripped past, a thicket of pine shiny along the circumference of a white sand turnout.

Past the Lancaster/Mojave exit.

Past Chilao Campground.

And the chain link gate of the Cal-Trans compound.

Past Newcombe's Ranch hamburger-and-beer joint. The parking lot empty except for a few pickups, a black-and-white sheriff patrol car, and a dark green dumpster.

Tamara's hands up beneath his jacket, clinging on as he opened up, leaning out of the turn. White cirrus across the desert sky. A blue zipper of ski lift chairs dangled on the stony slopes of Waterman Mountain, traces of ice in the pockets of shade. Air chilly and thin above the city. The short winter dead.

Tamara pinched his nipples, then thought better of it and slid her hands back down across his stomach, hooking her thumbs in his belt loops. Their helmets tapped with bursts of acceleration.

Jack banked around a series of S-turns. Consumed, dreaming of some big Japanese rice rocket. Something that would just *hum.* A lazy feeling followed the sweep of Tamara's cold hands. Something fast. He could get into a big machine that went really fast. Speed. He wanted to learn the Japanese word for *speed.* He was dreamy with the speed of everything.

21 ◄ ◄ ◄

Rick stepped into the fallen evening as a red Corvette Stingray crept up, waiting for the stoplight to change from red to green. The windows were smoked mirrors. Rick couldn't see the license plate.

He sauntered across the crosswalk. That last movie had done something, tripped some switch. He felt righteous.

The signal changed and the Corvette prow lurched, then stopped. Could it be?

The Corvette considered Rick.

Cars flashed around him as the Corvette's engine scratched at the air. The window lowered.

"Hi," said Ginger. "I had a feeling I'd see you . . ." Her tongue traced her lips. Her gaze moved once up the length of his body, hands on the steering wheel. "Recovered?"

Weird. Ginger. "*Fully.*"

Ginger shifted the car into Neutral and reached out. She caressed his Levi's.

Rick thumbed toward the theater. "Just caught one of your classics. *Pleasure Quest.*"

Ginger continued to rub, fingers closing on his erection. "What'd you think?" she asked.

Rick smiled. "As long as the girls really come, I'm satisfied."

"And you can tell?" Perfume lifted from her. Rick also noticed the faint smell of salt. "Maybe."

Ginger let go of him. "I've got to go. I've got plans . . . but I'm going to be out in Cathedral City, you know, around Palm Springs for the weekend. Do you have a car?"

Rick nodded. "A big one. And fast."

"Big *and* fast?" Ginger smiled. "Come out and meet me on Monday. Take the Gene Autry Trail exit and go down it to Palm Canyon Drive. Meet me at a place called the Vesuvius. Around six. They've got a *killer* happy hour. Okay? The Vesuvius."

"Why Monday?"

"I've got stuff to do, you know, *work.* But show up. After."

Rick moved close, pressed his hips against the Corvette. "Work?" he insinuated. Then touched her on her bicep. Her skin was warm. He ran his fingers back under her sleeveless boat shirt. Her skin was warm all over, her face slightly wind-burned. "What've you been up to?"

She looked at him. "You better go. You'll get hit."

Rick shrugged, then bent for a kiss. Their tongues tangled.

Rick glanced at the oncoming traffic. "Monday," he repeated. "Six o'clock."

The smoked glass curtain. The Corvette lurched. Smoothed out, built velocity. Was gone.

Excellent. Rick skipped ahead of a Ford Econoline.

Time for the first beer of the day.

22 ◄ ◄ ◄

Tamara stood on the rim of the turnout, her back to Jack. She was tossing rocks toward the yellow skeleton of a yucca. Jack was making triangles in the dirt with his black steel-toed boot. He had climbed down the frail slope to retrieve a cone from a Douglas fir. Tamara had dropped it in her struggle to climb back up to the lip of the turnout, arms full of dried yucca fans and wads of thistle sage.

They hadn't spoken for what seemed like a long time. They hadn't spoken since the kiss. Jack drew triangles in the dirt and watched Tamara throw her rocks. Tamara's head dipped slightly as she looked around. She wanted more ammunition. She held the fir cone, considering. Stared off into the dark green arroyo. Jack and Tamara motionless. They contemplated the canyon of pine that spread below them. Her long hair rustled against the red leather jacket.

Jack was exhilarated that *she* had done the kissing.

That's when Tamara turned and walked over, holding the pinecone. She performed a girlish arabesque, long, gawky. Her pale arms a vase above her, painted out of the purple sky. Shivered and moved so close Jack was forced to step backward, her fingers against his chest. "I'm sorry," she breathed as her lips returned, at first with hesitation, then desire. Something exquisite, yet unimportant, collapsed inside of him when her arms slipped around his neck for the second time. Her hair lush with the fragrance of cigarettes, exhaust, cream rinse, and sage. Stain of mesquite on the fingers that moved across his cheek. The sun quenched behind the ridge and the distant glint of the Pacific Ocean. Tamara's apologies whispered as she kissed him and everything began to sink and get very warm. Distant headlights sliced up the night. Tamara leading him behind the final breaths of orange that lit the green abdomen of the Suzuki. String of his spine twined with translucent silver microphones. Jack's hands follow Tamara's as she unbuttons his jeans, cradles him against the hush of her soft belly.

Lights of a big black car spear their bower of thin starless sky. Dissolve.

▶ ▶ ▶ *23*

Before heading back to Burbank, Rick decided to take a run by Tamara's and leave her a note. He had called twice from the Frolic Room. No answer. Just the phone machine clicking in.

The door of the Buick closed behind him. Two lamps burned luminous at ankle height on either side of the simulated-marble Sheetrock pathway. They cast a yellow sheen over the camellia. There was a pile of green leaves raked up against a tar-veined railroad tie. Rick took a kick at the leaves, his foot snapping in the jaundiced light. Grazed the pile, lost his balance, and almost fell.

There was a serene clipped-branches kind of smell in the air. The hint of a rainstorm. Rick sidestepped a chaise and looked up just in time to catch Tamara and Jack, bodies hazy in the entryway.

Tamara's front door was open. Jack had two jackets draped on his arm. His hands were on her hips.

Rick stepped back and bit his breath. This was a strange gig.

He watched Tamara slide up and put her arms around Jack's neck. Jack smiled as she whispered something. They kissed.

That fucker! Rick pressed back into the darkness, took a few steps to the side, and groped around the shingled abutment. Ivy crackled under his feet. He was able to make out a pillow of brightness from the direction of the open door.

He took a deep breath. *Jack and Tamara?* And only like on the *same* day he and Tam were calling it quits? That was hurting. Harsh behavior from like your two best friends. For all he knew, they could have been going at it behind his back for months. And here *he* was feeling guilty about Ginger? What a joke.

Rick balled his hand into a fist and held it against his chest. He should clock the motherfucker!

The pillow of light dissolved. Rick heard the *slump* of a door.

No footsteps.

Jack and Tamara. Jack and Tamara. And while Rick's hands still tingled from holding her!

Rick stepped around the corner and faced the entryway. His tongue tasted like Styrofoam.

Who was he kidding? *It was his fault.* But like maybe the only thing to do was storm in and grab her, take her in his arms. Tell her he was sorry. Tell her he'd always love her.

Either that or bail.

'Cause this whole thing was going to happen one way or the other. An idiot could see that. Jack and Tamara. It was just the answer to his own horny history.

He listened as a lively bebop leaked from the screen of a second-floor apartment. Moonlight caught the edges of the cement steps.

The light in Tamara's kitchen snapped black.

► ► ► **24**

Rick was awake. The carpet littered with Colt .45 malt liquor cans. His face burned from carpet fibers. And there was this smell. A smell that reminded him vaguely of Cheerios. Oaty. Sour. He moved his head, face sticky. Touched his finger to the carpet and sniffed. Yep. Urine.

He pulled himself upright and blinked, scratching at his eyes. The clean square of carpet where his stereo used to rest winked back at him. He waited, prepared to remember why he was in hell.

Then it lurched through him, that conclusive snap of Tamara's kitchen light.

Sitting in the Frolic Room and Boardner's Lounge, throwing back tequilas. Doing the white-trash-no-count-broken-heart bar gig.

Rick stretched out his legs, grasped his instep, and touched his chin to his knee. His brain throbbed. He yawned. Saline filled his eyes as he braced himself against a burst of disequilibrium. He remembered some girl named Lucia who had this boyfriend who weighed about a hundred pounds and kept shotgunning Colt .45s. The three of them bombing around town drunk off their butts in this trashed long-bed Jap pickup with a camper shell and a monster tape deck rig. X cranking. *Live at the Whisky a Go Go on the Fabulous Sunset Strip.* Which was perfect. Took Rick back through the Eighties. Except the one hundred-pound dude kept talking on and on about the CIA. The sabotage. The political stuff. The people they killed. Etc. Etc. It was getting on Rick's fucking nerves. He hated whining. The glittery highway taillights stringing down the 405 freeway. What was he doing in a car with these squids *anyway?* He was getting fucked up, that's what. Seriously hammered. There are no angels, there are devils in many ways. The world's a mess. Tamara and Jack. Yeah, thought Rick, nursing a Colt. 45. It's in my kiss.

Rick heard a rattle behind the bathroom door. Then the sound as someone unscrewed the lid from a jar. Outside the apartment a riff of frayed car horn brayed at Rick's ears. His stomach full of evil sickness.

He placed his head in his hands and wondered if there was a way you could just sweat all the toxins out of your body. His skin a field of silver rats. A fried metal smell at the back of his brain. That's when the bathroom door splashed hard against the wall. Rick cringed.

A woman in the doorway, legs spread, wide hips set off by the black fringe of her red corset. She looked like an angry red pear.

Lucia. "What's with the mask?" asked Rick.

Her response got caught in the zipper that covered her mouth. She raised a braided rawhide whip. Very Tijuana. And tugged at the top of the mask, pulling it into a black cone. Mascara blotched her low-slung cheeks. Her voice was as sweet and small as a child's. "Want to play?"

Behind her Rick could make out the salmon wisp of her boyfriend soundless behind the drawn shower curtain. Colt .45 cans lined the edge of the sink. A blackened glass pipe rested on the toilet seat beside a turd of pink wax. Lucia wiggled. "C'mon. We'll whip you right into shape." Her laugh was a wind chime. She lowered her arm, pleased with her facility for puns.

"I'll take a rain check," Rick mumbled.

Lucia shifted her weight onto her right foot, arms akimbo. "I *knew* I shouldn't have let you pass out. Gee, I must be slipping . . ." Her eyes shone with sexually explicit glee. "Oh, well. Them's the breaks . . ." She peered back over her shoulder to where the salmonoid shadow hung behind the shower curtain. "I gotta get back to work, I guess. You don't mind?"

Rick shook his head and made his hand wave bye-bye.

"Thanks!" She twinkled. Her face disappeared in the mask. The door closed behind her.

"*Jesus,*" Rick whispered into the carpet. He was seriously thankful he'd passed out. Saved from getting chained to his shower and whipped by some pear-shaped bimbo wayhone nectar scruff with a zipper grin. Wow. Ugly reality all over the place.

"Mr. Jeffers? Brother?"

It was The Manager.

Rick rolled onto his back and looked up at the ceiling. Would they ever end, these terrible things called *morning?*

Rick said, "Yeah?"

No answer.

"*Yes?*" he croaked.

"Well, *brother,* look's like your time has finally come . . ."

Rick lifted himself to his feet. The Manager held the rental contract in his yellow fingers. Rick watched as the sheets were torn in half and then in quarter sections and then into a fine triplicate ash of green, yellow, and white. The Manager on the balls of his feet now, yellow fingers quivering. His breasts and belly jiggled. "That's it, *brother!* There've been just too many complaints . . . and now *this!* Our good tenants live respectable lives . . . *and* they pay their rent on time . . . and *they* don't get robbed . . ." His eyes blinked rapidly. He reminded Rick of a big fat hyperactive rat. "I could have you arrested. For vandalism. I *know* you're the one that did it."

"Did what?" asked Rick.

The Manager motioned for them to go outside. Rick stood and they did, shoulder to shoulder above the green water of the swimming pool. Rick was impressed. *Now* he remembered.

Last night they had driven to Bob's Big Boy for a hamburger. The restaurant was closed and Lucia's boyfriend lifted his toolbox out of his pickup. Yeah, it was all coming back to Rick.

He remembered.

The life-size polystyrene Big Boy smiled back up at them from the bottom of the moldy pool. He was on his back, holding his plate with the hamburger on it. His red-checked overalls muted by the algae.

"Wow," said Rick. "Who could've done that?"

"You did it!" snapped The Manager. "Who do you think did it?"

Rick stepped back from the rail and looked The Manager in the eyes. "I was just fucking raped of all my goods and now you're trying to stick me for some college prank like this? That sucks, man. *Really*. Besides, I was out with my girlfriend last night."

"Oh?" asked The Manager. "Which one?"

"Ha, ha, ha," Rick answered flatly, staring at The Manager's new ugly golf shirt, his double-knit slacks. That skin that must have been scoured daily with Comet or some other name-brand cleansing agent. "Ha, ha, ha," Rick repeated. "Maybe you're right. I'm being greedy, aren't I? I should learn to share, huh? Like maybe I have an extra girl that's, you know, too ugly and stupid for *me* to fuck. That'd be new for you, wouldn't it? An actual girl. Kind of living and breathing and sort of three-dimensional."

The Manager's eyes were miniature vestibules of spit.

Rick laughed. "What'd you say, champ? *Brother?* Want an ugly little slit to twist one off with? Would that make your day or what?"

The Manager whirled as a heavy groan catapulted from the bathroom. "What's that?"

"Just one of my spares, dude. Want to check her out?"

The Manager was confused.

"No shit," assured Rick. "Just go in there and take a peek." A peal of chirping whip noise followed Rick's offer, followed by a drawn moan and a ruffled *sigh*.

Rick winked. "Sounds wicked, huh?"

The Manager faced the door. He withdrew a cigarette.

Rick decided to act quickly. "The only way I'm leaving is if I get my last month's back *pronto,* plus cleaning deposit. Otherwise, I'm hanging and tearing this shithole apart. I can do that, you know. You haven't given me proper notice and now you're trying to evict me and that makes *you* the asshole. I could probably even take you on *People's Court* and let Judge Wapner fry you in front of half the country. Shit, for all I know you ripped my place off just to *try* and get rid of me! I've got friends too, *squid.* I could get myself some monster character witnesses and you'd be dicked. Fully dicked. I figure I could get about three months of hard-core thrashing in here before you'd ever be able to get me out."

The Manager stepped toward the bathroom. Lucia traipsed out in all her dominatrix glory. "Howdy!" she perked. "Oooh, another!" She held up her whip. "First time's free."

Her proposition fell through the empty light.

"Look, Jeffers," snapped The Manager. "I'll give you last month's and the deposit, less the damage to the door and whatever the charge is for removing that thing from the pool."

"Ha!" barked Rick. "No deal, squid. Hamburger boy's not my problem and it's not *my* fault the fucking key broke in the lock. Shit happens. Deal with it. Like I said . . . otherwise I'm cool and I'll just hang and make you kick me out. *Legal like.* No, I think if you want me gone you best fork the five bills, plus the two-oh-oh cleaning deposit."

"Neat." Lucia whistled. "You guys are having a fight."

"Fuck off," Rick spat. "Go uncuff your victim and take a hike."

"I thought we were friends," she cooed.

"Yeah, we're cool . . . just do me a favor and get Bozo the Whiner out of my shower. I'll give you a call if there's going to be anymore wackiness, okay?" Rick grinned at The Manager. "Come to think of it, we might just be having a little get-together tonight, you into it?"

Lucia thought for a second, turning toward The Manager. "Is *he* going to be here?"

"Yeah, probably. Why, do you like him?"

Lucia wrinkled her nose. "He kinda smells. But sure, I guess. Is he your dad?"

The Manager worked his knuckles. Rick smiled. The Manager didn't have the balls to take a swing. No, The Manager was a stab-you-in-the-back kind of squid. A loser's loser.

"I'll go write you a check."

"*A check?* Kick me out of house and home and stick me with a check? Fuck that. I want cash. *Solamente.*"

The Manager stepped into the hallway and ground his cigarette out with his corduroy slipper. The sun made a white cross on the casement window. "I'll be back in two hours. Then I want you out of here for good. I'll be changing the locks this afternoon."

Rick grinned. "Fast," he suggested. "That's the deal, *brother. Do it fast!*"

The Manager watched him with the same tiny, flaming spit eyes. Then disappeared down the hallway.

Rick laughed. Fuck this place. Breeding ground for memories of Tamara. Tamara and Jack. No, he needed a major road trip. Just pile his gear in the heroic Buick Skylark and cruise. Ramble on. Rage forth. It was Saturday. That gave him two days to kill before hooking up with Ginger out in the desert. Why spend it sitting around and waiting for Jack and Tam to come and bum him out, mess with his party head? No way. Hit the road. Drive fast. Drink beer. Litter.

Lucia stepped from the shower curtain. She was humming "Whistle While You Work."

Rick opened the fridge. Yeah, it was definitely time to hit the road. Some drunk dude cuffed to his shower and a singing Bondage Pear with a Tijuana whip and a shiny, metal grin. . .

And nothing in the fridge. Mustard. Onions. A stale hot dog bun.

► ► ► **25**

Tamara's eyes were closed. She rolled onto her hip, pushing herself back against Jack. She loved spooning. Particularly when the curtains were backlit with late-morning sunlight, a man's warm breath against her neck.

"You awake?" she whispered.

Jack mumbled, his arms tightening around her.

She almost expected Rick to come wandering in from the kitchen. The thought made her very uneasy. Guilty. But that was inevitable. And guilt was much more bearable than sitting around waiting to be betrayed. Besides, Rick had made his bed, let him sleep on it. Alone or with his little triple-X Ginger. Either way. She didn't care. She'd had enough.

Jack's hands against her.

He wasn't bad. Cautious and delicate to a point, but that point had passed and they had moved on together. Everything a little scary.

She *should* call Rick, though. Duplicity was unfair, regardless of the situation. She'd feel much better if everything was out in the open. And she'd also need to talk to Jack and explain to him that she didn't really know what was happening. Didn't know exactly what it meant. Because she didn't want Jack to fall in love with her. But then, why did you sleep with him, Tamara? Just looking for revenge? Trying to get back at Rick? Things aren't that black and white, are they? Rick's influence was strong and she was caught up in it . . . yet, Jack excited her . . . had excited her in a way that made her feel absolutely great. That was okay, wasn't it? Feeling great?

The wind outside dragged the branches of the blue hibiscus across her picture window. Tamara watched the shadow branches through the drawn curtain.

Jack's hands cupped her breasts.

Tamara took a deep breath. Her worrying was familiar and it was not welcome. It was a bad habit. Sort of like smoking. A habit Rick had only stimulated. *Think, think, worry, worry, suffer, suffer.* That's what he said. And that's how it felt sometimes. Like something that held her too tight and made it hard to breathe.

She concentrated on the shadow of the blue hibiscus.

Crushed against Jack's strong chest.

She shouldn't be afraid to save herself. She wasn't like Rick. She wasn't capable of acting the way he acted. And Rick had given her no other choice.

And Jack cared about her. Maybe needed something like this.

Maybe, maybe not.

26 ◄ ◄ ◄

Rick was wearing a black cowboy shirt. Pink flamingos embroidered on the yoke. His Levi's were held up by a black leather belt with metal *X*'s stitched on it. He had on two earrings, the ear clasp, and some silver bracelets he'd bought in Mexico. A new yellow toothbrush stuck out of his shirt pocket, still wrapped in plastic wrap.

"Certainly looks delicious, a meal fit for a king. Mind if I join you for a moment?"

Rick looked up from the murdered chiliburger in his hands. Puddles of glutinous chili spotted the molded plastic table at his elbows. "What?"

"I was simply commenting on your meal. I take it those jalapeños are a kind of hors d'oeuvre. A delightful pre-entrée tidbit. And the fries? The critical *entremets*, correct? Of course. It all looks wonderful. And a Pepsi?"

"Water," said Rick with suspicion.

"Water? Critical to all species, but isn't that . . . *pedestrian?*"

Rick slurped some excess chili off his wrist, keeping the stranger locked in the corner of his eye. "I don't like Pepsi *or* Coke. I like Dr Pepper. I like liquor. I need water to live. So I drink it."

The stranger appeared to be in his forties. He had a soft complexion, patches of crow's-feet around his eyes. He watched the action around him with an enthralled and skittish energy. His voice was musical. This made Rick testy. Rick shifted his weight and prepared for any sudden movement. The stranger's shadow fell across the plastic table.

The stranger wore a clean white oxford shirt and a pair of creased khaki slacks. His hair was thinning, pale jute. Like a wave of dust. He had the bulging pink forehead of a perplexed extraterrestrial. He stood under the vacant sun with a smile on his face.

Rick finished his chiliburger and wiped his hands on the industrial-strength paper towels available in the dispenser bolted on the wall. This was Rick's favorite hamburger stand. Tommy's Original World-Famous Hamburgers. The stranger was wearing penny loafers. The face of his wristwatch slipped to the inside of his wrist.

He must be a Mormon. Either that or another management casualty. Some dude who'd sold his soul to Corporate America and just couldn't hack it anymore. Another loser suffering from slow yuppie rot. Too much paperwork. Too much time daydreaming under electric ceiling grids. Yeah, Rick saw men and women like this every day, usually in the supermarket aisles, drooling at the shelves of imported water and frozen dinners with fake French names. People with the same colorlessness to them. Lost. Ruined by the recent recession, the increased expectations of senior management, the competition for jobs. Each evening punctuated by a few pages of *The Wall Street Journal* and that slow spiral to the worms. The stranger's eyes chloritic, flecked with diluted ash and a micaceous green, yet you'd be forced to call them blue. Sort of an aquatic, fragile blue. The stranger wiped at them with a linen handkerchief. Teeth shellacked with saliva.

Rick looked away.

"And I assume you have already decided upon dessert?"

"Get lost," said Rick. "Fuck off. See you. *Bye.*"

The stranger offered his hand. "Langdon. Jules Langdon."

Rick stared back. The stranger's eyes flickered. The stranger's hand unmarked by callouses, unfettered by rings. Nails manicured, smooth. While below the cuff, a series of creamy scars wound together into a knot. No, our stranger was not a happy camper. And lame when it came to suicide.

"Get lost," Rick repeated. "Go play in traffic."

Jules Langdon retracted his open hand, his face darkened. He turned around as if someone was calling his name, then pursed his lips and got ready to try again. He looked at Rick.

Rick twirled his straw in the ice.

Jules pushed his hand forward. "Langdon," he repeated. "Jules Langdon." His teeth glistened. He gestured at Rick's shirt. "Nice flamingos. Do you like birds?"

"Love 'em. Fried chicken. Roast duck. Turkey sandwiches. Now go away, squid. You're interrupting my chow."

"I'm afraid," said Jules pointedly, "that you are not a very friendly man, not very sympathetic. I was simply suggesting you might have an interest in our avian partners. Flamingos are fascinating creatures. They can live for as long as fifty years . . . monogamously. In Africa, they raise their young in the caustic remains of an empty lake. This was possibly the beginning of the myth of the phoenix—the flame that rises from the ashes. Yes, flamingos . . . effective predation avoidance. Filter feeders. *Very* communal. Interesting preening habits. Roman emperors used to kill them for their tongues. It was considered quite a delicacy. But this doesn't interest you. It is obvious that you don't trust me. Here it is a beautiful day and my overture can't be greeted with a little warmth . . . a trace of faith? I'm not a *threat.*"

Rick stood and deposited the remains of his lunch in the trash can. He *loved* when complete strangers started babbling *and* passing judgment on his behavior. Yeah, that was *really cool.*

"I understand that it is quite reflexive to distrust a newcomer. A typical behavioral response. Most species do it instinctively, yet I would draw your attention to the tale of the Good Samaritan."

"The what?"

Jules retreated a few steps. "Not the *what.* The *who.* The Good Samaritan. It's a story from the Bible."

Rick wiped his mouth with the back of his sleeve. "Look, squid, you got it totally correct the first time . . . I'm not a *sympathetic* man . . . in fact, I eat sympathy for breakfast. Dig it? So take your fucking *Samaritans* and your fucking *typical behavioral response* and go for a hike. Okay? Swim in traffic. Fly off a freeway. Do anything. Just do it far away. I'm not in the mood." Rick paused. The eyes watched him. There was such a *fragile* blueness.

Despite himself, Rick asked, "So where're you from?"

"Arcadia."

"Huh?"

"Arcadia."

"Like near Pasadena? That Arcadia? Out the Two-ten freeway?"

"Of course. Are you familiar with any other Arcadia?"

"No," admitted Rick. "I figured it might be . . . uh, like a hospital . . . I mean, like Arcadia General or the Arcadia Glade or the Arcadia Psychiatric Ward or something like that." Rick touched his ear clasp, watching the stranger. "So who let you out anyway?"

Jules was confused. "Let me out? From where?"

"Wherever they keep you tied up. Samaritan Land. You know, the *safe place.*"

"Where? Sandpiper land? *Safeway?* Do you mean, Safeway, the supermarket chain?"

A heavy man wearing a medical smock and a Dodgers cap watched them while he ate his chiliburger. Rick motioned toward Jules. The man shrugged and continued to eat.

"I'm not sure I understand," Jules reflected. "Sandpipers? Safeway?"

"Shut up," said Rick. "Look, I gotta bail. Bye-bye. Farewell. *Later.*" Rick waved.

Jules followed. "Excuse me . . . ? Ah—"

Rick took a swallow of boulevard air.

"Ahem . . . excuse me?" A finger tapped at his back.

"*Yes.*"

"I am forced into honesty."

"Yeah?"

"I am without recourse to . . . well . . . in truth . . ."

"Spit it out, squid."

"I happen to be very hungry at the moment. I am also, presently without the means to—"

"*Fuck!* You're the worst! First that Samaritan rap and *now* you're spare-changing me?" Rick was incredulous. "You've got balls, dude."

Jules's voice went flat. "I would never ask, unless . . ."

Sunlight reflected off the speeding traffic. Rick squinted. "Okay. You're lucky I happen to be a little flush at the moment."

He turned so his back was to Jules and pulled out his wallet. His shirttails flapped in the heat. He peered at the six crisp hundreds and the loose bills left from his beer-cigar-condom-ice run to the liquor store. Pulled out three singles and turned around. Jules was politely watching his handkerchief, his mouth tucked at the corners. Rick took satisfaction from the situation. "Here," he said, handing Jules the money.

Jules looked up, the green paper closed in his fist. "Thank you."

Rick shaded his eyes. "Whatever."

Jules walked over to the take-out window.

27 ◄ ◄ ◄

Rick was sitting in the Buick, absently brushing at his teeth with the new yellow toothbrush, while listening to the monotonic hum of the shorted radio. He had on his sunglasses. He had lifted the hood and messed with the wires. No luck. He had slugged the dashboard. No luck. He had kicked the dashboard with the heel of his boot. He'd even crawled down into the luxurious seat well and stared up at the underbelly of the dash. No luck. Stock molding. He couldn't tell if any of the wires were loose or crossed. Rick hated mechanical problems. And he was still tuneless.

Fuck it, he decided. The stations all suck anyway.

He slipped the toothbrush into his duster and worked a cold Hamm's out of the Styrofoam cooler. Washing his mouth with beer, he traced his finger along the blue artery of the Ventura Freeway, onto the 210 and out to red Interstate 10. East . . . toward Palm Springs and Cathedral City. The Vesuvius. Happy hour with Ginger Quail. Yeah, *she* was going to be his dessert. Ginger Quail. And he'd need some major bliss protection if he was going to take on that fierce scruff again. She wasn't a job, she was an adventure. One random package of girlness. The perfect genetic expression of the word *fuck*. Make your eyes bleed and your skin blister. Yeah, he'd need a *major* bliss screen. Liquid protection would be *crucial*. Rick laughed aloud. Solarcaine for your dick. Bain de Soleil for your brain. Coppertone for wayhone moan. Bliss Factor 30. That's what he'd need. 'Cause she was sunlight. Pure sunlight.

He was glad he'd given that squid a few bucks. It made him feel kind of Christian. Kind of fat, sassy, and Christian.

Rick refolded the map and dropped it in the seat well. He kicked his feet up on the split upholstery. Yeah, if you weren't driving, you might as well be parked.

He stared out the passenger window and nursed his Hamm's, happy he'd got that cash off the manager and was doing something cool for a change. Like a road trip. The only drag being the couple of days to kill before hooking up with Ginger. Normally, it'd be no biggie, but now that Tamara and Jack . . . well now it was sort of like he didn't really have anyone to hang with. It'd be too weird to hang with them. Tamara and Jack. Whatever. It definitely made sense to hit the road. Lose himself in the desert. Piss on a lizard. Throw rocks at the sky.

Rick yawned, turned the ignition key, and was about to back out when the stranger returned, peering down into the open window, forehead glittery with sweat. There were traces of chili on his chin. "I would like to offer my thanks for your kindness."

"Later," said Rick.

"And," Jules continued quickly, "ask you for one more favor."

Rick clicked the gear lever on the steering wheel column; the parking brake released automatically.

"I understand that it's an imposition—"

"Yeah." Rick gave the car gas and began to back out. Jules Langdon clung to the edge of the window. "An imposition . . ." he repeated, "an imposition, yet something that . . ."

The Buick squealed as Rick careened over the curb. Forced to hit the brakes just as a guy on a ten-speed clicked past, juggling his handlebars over the crenulated cement and showing Rick a sour face.

Jules appeared at the windshield, palms spread in a plea.

Rick mouthed *no* and turned to guide the Buick back into the oncoming traffic. The river would not part.

The radio whined. Jules knocked on the windshield. Rick clicked the radio off. This Christian gig was fun for about five minutes. Twenty-four hours of it would be a major drag. But the squid was still there, forehead still bulging. Ugly face still staring. Rick gave up. "So what's the imposition? Got some Samaritans after you?"

Jules composed himself. "As I was without the means to feed myself, I am also temporarily without the means to return home . . . to Arcadia. I fell a little short of money. If you could see your way clear toward assisting me . . . I will gladly reimburse you by mail in the very near future."

Rick laughed. "Yeah, I bet. Why don't you just click your heels together three times?" Jules's face clouded.

Was the squid going to cry? "Look," continued Rick. "I'm heading out that way . . . why don't you just get in. But there's no way I'm fronting you more cash. For all I know, you're just a wino in yuppie clothing."

"Really?" asked Jules brightly. His pale hair whispered.

"Yeah, *whatever.* Just hop in. And hurry. I'm not into getting killed."

Rick leaned over and unfastened the bungee cord, hitting at the door. It sprung. Jules lurched around and began to wipe at the seat with the handkerchief.

"Get *in!*" barked Rick.

Jules did and leaned back, smoothing his hair with his hand.

Rick sighed, rehooked the cord. The traffic parted with eerie suddenness and accepted the Buick Skylark. Acceleration. Jules's fragile blues beamed.

 **28**

"Going traveling?" Jules clung to the headrest and looked over into the backseat, where Rick had stashed his belongings. Milk crates of his remaining albums. A couple Hefty bags of clothes. "I'm a man of the road myself. Always loved the vistas and the great *leks.* The swoop of the kestrel."

Rick's hangover had returned with a vengeance. The Hamm's had done nothing to soften the edge of nausea. "Who taught you to talk . . . Walt Disney?"

"Ah!" exclaimed Jules. "Walt Disney. What a wonderful man. Defined the standards for animation. A visionary. A pioneer. Rather like a Marlin Perkins. A modern Darwin or Audubon for the entertainment industry."

"Yeah, like that. That stuff. *Defined the standards. Visionary. Rather.* Why don't you holster that shit and talk normal?"

Jules's expression went cloudy. "Yes," he said carefully. "Quite. If that would make you more comfortable."

"It would," snapped Rick. *"Quite."*

They drove without speaking.

Rick couldn't believe it. It wasn't even morning anymore and here he was, still dealing with weirdness. No tunes. The beer hurt his head. And *sympathy* had trapped him with this serious vegetable who drooled this strange squid language. Yeah. Well. Whatever. It *was* a road trip. The idea was to *enter* the wilderness. Make it strange. Make it vicious. Make it weird. "So you like Disney?" Rick finally asked. "Mickey Mouse, Donald Duck, Dumbo? The whole crew?"

"Yes," answered Jules. "Although really his features, *Snow White, Fantasia.*"

"Uh-huh . . . and Marlin Perkins? Wasn't he that dude from *Mutual of Omaha's Wild Kingdom?* That sixties show where they were always out in the jungle and desert filming wombats and pumas and whatever?"

"Yes," repeated Jules. "Excellent. Strong habitat focus."

"Darwin? Audubon? Like Darwin did that Galápagos gig?" Rick watched Jules out of the corner of his eye.

"Yes," repeated Jules, struggling not to elaborate. "*Origin of Species. The Ornithological Biography.* We all know their work . . ." Jules shifted against the upholstered bench seat.

"Okay," said Rick. "Forget it, spew away. Do your gig, squid. Twenty-four and seven, three sixty-five."

Jules's expression was inquisitive.

"Just talk however you want. Like twenty-four hours a day, seven days a week. Three hundred and sixty-five days a year. Whatever. *Visionary* and so forth. I was just hassling you. Go with the fierce wordage, hombre."

Jules sighed. "I certainly would find it preferable." He looked back out the window. "You must include Tinbergen. Nikolaas Tinbergen."

Rick said, "For what?"

"Niko Tinbergen. Dutch biologist. Born in 1907. His influence has been substantial thanks to his book *The Herring Gull's World.* Virtually all of the work done today owes something to Tinbergen's research."

"Of course," said Rick. "Crucial. But what are we talking about?"

"Shell-disposal behavior, for example. *Avian ethnology.* The study of bird behavior in natural settings. Tinberger shared the Nobel Prize with another great ethologist, Konrad Lorenz, as well as Karl von Frisch. Frisch was the forerunner in honeybee communication— distance, direction of food source, ritual dancing on the honeycomb."

Rick sighed. Hello. Earth to squid.

"Now Darwin's work *was* with the finches of the Galápagos Islands, well of course you know the history of natural selection theory. The struggle. The great sacrifice. The voyage of the H.M.S. *Beagle.* But from a contemporary ornithological perspective, it was really Audubon and his contemporary Alexander Wilson who did the ground-breaking *discovery.* The seminal *investigation.* The incomparable engravings, the hand-colored lithographs. The five-volume study. Absolutely essential. *Visionary.* One thinks of Audubon's description . . ." Jules looked up into the blank Los Angeles sky. "Imagine passenger pigeons, those now-extinct flocks of the deciduous forests that once carpeted the eastern United States. Nesting colonies could be several miles wide and up to *forty miles* long! Their droppings were at such a capacity as to destroy the forest understory . . ."

Rick looked at Jules. This dude was amazing. Nonstop babble. That was the thanks Rick got for letting the squid hitch a ride. Nonstop babble.

"Audubon described a flock that flew over his head for *three* days. He estimated three hundred million pigeons flew by sometimes *each hour.*" Jules gave Rick a pregnant look.

"They're gone now, right? Like *history*?"

"Very severe habitat destruction. Very severe colony disruption. There were laws, but people ignored them. Some would sew the eyelids shut on captive pigeons and leave them as decoys. Put them on a stool. Of course, you see . . . *stool pigeon.* This would attract other pigeons. Who would be clubbed or shot. In nesting times you could simply pick them up. It seems that they had previously survived by *swamping* predators. The flocks were so massive, yet they covered such a large area migration-wise . . . they proved an ephemeral resource to predators. They were always moving so the *number* of predators never had time to adjust upward. Unfortunately, they could not adapt to the *new competition* of an increased *human* population. One killer in Michigan supposedly shipped three million birds east in 1878."

"Wow." Rick looked up at the sky. "Can you imagine what three million pigeons shitting would do to a freeway? *Heinous.*"

"I would argue that there are two points here." Jules fussed with his shirt collar. "One, if we are not careful, we will reduce our habitat so that it is incapable of supporting anything but very tenacious species. We will reduce our world to doves and starlings and sparrows. We will lose our global avifauna. And *second*"—Jules's voice got ominous—"the story of the passenger pigeon suggests that it is not necessary to actually kill the last of a species in order to guarantee its *demise.* Our own survival is *interdependent.*"

"Ouch," said Rick. "Spooky."

Rick thought of Ginger. She had been so yummy up against that clamshell headboard. She had arched her back. She had got all soft. She had fought with her hips. Opened her eyes when he needed to see them blue. This thin line of sweat between her breasts. The way her lips went *okay* when he told her to roll over . . .

"Do you require any assistance, maybe a companion for your adventure?"

Rick felt the high, thin blank sky and the way it hovered above them. He felt the sun and the way it burned through to the dashboard, upholstery, the floor carpet, his black cowboy shirt. "Oh, really?" he said. "How could you *be of assistance?* You're broke and you're seriously clueless."

Jules mulled this over. "I helped change a tire once."

"Brilliant. Mondo Road Warrior. What else?"

"In terms of applicable skills . . . as in the field of auto mechanics? Facility with tools, emergency repairs?"

"Whatever," suggested Rick pleasantly.

Jules concentrated, then his face brightened. "Motor oil?" he asked. *"Gasoline?"*

This is really special. Rick wished Jack were there to share in the road trip hell. Jack would have loved this guy. "Yeah?" asked Rick. "And?"

Jules watched him sadly. "I can't remember."

"You can't remember what?"

"The actual relationship . . . in terms of the eventual, well, of course, the gasoline is placed *in* the tank . . . and being flammable there's a clear intent for combustion . . ."

Rick smacked himself on the forehead. "What are you yapping about?"

Jules lowered his eyes; the wind of the speeding car pressed his hair into a skullcap. He was a man swimming underwater. His hands moved in supplication.

"What?" demanded Rick. "Choking or something?"

Jules's cheeks welled scarlet. He wiped at his eyes with his handkerchief. "I've never been very mechanical."

Rick reached over and ripped the handkerchief from Jules's hand, held it out the window, letting it thwap. Then released it. Jules's head snapped around as the handkerchief spiraled off like a clipped gull.

Rick shook his head and put the pedal down, guiding the Buick up the ramp onto the Ventura Freeway.

Jules's head bobbed. He turned away and faced out the side window. Yeah, Rick decided, he was *definitely* about to cry.

Rick slid his sunglasses down and peered over them. "Gasoline, huh? Like you know how to put it in . . . that kind of thing?"

Jules turned.

"Really," continued Rick. "Like you're experienced at filling the tank?"

Jules straightened in his seat. "I know my way around a gas station."

"Right . . . the pumps, the cash register, the squeegee bucket, the candy machine. Well, that's awesome. *And* you've changed motor oil? Or just poured it in?"

"The latter. On occasion. I used to be called upon to assist my father when necessary."

"Right. Anything else?"

"Yes . . . certainly in the nontechnical sector. *That* would be my special field. The nontechnical. I *do* consider myself a man of the road . . . with a particular emphasis on non-technical skills, appraisal of the environment, wildlife identification, seasonal changes."

"Really? Cool. That stuff is pretty damn *handy*. Like you can tell if it's raining? And you must be pretty good with roadkill? Can you tell the difference between a cat and an eagle?"

Jules ignored him, his head out the window. Rick sighed. Jules's hair a dim hedge, chin resting upon his hands. His eyes watering from the wind, the scarlet of his cheeks now earthy, vigorous.

"You like driving?"

Jules turned back and cupped his hand to his ear.

Rick yelled above the wind, "*You like driving?*"

Jules nodded.

"Yeah," Rick confirmed quietly. "Me too."

They drove on for a while. Eventually Rick turned up the radio, noise hungry. Even the whine of electricity might be okay. He twisted the whine down again to a low hum. "What were you doing today, squid? Just out begging for chiliburgers?"

"Early in the morning I was in Pasadena, watching the feral parrots in the park. Had a cup of tea. Then I decided to make a visit to the Los Angeles Zoo. The aviary is very cathartic. Walked in Griffith Park. Walked through town."

Walking? What a loser, thought Rick. The V-8 jumped beneath his foot.

"Feral parrots?"

"Yes, *feral* means when a nonnative species has gone wild. Established a breeding population. Parrots have escaped from cages and probably, smugglers . . . much like the red-whiskered bulbuls. Or even the greater flamingo down in Florida."

Rick had seen parrots in cages, but this was weird . . . were parrots just *flying around*? How come he'd never noticed?

The day had turned clear, windswept. The smog packed back against the mountains. The glass façade of downtown Glendale flickered with internal fires, an overpass clutched up against the rolling green hills dotted with church steeples, criss-crossed with power line, roods, and cable.

"Where's your ride? In the shop?"

"Excuse me?"

"Your ride, you know, your car?"

"My car? I've never owned a car."

"You're carless? What'do you do for wheels?"

"Oh, I don't usually go out these days and if I do, well . . . I use public transportation. The bus is my preference."

"*The bus?* Bleak. No one rides the bus. Only insane people and Mexicans ride the bus. Don't you have any friends?"

Jules thought about it, then shook his head.

"What'do you mean? No friends or no friends with cars?"

"I've just been rather solitary these days," Jules explained. "I'd rather leave it at that."

"Yeah?"

Jules placed his hand upon the bungee cord. "What is this?"

"What?"

"This." Jules pulled on the cord as if to hand it to Rick.

"It's required by law. You know, for your *safety,*" Rick said.

"This?"

"Yeah, it's like a seat belt only more awesome. It was designed by Lockheed to protect those supersonic pilots. You know, those guys who break speed records all day out above the salt flats? Yeah, well, duty demanded something mega-effective. But something that wouldn't *hinder* mobility. So Lockheed ended up swooping the contract and after five years of top-secret, high-tech R&D, they cranked out this baby."

"Really?" asked Jules, impressed.

"Sure. But you can't order 'em unless you've got special government clearance. Like you've got to get this stamp on your driver's license. That says you've been approved for reconnaissance and electronic combat procurement testing. The stamp says Supercool Airborne Product-testing. Anyway, once you've got that, you're *in there.* Then the government's constantly boasting you wicked, state-of-the-art test gear."

Jules's eyes widened. "*Super* what?"

"Supercool Airborne Product-testing . . . but they just call it SAP. Get it? SAP." Rick looked at Jules.

Jules nodded. "Impressive. SAP."

"*Jesus!*" Rick's hands jumped from the wheel. He smacked the dashboard. "*SAP.* Get it?"

Jules cringed. He didn't get it.

"SAP," repeated Rick. "As in dumbfuck-squid-retard-from-Arcadia-who-can't-tell-when-someone's-feeding-him-a-load-of-horseshit! *Understand?*"

"You mean—"

"Yeah!" Rick laughed. "Man . . . you're fucking *unreal.* Like how old are you . . . and not in bird years?"

"Forty-two," Jules answered evenly.

"Yeah, I figured you like to be in decline."

"I've certainly felt old lately," Jules admitted. "The last few years have been difficult. A rough road to hoe."

"Shit," said Rick.

The Buick battled a head wind. Rick stepped hard on the gas pedal. They sped past Eagle Rock and the exit for Rick's Arroyo College, entering the garden of terra-cotta tile roofs and brick that was Pasadena. Parrots lurking in the trees, a tenor of green unwinding in acacia, oaks, palm, and stunted pine. Eucalyptus shimmered to the south of the Colorado Street Bridge. *Suicide bridge.* Angela had called it that. The students at Arroyo had called it that. Told stories of high school kids lost against the sky, diving toward the red rose logo of the distant football stadium.

"So what's your destination?"

"Uh? What?"

"Where are you going?" Jules asked.

"Cathedral City. Out by Palm Springs."

"Where exactly?"

"Cathedral City," Rick repeated. "You know, like by Palm Springs . . ."

Jules was puzzled.

"You *do* know where Palm Springs is, right?"

Jules shrugged.

"How long've you lived in Arcadia?"

"Since my birth."

"And you don't even know where Palm Springs is?"

Jules shook his head. "I often have trouble with exact locations, cities, streets. I just don't think that way. It's environment-specific in an urban sense, but very limited. Arbitrary."

"Yeah. A *serious* road warrior . . . doesn't even know where Palm Springs is." Rick shook his head. "Quite a man of the road."

Jules was nonplussed. "I refuse to be restricted by *that*. I have my thought patterns. My chosen focus."

"What?"

"Simply because my mind is concerned with different issues, well, that's no reason to deduce I can't contribute. Rather—"

"Shut up. It's in the desert. You know, palm trees, dirt, tennis courts . . ."

Jules stared at him. "Of course." He turned away and gazed out the window. "What's the purpose of your trip?"

Rick guided them past a Volkswagen. Didn't answer.

"Why did you choose *that* destination? The desert? Are you planning to *camp*?" Jules pronounced the last word strangely, with a festive lilt.

"*Camp*? No. I'm going to the desert to get laid."

Jules stared out the open window.

"*Hose,*" said Rick. "I'm driving out to the desert to hose some bliss. Like a chick, *comprende?*"

Jules didn't.

"You know, bump uglies. Bonk. Screw. Do the antler dance. *Fuck.* C'mon, you know, like *fornicate?*"

"Ah!" said Jules knowingly. "Of course. That would explain the competitive, unfriendly behavior."

"What?"

"Yes . . . yes . . ." His head moved in acknowledgment. "I wondered about your tendency to *display.*"

Rick's hands were very tight on the wheel.

"Do you live in the desert?" Jules asked.

"*What?* No. I sort of live in Burbank."

"Oh." Jules was thinking. "And your wife? Or are you promiscuous?"

"No," Rick said with extreme patience. "And yes. No, I'm not going to see my wife. I don't have a wife. And yes, I'm sort of promiscuous. 'Specially as of yesterday. Friday. And now I'm going to the desert to meet a crucial wayhone . . . you know, like a *girl.* Then after I meet her, I'm going to fuck her. Assuming she's into it, which she will be. The desert's good for that kind of thing. Sunshine. Blue swimming pools. Air-conditioning. Cocktail bars."

Jules nodded. "Good *lekking* territory."

"What?" Rick was counting the last few miles to Arcadia.

"It's part of the mating system. Certain species travel to traditional sites year after year. They display in competition for females. It's very exciting as they inflate brightly colored air sacs on their necks. The central male generally ends up with the highest proportion of females. Very promiscuous breeding patterns at the lek. A central *position* is a sign of success in the male dominance hierarchy. This is very common with most grouse, prairie chickens, for example. Some people prefer to call this traditional site an *arena.* But of course, you get the picture."

"Yeah. Sort of a prairie chicken orgy. My . . . how *enticing.*" Rick reached for the radio knob, then let his fingers trace the impotent AM dial screen. "Now what exit are we looking for, squid?"

Jules was silent.

"C'mon, dude. What's your off ramp? Baldwin Avenue?"

Jules looked away.

"Let me guess," asked Rick. "You *did* escape from somewhere, right? A nuthouse or a prison? Some place mellow where they give you lots of sedatives?"

Jules moved his finger to his lip, started to say something. Stopped.

"Fess up, squid."

Jules looked down at his hands. "Well, in point of fact, I *did not* escape from some place . . . yet, I *am* temporarily without a home. I'd rather not admit it, but it *is* my situation. I was recently informed that my assets are tied up until I clear a few impending debts. My creditors are upset, as you can imagine, and recently have taken it upon themselves to unite with the bank to try and remove me from my home. I'm trying to avoid them."

"Yeah?" Rick felt a certain justified sympathy. "And what about your family? Parental units? Wife thing? Little creatures?"

"I'd rather not go into it," Jules said. "It's personal."

"And you're broke?"

Jules nodded. "At least for the moment."

"And no friends, right?"

"Yes," blurted Jules. "As a matter of fact . . . I have some good friends . . . in Palm Springs."

"Imagine that. What a *super* coincidence. You mean, you've got friends in just the exact place that I happen to be heading?"

Jules nodded.

Rick showed his teeth. "I doubt it."

Jules didn't know why.

"I don't believe you, squid."

"You don't?"

"No," said Rick with a laugh. Thinking to himself what *a major* drag it'd be to be over forty years old and be scared to go home. To not have a single friend. Or a car. Even retards in penny loafers deserved a better world.

Rick sighed and watched himself drive past the exit for Baldwin Avenue. Yes, it slipped by and along with it Santa Anita Racetrack. Rick looked off over the tops of the trees, wondering what the odds were on him ending up on the road with a squid like Jules Langdon. 30 to 1? 50 to 1?

Or how about getting ripped off and losing his apartment? Or Tamara and Jack?

Wow.

The odds were escalating. Probably up around 99 to 1. Yeah. At these odds he could have bet the trifecta and woken up in a house of gold! Apartment and the *ecstasy* to win. Jack and Tamara to place. And last but not least, Jules Langdon to show.

But sorry. Money was not his reward. Rick steered the Buick into the fast lane and motioned toward the Styrofoam cooler. "Get me a beer, squid. We're on the road."

29 ◀ ◀ ◀

Jack placed the phone back in its cradle and turned to where Tamara sat brushing her hair. She was wearing a cotton kimono patterned with blue dragons. "He doesn't answer."

Her hands continued to work the onyx rattail brush through the snags. "Do you have any idea where he might be on a Saturday . . . if he's not with one of us?"

"Nah, not really. He doesn't hang with those guys from the pizza place anymore. I mean, if it was Sunday he might be playing hoops in the park . . ." Jack's voice trailed off.

Tamara placed down the brush and tightened her sash. "What about that girl? Ginger Woodpecker?"

"Quail," said Jack.

"I know her name. Her *stage* name, Jack. I can guarantee you her real name is Lori-Anne or Theresa or Holly. And her last name is probably something like Chancre. Theresa Holly Lori-Anne Chancre. She might be from Encino. She's probably from Palmdale."

Jack made a gesture toward the unmade bed. "Is she why *this* happened?"

Tamara looked past him. "I don't know, Jack . . . I mean, *yes.* It had to do with it, but it's more than that. You shouldn't take it wrong."

"How *should* I take it?" Jack stared at her.

"If last night meant something to you . . . well, I think you should take it *that* way. Because that's how I'm taking it. Rick or no Rick."

Jack rubbed his jaw. "Are you *trying* to sound like a bitch?"

Tamara watched his bare feet, his crooked toes. "Sorry, Jack . . ."

She patted at a wrinkle in her kimono, smoothing it with the flat of her hand. She had too much control with Jack. It was new to her. "I don't see why Rick's disappeared. Doesn't it seem curious to you?"

"Yeah." Jack loved her legs. Even liked her bitchy voice.

"Would you mind if I took a bath?"

Jack slipped his hands into his hip pockets.

Tamara felt ripped between comforting and turning away. "I guess I shouldn't talk about Rick right now. You probably feel strange enough . . ." She kissed him. "What are you thinking?"

"About Rick? Or you and me?"

"You and me."

"I don't know, I'd never thought this would happen. I guess I've wanted it for a long time, you know, thought about it. But I never thought I'd do this kind of thing. Except Rick's kind of been lame lately . . ." Jack let the silence finish.

Tamara sat down on the edge of her bed and reached for her cigarettes. "Maybe he'd want you to take me off his hands?" She exhaled a thin stream of smoke.

Jack stepped to the window and looked out at the blue pool. A woman with brilliant red skin stood on the diving board, her arms together like the apex of a compass, head bent. "Maybe. But . . . I don't know . . . what's important is . . ." Then he stopped. He couldn't say it. Couldn't tell her how much he wanted her. He was surprised how easy it was to not say it. How really easy it was to not say anything.

The lights are so bright they almost make it black. This guy, Jay Stiff? Not psyched at all. Wish he looked more like that guy holding the camera. He's cute. Nice butt. Soft lips. And then what? Oh yeah, that hard-core shot. Of course. Yawn. But not yet . . . God, this is good. Oh,

okay, I should start picking out these guys' colognes. Oh, Oh, Oh, That sound is the hottest! I wish she would, I could come right now. Right now! Psyched over there, huh? Just keep watching. You're next. God, turn the lights up. Oh, that face he's making! It's the sponge, Hate the sponge, huh? Oh, Oh, Oh, Fuck me, Yeah, God, psyched, Fuck me, Fuck me, Fuck me,

36 ◄ ◄ ◄

Jack reached over and clicked off the TV. Tamara was asleep. One piece of pizza left in the greasy cardboard pizza box. Jack reached down and picked it up, taking a bite. He felt perfect. Perfect as the day he had stuck that halfback in the open field, recovered the fumble, and returned it twenty yards before getting dragged down from behind.

Jack ate the slice of pizza. The bed sheet draped across Tamara's turned hip. Like that little cotton kimonolike robe Tamara left on the chair. Everything was perfect just where it was, as if someone *designed* this moment. And part of the design was *exactly* that rush of adrenaline that hit you when you stuck some wimpy quarterback or recovered a big fumble . . . or maybe took a dirt bike over a rise of steep trail. He could smell the chaparral as he came down, gripping those handlebars, pitching sideways into the trunk of an oak. Exhilaration, velocity, pain.

Tamara rolled over and rubbed her eyes with the back of her hand, voice soft with sleep. "What's up?"

"Nothing, just finishing dinner. How's your nap?"

"It *was* fine." She slipped her hands behind her head. "How was yours?"

"I didn't have one."

"No?"

"Nah . . . I caught *Batman.*"

Tamara directed her eyes to the ceiling.

"On the box." Jack pointed to the TV, to the face of a woman in a red blazer, holding a microphone. "First it was *Voltran* and there was this saber-toothed tiger creature and this blue cat and they were all chasing these mice. It looked like *Speed Racer,* only not. The mice had little helicopters. They were all going to a place called Planet Doom. Extremely bogus. Nothing like Racer X. The Car Acrobatic Team. That cool *Speed Racer* jazz . . ."

Tamara made a face. "I wonder what my problem is . . . liking men who do nothing but watch TV."

"Then I tracked down *Bewitched.* Far superior. Darrin's mother thinks her husband is having an affair . . . and Aunt Clara and Doctor Bombay get involved. But things go haywire, 'cause Clara can't do her spells right. First Samantha's voice gets out of sync. Like in some Japanese monster movie. Then Samantha's face gets covered with green stripes. Love wins out in sort of a strange way, though. Darrin's mother decides she's going crazy because of the weird voice, the green stripes. She forgives her husband . . . says she must have imagined the lipstick on his collar."

"And? What do you think, Jack?"

"Guilty." Jack shrugged. "Flat-out guilty."

"Scintillating explication. You should go on public television, Jack. Share your insights with the world."

Jack smiled. "Let's try Rick again." He forced himself to sound easy with the idea. "Maybe he's home."

Tamara dialed, the sheet slipped to her thighs.

Jack wondered to himself what he'd say. The only thing to say was, Fuck you Rick. I'll kick your ass. Yeah, he could really hurt Rick. If he wanted to.

No answer. Tamara hung up. "When did you last see him?"

"Thursday night. When we talked about all hooking up for that video. I think I started to tell you about it at the sauna, I don't know. Then he never called until the next morning and it was about getting ripped off and needing some cash."

Tamara looked at Jack. She felt a quiver of that being-with-the-wrong-person feeling. She wished suddenly that he was Rick. It wasn't fair. But . . . maybe she was making a big mistake. Tamara tilted her head back, the curtains of the room lustral. The frustration, animal. Mobile. "Jack," she whispered. "What was I supposed to do? He wouldn't even explain to me why he'd slept with that *girl*. He *made* me drag it out of him." Quietly, she began to cry *again*. "Not even told me . . ." she repeated, frustrated for letting Jack see this thing that was inside her. This hurt.

Jack moved closer, a little dizzy from the long warmth of her. Jealous. He didn't know what to say. Couldn't explain himself.

Then he touched his lips against her cheek, tasted salt. Her eyes closed. He kissed the pillow above her. It was very quiet. He wanted to kiss her lips. It was all he wanted. That one kiss. He was surprised how easy it was not to do it. Now. Now that Rick's name floated right there between them. Rick. Rick. Rick.

31 ◄ ◄ ◄

Jules was talking about *coloniality*. Something about the way various species flock together to avoid predators. Like flamingos. Like the extinct passenger pigeon. The Buick Skylark, complete with clothes, blankets, pots, pans, trash bags full of clothes, two milk crates full of Rick's remaining albums covered with a Twister sheet, bounced over the curb and squealed a doughnut of tire rubber around the parking lot of Galaxy Bowl. The heart of San Bernardino right behind them.

"Look!" Jules yelped as they pulled from the gas station. "Bowling!"

Rick squinted, reached in the glove compartment for a cigar. "You like bowling?"

"Yes, most definitely." Jules smoothed back his hair with a movement of his hand. "It's my sport, actually."

"*Actually?*"

Jules nodded.

"Groovy," said Rick. "You're probably quite a man of the lanes, huh?"

Jules looked at him defiantly. "Yes. *I am.*"

"Whatever."

"No really," Jules insisted. "I've played in tournaments. I even owned my own ball. It was a Voit. Cherry red."

For all Rick knew it could be true. It was terrible to imagine what the asylum must look like with all those long white padded lanes. Oh, man, and the interns doling out sponge bowling balls and little disposable paper bowling slippers. "But I thought you were *solitary.*"

"My parents used to play," Jules explained. "They took me with them ever since I was a child."

"Jesus, when was that? 1950? What a blast. Like Dinosaur Days with the Squid Family. What a *great* time you must have all had, huh?"

Jules ignored him. "I came in second once," he explained, "in a junior tournament. I am actually *quite* good."

"Whatever," Rick repeated. "I bet I could put the serious hurt on you."

Jules looked at him inquisitively.

"That means smoke your ass," Rick explained.

Jules coughed. "I, ah . . . assume you've competed yourself?"

"Sure," said Rick. "You name it, all the big tourneys. The Belfast Pro-Am Rounder. Laguna Beach Bowl-a-Rama. Shit, I'm even a platinum key member of the U.S. Olympic Intercontinental League of Harsh and Very Awesome Bowlers Anonymous. Maybe you've heard of us? Like I practice *every* day. Sunup to sundown. Never miss it."

"Oh," said Jules unevenly. His hands went to his elbows.

This was too much. "Look. I just said I could smoke your ass, doesn't that mean anything to you? Don't you have some competitive *fire?* You better, 'cause otherwise you're out the door. I'm not road-tripping with you, dude. I'm not driving with someone too chickenshit to *bowl.*"

"Okay," Jules decided. "I accept."

"Great. What're the stakes?"

"Excuse me? The steaks?"

"Stakes. Like as in what are you willing to risk? I mean, what toys're we playing for here?"

"I don't know," admitted Jules. "I think I'd rather not gamble."

"No, I'm sure you wouldn't. Tough shit. What'do you have that's worth anything?"

Jules looked down at himself with an exploratory glance. He shook his head.

Rick shifted the car into Park and turned off the engine. "What about your watch?"

"My watch?"

"Sure. The wristwatch. What about it? Worth anything?"

Jules nodded.

"Like what, cashwise?"

Jules shook his head. "I don't know. It was a gift."

Rick rolled his eyes. "It'll have to do, 'cause I'm sure not risking my awesome bowling reputation for anything else you got. I *need* valuables. Loot. It's my rule."

"And what about you?" Jules asked. "I'm afraid I must know."

"Right, right," Rick interrupted. Moving around the inside of the car, he reached back and pulled out a carbon-stained frying pan. "This?"

Jules looked at it.

"Okay, dude, you caught me . . . you're just *too* sharp. But how 'bout *this* baby, seeing's how we're talking sentimental value?" Rick lifted the Twister sheet, tugging it free from underneath the milk crates. "What'do you say? Pretty killer, dude. It'd make for some serious yucks back in crazy Arcadia."

Jules touched the plastic. "What exactly is it?"

"*This*? It's fucking bliss, squid! *Twister!* Don't tell me you've never played Twister?"

Jules shook his head.

"It's like the Sixties *incarnate*. It's a party game. Very participative. You lay this out on the floor and then you spin the wheel, which is here somewhere . . ." He fumbled around for a few seconds to be convincing. "Anyway, you can always pick up a wheel. The important thing is having this—" He draped the plastic sheet across himself like a toga. "Then what you do is get a bunch of folk together and spin the wheel and everyone's got to do what the arrow says. Like if it lands on the space with the drawing of the sock and the blue circle, then you've got to put your left foot on one of these blue circles on the sheet. So all the folk get tangled, you know? And soon you're laughing and falling down and having fun. Get it?"

Jules shook his head.

"You know, it's something you do with *other people.* For fun."

Jules just watched him.

"Don't worry," said Rick. "It's fairly tough to get a handle on at first, you know, conceptually. The important thing is that it's a major winner in the yucks department. Capital *F* for fucking, hilarious party game."

Jules looked more perplexed.

"Forget it," conceded Rick. "It's over your head, squid." He turned. "I can't believe you've never played Twister. That sucks. I mean, Twister's like the Game of Life or Hot Wheels or Monopoly. A crucial step in normal childhood development. Proper social adaption. Dig?" He shook his head. "Bleak. Bleak. Bleak."

Jules waited expectantly.

"Whatever. But the key thing's that we've got to find something worthy. Something equal to that fine watch. Maybe music?" Rick slyly peered toward the crates in the backseat. "You into Foghat?"

"I've never actually owned a pair of sunglasses."

"What!" Rick removed his Ray•Bans, scrutinizing Jules. "My *shades*? For some bogus wristwatch? You're hurting, squid. Hodads don't look good in this kind of gear anyway."

Jules was unperturbed. "I think it'd be a fair exchange, considering you were in those leagues and have had much more experience than I have recently. Yes, I would accept those terms."

"Oh, you would? Big man, big wow. These shades are like worth seventy bucks if you buy 'em. They're topflight. I bet that wristwatch was worth a nickel back when Kennedy bought the farm."

Jules shrugged.

"Okay, for a retard you sure can drive a mean bargain. I respect that. Just put a leash on the pathetic expression. Deal?" He held out his hand. When Jules reached out to shake, Rick pulled back and laughed sharp and dry. "Ha!" he taunted. "You're dust, squid. Serious, serious *squid* dust."

That guy with the light rack isn't even watching?   He's looking at the fucking TV? Who's he think we're filming here?   Must be gay.   No, too ugly.   Maybe he's got money on that basketball game.   Definitely not psyched at that horrible.   Oh, okay. We want.   Check it out . . . she's so young.   Kind of like.   Oh, okay.   Like mirrors, those lights.   Hot mirrors.   Warm.   Everywhere.   These,   You could be

on a beach.   You're beautiful.   Pretty.   Mirrors.   Mirrors.   On the wall.
That way.   Put it right there.   Deep, bad little . . . deep.   Deep.   You know she'll
love this.   The little ones always act like . . . just so you'll.   Oh, bad.   Good!
Little . . . fuck me.   Not that thing.   God, look at that.   Okay.   Watch it.
Cute.   Not so hard.   Psyched.   Oh.   Not.   Okay.   Oh sure.   Sure you
will, sweet little.   Sure.   With it like?   Yummy.   Psyched.   Fuck.   Try it.
Try it.   Fuck.   Try it.   The little ones.   Fuck it deep.   So beautiful.   Like.
That's what it's like.   That.   Fuck.   She is.   You.   Like that.   Beautiful.
Really.   Okay.   Okay.   Okay.   Yeah.   Yeah.   Yeah.   Psyched!
Sweet little.   Psyched!

► ► ► **32**

"You got a special way of lacing 'em, lanesman? *Lane Warrior?*"

Jules looked up, his face lit in the soft radiance of halogen. He smiled politely and continued to thread the scuffed bowling shoes. Rick watched, while knocking back his first Olympia draft. He had been going pretty easy on the beers, what with the driving . . . but the stress of his life was beginning to get to him. He selected a bowling ball. Eager for the slaughter. Squid slaughter. So what if he didn't know what he was doing. The important thing was to find something heavy and roll it.

Rick selected a black ball with chipped finger holes. He held it up and watched the fluorescence dissolve in its muddied gloss. Turned and looked around as a man in the seventh lane delivered an explosive shot right into the pocket between the first and third pins, the white triangle of white clattering onto the pinewood. Swept away. The man pushed his feathered hair from his forehead and tugged at the band of his slacks.

Whatever, thought Rick. The trick was just to stay cool. Yeah. And drink beer. The trick on a road trip was always to stay cool and drink beer.

Then Jules walked up, pants cuffed to his calves. He had on argyle socks.

Jules went up the three carpeted steps that lead toward the register counter, the video arcade, and the racks of bowling balls. He returned with a cherry red number cradled in his arms. The bowling ball was flecked with gold.

"Nice," said Rick.

Jules smiled. "It certainly is a specimen, isn't it? Reminds me of childhood."

"*Certainly*," agreed Rick. "How come, Jules . . . you're so unique?"

"Unique?"

"Yeah," affirmed Rick. "*Unique.*"

"As in *rare?*"

"As in *special*," insinuated Rick, drinking from his beer. "*Really special.*"

Jules placed his bowling ball down into the retrieval mechanism. "Yes, well . . . I'd venture to guess that I'm simply a product of my environment, which, well—"

"Look. I've been to Arcadia. It's just like any other place. Same shopping malls, same gas stations, same prefabricated everything. Maybe a little more *protected.* Maybe a few extra trees, but the *environment* is basic. Seriously, what's a guy like you do in Arcadia for over forty years? Like *really?*'

This wispy shadow crossed Jules's face as someone walked past holding a young girl on his shoulder.

"I mean," continued Rick, "you must've had a job, right?"

Jules dipped his chin. "My father and mother owned the Castle of Birds. I worked with them. It was our family business."

"The Castle of Birds?"

"Yes. I assume you've heard of it, if not been there?"

"Afraid I missed it."

"That's too bad. We were the crème de la crème. The sun never set on the Castle . . . as my father used to say."

"What?"

"We were the only twenty-four-hour bird emporium in the United States. In the world. Our reputation was unparalleled. We were without peer."

"*Birds?*" asked Rick. "Like the winged things?" Then it all started to make sense. The endless babble. The stray bird *facts*. "You mean, like you sold parrots and stuff?"

"No, we had a little more range. Domestic species were our specialty, but we would work with everything from domestics like Arizona pyrrhuloxias, which means 'bullfinch' in Greek, to quetzals, toucans, hornbills, and even a Mauritius kestrel on one rare occasion when we assisted the Peregrine Fund. The bird of your choice. Domestic *or* exotic. As long as it was for legitimate reasons, such as aviculture research. We always went to great lengths to guarantee that we did not contribute to the nesting destruction so commonly the result of careless or greedy harvesting. The typical habitat *strain.* Imports are regulated by the U.S. government. We had a list of permits. However, international wildlife trading is not effectively managed. Many exporting nations don't have the resources to evaluate the potential impact on endangered species. Data is sloppy. International permits are subjective. Documents are falsified by smugglers. Consequently, the Castle chose to take particular care in selecting our suppliers. We judged all our business efforts on a long-term cost-and-reward basis. We only worked with professionals. People who took a quality approach to their efforts. Our captive-breeding support was considered some of the most successful in small-scale wildlife restoration, particularly with raptors . . . that is, birds of prey. But we also did highlight work with water birds. We had an indoor aviary complete with the proper aquatics. We had data base capabilities for providing graphics and inventory lists to assist in mapping out the necessary collocation of competing and adversarial *residents.* As well as providing coordination of external efforts focused at habitat support, such as monitoring the major production centers and customers for chlorinated hydrocarbon pesticides and the like. Doing our part about educating the public on the aesthetic and direct economic value of raptors."

"*Residents?*" asked Rick in disbelief.

"Yes, residents. *Guests,* as Mother would say. Both my mother and my father were dedicated ornithologists. Dedicated to a whole new *global* attitude toward biodiversity. Visionaries of the necessity to act as caretakers for the ecosystem." Jules looked at the beer Rick had placed in front of him, but didn't touch it. "They were often contracted out by the Los Angeles Zoo to act as intermediaries in the transportation and care of particularly finicky or endangered avian cases." Jules cringed as a girl screeched and waved a fist. She stared at the ceiling lights as if they were big white worms. The rattle of pins hung in the air. "I remember a number of times when, in an emergency, Father would be called off to do what he could to resolve a crisis. He was in the habit of leaving Mother and myself in charge, then, of course, after Mother's illness, *I* was left with the many responsibilities of the Castle of Birds." Jules's mouth went tight. His voice turned inward. He tried to smile. "Well, on one occasion, we were moving a snowy owl that had been delivered upon request for research in cyclic population in boreal areas . . . the result of some university grant, if I remember correctly. My father was involved in the prefledgling care of certain Andean condors . . . a captive-breeding program with releases in the Los Padres National Forest mountains. I was left with our small staff to hold down the operations. He had hired an inexperienced student and she forgot to close the second door to the vestibule leading into the cage we often used for the temporary housing of raptors . . . so there I am, trying to handle this owl and my left hand is restricted by the glove, you see . . . I opened the door to the vestibule and, it was really all my own fault, it certainly wouldn't have happened with Father present. Out bursts this Cooper's hawk and flies right into the grille of the air-conditioning unit, catching its wing . . ."

"Yeah?"

Jules shook his head sagely.

"What happened? Frosted hawk-on-a-stick?"

Jules shook his head. "It was terrified and tried to free itself. Its beak wedged in the grille and as I was working at helping it, the talons clenched. I pulled back. . . . " Jules stared at Rick. "Snapped its neck and asphyxiated before I could liberate it." He held up his scarred wrists. "I removed my glove in the attempt. Father returned that evening. They had been raising the chicks with the aid of hand-operated raptor puppets. At seven months they fitted them with radio transmitters—"

"So?" prodded Rick. "What's the big deal 'bout a hawk here or there? It couldn't have been *that* bad?"

Jules shook his head. "No, you're wrong. It *was* bad. Mother and Father were very proud people. The Castle of Birds had never *once* lost a resident due to negligence. I've always felt that *that day* marked the beginning of our demise. After that fateful day we were cursed, losing residents right and left. Accidents like a curse. Father actually blamed me for it once. And he was right."

"You're breaking me, squid," said Rick. "One fucking bird and you're all tense. And it was only a hawk, right? That's not too exotic."

"Correct. Cooper's hawks are indigenous to the greater part of North America, but still they have been blue-listed. Targeted by the National Audubon Society's field journal *American Birds* as suffering population reduction. They have undergone severe noncyclic decline. This is a real concern. My family took pride in our work. We were *very* devoted."

"Sounds like it must've been sort of mondo?"

"What?"

"Big," said Rick. "Your castle. What with aviaries and aquatic whatevers . . . sounds like a fairly spacious situation."

Jules shook his head. "Not actually. We had what literally was once a supermarket and so, considering the range of our duties, space was at a premium. Organization was fundamental to our success. Management was everything. Father had familiarized himself with leading-edge business concepts in total quality management. In just-in-time. Feed, cage structure and arrangement, client requests . . . everything was organized to limit a backlog of unnecessary supplies and extraneous equipment and effort. Time became a resource. We had excellent relationships with our customers *and* our suppliers. We were *lean.* We concentrated on making sure that what we did ended up bringing *value* to those who required our services." Jules looked at Rick. "The majority of our supplies . . . *and* our office space was concentrated in the turrets."

"Turrets? In *Arcadia?*"

"Yes." Jules's mouth curled and he looked away. "Father's idea. It was quite an adventure."

"Was?"

Jules bent and picked up his bowling ball, stepped to the foul line. He counted back four paces, slid his shoes back and forth, testing for slippage.

"I guess we're on," acknowledged Rick. He sat in the molded plastic chair behind the illuminated table. The score sheet confused him.

When he looked up, Jules was wiping his hands on his khaki slacks, lips twisted in a pale bow of pleasure. Rick saw all of the pins were spilled. A red *X* glowed inside a red square.

"Your turn."

Rick motioned to the fluorescent table and score sheet. "Handle this, squid."

Jules nodded. Rick fit his fingers into the grip of the black bowling ball. Then, attempting to balance the ball, he stumbled and dropped it with a resounding *melon*!

He picked the ball up and stepped to the foul line. Mimicking Jules, he traced back four steps. He had bowled once in the seventh grade.

Rick tested the flex in his knees. He was filled with longing for a fluid delivery and the sound of destruction. A few seconds later, the pin machine lowered its cargo unscathed. Rick tried again. The ten pin clittered.

Rick sat down with the dregs of his beer.

Jules missed cinching a split, leaving the seven and eight pins. As he returned to the scoring table, Rick bumped him with his shoulder and grinned a thin grin. "Sorry," he lied.

"Good luck," Jules offered politely.

"Missed a couple, huh?"

"Yes."

"Yeah, well, I guess it happens to the best of them."

"Quite," agreed Jules cautiously.

"*Quite*? What's this constant *quite*? Is that bird people talk or something? Makes you sound like a *serious* tool."

Jules chewed his lip. "I'd rather you not make fun of the way I speak."

"Oh, really?" challenged Rick. "Then don't talk like a squid all the time. Talk normal. I thought I already told you that."

Jules was silent.

Rick stared at him. "Man, you were definitely in that castle too long."

Rick was not above psychological terrorism in the pursuit of victory.

Jules looked away. "Why don't you continue to bowl?"

"Because," Rick suggested insouciantly, "our greatest worry here is you. Like who taught you how to talk? I mean, speak American, why don't you? You grew up in America, didn't you? You didn't just make up the whole bird thing, right? You're not *French*?"

Jules shook his head. "I simply choose to speak the way I do. I was an insular child and I've spent the greater part of my life working and living with my family, my parents. *They* certainly had no problem with my deportment *or* my diction. In fact, my mother used to compliment me. She used to say that I reminded her of the Princess of Monaco, Grace Kelly."

"Great." Rick smirked. "And you *like* sounding like a princess?"

"I don't know if you are aware of it, but there was a time when people were not afraid to carry themselves with a little dignity in this world."

"What, like some bimbo—"

"*She was not a bimbo!* She was a talented actress who followed her heart and married a prince. It was a storybook romance. That is, until tragedy struck."

"Yeah? I think I read about that one in *Penthouse.* Didn't the horse fall on her?"

Jules was confused. "No, it was a car accident. The brakes failed. Stephanie was in the car. It was terrible, just terrible."

"Yeah," said Rick. "Cars. They're brutal."

Then he stepped to the line and bowled his first strike.

33 ◄ ◄ ◄

Tamara moved above Jack, grinding herself against him. She folded over slow. Jack pressed back, kissing her under her arms, eyes closed amid her hair.

He knew three things:

1. He was glad Rick was gone.

2. Love was not only like a good open-field tackle or a fumble recovery or dirt-biking or even going down the start stretch and feeling that midflight rush, love was like punching someone in the face.

3. Touching Tamara's hips would be *too* much.

OO

Tamara ran her fingers down the grillwork of Jack's stomach. "I love your body," she said. She took his hands against her own. His were so large. Strong from those first years after high school when, according to Rick, Jack had got *seriously* into riding his Suzuki 250 off-road after working his eight hours of construction, shoveling cement in Glendale.

Just hanging out, hopping up his old off-road 250 in his mom's garage and smoking bowls.

Then he'd put himself and the 250 into an oak tree and busted his hip.

Rick had always said Tamara should have seen Jack back then. What a brawler. Nothing could stop him. But now? Rick would shake his head. Sure, he fights. But that's about it. Man, when we were kids! Jack could *ride* some fucking piece-of-shit bicycle and make it look like it had an engine. He was fierce. Flying off of everything. And football? Fucking A. I saw him hit this dude so hard they just *rolled* him to the sideline. I think Jack's just letting loneliness take him down. Smokes bongs. Reads Wolverine comics. Watches *Cupid's Arrow*. Just full-on nowhereland. Burning the sofa with his ass. Scared've becoming his dad. Scared've ending up evil. With a pricey car. Creepy *families* piling up. A dead ex-wife. Just another asshole with a taste for expensive champagne.

Scared, Tamara thought, his chest and arms around her.

Jack plus scared. Her minus Rick.

The equation was dangerous.

34 ◄ ◄ ◄

The bowling alley PA system was mumbling names, the wall unit stereo alive with the sounds of some *poseur* band Rick hated. Rick tried to suppress the horrible whining and imagine a cool tune instead. Something like Motörhead's "Eat the Rich" or "Killed by Death." It was no use. He was trapped in the horror of a foreign environment. "I hate this shit," he said to Jules, pointing at his ear.

Jules was working on his second strike in the final frame, five total. Rick was drinking his fifth draft. His moment of glory had come and gone. "Hey, squid!" He watched Jules pace backward. Rick had not abandoned his strategy of intimidation. "Hey, squid, it's hard to bowl with both hands on your throat. You're gonna choke, dude . . ."

Jules looked back over his shoulder, wings of sweat darkened his shoulder blades, his oxford shirt rumpled. "Excuse me?"

"You *suck!*" Rick offered.

Jules made his approach and released. The one, two, and eight pins left standing. He returned and began to tally the score.

"Forget it!" barked Rick, eyes cowled under heavy lids. "You crushed me. Let's just go celebrate. I'm thirsty."

"You're intoxicated."

Rick stared back.

Jules shook his head sadly.

Rick exhaled and kicked off his bowling shoes. "Not yet, but soon come. You're the DD tonight, squid."

Jules was startled. "What?"

"*Designated driver.* You know, the guy who handles the wheel so I can get comfortably numb."

"But I can't drive."

"*What?*"

"I never learned. My parents forbade it."

"Of course," said Rick helplessly. "You guys trained the birds to drive, right?"

"No, but Mother and Father were very concerned about the increasing odds of becoming another traffic fatality. The thought upset them greatly. Consequently, they chose to limit our driving as much as possible . . . that is, our chauffeur's driving. When possible we would walk, or arrange for deliveries. And I was *strictly* forbidden to learn to drive myself."

Rick was dumbfounded. "*No cars?* Living in L.A.? And *no cars?*"

"In emergencies my father would commandeer the Castle of Birds' Land Rover, but that was very rare. Otherwise it was deliveries and the chauffeur. It was quite sufficient and undeniably relaxing. Why I remember one beautiful day on the way to Lion Country Safari, when—"

"But, if you were getting into a car with a chauffeur, why not drive anyway? You might as well trust yourself, squid. You could end up dead no matter who's dealing with the wheel."

"Granted. We were simply concerned with lessening the risk. Thus, Father and Mother decided on using specialists, allowing us to concentrate on the tasks at hand. We could relax and discuss our duties regarding the guests."

Rick rubbed his eyes. "Why not buy a tank?"

"Well, now *that* would have been impractical. A tank?" Jules chuckled. "A tank?"

Rick stared at him. "*Real man of the road,* huh?"

Jules shrugged. "I never learned to drive. So crucify me."

"Look, squid, there are *rules* on a road trip. And *you're* worthless baggage if you can't *drive.* It's that simple." He picked up his bowling shoes and wagged them under Jules's nose.

"You *can't* drink. You *can't* drive. *And* you talk like a fucking dead princess." Rick's arms dropped to his sides. He shook his head. "Okay. I can deal. Whatever."

Jules stared down, face red.

"Okay," repeated Rick to himself. "So what if the squid can't drive. Big deal."

Jules turned away and began to unlace his shoes.

Rick poked Jules on the shoulder. "It's cool. *I'll* just do the drinking and driving and hosing of tasty wayhones. You sit tight. Besides," he added, "you won, dude. You took the big risk and came out of the flames alive. Proud owner of one pair of killer shades. Here." Rick pulled the Ray•Bans out of his pocket and held them toward the hunch of white oxford shirt. "Here. Take 'em, squid."

Jules turned, eyed the sunglasses. "I'd rather you not call me that name."

"*Squid?* You don't *like* that? Well, that kind of changes things. How 'bout *dipshit?* Or *horseface?* That's catchy. It's really all the same to me . . . I mean, it's kind of harsh, but whatever, right? The crucial thing is that we find you *something.* A *name* that'll really get the job done. What do you say?"

"No."

"No to what?"

"Those names . . . any one of them. I don't think any one is particularly suitable."

"But . . . squid, there are only three choices. And since I think *dipshit* is a little harsh, and *horseface* is kind of wrong rhythm-wise, we're gonna have to stay with *squid.*" Rick lifted his arm in a florid gesture, bowling shoe in hand. "I now crown you . . . Sir Squid, Full-on Bowling God." He reached over and tapped the shoe against Jules's bulging forehead.

Jules looked back at him erratically.

"It's a joke. I was kidding." Rick held up the sunglasses.

Jules reached over and grabbed the Ray•Bans.

"C'mon," said Rick. "Let's bail."

Jules slipped out of his shoes and wiggled his toes. Streaks of fluorescence wavered across the green lenses. "Whatever . . ." He whispered as Rick walked away. "*Whatever, dude.*"

► ► ► **35**

The Buick pulled into a parking space beside a row of shopping baskets. The neon sign above them CODY LIQUORS.

"First stop, frosties." Rick scrunched down on the emergency brake pedal and kicked open the door. "You hang. I *will* return."

Jules stared forward, eyes hidden behind the plunged reflections.

"Right," Rick answered himself, and slammed the door.

A pair of high beams cut across the plate glass of the storefront, slashing the cardboard advertisement of a helicopter pilot with a pack of Winstons in his hand; a dark girl in a leopard-skin bikini on the back of a tiger, Santa Claus with a green margarita. Another red Winston poster of a golden eagle. Silver spurs, a lariat, a hand-tooled saddle, the Marlboro Man. Jack Daniels. Old Grandad. Wheat fields roiled under a combine as the afternoon light dissolved and a man in overalls held up a glass of bourbon whiskey, his overalls blue against the white porch swing.

Rick pushed open the door. A brass bell on a string jingled.

The man behind the counter was rail-thin, except for a slight cushion of gut that pressed against his red plaid wash-and-wear rodeo shirt. His face was a yellow paper fan that folded up when he put down his Lucky Strike. "Can ah he'p ya?"

Rick pointed to the seven-by-seven-foot cold-box at the rear of the store. "Just grabbing a couple." The rail-thin man watched as Rick ambled back and selected a twelve-pack of Hamm's.

"Any smokes?" he asked as Rick returned.

"Yeah, I'll take some cigars."

"Garcia y Vega? White Owl?"

"Shit no. Tiparillos. Yeah, those right there—"

The rail-thin man turned and dropped the package on the counter, the fingers of his other hand worked the register. With a *ching* he disposed of Rick's twenty and thumbed out change, tossing a pack of matches into the deal. "All set. Stay outta trouble."

"Not if we can help it, Cody."

The rail-thin man narrowed his eyes. "Name's Bill."

"Sorry, hombre. Just figured it was your place." Rick motioned over his shoulder. "Just figured you were Cody."

The rail-thin man thought it over. "Nah, name's Bill. Bill Kuzma. But ah'm from Cody. Cody, Wyomin'." He tapped out another Lucky and snapped a bluetip lit on the edge of the counter. The end of the cigarette fizzed red.

"Wyoming, huh?" asked Rick generously. "Well, that's *killer.* Welcome." He spread his arms like a dazed vulture.

Bill gave him a significant look. "Thanks for the greetin'. But ah figure ah'm either welcome now or ah ain't. Been out here 'bout thirty'r so years."

"Sure," said Rick. "You're either welcome or you ain't. I guess that's the deal. Take her easy, Bill." He held out his hand. Bill looked at it. "Ah'd take a rest from the beer drinkin', son. Lots a trouble a man can find himself when he's lookin'."

Rick nodded somberly. "Solid advice, Bill. *Solid.* Just say no, dude. Catch you—" He raised the paper sack and disappeared out the door into the night.

Jules watched him from the front seat of the Buick.

Rick flashed a peace sign and pulled a beer out of the paper sack, crackling up the pull-top and taking a long guzzle. He wiped his mouth just as a pack of teenage girls walked by, voices shiny and sharp. Rick watched and sipped.

The girls walked in the direction of an El Camino parked alone near the entrance of a Sav•on drugs. Rick relished the fine skin, the soft spring in their step, the distant drift of the incongruous *arty* gloom-romance pop that drifted out of their bad-girl American seventies muscle pickup. These girls were *girls.* Yeah, and everything that went with that. Like the *girl* bodies. The arty *girl* clothes. Like the *girl* fuck-you-dude attitude. Yeah, they had that edged-out *girl* gig going with wanting to be above it all. With wanting to be *older.* Cosmopolitan. It was crucial the way it went against the image of the truck. The way they walked. The noise of their car stereo. I mean, loud and clear. The whole image was *girl,* cranked up so high Rick could hear it in the back of his skull.

Rick placed the sack on the hood of the Skylark and whistled.

Two were already in the cab, skooching over. The third turned. Brushed her hair away from her eyes, smiled, and said something to her friends. Rick waved. The third girl waved. The two heads in the truck swiveled.

Yeah.

Rick finished his beer. "I'll be back," he muttered over his shoulder. "Stay cool." He sauntered toward them.

The third girl's smile softened as he crossed the empty parking lot. He felt warm. Like if you've been sitting in front of a campfire. Her skin moonlight. She used the open truck door as a shield and leaned through the open window. Burgundy upholstery and her black wraparound blouse. Rick closer, closer.

"Hey," he asked. "You from San Bernardino?"

She nodded and cut her eyes up at him.

"Great," said Rick.

"What's so great about it?"

She was wearing blood-red lipstick. Rick leaned against the front flank of the truck. He loved blood-red lipstick. The two girls in the cab conversed in a desperate whisper. "I don't know," he soothed. "It's just great. Great gas stations. Great bowling alleys. Great down-home folk."

The girl flicked her bangs. Rick figured she was about nineteen years old. A fairly curvy nineteen.

"How old are you?" he asked, shifting his hands to his pockets.

Her lips paused, blood-red and yummy. Her tongue was frosted pink under the parking lot lighting grid.

"Yeah?" asked Rick. "That's awesome. Really?"

"How old do you think?"

"Twenty-one?"

She leaned back casually, so that her breasts welled up in her shirt. "Six*teen.*" Her voice traipsed across the second syllable.

"Sixteen? You're kidding? And chatting with strange dudes in parking lots? That's a little out of control."

The girl smiled, and extricated herself from the truck door. She raised the electric window, smiling at Rick. Then shut the door. Her friends snagged their hands in the light as it *clumped.* "I'm like that. My name's Tracy."

"Hi, Tracy."

"So why did you wave at me?"

Rick looked her up and down. "You were just too waveable. But I didn't figure you were sixteen."

Tracy stepped back and looked down at herself. "Sixteen's kind of young, huh?"

"What do you think?"

"Probably most of the time, but I don't know. Not for me."

"Why not?"

"Like not *too* young," she explained.

Rick nodded, stretched out his arms, and stifled a yawn of adrenaline. "So how *is* high school these days?"

Tracy leaned out with her hips. "Fine, thanks."

Rick was at a loss for words. He watched her stretchy knit shorts, her white shiny thigh-high vinyl boots. This black arty thing that wrapped around her like a blouse, but wasn't. Tracy had small feet.

"You're kind of high, huh?"

Rick looked up.

Her eyes searched his face.

"I had some beers," he corrected.

"Some?"

"Some."

Tracy's eyes flickered. "I don't know if I like it when boys drink. They always end up acting like jerks."

"Boys *are* jerks," Rick pointed out.

Tracy laughed, cocked her head to one side, and let her eyes glitter through her bangs. "Where're you from?"

"L.A. Like around Burbank."

"Then how come your skin's so white? Don't you ever go to the beach?"

Rick shrugged. "Why should I?"

Tracy shrugged back. "I don't like the sun either. It's dangerous."

"So what'you do here?" He stared off toward the turgid glow of the Sav•on drugs. "I mean besides puberty and stuff."

Tracy smiled. Swayed forward and threatened to electrocute him with the points of her hips. "I don't know. I think I want to be a painter."

"A painter? Like in art?"

Tracy turned sideways. "I don't *really* know . . . but I think maybe. I'm pretty good at it."

"In school. Like in art classes?"

"Uh-huh, it's about the only thing I like. I'm *terrible* at math. I mean, *the worst.*"

"Yeah, I kind've always hated math. Math and English and science and history."

Tracy made her arms cozy. "What *did* you like?"

"Stuff."

"*Stuff?* Aren't you being too . . ." She searched for the word. "Specific?"

"So?" Rick leaned his hips back at her. Their bodies were silly. Violence crackled between them.

"Stuff," she repeated.

"Stuff and things," he affirmed, stepping away from the side of the El Camino.

"Such as?"

"Your friends're probably bored."

Tracy's eyes were bright. "You're not *that* cute," she challenged. "I can *tell* you think you're super cute or something."

Rick shrugged at the ceiling of stars. "What does it matter to you?"

The window of the El Camino lowered. *"C'mon, Trace. We're goingtobelate!"* The engine turned over, revved.

Rick took a polite step backward.

Tracy rooted around in her purse.

"Need a ride?" Rick offered.

Her eyes experimented with shyness, then she smiled and withdrew a diaphragm case, shielding it from her friends in the car. She arched her eyebrow. "I only live six miles out of town," she added.

Rick eyed the sphere of plastic.

Tracy leaned into the open window and cupped her hand toward her friends, whispering. One of them laughed and flashed her teeth at Rick. Tracy turned on the radio and the three girls continued. Then she was beside him. "I've only got an hour and a half. But I live real close. *Really.*"

Rick touched her shoulder. "You don't drink?"

"It's fattening." She looked down at herself; the El Camino pulled away. "But who cares, huh?" Tracy bared her white fingers at the night and stretched her white arms up. Swinging her purse across her shoulder. "Rick? It's Rick, right?"

Rick nodded as they walked back toward the Buick and Jules. Tracy stared into the liquor store. "Need something?" Rick asked.

Tracy smiled at the bright face of glass. "I like Southern Comfort and Pepsi."

Rick pressed his hand into the small of her back, guiding her up the sidewalk. A man with a Confederate flag printed on his T-shirt wheeled out a keg of beer on a handcart. "Scuze me," he mumbled.

They sashayed past.

And before you knew it, Bill from Cody, Wyoming, was sacking up the sweet bourbon, a liter of Pepsi, a sack of ice, and a cone of sixteen-ounce cups. His yellow face tipped at them. "Ah'll remind ya, son . . . ah'd have a mind to be careful . . ." Bill looked with disapproval at the girl and then at Rick, adjusting his rangy posture. He exhaled.

Rick just nodded, grabbed the sack, and headed for the door.

Tracy said, "C'mon, I'll show you my favorite place to park."

It wasn't that he didn't like Bill. Bill was cool.

But caution was fear. And fear was no excuse for anything.

36 ◄ ◄ ◄

These towels?   God, not psyched.   Like a cheap.   Five minutes?   Okay.   At least, it's him.   He's cute.   Oh, bad.   Concentrate.   Think of the camera. Concentrate.   One down.   Then her and walking up the path.   Get started with the hair, that skirt.   Then that scene set change.   Raphael.   Shannon.   Felina. Something like that.   Raven and the balcony scene.   God, I'm sick.   Looks like she is too.   Nikki and Ashley meet.   The pool table.   Shannon and Felina and the psychologist.   Okay, I said!   God, did she have a kid?   But the cameraman!   And not too big.   Just cute.   Always acting like the boss.   Kind of hate that.   Then, isn't it Raquel?   Shannon.   Felina.   Raven and me?

And the hilarious thing, Rick decided later in the evening, is that sometimes life is just so *there*. And endless road of heat and traffic and then the dust lifts and you're free, going fast. *Driving.* Or, like right now, *partying* in a vacant lot on the fringe of San Bernardino. Southern Comfort spilled down your chest and some jailbait wayhone with blood-red lips and a frosty pink tongue climbing your dick to the stars. Her shoulders dipping in the shards of color reflecting off the freeway off ramp. ANARCHY sprayed on the cement wall that girds the tract of a housing development under the streetlights.

"You live over there?"

Tracy nodded, shaking out her breath. "Me. My brother. My dad . . ." Her back arched. "Dad says there's going to be houses all over here by the end of the year. Schools, Seven-

Elevens, McDonald's. Wendy's. Everything. It's going to be like a neighborhood."

Rick slid against the armrest and the wad of his duster. Condensation bloomed on the windows. The upholstery was chilly.

Tracy snuggled down into the crook of his arm. "You like this?"

"Uh-huh."

"What about your friend?"

Outside, Jules sat patiently on the hood of the car, his oxford shirt a white glow.

"No problem, he's cool. A professional. Trained to deal with these sort of situations—"

Tracy arched her eyebrow. "And he's really your chauffeur?"

Rick nodded.

"Then how come you did the driving?"

"It's his coffee break and like I hate to impose on him. But normally, forget it, I'd have to pay him *not* to drive. He's a serious driving machine. He's just a little burnt now 'cause we've been on the road . . . but, I mean, this guy went through *all* the top chauffeur programs in Europe . . . loves to open doors and clip your seat belt shut, roll down windows. Mix martinis."

"Really?"

Rick gazed deeply into Tracy's eyes.

"Oh, you were teasing, huh?"

Rick smiled. Then stuck his tongue in her mouth.

She murmured, accepting it.

And the hilarious thing was that sometimes life was just so *there.*

Her tongue a petal of butterflies. The armrest a cold brick in his back.

Rick intent, concentrating on the tide of Tracy, her fingers on his stomach. Intent. Intent. So intent he actually screamed, blinded when the open Buick door slammed into his knee, arrows of glory and pain sinking into his shady garden of sweat and sweet odor. Confusion spreading across Tracy's face as her hands go to her breasts. The rear window flexing under the strain of a baseball bat. Shattering safety glass, prismatic, drifting onto Rick's stomach. Trying to free himself. Glass like snowflakes upon the vinyl. Tracy squirming, mouth stuffed speechless. Rick staring at a black log of homogeneous sound and depth. *A baseball bat!*

The lid came down.

37 ◄ ◄ ◄

Rick remembered crawling from the car and puking. His mouth tasted like moldy rice. His knee throbbed. Throat filled with a sour fluid. His jaw, white velvet beneath the skin.

The night an enormous room.

But all right, whatever. It was just pain. He could deal. It'd be better later. Everything always got better. Later.

The enormous room shifting, collapsing. Filled with silence and starlight and the smell of sage.

Day of Reckoning

38 ◄ ◄ ◄

Tamara was on her stomach, the morning light tangled in her hair.

Jack watched the ceiling.

Tamara reached for her cigarettes. Jack rolled over, a smile on his lips.

"What's so funny?"

"You." He touched her shoulder.

"Me?" Tamara exhaled, blowing the smoke past Jack's ear.

"You're a pretty serious girl."

"Serious?"

"Pretty *and* serious." Jack looked at her. "And I guess *woman* is the correct word."

"Jack . . . it's . . . well, it's not easy. I appreciate your understanding, and it's my own fault, but I feel sort of weird about this. And I don't want to feel like anything's wrong. I want to feel like I'm treating people fairly. I want to feel that we can just be *together.* Without it being weird. But the more I think about it, the more confused I get."

Jack knew plenty of men who probably would've assumed that a woman who seduced you and *then* demanded room . . . well. But Jack knew how he felt. He wanted her. But she'd said she still had strong feelings for Rick. Couldn't just move between two men—two *friends*— like that. She'd said Jack needed to make up his own mind about whether or not he could accept the situation. Jack wanted to laugh. Rick would've played it cool. But so what? What did Rick really know? Rick didn't know shit. Because if he did he wouldn't have messed around behind Tamara's back and Jack'd still be at home watching *Cupid's Arrow* reruns, listening to Nazareth, and reading back issues of *Fitness Times* and *The Uncanny X-Men.*

Tamara stubbed her cigarette out in the ashtray.

"If you can take the indecision, I guess I ought to be able to, right?" Jack looked her straight in the eyes.

Tamara smiled and reached over, touching his wrist. "Maybe I'm just scared . . ."

Jack took her finger. His fist closed around it.

Her eyes flickered. "You better go. I need to get ready . . . I've got a long day."

Tamara leaned back into the hot bathwater, pulling her hair into a loose knot, then picked up her glass of iced tea. The bathwater was scented with chamomile oil. Her portable JVC CD box sat on the closed toilet seat. Candles flickered in small iron-petal holders. The ice crackled. The singing was soft. *Shadowland* by k.d. lang. That's when the phone began to ring down the hall and the answering machine clicked in. Tamara listened to the recorded muffle of her voice. It must be Rick, she thought. He's probably bored with his cheap freedom. Probably ready to talk in that soft voice. But *no way.* No. The water rippled across Tamara's stomach. Let him stew for a while. She took another sip and listened.

It didn't really sound like Rick. Wait, it was Jack. Calling already? Wanted her to call him back.

Jack. Muscular, yet soft. She liked being with him. But that was it. Nothing serious. It just wasn't *compelling* enough. She would wait awhile before returning the call. She didn't want to send the wrong message.

She flipped her ankles and listened to the sound her legs made in the water. She needed to shave them. Certainly before work that evening. Maybe she'd even wear her favorite burgundy stockings. The ones Todd Mann had once told her he thought were sexy, the stockings she subsequently never wore to Deacon's Garden.

But she felt like looking nice, if only for herself.

Tamara shook her head. Todd Mann was enough to drive her to burlap. To hair shirts.

She closed her eyes. Wind scattering eucalyptus leaves against the bathroom window. This thing with Jack was okay. Nothing to feel guilty over. When it came to sleeping, his beautiful muscles turned to silk. *That* was delicious. The sleeping part.

She just needed to relax. Not worry about acting. Not worry about Deacon's Garden. Not worry about love. Not worry about anything.

The sky beyond the hibiscus and eucalyptus stacked with black clouds. The swimming pool scarified with needle wisps.

Los Angeles revolving on its axis.

Tamara's rumpled bedroom rank from her rose cachet and the perfume of pizza. Her burgundy stockings clean, folded, waiting in the bureau in the closet.

39 ◂ ◂ ◂

Strips of heat simmered across the back of Rick's neck. The sun already high up in the hot sky. He opened his eyes. Groaned and rolled onto his back. His arm went over the left side of his face as the sunlight drained off. Footsteps. He smelled sage. No, not to open the eyes. Save the eyes, Rick. He took a backseat in his brain. Time to regroup. Frantic discombobulated figurines twirled in a mad dance on the blood-red curtains of his inner eyelids.

The footsteps a nursery rhyme.

The frantic figurines twirled. Footsteps closer. One eye ached, parted into a steel rim of blue. The other wouldn't open. Swollen shut. He touched the side of his face. Someone bent over him. Rick's good eye flickered. It was the squid. Jules. The Road Warrior. Then something cold stuck to his face. It stung like a motherfucker. It smelled like soap.

"Quite the inhospitable neighborhood for dating." Jules's voice was musical. "We really crossed into the wrong feeding site."

"Quite," croaked Rick. "You cool?"

"Well, I hurt. And . . ."

"Yeah?"

"I'm rather sore and . . . just weak."

Rick tried to raise himself. Couldn't. Jules's fingers moved across Rick's face, mopping soap into the abrasions and welts and scrapes and pain. Jules's voice far off in the red light. "I walked and managed to find this ice and disinfectant over at the realty office. They were actually closed for business on account of Sunday, but the gentleman let me in regardless . . . a very kind man. Rather lonely, I think. Still. He even offered to telephone for an ambulance, but I wasn't convinced that you'd want—"

"Definitely not," Rick grunted, concentrating on the white spike that began as pain and ended as a violent urge for reprisal, revenge, acts of carnage, bloodletting. "They'd probably get the police and I'd get popped for statutory rape or willfully bleeding on their vacant lot or some such hilarity."

"Sam T. someone," Jules continued. "I mean, that was the gentleman's name. He was very kind. He even let me wash up."

On the other hand, thought Rick, paramedics *would* have the *serious* painkillers. They were always pulling people out from under heavy wreckage. Dealing with grief. Dealing with mayhem. Like on that TV show *Emergency.* He'd always been into that show. Those two EMTs, Johnny Gage and Roy DeSoto, racing around, flipping on sirens. Having a big truck full of gear and knowing how to use it. Must've been kind of like the Army. Maybe. Only cool. Less stupid.

Rampart . . . Rampart . . . This is Squad 51 . . .

"Sam T." Jules repeated absently.

"Where's what's her name?"

"You mean your friend, the young lady?"

"Yeah . . . the young lady?"

"The last I remember, I was being restrained facedown and struck repeatedly in the ribs. I think the young lady was screaming. Her name was Trixie, correct? Anyway, she screamed . . . kept addressing one of our assailants as *Brad.* I surmised he was the larger of the two, that is, the one with the baseball bat."

Rick could feel Jules's hand support him. "Did you see if they were messing with her?"

"No, to the contrary. I think Brad demanded she get dressed. He said something about *home.* I think maybe he was *protecting* her." Jules looked at Rick.

Boyfriend or brother, Rick decided. "See their car?"

"No, I'm afraid I didn't. I was caught unaware."

The pain was adjectival, but Rick decided he could handle it. He just needed to concentrate on the smell of sage, the solid weight of Jules's hand. Then he was on his feet, nausea and fever draped on his shoulders. He shivered, opened his eye. That's when he saw the Buick Skylark.

The side had been pummeled with blunt objects, a can of red paint dumped through the smashed rear window. The side windows—driver's, passenger's—hammered clean into threads of safety glass. The rear a face of tiny cubes. Rick stumbled to where the taillights had been tamped into a diamondy web, the brake lights little stacks of rubies.

Jules guided Rick into the front seat, placed his hands on the steering wheel for him. The backseat rifled. The milk crates gone. The plastic trash bags of clothes were covered with red paint and sticky glass. "Your records are on the freeway. I tried to collect them, but I was too late due to the morning traffic. I found this one . . ." Jules held up a blue-black album. A blue-black *X* burned with white flames. Red letters went *Los Angeles.*

Rick fumbled at the remains of his Styrofoam cooler and extracted a bruised can of warm beer. Fuck those assholes! His tunes! His history! First that shitty little Burbank metalhead thief and now these fuckwads from San Bernadino! He popped the top and nursed down the warm liquid. The soft sky gray in the distance. It was difficult to figure out where one streak of pain stopped and another began. He was a canvas of hurt. His jaw and his leg fully verbal.

The windshield cracked, not broken.

Jules crawled in the passenger's side and leaned back with a sigh. One of the lenses had popped out of his Ray•Bans. His pale blue eye watched Rick. "Did they take your money? Territorial behavior is essentially protective." Jules coughed, wiped some sweat off his fore-head. "An attempt to monopolize resources."

Rick grunted, reached down, and patted his thigh. His wallet was present and ac-counted for. He dragged it out and checked. He had the cash. He noticed a purple bloom on Jules's mouth. "Got you in the kisser?"

Jules touched the lip with his forefinger and nodded, his breath raspy. "Another example would be kleptoparasitism . . . for example, during nesting season, turkey vultures are known to force great blue herons to regurgitate their last meal, which they give to their own chicks. Or dabbling ducks often pirate vegetation—"

Rick held his hand up to Jules's mouth, motioning him to be silent. Then tilted down the rearview and searched the wreckage of his face. His lips raw. The left side of his head a black galaxy of dirt, pus, and the rubefacience of contusion. Rick traced the fingers of blood that reached down from his scalp. He touched the bridge of his nose. It wasn't broken. He must've rolled and taken the ass-kicking sideways. Eyes closing as he sipped his beer.

And for what?

Rick grinned, twisting his lips. He was glad he'd seen Tracy's perky mouth go all soft.

He just wished he'd had the foresight to take a few Polaroids for his buddy Brad. Dead Brad. Bradley the Later. Bradley the Dust.

He looked over at Jules, eyes closed, mouth agape.

Poor squid, Rick thought. Didn't even get his dick wet.

4ơ ◄ ◄ ◄

Psyched? Not! Yuck, Oh there, Here, He's like a tractor, Get over here! Little thing, Felina, No, Make it, There, Yuck, Got to, Ouch, Her, Can't get stuck on, Yuck, Hate this, Right, Bright lights and I taste my lunch while this fat fuck rams, God, God, God, His, No wonder? Yuck, Oh yeah? Yeah, Sure, why not? Fuck, Fuck, Get out of there! Come over here, little, Oh, right there! Oh, don't let him! You're not mowing the lawn, asshole! Baby, use that, Use that, Use your, G spot, baby, Felina, Felina, Psyched, Sexy! Oh, Shred, Ginger, Let him look, Let him dream, Oh, little, Yeah, Felina, Felina, Kiss me, Felina! You soft little, I, I, I, Get, Make me, Yeah, This is, Oh, Little thing, Little thing, Felina, Felina, Felina!

Just a nice Sunday afternoon. Rick forking at a burrito. "It's better than being dead, squid. You know, baseball bats to the skull can mean like *see you.* Big-time." Jules looked up, his grape Slurpee had purpled his teeth beneath his purple lips. He still had on his blood-stained oxford. His eye blinked through the broken lens. "Can't we just leave? Revenge resolves nothing. Revenge will only lower us to their level."

"I know," said Rick. "I *want* that level. To get right to their level."

Jules resigned himself to his Slurpee.

It was Sunday afternoon and the streets sizzled. The Mojave to the north. Dark clouds mortared the horizon to the west.

Rick took a sip of his Dr Pepper and another bite of his burrito. Violence wasn't his idea of a good time either. Especially with a face like roadkill. But tough. The situation required it. His duty was to deal. Make the future livable. Make Brad *history*.

"So we just chow," he started, convincing himself. "We build *crucial* strength, keep an eye peeled and then like go back and hang by those tract houses Tracy said she lived in. That'll be the place. Brad Town. And we'll be waiting. *Fully.*" Rick was lost in images of destruction when he looked up to where Jules pointed. A sparkling jacked-up Dodge pickup with fog lights idled by the curb. A stout guy with mirrored wide-lens sport sunglasses with lime-green frames watched them. He wore shorts and a polo shirt. He smiled at them from behind the steering wheel. He waved to Rick, then opened the truck door and reached behind the seat, withdrawing a baseball bat. Some other guy hovered behind his shoulder . . . he wore the same mirrored sunglasses with bright pink frames. The stout guy let the bat tap the pavement three times, then waved again. The truck burned a patch. Tire rubber drifted to where Rick and Jules sat stunned amid Styrofoam plates and greasy yellow burrito wrapping paper.

The Dodge fishtailed, crunched at the sidewalk, then roared down the boulevard.

Rick's voice was pinched. "C'mon." Styrofoam plate in his hand. He slammed the leftovers in the orange trash receptacle.

The Buick screeched back out of the parking lot, spraying safety glass. Cardboard taped over the windows. A wide strip of gray tape on the windshield. Red paper taped over the brake lights. Red paint clawing at the flanks.

41 ◄ ◄ ◄

Rick crouched behind the car, held down the spring-loaded license plate, and fed some gasoline into the ticking car, popped a bottle of 30-weight, and leaned under the hood. He reached into the pocket of his duster and dragged out the toothbrush. He absently began brushing his teeth as he stared across the hot cement.

The black Dodge was parked across the boulevard in the lot of a chrome-and-redwood athletic club with a candy-striped portico. The Dodge sat back from the rest of the cars. The fog lights had yellow smiley-face cloth covers. Very sinister.

Rick handed a twenty-dollar bill to the attendant and climbed back behind the wheel. He looked at Jules: the dried blood, the fear. It was as if he was driving with a reflection of his own weakness, his own vulnerability.

Rick took the change, eyes on the rearview. He figured the Dodge would be there for at least an hour or so. Maybe longer. Those fuckwads had that top-heavy look. Kind of dudes who'd camp in the weight room all day watching their pecs inflate.

Rick's adrenaline was pumping.

He backed out the Buick and headed for the chain of buildings down the road. Signs blinked in the distance. Indecipherable bits of color beyond MIDAS MUFFLER. LOVE'S WOOD PIT BARBECUE. STEVENSON RED-Y-MIX. The Buick rolled past a vacant berth of tumbleweed and rusted metal siding. A sign was jerry-rigged onto a cross of soldered pipe and an I beam. "There's your Sam T. Hombre. No wonder he was cool, looks like business is a little limp."

Jules nodded. The sign was not impressive. The paint had bubbled into sores of mold. Gray primer showed. The logo was of a hillbilly holding a jug, feet kicked up on a railing.

Out-dated, if not poorly conceived. The black lettering had been touched up recently. SAM T. NOTREM'S REALTY. PURIFY YOUR HEART AND RELAX. WE MAKE THE DESERT YOURS.

"But he was still very nice," Jules offered.

Rick nodded. He wasn't in the mood to talk about niceness. Wanted to talk hatred. The lovely sounds of hatred. The wind tore the cardboard from the driver's side, slamming it past Rick's face. It spiraled into the backseat.

He wasn't sure what he wanted to do about Brad. Bradley the Corpse. But whatever it was, it had to be big. That asshole had handed Rick a world of serious misery.

On the right he saw a sign for OASIS ARMY/NAVY SURPLUS. He pulled over and parked the Buick against the curb in front of a cut-rate electronics store. They walked back to the racks of reversible hunting vests that swayed beneath the canvas awning of OASIS ARMY/ NAVY SURPLUS. Rows of knives glistened behind the plate-glass window. "C'mon, squid. I feel like shopping."

Jules looked at him with apprehension. "I think that—"

"*Look,* this is normal. We got fucked with royally. This is business."

Jules stood in the heat and watched Rick.

"You think it's *my* fault? Is that it?" Rick glared.

"I don't think you are to blame, exactly . . . but I *would* rather end it all right now. I don't see what we have to gain by—"

"Respect!" Rick snapped. "Try fucking *self-respect.* Like the mirror and looking in it and all that shit!"

"And that justifies revenge?" asked Jules, his lone visible eye ablink.

Rick turned and punched at the air, almost kicking over a display of war medals on top of a card table. "Yes!" he snapped. "Yes, yes, yes!" He took a looping right hook at the sky. "Fuck those losers!"

Jules followed, peering down at the polished bars and bits of bright cloth. The swinging glass doors like the wings of a great silent spirit. Chilled air blasted Jules. The doors bumped behind him. He closed his eyes. The cold air was a collision, a delicious collision. But then Rick was there, whispering with a grin through the scarlet edges of open, purpled skin. The pus on his face drying into crusty twigs. "Look." He held up a curved blade with a jagged spine and a bleeder that ran the length of the inch-thick six-inch-wide knife. Store light glittered on steel. "I bet they used these in Nam."

Jules cleared his throat. "Yes, most likely."

"You're that age . . . weren't you there?"

Jules shook his head.

"Why? Bird business?"

"No. I'd had a rather difficult surgery. It exacerbated some problems."

"Like?"

Jules brushed his neck. "It was for my sister. She was very ill. Leukemia. She needed bone marrow."

"And you were sporting a little extra?"

Jules shook his head. "I just did what I could. My sister and I *matched*. That is, the bone marrow. There was no one else. They take it out of your pelvis with a needle. The operation had lingering effects. My health was never robust, even before. The doctors claim there is no correlation . . . but—"

Rick lowered the knife. "Did it help her?"

Jules walked over to display case of Swiss Army knives, touching the clear glass. "I think it's the scissors," he said. "I always liked the idea of the scissors. And I've always appreciated well-made products."

▶ ▶ ▶ 42

Jack picked up the remote control and waved it at the TV.

"Well, Chuck, if Theresa'd like to . . . I sure would, Theresa?"

"Theresa, would you accept another date with Ron?"

"Gosh, Chuck, sure, I'd love to. As long as it's not to another museum . . . and I want a good restaurant this time. You know, Ron? Some place fun, okay?"

"Sure thing, Theresa . . . anything . . ."

"Congratulations! Ron . . . Theresa . . . Cupid has found his aim!"

Ron lurched around the corner of the cardinal-and-gold stage set, arms out. He bore down on his future partner-in-love, Theresa, with the eagerness of a walking zombie, the eagerness of the undead.

Jack watched as their mouths met. It was ugly. Theresa deserved something tangible like a diamond broach or a jet ski. Still, Jack liked *Cupid's Arrow*. It was a hopeful show. All these people looking for love. Or looking for the next best thing . . . someone to tear apart on nationally syndicated television. The rush of being on TV. But generally, you got the feeling they were chasing something fundamentally good. And it was hilarious. He imagined himself turning the corner . . . Tamara, her arms shyly at her sides, eyes bright. The two of them holding brand-new plane tickets to Tokyo. Travel by train down to some fishing village with plum trees and those gardens made of little rocks. Those shiny ponds filled with fat orange fish.

Jack watched the TV. Ron and Theresa. You could see her eagerness to get Ron back home to show off to Mom and Dad. Ron: eye-hunting her curvy knit dress with a dim, fraternity grin.

Jack sighed. Love translated badly on TV.

The host held up his hands, good-natured as a drunk uncle. *"Whooaa!"* he laughed as Ron's and Theresa's mouths flowered again into a wet kiss. Theresa pinched Ron, then pushed him away. The two smiled into the audience noise. The voice-over rich as aged whiskey:

``Love's battle, Passion's bull's-eye, The arrow and Cupid's trusty aim, Cupid's Arrow, The only game in town, Where the money's on us and love could be yours today!''

Jack had videotaped some shows earlier that month. He liked to get stoned and watch. Just sit back and listen to the bong bubble. But now, after the last few days with Tamara, his old life seemed dull. Pathetic. He clicked his way out of the VCR mode, returning to the regularly scheduled possibilities of Sunday afternoon: golf, tennis, an evangelist. A special on the bombing of Dresden. Uh-uh. *Bad move.* He flipped back to *Cupid's Arrow.* Hit Play and watched as an attractive Asian American named Lucy began to explain why she chose only men who understood *seriousness.* She had little teeth and the kind of silent liquid eyes that made Jack reach for the bag of marijuana. If he squinched, she could be Mariko. Only maybe even hotter. He thought of Wolverine in the Citadel. That time Horde had transported the X-Men team in an attempt to enslave them. Each of the X-Men was tempted by a vision. Storm. Rogue. Longshot. Dazzler. Etc.

Wolverine had found himself in the garden behind the Yashida ancestral castle. He was succumbing to the vision. The desire to find what he had always wanted. Pouring his heart out to the woman he loved. Mariko. It was only an illusion. Created to deceive him.

You're everything I'm not—soft where I'm hard, gentle where I'm rough, A woman of breeding an' culture, I'm a backwoods brawler, darlin'.

Jack thought of Tamara. Of Rick and the way Rick could turn the words and make the world jump. Even Tamara would jump for him. But not for Jack.

I'm a backwoods brawler, darlin'. What the blazes do you see in me?

He watched as Lucy's three prevideotaped date options flashed on the screen. Three Asian men chatted insipidly. After a few seconds, each face locked in midsentence.

Jack clicked the TV off; the picture bottomed into a marble that rolled away.

No one, not even Rick or Tamara knew it, but *he* had been a contestant on *Cupid's Arrow*. He'd selected a girl from Newport Beach. Twenty-four years old. He'd taken her to Anaheim on the back of his bike to see Ford's Bigfoot in the Battle of the Monster Trucks. One and a half tons of customized machine stacked on Goodyear terra tires. They were also going to get to see Robosauras, a forty-foot, thirty-ton monster robot that ate cars. Not Japanese cars, but full-size Cadillacs. Two copilots sat in the Tyrannosaurus-like head and and operated the controls, spitting fire and chowing on metal. Twelve thousand pounds of crushing power in the jaws. Jack figured she might have gotten a kick out of it. And who knows? Maybe she would have . . . except she had an anxiety attack in the middle of the mud boggin'. Was completely losing it when the sled pull came around. Did nothing but whine in Jack's ear until they had to leave. Not even seeing *one* wheel stand. Bigfoot grinding out under the clouds of burning Castrol and the pop of a million flashbulbs, an American flag flapping on the chrome roll bars. The girl begging him to move faster and get her outside, away from the long corridors of cement. So he'd taken her back to Burbank and they'd gone to a Mexican restaurant where he'd ordered a chimichanga and a Tecate and she'd ordered lobster and then sent back the sauvignon blanc, complaining it was *vinegary*. Jack avoided the pissed-off looks from the waiter, watching the traffic on

Victory Boulevard. His *dream* date. While the girl stuffed her face and showed her teeth to every man in the restaurant. Wiping butter from her chin and getting Jack to pay for a cab back down to Newport Beach. She said his motorcycle was dangerous and tacky. *Tacky?* So okay, it *was* your basic low-rent rice-rocket, but what'd she expect? He was paying his bills from bartending and he was still trying to get a little cash put away for a big trip someday, his road trip to Japan with someone who wouldn't complain. Maybe road trip with a woman who wouldn't choose the Battle of the Monster Trucks as the moment to face her fear of eternity.

Understandably, he had been a mess the morning he'd returned to the studio to recount his side of their date to the studio audience, as well as the syndicated national audience called the United States of America. He was glad he was backstage talking at a video camera.

Especially after she turned her nose up and informed everyone that he had been a compete *valley*. Like a *hessian,* she said with a knowing look at the audience. *Him?* Fine. Fuck her. So maybe he wasn't some spoiled Newport Beach twat. At least he was a nice guy, right? And he'd *tried* to show her a good time . . . which was more than he could say for her and her jillion gold bracelets. Calling *him* a *hessian* just 'cause he liked motorcycles and didn't mind breathing a little exhaust. At least he knew how to eat a chimichanga and didn't have to order the most expensive thing on the menu just 'cause. And at least *he* wasn't having anxiety attacks. I mean, wake up and smell the coffee. It wasn't *his* idea of fun to sit and watch her greasy chin and the whites of her eyeballs.

After the *hessian* remark Jack had lost his temper and stormed out the door and into the hall before he found himself restrained by two men in satin *Cupid's Arrow* windbreakers. They talked nice while trying to clamp his arms against his sides. A secretary demanded he sign some misplaced clearance forms he never remembered signing in the first place. His head filled with shadows after hitting the bong all morning. He had jumped when someone touched his shoulder. It was the game show host, Chuck Venison.

Jack remembered Chuck's easy smile. Chuck's hand firm on his shoulder. Chuck reminded Jack that love was a finicky mistress and Jack oughtn't to worry about it. "Let's go back in there and finish up, what do you say, amigo?" Speaking with this mock camaraderie that struck Jack as okay. So he went back in front of the TV cameras. But when it was his chance to ask the girl out again, he declined. No thanks. Then got on his Suzuki and bailed. The funny thing was that the girl had phoned him up, just a couple of days before . . . when he was on his way out the door to see Tamara. Had asked him down to her parents' condo on Fifty-second Street. But Jack didn't care. He was over it. Completely. He just wanted to talk to Tamara.

Jack's thoughts turned back to Rick. It wasn't strange for Rick to disappear. It happened sometimes. Normal. But not normal for Rick to ask for money *and then* disappear before collecting it. Jack wondered if he was hanging with that porn star. Ginger Quail. No matter the deal with Tamara, Jack was not into the idea of Rick getting serious with some X-rated Ginger. The idea of girls like Ginger made him think of big orange flags, blinking yellow lights, octagonal red signposts. Men in heavy-impact plastic construction helmets, smoking cigarettes by the side of the highway. STOP. WARNING. DANGER.

Jack picked up the phone and rang Rick's number. A recording told him the number was no longer in service.

Jack slouched further into the couch and kicked his feet up on a pile of phone books stacked on the carpet. He reached into the Ziploc and pulled out another bud, stuffed it into the bowl, and sparked up his Bic.

Why was Rick's phone disconnected?

The bong bubbled.

And what about Tamara?

He began to daydream of Tamara in a wedding gown, one with gauzy sleeves and a veil. Maybe a silk train.

Tamara walked down the aisle, her legs rustled in the sleepy cathedral. *Dum Dum Da Dum . . . Dum Dum Da Dumm . . .* Turned among a carousel of chapel lights. Their lips touched.

Tamara in his arms forever.

43 ◄ ◄ ◄

Jules admired himself in the dressing mirror. He was wearing striped workman's Ben Davis coveralls with short sleeves and a zippered front.

"You're definitely missing something," Rick said. He handed Jules a camouflaged bush hat and wide-webbed belt. He looked down at Jules's loafers. "How 'bout some boots? You know, those mesh kind with lug soles? That jungle Army kind of gig?"

The salesman nodded. He watched the blood-stained clothes clotted in Rick's hands: Jules's khakis and the remains of the oxford shirt. Looked at the blotched-red black cowboy shirt Rick was wearing, the blood on Rick's Levi's. The swollen faces of his customers. "What size? Nineish? Tenish?"

Jules nodded, hooking on the belt. "The latter, please. Ten and a half." The salesman threaded his way down the stacks of shoe boxes.

"These ain't government-issue," he said upon returning. "But just as good if not better."

Rick stared at the ammo belt looped around Jules's waist. "Forget it, dude. You look like one of the Village People. But go with the boots and the hat, they're crucial."

Jules fluttered the bush hat. "Isn't it awfully warm in here?"

"It's air-conditioned, squid. Colder than a witch's tit in a brass bra."

The salesman handed Jules the shoe box. "You'll have to try 'em on yourself. I've got to get back to the front." He motioned over his shoulder.

"Yeah, I think we can handle it," Rick said.

The salesman clicked a pen out of his shirt pocket. He watched Rick, clicked the pen again, and walked away.

Rick began to search through a rack of nylon flight suits. He selected a silver one and stepped into a small cubicle created by an olive wool blanket stapled over a dowel.

The silver flight suit was loose, but it stuck to the raw wound where the car door had sliced Rick's knee.

Rick stepped from behind the curtain. The blood-stained clothes wadded in his arms.

Jules looked up from admiring his boots.

"Now all we need is weapons," Rick said with a grin.

"*Weapons!*"

"Yeah, weapons . . . you know, guns and stuff."

"I don't want any weapons. I like these boots, if you must know, but I have absolutely no use for weapons, none at all."

"Okay," agreed Rick diplomatically. "But I'm getting weapons. Just for kicks." He began to scan the interior of the store. A wall display of hunting bows caught his attention. "Wow. Speaking of *serious* toys."

Jules turned his head and went back to admiring himself in the mirror.

Rick shouldered past, reached up, and removed a bow from the hooks in the particleboard paneling.

The salesman returned immediately, the thicker chunks of his face moved in consternation. "That new kid . . ." he breathed, shaking his head. "He'd need a backhoe just to scratch his ass. You do a little hunting?" He noticed Rick was holding the bow.

Rick looked down at the thing in his hands. "Not really, but what'd you recommend?"

The salesman directed himself to the wall, eyes asquint. "You a virgin? Bow-wise?"

Rick nodded.

"Then I'd say we start you out with around forty-five pounds draw and maybe try you on one of those compounds . . . like what you got right there in your hands. You could go recurve, but I'd stick with this, considering you're starting fresh."

"Right."

"You got any friends that shoot? Either way, you'll need to go to a range, otherwise, you'll get backcountry and end up nailing some Sierra Clubber or park ranger. Some innocent nature lover."

"And that's a bad thing?"

The salesman laughed. "Depends who's asking."

"So I'll take a class or something at the YMCA. But for now, I can just go out and *test* it, right? Take some *practice* shots?"

"What you got in your hand right there, that's called the Bronze Eagle. That goes for 'bout close to two hundred, 'cluding tax and your glove and armguard and three shafts complete with field points. You just screw those suckers in and let fly. If you need some backup, I'd recommend these Gamedriller J-twos." He held up a green arrow with green rubber fletching beside a small Day-Glo yellow cap. "Just use some common sense."

"Like?"

The salesman withdrew his pen and pointed it toward an imaginary target. "Well, for starters, I tell everyone, I say don't try it out around someone's yard, 'cause 'fore you know it, it's Hatfield and McCoy time. You hit the neighbor's favorite cocker spaniel by accident. . . flick one in their kid or something. Hear what I'm saying?"

"I guess I see your point." Rick winked at Jules. "Random killing can mess up the neighborhood."

"I'm not kidding," the salesman continued, still eyeing off toward the neighbor's ugly, loud, imaginary cocker spaniel, the neighbor's fat, noisy children. "You'd be surprised. I've heard of barbecues turning into fire storms. Last summer some character put one in this Chinese gardener's back . . . another put one through his wife's foot."

Rick held up the bow. "So what's the deal with gloves and whatever?"

The salesman pulled out a long box. "You want that *camo* finish?"

Rick nodded.

"Here, you take this one here and leave me the floor model. This one'll have your eccentric wheel and cable setup . . . then you attach these rubber strands and the shooting noise goes down to zilch. I had one way back and it was a whisper. Then you've got your insulated grip, which don't hurt. The glove and armband're in there, too."

"And what's their trip?"

"Keep you from tearing the bejesus outta your arms is 'bout all. Here go like this." He held up the bow and pretended to draw back the string. "You'll meet up with some resistance right here, then it'll go easier and you'll take her to here." He paused, his fingers around the imaginary string and shaft. "This here's your anchor point . . . when you get your right hand right alongside your face and finger here, the index right practically in your mouth, see?"

Rick nodded.

"Get your thumb down like here, under the jawbone, then sight like this, right along this notch. And if she starts to porpoise, you know, the shaft's wriggling in the air . . . then just experiment here with what's called the nocking point." The salesman then adjusted the imaginary shaft of the imaginary arrow up and down. "Truth is," he added, "you won't hit diddley till you've worked at it some."

Rick nodded, thinking about his buddies in the Dodge. "I'm going to take it easy," he assured the salesman. "Nothing that moves *too* fast."

The man nodded, looking back toward the front of the store. A teenage clerk with long stringy hair was staring down at the register, his face in remission. "Oh shit," muttered the salesman. "Looks like he just pissed his pants."

"Uh-huh." Rick turned to Jules. "Want a job?"

The salesman sized Jules up.

"No," Jules answered. "I don't really feel good. I'm sure that I'm fighting a fever." He fanned himself with his bush hat to make his point. "Besides my experience in retail is highly specialized."

Rick grinned at the salesman. "See? Grass's always greener."

The man nodded. "I'd also suggest this seven-arrow quiver. I'll attach it for you." The man watched Rick, "Ring it all up if you're interested?"

Rick handed him the box. "Yeah, the quiver looks crucial. Count up all this stuff and those boots my partner's got on . . . and make sure that bow's fully operational."

The salesman nodded. "You boys from these parts?"

"Nah," said Rick. "From up in Utah. We're just down to look up a little real estate and do a bit of, ah . . . you know, dirt-biking. Wheel out the old off-road machines."

"And where is it you do that?"

Rick looked over to where Jules fanned himself. "Oh, out in the desert. Just load 'em up in the pickup and go till we're there."

The salesman looked at the bloody clothes in Rick's hands. "Don't got enough desert up there in Utah?"

"Yeah, well . . . see it's different up there." Rick grinned. "Up there you got yourself all those Mormons. Can't even get yourself a cold beer on Sunday."

The salesman stared back.

"'Course Mormons are great people," Rick continued. "Real honest folk."

"Met my wife up there in Utah," the salesman said. "A real lady. She's a Mormon though . . ."

"Like I said," Rick faltered. "Salt of the earth . . ."

"Yep, a *real* lady. 'Cept a course for the fact she *married* a Mormon."

"Right," said Rick, squinting at his imaginary wristwatch. "Give'r my best. We got to get a move on."

Jules looked down at his watch and shrugged.

Rick found his wallet. "Guess you made yourself some sales, huh?"

But the man had already turned and was muscling up the crowded aisles of olive fatigues and red-and-black mackinaws.

"*Asshole,*" muttered Rick. He shoved Jules forward. The sudden movement flashing in a rich, candied pain. "Nosy redneck Mormon *fuck.*" Rick touched his jaw, winced.

On their way back to the car Rick motioned to Jules. "Hang on, squid. I got an idea." He walked into the electronics store while Jules stood under the sun in his new Ben Davis coveralls and broken Ray•Bans. Rick walked out a few minutes later. In his hand was a small Panasonic cassette player. "Got it for a song, squid. *Tuneage.* Way crucial." He held the small black unit up against the sky. It had simple push buttons and a metal grille. "They must've had this thing back there for two hundred years." Rick grinned. "Onward. Hail to victory."

They climbed back into the Buick, Jules's lone eye watched Rick from the broken sunglasses. Rick nodded. "Now all we need is batteries, maybe some cold beer . . ." Jules's coveralls were brand-new and stiff, they went nicely with the lone eye and split lip. Jules's forehead orange from the sun. His fingers worked the retractable scissors of the Swiss Army knife. His eyes sad.

Rick had paid for it in Oasis Army/Navy Surplus. It was this Christian gig. Being nice to the birdman, the road squid. How could he help it?

"Forget it," said Rick. "I just felt like being cool. It's only a pocketknife, squid. It's not a fucking *engagement* ring."

44 ◄ ◄ ◄

They made a quick stop at a hardware store for a hammer and an awl. Then onwards, where Rick and Jules stood in line at the ARCO am-pm Mini Market counter. Rick was holding a twelve-pack of Hamm's, a bag of Frosty Man ice cubes, a package of Black Cat batteries, and a cassette of Lynyrd Skynyrd. Some greatest hits gig. Rick eyed the man at the register. Then, when he wasn't looking, slipped the batteries and cassette into the pocket of his flight suit. Reached over and snagged a box of Tiparillos. Jules was in front of him, reading *People.* Rick slipped the cigars into the big pocket on the back of Jules's coveralls. Rick had to go with the Lynyrd Skynyrd. He *needed* tunes. And his choice was limited to the predictable shit that sat in the wire dispense-a-twirl. Shit, it was too bad, 'cause he could go for something fast. Something just like Black Flag. Or Hüsker Dü. A real dose of hard-core *history* to get him in the mood for dealing with these losers in the Dodge. Either would go nicely with his plans. Angry, fast, fierce. But what was his choice? Maybe that Waylon Jennings. Waylon Jennings was kind of cool. Sort of a David Allen Coe gig. Almost. But cool, when you wanted cowboy noise. Rick didn't. Rick wanted destruction noise. Lynyrd Skynyrd was his best bet in this one-horse redneck convenience shack chain gas station. And "Free Bird" would certainly have a creepy youth-is-gone feel. Anthemic concert buzz. Millions of people waving matches over their heads. That sort of thing. He could have gone with the Aerosmith retread in the dispense-a-twirl, but you know, there was that Boston connection and that troubled him. Not a good omen. Didn't leave much else. Tanya Tucker? Neil Diamond? The J. Geils Band? They all had something to offer . . . but he went with Skynyrd. He just felt it would be more *spooky.* Rick looked around. No Styrofoam coolers for sale. He was grinding his teeth, eyes locked on the Road Warrior as he flipped through the pages of *People*, cradling a thirty-two-ounce bottle of Squirt in the crook of his arm. Jules was humming.

"Oh my," he said. "Princess Diana is coming!"

"Great," snapped Rick. "Who's holding the dildo?"

Jules turned. "Excuse me?"

"Forget it."

"Oh, she's so radiant. And she'll be arriving in Los Angeles next week."

Rick's fingers clenched the box of beer. Fucking squid did not have the proper *anger.* Rick reached out and swatted the magazine to the parquet flooring.

The man behind the register peered above his mustache, unaware of the perfect square of overhead light that quivered on his bald head. "Ahem," he coughed, staring down at the floor.

Rick stepped on the magazine with his boot. "*What?*"

The man's fingers clawed the air above the register keys. "Is that yours?"

"I *don't* think so, dude . . . or we'd be holding it."

"Then will you try not to step on it?"

"I am trying," Rick said.

The man sized Rick up, popped at the keys with his index fingers. "Would you?" He nodded toward the floor.

Rick pointed to the magazine. "Jules? Do you think you'd mind picking that up for the gentleman?"

Jules eye blinked through the broken lens. "Yes. I *would* mind."

Rick stared, surprised. "Why not, squid?"

"I have no intention of picking up that magazine. *You* knocked it down there. It is clearly *your* responsibility to retrieve it."

Rick laughed. "My *what?*"

"Responsibility," Jules repeated, eye blinking in the broken sunglass frame.

Rick turned to the man at the register. "Just ring it in along with the *refrescos.*" Rick slammed the twelve-pack box on the counter. He slipped a pair of mirrored cop shades from the sunglass dispenser, using the twelve-pack as a shield. Rick slipped the sunglasses into the pocket of his flight suit.

The transaction completed, Rick faced Jules, pointing to the floor. "Want it?" Rick's stomach was framed by discount three-for-one shrink-wrapped cigarette displays.

Jules looked down at the *People.* Then pointedly at the pocket holding the sunglasses.

Rick understood the threat. He reached around and patted the cigars, nestled in Jules's own pocket. "Pick it up, squid." He gave Jules a hard face. "You owe me a favor, right? The *knife?*"

Jules looked up. "That was a gift."

"Suit yourself . . ." Rick looked toward the hidden cigars. "*Shoplifting,*" he whispered. "*We prosecute.*"

Jules gazed at the *People.*

Rick laughed and walked out. Dumped the sack with its ice and box of beers into the remains of the Styrofoam cooler.

Jules leaned out of the glass doors. He was kicking the ruffling *People* toward the parking lot.

Rick watched the magazine flap, belly-up on the cement. He sighed as Jules scuffled his foot against the magazine until it was beside the car. Jules opened the door and braced himself, clasping the magazine between his heels. He hopped up and dropped the *People* onto the car floor, stumbling backward. His lone eye blinked.

"Yeah," said Rick as he put the batteries into the tape player. "You made your point. Now give me that box of cigars." Rick punched On. The sound chintzy, yet clean. The Buick filled with barefoot Southern guitar wounds. Singing about whiskey bottles and too much smoke and too much coke. Man, that big oak tree is in my way. Twanging bad-ass Seventies bitcheness. The angel of darkness. Tomorrow might not be here for you. Man, the smell of death *surrounds* you.

Rick shook his head. "Get in the car. *Please*?"

Rick guided the Buick back up the boulevard to where the Dodge glistened under the late-afternoon sun.

Jules was talking about birdsongs. Saying they are essentially announcements of ownership and threats of possible violent reprisal. Defense signals. Rick's puffed eye narrowed for a moment. "That's right. That's why this Lynyrd Skynyrd is so crucial. I got Confederate flags flapping in my brain. Gimme back my bullets. Saturday-night special. What's your name." Rick began to sing. "It's eight o'clock in Boise, Idaho. I'll find my limo driver, Mr. . . . take us to the show. . . . Police say we can't drink in the bar, what a shame. Little girl, won't you come upstairs and have a drink of *champagne?*" Rick turned. "Know what I mean?"

Jules looked confused.

"Squid, what's your trip . . . are you like a fag?"

"Are you referring to my sexual preference? If so, the answer is no."

"So you're into chicks?"

"*Into?*"

"Yeah, like literally?"

Jules shrugged.

"Yes or no? Fess up."

"I guess," said Jules without conviction.

"You guess? What's that mean?"

"I don't know."

"Well, *c'mon* . . . if *you* don't, who does? Like who do you sleep with in the getting-off capacity? You don't like mess with pelicans or something twisted like that?"

Jules gave him a sour look.

"Then who?"

Jules shrugged.

"Are you a virgin?"

Jules dipped his chin.

"*Squid!* Get a clue! No wonder you're so strange . . . not even once, like on top of a bag of seeds? Wow. Critical. *Crucial* missed opportunity."

"It's not so long," Jules answered evenly.

"It's a seriously long time." Then Rick's eyes lit. "You just wack, right? Just sit around and do the fantasy gig about Princess Grace and flog the dolphin, right?"

"No."

"C'mon!" Rick laughed. "You just lean into the sofa with some back issues of *People* and shine the pony to some fierce princess wayhonage?"

"No," insisted Jules. "I don't do that."

"Don't do what? Wack . . . or wack and think about Grace Kelly? Don't tell me you don't wack. That's impossible. That's what makes us mammals . . . you know, opposable thumbs. Don't tell me—"

"Okay."

"Okay, what?"

"I won't tell you."

"Tell me what?"

"That I've never done that thing . . . that thing with the dolphin and the pony."

"No way!" Rick smacked the dashboard. "You're so *full* of it!"

Jules shook his head.

"Okay, squid . . . but that only leaves wet dreams. Now try to tell me you've never once in all these years in the Castle . . . never once hopped in bed and dreamed about all the whooping pigeons and barn condors and then . . . bam!" Rick slapped his hands together loudly. "Spunk in the bunk."

Jules was embarrassed.

"Ha! The truth wills out."

"Yes," admitted Jules. "I *do* remember something like that occurring some years back."

"Some years back?" Rick tried to regain his composure. "I think this confirms a theory of mine. How much did you work? Like hours a day? Eightish plus, right? Five days a week?"

Jules nodded. "Saturdays too. Sundays we spent at the house together."

"Right. Anyway, I think your natural *tendencies* just sort of dried up . . . like too much of the old *trabajar*. It'd probably've happened to anyone who spent his whole life cleaning up birdshit in a supermarket—"

"No," interrupted Jules. "My life wasn't that way at all. It was marvelous and very soothing."

"Yeah, soothed you right out of all your jism. No thanks. I'll pass on the bird-hell impotency plan."

Rick guided the Buick beside a chain link fence and a stack of pallets loaded with cinder blocks. He peered off to where the Dodge sat in the large parking lot, removed from the distant cars lined in front of the entrance far across the matrix of white parking lines. The Dodge cab and bed jacked free of the knobby oversized tires, yellow struts visible underneath. Rick pulled a beer out of the sack. He held up the shiny can. "Here. Jules. Beer. Drink."

Jules was sweating.

"Beer," Rick repeated somberly. "C'mon. It's like medicine."

Jules shook his head. "I don't think so."

"Drink!"

Jules shook his head again and slouched back against the seat.

Rick shrugged and drained the beer. "Hey, squid," he said with a belch. "Get me another."

Jules pushed his head against the shredded upholstery and sighed.

"Another beer," Rick repeated.

Jules gave a wan smile. "I'm used to hearing the P word."

"Pussy," Rick said as he watched the Dodge. "That's my *P word.* Forget it. I'll handle it. I forgot you were just the squid . . . the *road squid,*" he added, leaning over with a huff and extracting another Hamm's from the leaky cooler. He punched the top and watched as a pair of housewives in lumpy tights stepped from underneath the candy-striped portico, canvas gym bags swinging against their knees. Rick watched them walk toward a Ford Aerostar. "How long do you think since we got gas?"

Jules's shoulders hunched in a shrug.

"Then look at your watch. Like almost two hours? Guesstimate."

Jules shrank lower against the entrails of the passenger's door, peered at his watch, and nodded.

Good, thought Rick. He reached into a yellow plastic hardware store sack and withdrew an awl and a hammer. The salesman had claimed the awl had a "diamond" point. The hammer was just heavy. Real heavy. "C'mon, squid. Pay attention." Rick grabbed the clump of Jules's stained oxford shirt from where it was wedged into the seat. He slipped out of the Buick. The Skylark door ajar. To the west, the boulevard ebbed along at a Sunday pace. "Jules. Hey, man, wake up."

Jules mumbled.

"*Look!*" Rick whispered. "*I'm really serious. You're lookout. Don't space on me. Watch those doors at the front and if Brad and his buddy are coming out . . . just sit on that horn. Got it?*"

"I'm really feeling exhausted." Jules's face was bleary, pale.

"I'm *serious*," Rick threatened. "This is show time. Serious dealing weather. *Crucial*."

Rick straightened, the entrance to the health spa about forty yards across the parking lot. The Dodge about ten yards less. He took a deep breath to calm himself. His temples throbbed, nausea mixing with nerves and the soreness along his knee and calf. This was nothing compared to the ache in his jaw. A deep itch of pain. He walked.

He crouched down beside the Dodge and bent underneath the chassis. Found the gas tank, placed the point of the awl against the tank and swung the hammer. The awl made a spark-less *ting*. Rick looked over at the visible section of the glass door unobscured by the tires. He swung again, his hands shaking. Then again, the hammer against the handle of the awl. The bright speck of steel eased eventually into a hair-thin leak. Gasoline. Rick slipped the point of the awl within the hole and tapped lightly at the handle from the side. The leak thickened.

He removed Jules's oxford shirt from his hip pocket and wiped it up against the leak, allowing the gasoline to soak in.

He waited. The cloth soaked.

Then he turned and walked back to the Buick, ripping the wet shirt into strips. When he was back at the car, he laid the strips carefully over the trunk, pulled the hunting bow out and laid it beside the rags. He had watched the salesman clip away the protective plastic twists that cinched the bowstring, and now he held up the arrow shafts and began to screw in the field points.

Jules looked out the window with a mixture of curiosity and dread.

"Eye on those glass doors," reminded Rick, looking up. He took a strip of the soaked cloth and knotted it to the shaft beside the feather fletching, placed the arrow on the asphalt. Repeated the procedure with two more arrows. Wiped his hands and popped another Hamm's. Drank at it. *Matches!* He forgot the fucking matches! He fumbled around at the toes of Jules's jungle boots. He came up with a pack. The matches soaked in the melted ice from the leaking Styrofoam cooler. Rick removed a cigar and put the box in the glove compartment. The car lighter! Yeah. He sighed. Oh, the beauty of this Buick! Knocked his hand into the knob, then lit the cigar and exhaled a blue veil of smoke. Jules coughed, the sound wet in his throat. Rick pointed at the ignition keys. Then turned them to the right. "Don't touch these. If things look bleak, just hit the horn. Otherwise, kick back and I'll finish this gig."

Jules nodded, coughed. Behind him, dirt swirled beside mounds of construction debris: rags of concrete sacks, broken bricks, drywall fragments, stacks of two-by-fours. Perspiration gathered on Jules's brow. The sky along his shoulders the color of sheet metal.

Rick buried the cigar between his lips, dumped out the box, and scooped up the glove and armband. He clawed at the beer with his elbow. "Can't forget this," he explained. He stripped his belt out of his wadded Levi's and threaded it through the handle on the Panasonic, cinching it around his waist. The tape player bounced at his hip. The mirrored cop shades hooked over his swollen face. The paint-spattered Lakers cap. The silver flight suit. The tape player had a nice monospeaker kind of late-sixties tinny sound. But it would be cool if he could just rig a whole *system* around the parking lot. Get a road crew. Stack the speakers up to heaven. Go for something flat-out like Sepultura, Pantera, Sacred Reich. Something *so fast* you'd kill just to listen to the screams of your victim dissolve in the noise. A *serious* truck-annihilation sound track. But then, Lynyrd Skynyrd had poetic force, an undeniable seventies resonance. What he lost in pure speed and psychotic meanness, he made up for with the weird nostalgic beauty of crouching with a hunting bow in San Bernadino and listening to Ronnie Van Zant calling himself the breeze. Just rolling down the road. Rick crabbed along the fence until he had clear view of the glass doors and striped portico. He slunk back and grabbed the arrows. Gasoline gathered in a puddle beneath the Dodge. He leaned against the chain link and slipped to the ground, crossing his legs with a wince. Careful to avert his cigar, he lifted one of the strips of rag to his nose and inhaled.

The cloth stank beautifully.

Rick took a sip of beer, then fitted himself into the glove and armband. This was as cool as being a kid. He turned the tape player volume to High. He was the hero of the Saturday *Million Dollar Movie* on Channel 9. Cutting his sweatshirt off at the elbow like Steve McQueen in *The Great Escape*. Schwinn Sting-Ray skidding across the asphalt playground, tangling in the barbwire as the Nazis moved in with their Darth Vader helmets. Rick and Jack scaling the ridged, institutional bricks of the elementary school cafeteria . . . Mallory leading them up the cliffs in *The Guns of Navarone* . . . one brave final effort to silence the monster Nazi howitzers that haunted the primary strategic access to Allied supplies, before pedaling home for a bowl of rocky road ice cream or a chili dog or a microwave pizza.

Rick sipped his beer. Pureness ran through him like a blue mountain stream. Remembering when he and Jack used to steal sacks of oranges and lemons from the neighbor's citrus trees and carve cylinders into the fruit with a switchblade. Carving cylinders into the navels and nestling firecrackers in the fruit. Slipping like smoke behind the hedges, over the ivy, a soggy shrapnel of pulp splattering the skin, stinging the eyes. Jack, only twelve years old, scrambling back over the hedge.

But now what? Now you take off on a casual road trip and some motherfuckers decide to sucker-punch you with a Louisville Slugger?

Rick shivered. The pain in his jaw unholy.

It was all your basic yuppie Republican bullshit. He could deal with having to figure it all out about Tamara and Jack. They were his friends, and if things were tense . . . well, it was basically his own fault anyway. But these dudes in the truck were different. They were like everything he was tired of. People feeding on their small-town judgments. Everyone smiling as they served themselves. Smiling and serving themselves. Not even thinking about it. Just passing judgment and burning cash. One big target-market of losers. *It's not a job, it's an adventure.* The Army. The Navy. The Air Force. The Marines. Pepsi. Coke. Sugar water and military equipment. That was America. MTV ripping the balls off rock and roll. Everything organized. Everything safe. Everything cute. Drugs, drinking, driving, sex. Everything equaled death. Death. Warning, don't miss it! Conserve, prepare, invest. Be *ready*.

Don't do anything risky, dude . . . just sit down, shut your face, and save. Money, sperm, strength. Wait for the end.

Oh yeah . . . and be sure to wear a tie. Something pricey. Something silk. Yeah, *that* was cool. Just stay in shape and don't bother anyone. Shit, at least when Rick was a kid, people gave a shit. There was Vietnam. Helicopters cutting over the top of the jungle. Civil rights riots on the box. People ready to stand up and make some *noise.* Now it was just all about covering your ass. Fuck everyone else. But when Rick was a kid, life felt cool. *Real.* And the older kids knew how to party. Everyone wasn't just hanging around hiding from Death. Dreaming their ugly yuppie dreams twenty-four and seven, three sixty-five. There'd been promise. There'd been faith. There'd been a reason to fight.

> *Rick B. Jeffers shading his eyes. Dust and concrete powder swirling.*

He watched the shiny Dodge and the string of bleeding gasoline. Yeah, it was a nice truck. Too bad he had to torch it.

And it wasn't even Japanese.

He focused his good eye on the puddle of premium.

Yawned, pumped his arm, and held up the bow, experimenting with the proper sequence of motions. His eye narrowed as he imagined the baseball bat clipping into the silence of Tracy's jiggly dance.

He looked back at the Buick. Jules's bush hat barely visible.

Billy Powell's keyboard noise just drifted up into the white sky.

Rick stared at the glass entrance. Patches glared on the candy-striped portico.

"C'mon," he whispered softly. "*C'mon.*"

► ► ► 45

When Brad and Jim, Tracy's older brother, stepped out into the afternoon, they were forced to shield their eyes, the sun hanging above the horizon with all the loud fire of hydrogen and love.

Then they saw the Dodge and began walking toward it.

Rick had been pondering the idea of Tamara in those new green pumps. Tamara reclining under the Robert Frank print, hair fanned out on the pillow. Tamara. But the sight of Brad and Jim lifted him, a hot wire searing him right up to his feet in a pulse of cinematic confidence. He held the glowing cigar against the gasoline-soaked rag and blew. The rag took, Rick leaned back, rich scent of his own singed hair filling his nostrils as he held the shaft of the arrow away from the bow limb and walked. Rag smoldering at one end, a string of red burning up the edge.

His two assailants were about halfway to their truck.

Rick quickly hooked the string into the nock. Drew back the string, remembering to bring his index finger to the corner of his mouth. He got himself a mouthful of smoke and coughed.

"*Hey!*" he yelled over the rock and roll whining out of the tape player strapped to the hip of his flight suit. "*Bradley!*"

Brad and Jim stopped and turned. Rick watched as recognition wove through them. Brad tensed, shoulders lowering, feet spread for balance.

Rick held the point of the arrow, the rag burned waist-length creeping up. The point in line with Brad's chest. "*You're fucked, Bradley! You thought you were cool . . . and now you're just fucked!*"

"*What's your problem?*" Brad yelled back.

"*You're my fucking problem, Bradley!*"

There was silence.

Weakly, Jim called, "We didn't mean—"

Brad spun and stared him into submission, looking back at Rick. "*Fuck that!*" He pointed. "*You faggot!*"

Rick admired Brad, but there wasn't time to play around. "*Nice!*" he yelled. "*But you're the faggot, faggot! Sneaking up on me while I was hosing your little pal . . . and I mean seriously hosing!*"

Brad stepped toward him, then reconsidered.

"*Ha! Ha!*" Rick goaded. He lowered the bow and turned it sideways. He let the arrow fly. It lashed across the parking lot, but missed the truck by about five yards. Rick could smell the burned hair on his forearm.

Brad and Jim watched as the arrow skidded off. The rag left a trail of white stars skipping across the cement.

Rick lit and fired again. *Fast.* Too hard. Shot too hard. He couldn't believe it! The second arrow flamed directly into the right front tire. The truck slumped. Brad and Jim didn't get it. Why was this stupid longhair trying to kill their truck with an arrow?

Rick had trouble igniting the last rag, but it went and he drew as Brad moved toward him. Yeah, crucial! "*Stay back!*" Rick yelled. Released the bow string softly . . . imagined a feathery jump shot. The arrow skimmered underneath the Dodge, a thick cord of white rising from the puddle of gasoline.

Brad stopped and turned, then stepped toward the truck, his face grim.

The flames magnificent in a systolic dance of crackling blue fingers and lacerated white. The initial explosion as simple as a fist and the sound of kinetics.

Brad, Jim, and Rick all stepping back.

The air adrift with fouled upholstery smells. The Dodge lurched to the right, then blossomed in a tulip of crayon yellow.

Rick back pedaled toward the Buick, finger in the air. Brad running, eyes stubbed into black points. *"Number one!"* Rick yodeled above the noise. *"Number one!"* Slipping into the Buick, still clenching the bow, turning the key, Jules trembling. Brad just close enough to get his hand around a fistful of safety glass, stumbling as the Buick lunged. Churning backward. A plume of black smoke flapped across the rearview, a second crackling brightness against the sky. Rick stuffed his fist on the horn and his foot on the gas pedal.

"Ha! Ha! Ha!" he screamed coyote-happy. *"Ha! Ha! Ha!"* Brad waved a red hand at the sky.

The entrance to Interstate 10 a gift under the green traffic light.

▶ ▶ ▶ 46

The horizon was tangerine as Rick pulled the Buick off the freeway, guiding it toward the hedge of cars parked under the yellow-and-red Hadley's Fruit Orchards. Bins of dried fruit, nuts. Walk-in cold boxes of juice: bee pollen, carrot, beet, six kinds of unfiltered apple, fresh orange. Produce of every sort visible behind the electric doors of glass, milling bodies. The silver row of shopping carts, the stacks of plastic red or blue carryall baskets.

"Hey, hombre, you want a date shake? Hadley's makes these great shakes . . . you know, out of dates. Want one? You could use some liquids."

Jules's chest moved rhythmically beneath his stiff coveralls.

"You sleeping, squid?" Rick leaned over and tugged at Jules's sleeve. "C'mon, wake up a second."

Jules stirred.

"Date shakes!" repeated Rick loudly.

Jules lifted his head and rubbed his eye through the broken lens, cleared his throat and straightened against the seat, his skin glossy.

"Liquid . . . for the desert heat. *Date shakes.*" Rick explained.

Jules looked around, confused. "What is this place?" A man walked past the car with a Labrador on a leash. The man's belly jiggled over the waistband of his cutoff jeans. A sack of apples glistened in a red mesh sack on his shoulder. He smiled, showing Rick and Jules the places where his lunch had stuck in his teeth.

Rick grinned back and lifted his hand. "Like I said, squid. Hadley's. Frosty-date-shake-central. The full-on I-ten oasis. Last crucial stop on the road to Palm Springs. On the road to bliss."

Jules nodded, unzipped his coveralls, and began to fan his chest. "It's difficult for my body to handle shock . . . I'm rather anemic . . . a state of *torpor* takes over. Much like with hummingbirds when their metabolic rate drops to a third the basal—"

"Yeah? Get to it."

"A response," Jules continued. "Or, as I mentioned, consequence of the transplant. I have difficulty responding to physical trauma . . . I don't *adapt* well. I prefer stability and compansionship . . . like parrots."

"Sounds like a drag."

"I just require rest . . . the fever is not unusual, but the cough . . ." He looked at Rick.

"Okay, maybe we shouldn't have wasted time back there. I mean, I'm sort of trashed myself . . . but shit, those losers had to suffer."

Jules turned his eye downward, concentrating.

"C'mon." Rick laughed. "Did you see that truck? We smote those losers *big-time!*" He let out a whoop and smacked the dashboard. He smiled up at the thread-worn material above his head. "History. Crucial history in the making!"

Jules stared.

"Enough said," Rick continued. "Date shakes. *Pronto! Y hielo* for my jaw. Coming?"

Jules turned back, the damp stain extended down from his shoulder blades.

"You know, I *know* you think that business back in San Bernardino was stupid, but you're like wrong. Way wrong. Sure, we could have just dropped it, but you can't fully. That stuff'll come back to haunt you . . ." Rick waited for Jules to agree. "It's not like we killed 'em or anything *heinous."* Jules's eye was closed. He had fallen asleep. Rick watched him. "It's our *lek,* dude. They don't own the fucking desert."

Out the window, a pair of young girls chalked a hopscotch court onto the asphalt beside a Winnebago. Rick watched as the little girls hustled around, pointing at the scraggles of chalk. The smaller of the two produced a pebble and tossed it, popping along. One small tennis shoe lifted behind her against the giant lighted claws that glared in the orange parking lot sky.

"I mean, sitting there?" Rick asked aloud. "Doing nothing and just letting people hurt you?" He shook his head, watching as the older girl made her approach to the pebble. Usually little girls made him think of Tamara, but this little girl reminded him of Ginger. *What a surprise.* He watched as the older girl returned, triumphant, with the pebble. She handed it to the younger one. Rick guessed her at about five years. Rick wanted the younger girl to look like Tamara. But she didn't. The younger girl looked like a small hairless baboon in terry cloth. She threw the pebble against the side of the Winnebago and began to cry. Little Ginger slapped her and the two girls began to fight. Little Ginger was about eight years old. She made short work of the younger, grinning a curlicue of little white teeth as she pushed the young girl over and began to kick her. Little Ginger turned and spied Rick. She held up her pink fists and punched at him, her snarl opening into a smile. Rick waved and blew a kiss.

Jules moaned. Yeah, they'd definitely need to get a motel and catch some Zs. Rick figured Brad and his buddy would lie to the cops. He figured Brad would rather claim innocence and bag the insurance, instead of risk some ugly court scene. Risk getting prosecuted for attempted murder with a blunt instrument. Of course, Rick didn't want to sit in court and have to explain about the ultra-yummy, jailbait little sister in the moonlight . . . Yeah, the cops could already be after them. Tasers in hand.

The door to the Winnebago opened and a muscular man in double-knit shorts, a Raiders T-shirt, and Riddell referee shoes stepped out. Rick watched him and thought of that one Raider he'd heard was in some porn flick . . . *Babyface?* What was that dude's name? Some big bad bald dude.

Little Ginger waved to the man and returned to her hopscotch, the sky behind her indigo. The man watched as the younger girl ran up and wrapped her arms around his thigh. He patted the side of her head, looked down, and yawned. Then guided her back into the trailer, the door soundless when it shut. Little Ginger hopping, bending, skipping.

An obese woman in a yellow sundress walked by the front of the Buick. She was shelling peanuts in her mouth and spitting the wet shells back out into her open palm. Rick envied her peaceful life. No trucks to destroy. No endless road trips. Nothing to do but slide TV dinners out of the oven and kick back on the sofa and look out at the pecan trees and the hot daylight.

The woman stared at him and spit a shell onto the weathered gold hood of the Buick.

Rick grinned as she waddled off. Fragments of seed gyrated above her head.

Oh, not everyone can do this.   You know.   Take it.   God, those guys.   Oh.
Not watching TV?   Psyched, huh?   Uh-huh.   Oh.   Get it slow.   Concentrate.
Slow.   No, fuck you, stay out.   Slow!   Slow!   God . . . not now!   Okay, like
you're.   There!   Make it.   Good!   Oh.   Oh.   Oh.   Give it.   Uh-huh.
Just get it.   Here.   Here.   You've always.   Can you believe it?   So much.
My.   That's.   What.   Okay.   Now stay.   God.   Psyched.   Concentrate.

Oh yeah,   Can't,   Can't,   Can't,   Oh,   Oh,   I don't, just,   Bite, little,
That,   You know,   Oh?   Think you?   These,   Bright,   Oh,   Big,
God,   Fuck,   Yes!   I love this,   Fuck yes,   Oh,   Stay there,   Stay
there,   This?   Think she's,   Kind of!   Can you,   Oh,   Oh Yeah,   That
way,   That way,   Oh,   Psyched!

▶ ▶ ▶ **47**

Tamara understood that if Rick chose to cut her out of the dialogue at a certain point in their relationship, that is, to ignore her speaking role in his life, then she had no alternative, regardless of how much she cared for him. Because to insist on trying to love him would only verify his own arrogant assumption that she *needed* him, and was weaker because of that need. Consequently, she had decided to allow herself this thing with Jack. At least for now. The decision had crept up within her without her expecting it. And here it was. Real. As she tried to find room for her feelings. It was the realization that passion led to some deeper emotion . . . love, she guessed. For her at least. She sometimes wished she had Rick's casual attitude. But she didn't. And now she had to admit she was thinking about Jack more and more. This irritated her. There was this thing called *control.* She was losing it. Rick the outlaw. But Jack might be that guy who would actually build the ranch. You know, that other guy in all the Westerns and everything. That strong, quiet guy you always thought would just *bore* you to death.

Tamara picked up the two orders of blackened redfish and backed her way through the swinging doors, serving them to a tall woman with high cheekbones, a nice smile, and a nose like the corner of an ax. She had broad shoulders and large soft breasts that were incongruous with the general feeling of muscle that brushed the air around her. At least they look real, thought Tamara as she placed the plates in front of the woman, admiring the dress and the way it snared the wide woman into an elegant hourglass. Tamara had a woman's appreciation of breasts and she caught herself glancing down. The woman was an actress on a popular television situation comedy. Tamara remembered reading about her in *People*, a publicity bio where the woman admitted that she lived with two men, both her lovers. One, ironically, the host on that game show *Cupid's Arrow*.

The woman finished her mai tai and motioned toward two other empty glasses and two soggy paper umbrellas on the tablecloth. "Two more, please." She was flushed. "I'm doing everything in twos these days."

Tamara conspiratorially, "Everything?"

"*Everything,* honey. Even husbands. I've got two of the little darlings . . ."

Tamara nodded. "I know. I read about it . . . uh, I mean, I read about you. Are they . . . are you married to *both* of them?"

The woman smiled. "Officially, no. Only one. My agent suggested that prosecution for bigamy could hurt our Nielsens."

"Do you like it . . . that is, living with two men?"

"Oh, honey." The woman's eyebrow arched.

She was pleased and in no hurry to eat. Her fingers glanced across Tamara's arm. "Really, you ought to try it sometime. Appetite'll shoot right through the ceiling. Put some meat on your bones." She pinched Tamara.

Tamara looked down at herself, scrutinizing the way her dress clung to the sloe cant of her breasts and her slender stomach. "I'll keep that in mind," she said. "One of your husbands is on TV, isn't he? Doesn't he host that love game?"

The woman beamed. "Chuck. *Cupid's Arrow.* He's a very popular guy at the moment. It's wonderful how happy it's all made him. The success of the show. He *lives* to talk about love . . . and if I don't mind saying so, he *does* know what he's talking about." The woman winked and patted her chest. "He's my *official* one. He says that the best thing in life is a good wife."

"How did you meet?"

"In the business, years ago. We were shooting a movie of the week for television, both attempting to hold down roles that were somewhat more substantial than we were accustomed to. The production was essentially an update of *The Count of Monte Cristo.* It was called *The Tower.* Anyway, I played this wholesome American woman who the count meets while playing shuffleboard on a cruise ship. You see, he's plotting his revenge upon the oil tycoon who finagled to have him locked in the tower. The tower he just escaped from . . ." The woman looked at Tamara. "Well, you get the picture. Chuck was the count's aide-de-camp, a lawyer. Speaking of which . . . ?"

Tamara shook her head. "No . . . no husbands. Not even one."

"That's too bad. Any possibilities?"

"Oh sure. But just my luck, one's my *ex*-boyfriend who I don't trust and the other's *his* best friend."

The woman thought this over. "Well, you let *them* worry about that. Whatever happens, you *know* it won't be the first time it's happened in the history of Western Civilization. You just treat them nice and make up your own mind. Or take them both. Two was *my* choice and I couldn't be happier."

"I don't think that would work out."

"Maybe not. In any case, I wouldn't worry about it all too much. You seem to be a very sweet girl and I'm sure that everything will be fine. My best advice is to just have yourself a ball."

Tamara frowned. "I wish it were that easy. But I get worn out worrying about it all the time."

"I know," the woman assured her. "The way I see it, though . . . what's to worry? Ignore it and it disappears."

"I guess . . . at least that's what I keep telling myself I *should* think. But I always end up staring at the mirror and seeing wrinkles and circles under my eyes and stupid stuff like that."

The woman laughed. "Who doesn't? You can bet your men think the same thing . . . but what are you going to do? It's your life, you might as well live it while you're still young and beautiful."

Uh-huh, thought Tamara, looking at the expensive clothes, the comfortable career, the general feeling of contentment. The pampered glow.

The woman arched her eyebrow again and gave Tamara's arm a squeeze. "How old are we?" she asked.

"Twenty-five."

"Maybe you'd like to be on Chuck's show? We could certainly arrange it."

Tamara shook her head and smiled. "Think not."

The woman breathed a small laugh and introduced herself. "My name's Vesta. Vesta Miles."

"I know," repeated Tamara. "I've seen your show."

"I admit I really didn't think you were *Cupid's Arrow* material. Nonetheless, I always like to ask. You certainly are an attractive girl. What is your name?"

"Tamara. Tamara Jenson." Tamara thought maybe she should tell her she was an actress *herself*. Unfortunately, she couldn't do it. It felt manipulative.

"Tamara, honey, my food's going to freeze up on me if we keep chatting, but it *has* been nice . . ." Vesta seemed about to continue, then sealed the conversation with a lift of her fork.

"What does your other . . . friend . . . do? If you don't mind me asking, I'm curious," asked Tamara.

Vesta smiled politely.

"Is he also an actor?"

"No, he's really not involved in much of anything at the moment. He handles real estate occasionally for his brother's firm, but then, *everyone* handles real estate in Los Angeles. I don't know what we're going to do when Los Angeles County annexes everything from Santa Monica all the way to the Atlantic. But my *other?* He's quite the cook also. He can make fried chicken like Dad did when I was little . . . back before I became a *celebrity,*" she added with a self-mocking flourish. "What's really important is that he and Chuck get along famously. They watch football together on Sunday and both play a mean game of tennis. It's very cute."

"And they're never jealous?"

Vesta took a bite of fish, winked. "Jealous. They're always jealous. Just like small boys. But a woman must learn to appreciate the good with the bad, one man or two . . . am I correct? Stay happy, healthy, and keep 'em guessing."

"Sounds a bit calculated."

Vesta shrugged. "You mean deceitful? Or do you mean *controlling?*" Her eyes twinkled.

"That doesn't bother you?"

Vesta looked past Tamara's shoulder, then nodded.

Tamara turned, instinctively picking up the empty cocktail glasses. It was Todd Mann.

"*May I speak with you, Ms. Jenson?*" Todd asked in a mean whisper, grabbing her at the elbows. "*Remember what I said last week . . . about fraternizing?*"

Tamara glared at him, then looked with disdain around the empty restaurant. "I'm doing my job."

Todd looked down at her burgundy stockings, his expression tight. He was somewhere in his mid-thirties, his face dissolute, dulled by handsomeness. He reminded Tamara of an empty elevator in an expensive hotel. His sunburned nose blinked like a little red light. "Jenson," he started.

"Fuck off. I said I *know* what I'm doing." She turned and stamped back toward the cashier. "Has anyone called for me?"

The cashier shook her head, eyes barbaric, vague.

When Tamara turned back around, her anger sequined with wonder at how good it felt to finally tell Todd Mann off, she found the elevator door open. Her boss's voice hoarse. "You're fired, Jenson! *Fired!* You're out of Deacon's Garden forever!"

48 ◄ ◄ ◄

It was very late on Monday afternoon, getting dark, Jules working his way through sleep, his breath ragged. Rick, freshly rested and showered and naked in the curtained motel room. The Twin Daughters Hideaway, at the fringe of neighboring Palm Desert. A *Magnum, P.I.* rerun droned on the TV. The floor was littered with white Del Taco sacks and empty Hamm's cans. A bottle of hydrogen peroxide sat on the bureau beside a blood-stained motel towel.

Rick stared at himself in the long mirror above the bureau. A square of bandage covered the most severe section of his fucked-up jaw, a discoloration the size of a silver dollar and the color of a crow visible above his swollen eye. He winked, then closed his good eye and peered through the swollen eye at his fuzzy reflection. Touched the discoloration and cringed. Took a bottle of Anacin from the nightstand and popped three tablets into his mouth. The chalky taste was strangely refreshing. He washed the aspirin down with bubbly beer.

The compound bow lay on the carpet. Rick figured he should toss the evidence, but he couldn't. He had grown fond of it. His first real weapon.

He stood and slid the bow and nylon flight suit under the bed with his foot, wrapped a towel around his waist, and yawned. Opened the door, squinted into the bloody belly of sunset. Somewhere above, a thousand points of light went *twinkle, twinkle.*

The entrance to the Vesuvius was an atrium of spiraling strobe, lush green plants, parqueted teak, and beveled glass. The long doors inscribed with mallechort.

Rick's boots clicked against the tiles as he entered. His black Levi's were accordioned at his green boots. The Levi's streaked with red paint. He was wearing a peach *guayabera* with a wad of Sheik condoms in his breast pocket.

The atrium led into a crowded bar filled with the kind of people who drank champagne in the parking lot of UCLA football games. Faces proud with relaxation, spidery from the sun.

Rick hustled his balls and sidled up to a barstool, a nagging Top 40 major rotation tune with an obsequious melody and a pseudo-reggae bass line thrupped, the singer Britishy in sort of a private school Los Angeles way. The plants, the music, the crowd umbrellaed by a lofty ceiling and the pervasive hum of a gargantuan air-conditioning system. In the center of the room, a monstrous crystal fountain coursed with crimson and gold streams; an octopus made of fire. The streams wound down from the apex of the fountain. Lava. There were blue Malibu lights in the jeweled dark water that swirled in the bay below. On the base of the fountain was carved the inscription A.D. 79 in black marble.

Rick motioned to the bartender, ordered himself a shot of Sauza's Conmemorativo and a schooner of draft. Something American. Like Miller. The bartender watched him with uncomplicated eyes, a splash of freckles on her chest. She had long, amber hair. Her breasts pushed against the gilt brocade X of her silk toga.

Rick downed the liquor and chewed on the wedge of lime. She smiled with concern and touched her cheek with the pewter limit-spout on the tequila bottle.

Rick shrugged.

"You look terrible," she said.

Rick smiled and held out his hand. "Rick."

She moved toward him. "Iona." Taking his hand. "Iona Agave." Her skin rustled beneath her toga. "What happened?"

"Me and a friend were just, you know, horsing around."

"She must be some friend," Iona's eyes went sleepy.

Rick watched the curve of her abdomen as it brushed back and forth against the padded rim of the bar. She held the tequila bottle in front of him.

Rick nodded.

Iona Agave poured, watching as he drank, then reached out with a cocktail napkin and dabbed his lips. "*Horsing around?*"

Rick breathed in the jasmine air that floated off her skin.

Iona reached over and brushed back his hair.

"You must do pretty well in tips," he suggested.

"*Why?* Are you planning to give me one?"

Rick broke from her gaze, his reflection in the mirror behind the bar. Maybe he should get beat up more often. "Uh . . . yeah, maybe," he said deftly. Peering around for Ginger. "I've sorta got plans right now, you know, but if you give me your number . . . like maybe we'll figure something out tomorrow or something."

Iona's eyelashes were tender as she refilled his glass. She put the bottle down and proceeded to scribble out her phone number on a white cocktail napkin imprinted with a graphic of a fiery volcano. Then reached over and tucked the napkin into the pocket of his *guayabera,* behind the packet marked Sheik. Her fingers traced over the wad of condoms. "I like my tips *big,*" she added, her voice marbled with some shiny mineral.

Rick loved the desert. It was all very civilized and evil out here where the water dissolved into the sky.

She flashed her teeth and moved off to another customer.

Rick raised his glass. A woman who'd been paying high finance charges on her skin stumbled past. She smelled of orange blossoms and tanning oil, her hand on Rick's arm for balance as her lips tapped the ear of a man in a silky Nike warm-up jacket and linen slacks. The man whispered. She yawped back and brushed off the bottle of Evian mineral water he held in his hand, reaching instead for his Beck's and taking it for a gurgle. Behind her a man with a Mediterranean complexion, wearing a wrinkled cotton suit, smoked, gesticulating to an earnest sunburned high school kid in a tennis shirt. Rick looked around again for Ginger. His eyes snagged on a man with a mustache and rose-colored hands. The man was talking to a pair of teenageish women in matching waist-length nautical jackets. Their creased skirts billowed. The girls wore themselves with awe, shying from their reflections in the mirror only when the rose-colored hands flitted too close to their excruciating, new bodies.

One of the girls turned and showed Rick her smile. He raised his hand palm-flat and rubbed it against the air, baring his teeth.

The girl brushed her thighs together and made a pained face, touching the side of her cheek.

Rick nodded and tried to create an innocent face.

The girl watched him, but shook her head when he motioned for her to move on over and join him. She mouthed words he couldn't understand.

Then Iona Agave refilled his glass with tequila. A wedge of lime and a bubbly gold schooner of draft already in front of him. Rick looked at the freckles on Iona Agave's chest.

"Have you ever done body shots?" She leaned against the bar. "That's when you put the lime and salt on someone's body and then lick it off . . . before and after the tequila."

Rick sighed. He forgot about the nautical jackets. "No," he admitted.

"It's fun. Only it can sting."

"Sort of the snail effect, huh?"

Iona Agave lifted an eyebrow and smiled. "You better not try to discipline me," she admonished. "I'll struggle."

Rick laughed, put his hand to his jaw, and winced. "Don't worry. A little pain's good for you. Besides, struggle is like . . ." He had to think. "Makes your sweat sweet."

Iona Agave went very gentle in the eyes. "I hope so. I need it." Then slid her hand down the bar rail, following it. Started to mix a martini.

Rick shook his head and tilted back his beer, carbonation twisted in braids of tiny angels. He drank and belched, fascinated by a sudden urge to get hammered, lit, wrecked. He had a serious *throw-down* urge. The alcohol like the Santana winds in his stomach. His heart a shard of broken beer bottle. The sagebrush just red serious electric guitar crackle. That truck explosion had been the ticket! Gasoline slick fire stain! All the stupid hours of stupid jobs and stupid grief he'd had to deal with, motherfucker! Burbank life! Way crucial. Yeah, thought Rick. Let's dust some brain cells.

He drank.

"Hey, tiger."

Red fingernails. Same coconutty dry-ice fragrance.

Ginger's mouth greeted him. He shivered from the warmth of something darker and much more wet than her tongue.

She unstuck herself and smiled. "So, what's up?" She rubbed her hands against his chest. "I guess you already got your drink?"

Rick nodded, lingering over the scattered blush in her cheeks and the sheen of her fizzy rayon strapless.

Ginger gave the décolletage a tug up. "Pretty, huh? This friend of mine picked it out."

"Friend?"

"Yeah, this guy . . . the guy that directs some of my movies."

Rick nodded.

Ginger ordered herself a kir royale. "And tequila?" Iona looked at Rick.

"Yeah, I'll take a Herradura Gold."

"Hair of what?" Iona purred.

Rick watched her breasts as Ginger watched him. "Herradura Gold. You know, that expensive stuff with the horseshoe on the label?"

"Of course." Iona Agave was attempting to snare him again with her eyes.

"That . . . or if you don't got it, I'll just have a Sauza Hornitos . . . that green label stuff. You know, the bottled romance of Mexico."

"Hornitos?" Iona Agave's eyes flashed.

"Yeah, as in *horny.*"

Iona Agave turned to look for the bottle. "Hornitos?" Ginger asked archly.

Rick patted her thigh. "Give me a break."

"Hmmmm," started Ginger, imitating Iona. "*Hornitos?*"

"Yeah," Rick repeated. "As in horny."

"*How horny?*" Ginger batted her lashes.

"Horny enough."

Ginger moved closer. "Enough for what?" Her fingers clutched his chest. Twiddled his nipples beneath his *guayabera.* She watched him watch her.

"Enough to make your little blond pussy shred."

Ginger laughed a husky laugh. "It *always* shreds, Rick. Fast, loud. Just like a guitar." She let her tongue rub the back of her teeth. "Rick, the *feedback.* That's when the bad boys beg . . ."

Rick nodded. It was true. He'd been there. "Here's to it," he said, and raised the dregs of his glass.

Ginger raised her empty hand with a saturated look and recrossed her legs. "So here you are, I didn't think you'd make it."

They watched Iona Agave return with their drinks.

"Yeah, well, I couldn't really miss our first date."

Ginger was amused. "Is that what this is?"

"Sure," answered Rick. Ginger seemed more confident, capable. 'Course, in Hollywood she was a little on the trashed side. "When do I meet your parents?" he teased.

Ginger snorted. "*My parents?* That's a joke."

Rick downshifted, running his fingers across her calf. "Let's drop the parental *units*. The crucial thing is that this is our first date." He softened his voice, ". . . and I'm nervous . . ."

"Yeah?"

"Yeah, girls scare me."

Ginger laughed and fluffed a spot of her drink up with the tip of her tongue. "They do, huh? I don't remember you being too scared."

"That's 'cause it's different with you."

"Yeah. I bet." Then she wrapped her legs around him, pulling him forward. Her barstool tilted as she caressed the compress on his cheek.

"Don't ask."

"A fight?"

"Sort of. Sort of a mugging. But it's no biggie. Justice was had by all."

"Got him back, huh?"

Rick nodded.

"Why do people always fight?" This asked with a curveless curiosity.

Rick shook his head. "I don't know. Everyone just gets tense, I guess." Rick sipped his tequila.

Ginger's interest melted into something different. She touched the wad of condoms in his *guayabera*. Her fingers slipped over the folded cocktail napkin with Iona's phone number. She ran her nail across his nipple.

Rick watched his hand crawl up her calf, slip toward her relaxed thigh. "How'd the shoot go?"

Ginger smiled. "It was all right." Watching his reaction. "Except I had to do this scene with this real gross guy I hate . . ."

"Yeah?"

"Yeah. We were doing this hard-core shot . . . you know what that is? That's where the guy's doing you from behind and he practically climbs on your back so the camera can get up in there, you know and get the *action*. Anyway, this guy's been around forever and I just think he's sort of foul. I mean, they're basically *all* pieces of meat . . . but he's the *worst*. He's always telling these sick jokes and he's real ugly . . . about the only thing he's got is a big dick. And he never misses a cue. Like never. Old Faithful. But, yuck . . ." Ginger shivered to make her point. "You know?"

Rick nodded.

"So I've only done a few films with this guy 'cause I just won't. But this time, well, I said sure. I don't know why. Maybe the money. Anyway, we're doing the shot and he just starts trying to ram his dick into my ass, like really hard. I think it's 'cause he can't handle cunts anymore. Like he's too fucked-out. So I made him stop. I said *that* was out. I mean, *really*. Not psyched. You only do *that* if you're desperate for work." Ginger smiled. "Which I'm not, thank you. So like afterward, after we're done and showered, I walked by him in front of everyone, the whole crew and everyone, and told him he was just a life-support system for his cock. Those were my words, *life-support system*. And you know what? I think *he* thought it was a compliment!"

"Yeah?"

"Yeah." Ginger shook her head.

Rick nodded. He didn't know what to say. He figured ugliness and stupidity were occupational hazards.

"But we shot for two days, tenish hours straight, two movies. Then I got some sleep, which was nice. It's a real drag to act like you're into it really early in the morning. I don't know, something about mornings . . . and—" Ginger's face brightened as she thought of something. "I almost forgot. We had this new girl who'd just had her tits done. She was from the South . . . some place like Alabama or Kentucky. There was this scene where I was supposed to walk into the room and catch her playing with this big vibrator, but she was scared of it, you know . . . I mean, it was *really* big. I knew it could fit, but wow! And once I put it in . . . *forget it!* I just forgot *everything* . . . my lines, you name it. And the new girl opened the door and just stared. I tried to say my lines, but I couldn't *even*, you know? Then I just fell off the bed and this thing was making that weird sound . . . sort of like a vacuum cleaner under water. And then I looked up and everyone was clapping, you know the cameramen and the guy who holds the pussy light. *Everybody.* They were just standing there cheering. But I kept going 'cause, I mean, *c'mon*! And then the new girl wasn't so scared and she came over and tried to steal it from me. Can you believe it? Boy, she learned *fast.* Like wasn't scared. Like not at *all.* So we started wrestling and stuff and the director was *psyched!*"

"And the other girl?"

Ginger curved her lips. "She's all better now. But what a *kid.* She goes like, 'Hi, Ginger, I'm Lauren. I'm bicoastal.'" Ginger flapped her bangs down over her eyes and made a dopey look. Then laughed. "I bet she's like three days out of the talk booths, you know?"

Rick nodded. "Cosmopolitan City."

"Right. But I try to give each of them a little TLC. Everyone can't be a star. Not even. You need some cattle. And I like . . . I just don't think anyone deserves to be treated badly. Besides . . . she *is* cute." Ginger continued, "It's fun when you do it straight through like that and no one's too much of a jerk. But having to work with what's his name was really gross.

A complete drag. Guys like that leave you with an upset stomach and a sore pussy. I mean, a *complete* drag."

"I hate drags," agreed Rick, tilting his beer.

"Tell me about it. I think he was trying to get back at me 'cause of the last time . . ."

"Yeah?"

"Uh-huh. A while ago . . . we were out in New York and he couldn't get it up. He has to come twice each day . . . it's in his contract. So anyway, this was like the first time in forever he couldn't do it and I just laughed and told him to go home. I said, 'Go home, little boy.' He was *really* pissed-off. But so what? He deserved it. They asked me to fluff him and I just laughed. I said, 'I'm not going to touch that limp thing.' He was *totally* embarrassed. I think that's why he was trying to sneak that anal like that . . ." Ginger looked pensive.

"Fluff him?"

"Yeah, like that's what they used to call it. Like *fluff girls.* That's when it's your job to keep the guys hard when they're waiting."

"Oh," said Rick.

Ginger pursed her lips into a tiny red heart.

"And you've done that? Been a fluff girl?"

"Technically no," she purred. "But in an emergency . . . as long as they ask nicely, you know, treat me with respect. And I think they're okay."

Rick shifted on his stool.

"Otherwise we'd be there all week and I don't get paid enough for that."

"What *do* you get paid enough for?"

Ginger smiled and finished her drink. "Could you order me another one of these? I'm going to go freshen up."

"Freshen up?"

"Yeah, want a bump?"

"I'll pass," said Rick. "Maybe later."

"Suit yourself, tiger."

Rick watched as she walked off in the direction of the ladies' chipped out of the marble facing. The grind of her ass made his throat tighten. He washed the tightness away with tequila. Iona Agave watched him. She walked over and touched his hand. "That your horse?" Her lips were wet. The tequila helixical, wonderful.

"No. I mean . . . yeah. She's my horse. Sort of."

Iona Agave nodded. "You could do better."

"Yeah?"

"Yeah." She lifted his hand and rubbed her fingernails across the underside of his wrist. "Much."

Rick's reflection grinned back at him. *Unhinged.* Hungry, wild. His reflection? The long hair, the bandages, the bruises. Iona Agave put his fingers in her mouth and began to suck, eyeing him through her amber hair. They watched each other. Her lips moved.

Rick pulled back his hand. "Whoa."

She reached out and patted the pocket of his shirt. "Don't forget."

"Sure," he said, turning as Ginger uncoiled from a throng of lightweight double-breasted pastel suits and moved back toward him. Her breasts jounced merrily. Her lips a thin red line.

She slipped her fingers into the pocket of his *guayabera* and pulled out the cocktail napkin. She didn't open it. "Eat."

Rick looked at her.

Ginger turned away. "Eat it, Rick. Or you'll never touch me again."

Iona Agave watched them uneasily. There was a lonesome thing going on in her eyes. Rick took the napkin from Ginger's fingers and began to chew. He watched the crease where Ginger's arm pressed the side of her breast. He washed the napkin down with a mouthful of beer.

"Good," she said. "That's a good *boy*."

Iona Agave began to replace their empty glasses, head turned slightly to one side.

Rick picked up his fresh tequila, *eyeing* Ginger. He wanted to look ironic. She gazed back at him with soft, somewhat parental distraction.

"I think I'll have that bump," he added.

▶ ▶ ▶ **49**

Eventually it was last call. Ginger ordered a final round. Rick was nursing two more glasses of something . . . some kind of tequila and some kind of draft beer. He forgot their names. But the cocaine filled him with an eager appreciation for the shadows, the noise, the pauses in conversation. Then the lights fired down abruptly, the lava of the volcano fountain a blood of silvers. The blue bay so much tap water.

Ginger smiled and took him by the arm. They stepped out into the purple Coachella Valley desert. She led him around the corner of the building, nudging him back into an unlit doorway. "Here," she ordered, the smell of industrial cleanser mixed with her perfume. The taste of cocaine at the back of Rick's throat.

He lowered the dress, cradling her breasts.

"Squeeze," she whispered.

Rick did, eliciting a sigh, bent and took a nipple between his teeth.

She ran her fingers through his hair. "Is my good little boy going to fuck me now?"

Rick straightened and searched out her mouth, working his hands to free her from her zipper.

The dress fell with a puff.

Gingerly, Ginger stepped clear, picked the dress up and folded it over her arm, leaned back and turned her eyes on him. Her panties filmy black. She held her finger against her nose and sniffed. "Well?"

"I guess you better turn around and spread your legs."

She turned. Naked, her skin speckled with starlight. Swayed her hips for Rick. "Okay. Stick it in."

Rick tore a condom from his pocket and ripped open the translucent packet. He was weaving. He stroked himself with his hand.

Ginger looked back over her shoulder. "No! I'm sick of those. I'm not in the mood. Just fuck me right or don't fuck me at all."

Rick looked at the condom, then dropped it and ground it into the cement with the heel of his boot.

"Here," Ginger whispered, taking him in her right hand. Her panties were a shimmering crushed W that slipped to her ankles. Her dress draped over her arm.

She cooed as he entered her, shifting the dress and slinging it back over her shoulder, directly under the strain of Rick's chin. The fit and smoothness of her beyond him—an engine. The click of highway safety reflectors. Pure speed. Rick's eyes pegged open. He began to chew on the shiny material, biting and gulping at the desert air.

Ginger didn't care. They were fucking.

► ► ► 50

Tamara told Jack she needed a few days alone. No people at all, she'd said. I just want to be alone for a bit.

Fine, he answered, placing the phone back in the cradle.

Tamara knew he meant something else entirely, but she forgave him. He was probably just as confused as she was right now. Maybe more. And no one had the slightest idea where Rick had disappeared. Or with whom. That worried her. Made her jealous. Bugged her much more than losing her stupid job, although that was another reason she wanted a vacation from the past few days. Made her more certain she shouldn't fall into a relationship right now. Just more trouble, that's what a relationship would be—more trouble.

She tried the telephone again at Rick's. The recording said disconnect. She wanted to drive over to Burbank, but decided against it. She didn't want to invade his messy sanctuary and catch him flagrante delicto. No, but she would have appreciated some assurance that he was all right. Either that or comfortably in some sheriff's or LAPD holding cell.

She turned on the TV. Maybe that would cheer her up. As she looked around for her cigarettes, she realized she had made a mistake. The TV was talking about soil erosion. Deforestation that covered an area the size of China and India. The world's vegetated surface increasingly incapable of producing crops, lumber, livestock. At the exact moment she lit her Winston, the phone rang. She wasn't surprised to hear Jack on the other end. "Yes?" she asked in a coolish voice, irritated by what she perceived as his lack of patience.

His voice was formal, embarrassed. "Sorry to bother you again, Tamara. I know you're tired and everything . . . but my sister was just telling me that the Gold Star Theatre is holding auditions for *The Taming of the Shrew.* I think the group that normally does their thing there, you know, what do you call it? What's that word?"

"The *company*?"

"Yeah, that's it. Anyway, I guess her friend who was going to handle the lead just got some part on TV and they didn't have an . . ."

"Understudy?"

"Yeah, so they need to figure out a replacement . . ."

"For Kate?"

"I guess so, I don't know. I guess I've never really read the play. But my sister said she knew some other guy who'd done set work there . . . over in North Hollywood. Said it's a good atmosphere and that if you wanted to give it a shot . . . well, they even pay. It's real." Jack paused. "They did that *Three Nickel* thing last fall."

"*Penny,*" Tamara said. "*Three Penny Opera.*"

"Yeah, that must've been it." Jack's voice curled down.

"*Kate,*" Tamara said without elaborating. "Do you have the phone number? I've heard of it, the Gold Star . . ."

"Yeah. He said the place is somewhere on Victory Boulevard." Jack gave her the number.

"That sounds right. Thanks, Jack. I'm glad you called. Really."

"Anytime. I just want to see you make it. How much waitressing are you supposed to take, right?"

Tamara exhaled. "I got fired last night, Jack."

"What? Why didn't you tell me?"

"I *am* telling you. I was talking with that actress Vesta Miles—"

"Wait, isn't she the one married to Chuck Venison?"

"Yes. She also has another. Unofficial husband, that is. But anyway, I was fired for *frater-*

nizing with the customers. That means talking politely with someone when the restaurant is empty."

"He fired you for that?"

"*And* because I told him to fuck off."

Jack laughed. "You were wasting your time there, Tamara. You've got to try harder to do what you want to do. Acting. Just try and I bet you'll be on the cover of *Premiere* in no time."

"In an evening gown?" she asked, lighting herself a Winston and scratching the back of her calf. Her jeans were rolled up at the ankles. She was wearing sandals.

"Sure," said Jack. "One of those sequined numbers."

"That's comforting. I just hope they'll supply the cleavage."

"No problem. I'm sure that all comes with the deal. They'll probably even use one of those special lens filters that makes your skin all soft and awesome-looking."

Tamara leaned back, lifted up her T-shirt and looked at her stomach. "My skin already *is* all soft and awesome-looking, Jack."

"And Lee Press-On Nails," he continued, unperturbed. "I bet they give you all that. They probably even *make* you wear it. And in the breast department, I bet they use lenses or something that'll make your breasts look like watermelons, if that's what you're into."

Tamara laughed. "I'll settle for cantaloupes, Jack. Firm, ripe cantaloupes."

"C'mon, Tamara . . . your breasts are beautiful."

"Thanks." She exhaled a thin gray stream of smoke. "They get the job done."

"Champagne glasses," he agreed. "My sister always told me girls were just supposed to have enough to fill a champagne glass. That was the elegant form of measurement."

"A *crystal* champagne glass," Tamara added.

Jack was silent for a moment.

"What are you thinking about?" she asked.

"I'm wondering if you'd let me . . . measure you?" he asked. "I mean, when you're done hiding from people. I'll bring the glasses and something to drink. Wine. Maybe we could cook dinner together . . . have an *elegant* night." Wow, Jack thought. I'm flirting.

Tamara smiled, then made a thinking sound. "I don't know if I really want you to measure my breasts, but . . . why don't you come over and help me cook? *And* help me study the lines for this play, that is *if* I can get an audition. That way we'll be elegant *and* productive. You can bring whatever you want. Wine. Gifts. Assorted breast-measuring devices, I guess, if you must."

Jack smiled at the phone. "When?"

"Tomorrow night. Eight o'clock. Are you working then?"

"No. I've got a shift tonight and this interview in the City of Industry tomorrow afternoon . . . that's about it."

"Another job?"

"Yeah, I guess. I'm going to talk to this guy about selling cars. You know, pushing iron."

"*A car salesman?* Jack, that sounds horrible."

"Really? I must be twisted, but I thought it sounded sort of cool. I figure I might learn something and I need to make some cash if I'm ever going to get to Japan."

"Japan?"

"Yeah, that's my plan. Eat toxic fish. Ride the bullet train. Sing *karaoke.* Visit temples. You know . . ."

"Jack, you can do all that stuff here in Los Angeles. *All* fish is toxic. You can do *karaoke* at Sizzler, bet. And you can just take Amtrak down to San Diego if you want to ride a train."

"It's not the same. I want complete immersion. Also, I got some basic bills and that's going to tag me. It's no big deal, though . . . everyone's got to work. Unless you were born rich. Which we weren't. Even Rick's feeling the heat. I . . . I didn't really know how to bring this up, but I went over to his place and that fat dude, The Manager, told me he'd kicked Rick out after the robbery. He told me Rick had piled his stuff into that old woman's car and bailed."

"*Bailed?* What's 'bailed' mean?"

"You know, *took off,* I guess."

"C'mon, Jack, I'm worried . . ." Her voice flattened. "Is he with that girl somewhere?"

"Final word I got . . . I mean from him . . . he'd been robbed and needed some cash, but then he never showed. The Manager told me he'd taken the last month's and just split."

Tamara stared at the phone.

"Look," said Jack. "I'm sorry, but I'm sure he's cool. If I were you, I'd look into that *Shrew* deal and relax."

"*Relax?* Jack, It's hard to relax. What if he's in trouble?"

"I know, but he can handle himself. He's probably just out somewhere brawling around, spending that money, and doing what he always does. Let's drop it." Jack's voice got sharp. "Don't worry about him. He doesn't deserve it. Unless maybe you just miss him. Is that what this is about?"

"Maybe. Maybe I'm acting stupid . . ." Her voice changed. "Well, thanks."

"Look," said Jack. "I'm not that fair about the whole thing. But I think Rick's blowing it. He doesn't treat you right, Tamara."

"I know you feel that way, Jack. I'll let you go . . . just call me if you hear anything. Okay?" Tamara tried to make herself sound cheerful and confident.

"Okay," he said. "Later." Jack stared at the phone. *I'll let you go?* How fucking polite.

Tamara placed the phone down and crushed out her cigarette. Jack's concern? It was more than *boy* jealousy. She should be able to accept *concern.* Concern shouldn't scare her off. Especially since Rick had just hopped in an old Buick and disappeared from the face of the earth. Taking their love with him. *Love.* What an interesting choice of words to use. But what other word conjured up the frustration, desire, and vertigo that he caused? Maybe *sickness.*

She wasn't in love with Rick . . . she was in sickness.

The iced tea powder fell in a cloud. It stuck to the cubes of ice. Tamara held the glass under the faucet. The curtains in the neighboring wall of apartment windows were static, colorless.

It made her sad to realize that life in Rick's apartment was over. The clutter, the damp marijuana smell. All the things she used to complain about. Sad. But that's why this thing with Jack had to be temporary. She couldn't imagine a relationship involving another musky apartment that smelled of bong water. *And* Jack didn't even *have* his own apartment anymore. I mean, *really.* Was this what womanhood was all about? Stupid jobs and men who did nothing but watch TV and listen to loud music?

51 ◄ ◄ ◄

Ginger was talking about how *healthy* people don't die from cocaine. No, not really. It was just the ones with bad hearts.

"Yeah," said Rick. He handed her back the hollow ballpoint and sniffed. He watched as Ginger held her hair back and inhaled, running the pen along the white line.

"We're almost done . . ." She glared at the mirror.

Rick nodded.

They were in a motel room stacked with video equipment and assorted cardboard boxes; a glass breakfast table and some padded leather chairs stood in an alcove by a wet bar. Each of the boxes had Eurydice Productions stenciled in large black letters on the side.

Rick stared at the stenciling and listened to his heart. For some reason they were out of liquor. "Why Eurydice?"

Ginger shrugged. "It's the name of my friend's boat. I think he thinks it sounds real slick, so he just used it again."

"Not even a beer?"

"You can keep looking." She sounded irritated. Then began to brush at her hair with what looked to Rick like a lint brush. "But he keeps it all locked up."

Ginger began to check her face in her compact. Her lipstick had deteriorated, revealing the thin tilde of her lips. She reapplied more from an ebony container which fell from her fingers. It bounced soundless on the carpet.

Rick picked it up. "What color are we wearing tonight?"

"Wine in Heaven," she answered as she stuffed the gold-banded tube into her purse and started to dial out more lines.

Rick exercised vague mental images of fucking. Clinical images. Lots of close penetration footage. Then he thought about Angela. Everything she did, the way she moved, her scent. It clung like it had claws. Even now. Like the time Angela admitted to giving one of her girlfriends head in the front seat of her MG, had told Rick it was the polite thing to do after all the crystal meth. Polite and fun. *Angela.* Made him *hungry* for the dangerous sun, *hungry* for the cold moon.

Rick watched Ginger. Yeah, it wasn't surprising he thought of Angela now. Wired and beerless in a twilight of curtains. "Don't you kind of hate that stuff?" He listened to the click of the blade.

Ginger looked up at him. "I guess. *Sometimes.*"

"Like now?"

She continued to chop. "Do you want to leave?"

Rick shook his head.

Ginger grinned. The sign of her lips and teeth sent a terrible pleasure spilling down his spine. He moved his hands for the beer that still wasn't there.

She held up the mirror. "Here."

Rick finished the line. "Where're you from? Like in the Valley?"

Ginger watched him.

"That's cool," said Rick. "I'm from Burbank."

"I'm not from the *Valley*. I just stay there 'cause of my husband." Ginger smiled. "I grew up in Brentwood."

Wow. Kind of a pricey neighborhood. If she was telling the truth.

"It was beautiful. I used to go to the beach. Until I started taking care of my skin."

"And the folks? You'd acted like there was some trip going on with them."

"Oh, nothing like you're thinking. No Dad stumbling in drunk and pissing in the closet and trying to fuck me..." Ginger was dialing out another line. "They just aren't psyched about my work. They don't want me to act. Like not at all. Say it's sleazy." Ginger rubbed Rick's thigh. "It's not a problem. They've got their life. I've got mine."

It was early. Somewhere in the predawn of Tuesday. Rick's body forged in the glowing furnaces behind the gates of Valhalla. He was muscular, supple, brilliant.

Ginger behind the video camera. He watched himself on the screen, the bruises on his face black on the TV. "And then what?" Ginger asked.

"Well... then I got out of college and... you know, started doing the adult thing. Paying the bills solo. That whole gig."

"Yes?"

Rick stared at his reflection.

"Did we start a family?"

Rick hitched at his jeans, his shirt and boots crumpled on the floor. "No, *we* didn't. *We* just sort of fucked around."

"But a sweetheart? There must have been a sweetheart."

"Yeah, there was a girl."

"Was? Is?"

"Was," Rick said.

"Too bad. Do we miss her?"

Rick watched Ginger's legs.

Ginger giggled. Fiddled with the lens. The image on the TV screen zoomed in and out at Rick's crotch. Ginger started to make heavy-breathing noises.

"This must be a new role for you . . . *behind* the camera."

Ginger's giggle ended flat, a gruff laugh tacked to the end.

Rick's forehead was heavy. He blinked.

"And when we fuck our sweetheart, do we always remember to wear our rubbers?"

Rick stared back at the camera.

"Sor-ry!" she sang.

Rick's gaze fell to her hips, followed her legs out from her skirt and down to her naked feet floating in the carpet.

"Take off your pants."

"What?"

"*I said*, take off your pants."

Rick shrugged, stood, and crackled open the silver buttons of his Levi's, shrugging out of them.

"And put the boots back on," Ginger whispered.

Rick stared at the camera, sat back down, and tugged at his boots.

"Now stand and turn around slowly."

Rick snorted. "Turn around slowly yourself."

Ginger's head popped above the camera. "*Please*, Rick. A *complete* circle." She puckered and kissed the air.

Rick did as he was asked.

Ginger whispered. "Now caress it."

Rick snorted.

"Stroke for me, Rick. Jerk off for me."

He diffidently began to fondle himself.

Rick stared into the camera eye. "This your idea of a fantasy?"

"Just do it," she implored. "*Please . . .*"

Rick spit into his palm and began to masturbate, staring at the lens. "Like that?"

"Uh-huh," she allowed.

Rick watched his thickening cock, then back up at the image of himself on the screen. His swollen eye pulled his face up into a knot of shadow. Ginger's feet. Her dress drooped like a small blue animal, shinnying down her legs. She stepped out of it for the second time that evening, flipping it toward the bed with her foot.

Rick followed the curve of her thighs, his own pulsed.

"What're you looking at?"

"You," he answered, his eyes trained on the taut scimitar of leg above the knee.

"Don't!" she snapped.

"What?"

"I said don't."

Rick shrugged, looked down at the carpet, and applied some flux to his strokes. Ginger back in the dreamtime milky doorway, black panties high on her hips. Shoulder blades speckled with starlight.

"What're you thinking about?"

Nothing, thought Rick as he recognized the first pinching roots of orgasm. *Nothing.*

"And don't *think* about me either. That's an order. *Don't.* I just want you to think about you. That's how I want it. And don't think about *her.* What's her face. Your sweetheart." Ginger's voice went soft then. "I just want you to think of you. Rick. And you're all alone."

Rick closed his eyes. Body glinting. Flash-burned with the warmth of cocaine. His erection deflated. He imagined himself alone on a white sand beach, hair shiny from the salt water and hot sun. Skin syrupy. His muscles carved.

But it was useless. His hard-on was a bad metaphor. He tugged some more, spit on his fingers, and swept them over and around the head of his penis, then down the shaft.

Finally, he gave up and opened his eyes, surprised to find Ginger beside the tripod, fingers plying the tiny umbrella of light between her thighs, free hand clenched behind her neck.

Rick's mouth tight, shoulders squared at the TV. Ginger's fingers restless. Her eyes slivered curves. Hips awkward as she shivered at him.

Rick slipping against his hand as the umbrella of light clicked open and shut. Open and shut. Open and shut.

Thinking briefly of Jules.

Crucial Grace Kelly Fan. Crucial Monster Bowler. King of the Road Squids. Accomplice in Destruction. Bone Giver. Bird Saint.

► ► ► **52**

Los Angeles swirled with the sounds of rush hour as exhausted, coffee-yellow drivers piloted their machines into stopped left-turn aisles. Shells of broken bottle glistened on the cement. Stoplights vestry-red. The Hollywood hills spotted white with bungalows, mansions, funereal cornices glinting through the deodar pine. A rolling cemetary buried in smog, ocean haze, punctured sunlight.

Jack stepped from the porte cochere of Bullock's Wilshire, a silver box wrapped with ribbon in his hand. He shielded his eyes and looked around for his motorcycle. He couldn't remember where he'd parked. It frustrated him, just as it frustrated him to even walk *into* one of these department stores. He hated department stores. Just another trespasser in the vaults of fashionable merchandise. His chinos grimy, oil-stained in the citrus shadows, infinite rows of dressing mirrors and racks of shimmering cloth. It always confirmed his prejudice that, underneath it all, he was an Okie. A white-trash, Jewish Okie, stinking of black dirt and jalopy fumes. This feeling was the reverse of how he felt when he was in the weight room. Or on his bike. Or with Tamara.

He peered into the soiled city. Taillight of his Suzuki between a vintage Corvair and a Diplomat. He walked. The question was could he hold on to the box and manage his way over to Tamara's without breaking the crystal champagne glasses. He slipped on the DISCO shades and stepped on the kick start. The idling Suzuki was a blender full of rocks. He shifted into gear and readjusted his weight.

He'd talked to the guy about selling cars and it looked like he might end up with a second job. Maybe even be able to save up enough money to take someone with him on his big road trip across the Pacific. Someone like Tamara.

Jack could think of nothing better than eating peanuts on an airplane, watching the blue sky from on top. Knowing they were going somewhere together. Just elevenish hours of bad movies, reading Wolverine comics, and then touching down in Narita International. Where life was different. Where life wasn't America. Where life wasn't Los Angeles. Where life *was* Japan. Chosen land of the Wolverine. A place where maybe Jack could take the anger inside of him and figure out how to change it. Get that kind of *inner* thing he wanted. Walk under different signs. Look at different faces. Learn a new language.

► ► ► **53**

Rick was sweating. He opened his eyes. He'd been having a bizarre dream about Jules. In the dream, Jules was fishing, casting his line out over the water and grinning with a face that wasn't Jules's real face. The fishing line snapped and quivered. Tamara stood on the other side of the river, her dress blowing all theatrical at her ankles.

Then Ginger stepped from the bathroom, stretched out alongside Rick, and yawned. She was dressed, skin damp from shower water.

"What time is it?" Rick asked, touching his jaw with the back of his hand.

Ginger pointed to the digital 6:52 that blinked turquoise on the VCR.

"Oh," said Rick. "Jesus Christ. We crashed serious."

"Uh-huh." Ginger watched him with aquatic disinterest.

He lowered his head to the pillow.

"I'm going," she said. "I've got to meet a friend for dinner. That means you have to go, too. It's not cool for you to stay here."

"Yeah?"

"Yes," she answered, sitting up and sliding to the edge of the bed. "It's not my room. It's the Eurydice guy's and he's getting back from L.A. in about an hour."

"Boyfriend?"

Ginger looked at him. "Sort of. He's also sort of a boss."

"Does that mean like a director or a *pimp*?"

Ginger's mouth turned down. "I had a good time, but you have to go, Rick. I don't need to give you any excuses."

"Whatever." Rick regretted his remark. He stood and slipped off his boots, leaning back into his Levi's. Ginger swung her purse and watched. She had on a tight, shoulderless sheath dress that looked like it had been quilted out of green vinyl. Her eyelids were lemony. Her eyes as green as her dress.

"Hey?" Rick asked. "When'd you get the green eyes?"

"They're contacts. Just like the blue ones."

"You mean?"

"My eyes are brown, like my hair."

"You're not into brown?"

Ginger shrugged. "Brown's *normal.* I just like to play with it. Like accessories."

"Yeah . . . you should make your hair that same green. That'd be wicked."

"My *pimp?*" Ginger asked. "Aren't I allowed to have friends?"

"This the same dude that buys you fancy clothes and takes those photos of you?"

The air tasted of blow dryer, burned shampoo, and air-conditioned air. Ginger shifted her weight and opened the door. The smell of desert. It was night again.

"So you think *you* want to start paying for my clothes?" she asked.

Rick walked over and stood in front of her. He should say something and he knew it. He was acting like a baby.

Ginger was motionless, backlit by a yellow bug light. She stared at the parabola of muscle along his neck. Her emerald eyes glinted.

Rick snapped his fingers.

She looked at him strangely. "Was I staring?"

"Totally."

Ginger teased at the blond hair above her forehead. "Do I look okay?"

"Yeah, fine . . . but what's the matter? I thought you were about to fight with me and then you just *spaced?*"

Ginger smiled. "I don't fight. Not with you. Not with anyone." She adjusted the snaky hem of her dress. Smoothed it against her stomach. "Don't come back around here. I'll call you in L.A."

"I don't have a phone." Rick moved to kiss her. "No apartment either."

Ginger stopped his hands, taking him by the wrists. Held him back. "You could call me, maybe at . . ." Her voice stopped. "No, forget it."

"Forget what?"

"I can't see you again."

"Fuck that. Why not? What's the problem?"

"No," continued Ginger, to herself. "I can't."

Rick snorted. "What's your trip?"

Ginger looked at their hands together. "No. I shouldn't have even invited you here."

"Look," started Rick.

"I'm tired of men like you," she added. "Men like boys. Men who want to screw up my career."

"Your *career?* What career? You're a porn star. An X-rated party girl. That's the bottom of the barrel career-wise."

"Fuck you," she snapped.

"Look, okay. We're just hanging out, right? How'm I going to fuck up your life by *fucking you?* Isn't that like *practice?*"

"Because, if I start fucking you seriously . . . it's just *different.* Even *you* probably know that." She turned and began to click down the tiles toward the parking lot. "I need things," she said over her shoulder. "I *need* to be taken care of. I *need* my concentration."

"Well, I need a ride. If you don't want to fuck me anymore, that's your problem. But don't leave me out here. My car's back at the Vesuvius."

Ginger faced him, arching her eyebrow. "My aren't *we* independent?"

"At least I don't call being a whore a *career,*" Rick said despite himself.

Ginger's eyes narrowed. "I'm not a *whore*. I'm a star. There's a difference. People all over the world watch my movies. Millions of people. I was even invited to New Zealand to give a press conference on the adult movie industry. I have dinner with famous people *all the time*."

"Yeah." Rick laughed coldly. "You're a star. Big deal. You're still a coked-up slut who's taking herself too seriously."

Ginger spat. "*A coked-up slut?* And what's that make you?" Her hands opened and closed, flickering pink. "*You're* the slut!" she snarled, before the spin and the clatter down the tiles. Her purse bounced at her hip. Her legs sliced like swords. Her little angry ass the end of the sentence.

The black dunes awash with stray headlight glare.

Rick was confused. Mad at himself. And two miles from his car. Because why? Because he couldn't keep his mouth shut. Everything was easy and cool and he had to fuck it up. Tonight he was a fuck-it-up machine. And it wasn't like him to blow it. He was Rick. The cool one. Our hero.

What gives?

And he'd kind of thought they were having a good time. He'd kind of expected more of it. Wanted more of it. *More. More* was crucial.

54 ◄ ◄ ◄

Tamara woke after a deep sleep. She was under her comforter. A muscular warmth crept down her legs. She stood and stretched.

The coffee grinder whirred as she tapped out the number for the Gold Star Theatre. Tamara poured the tap water into the Mr. Coffee. An answering machine informed her that auditions were currently available by appointment. Emergency auditions for the role of Kate of Padua set for the eighteenth of March, the phone number of the director followed.

Tamara called her agent. Motes of dust swirled up through the sunlight that slanted past the kitchen curtains, a wedge of marble cast across the chopping board beside the sink. Tamara's agent said she would see what she could do for Tamara. Agreed to *really try.* That meant the first thing to do was drive down to the bookstore and grab two copies of the play.

Practice.

She went into her bathroom and turned on the shower. "Kate," she whispered as the hot water swamped her. How had that one line gone, the one she remembered from when she was in Venice Beach?

My tongue will tell the anger of my heart . . .

Tamara reached for the Dr. Bronner's Eucalyptus Soap and spread her palms with it, lathering the scented liquid across her shoulders and arms. She could only remember the beginning of the speech and it bothered her.

Why, sir, I trust I may have leave to speak; And speak I will. I am no child, no babe; Your betters have endur'd me say my mind; And if you cannot, best you stop your ears. My tongue will tell the anger of my heart . . .

She rinsed off, squeezing the excess water from her hair. She probably *should* act more like Kate of Padua. Because it was something about her heart. Something about the anger of it and being *free* with words. Fighting with words.

The kettle on the stove whistled. A pack of Winstons untouched in their cellophane wrapping by the ashtray.

She wondered who they'd cast as Petruchio?

Before the Mr. Coffee pot was full, the phone was ringing.

Tamara answered and heard her agent's voice.

55 ◄ ◄ ◄

Rick pulled the Buick Skylark into the entrance of the Twin Daughters Hideaway outside Palm Desert. Shut off the engine and stepped out, cradling a damp paper sack in his arm. He wasn't *exactly* sure what his plan was but he would figure it out. He was pissed for eating Iona Agave's phone number . . . he could've called her tonight. That would've been cool. But whatever. And now it was lonesome Tuesday. Just him and the squid. The bartender at the Vesuvius had told him that Ms. Agave had gone to Barstow for the next couple of days to see her family. S.O.L. For now. So here he was with a sack of goods. And tired legs. His eyes ached from the flash of head-lights. Eventually someone had stopped and given him a ride. And now there was nothing to do but kill some cold beers and read some fresh literature to go with the Adult Channel and *King-Size Water Beds* advertised on the cracked plastic marquee.

He freed the motel key from his pocket and fumbled it into the doorknob. Put his weight against the door. He stumbled into the motel room. Brusque traffic babble and the pink neon glow filtered through the curtains. The room was freezing. Air conditioner unit making the sound of ferns at dusk.

Jules lay asleep, curled in a drenched sheet.

Rick placed the sack on the bureau and turned the dial up on the thermostat. "Jules, you awake? Hombre?"

Jules stirred.

Rick sat on the edge of the bed, touched the damp, thin hair. Wiggled the edge of the water bed.

Jules sighed a pale sigh.

"Shit," mumbled Rick. He stood and walked over to the paper sack. He hated when people were sick. It always made him feel lame. Like it made him feel when Tamara led Jack inside her apartment. Or when Tamara used to cry. That same thing inside him going nowhere. Running around and around.

He tugged out a brown bottle and twisted off the cap. The beer had that perfect Budweiser consistency that was probably just tastelessness. He flipped the channel control on the TV, turned up the volume, and found a Sergio Leone Western, complete with Clint Eastwood chewing a rapier-thin cigar.

Rick leaned back beside Jules as Clint sent a stick of dynamite sputtering underneath a Gatling gun. "Hey, Road Squid, you been drinking water like I told you?"

No answer.

"*Have you?*"

The damp colorless head of hair moved *Yes.*

"Then start getting better, dude. That's an order. Here, keep these blankets cranking and make yourself sweat. Crucial to the whole healing process." Rick picked up his Lee duster and placed it on top of Jules.

"Thank you," Jules said in a tired voice. "I certainly appreciate . . . " He shrugged moistly. "*Torpor . . .* "

Rick turned as the wagon of explosives careened into a saloon. He drained his beer, checking his wallet. They had enough cash to cover their motel bill, get a little extra gasoline and some Egg McMuffins in the morning. Maybe some necessary cheap beers. After that?

He thought about Tamara. Turned the sack and dumped out a bag of sunflower seeds and a copy of a magazine called *X-Rated Neighbors.* His empty burrito wrapper clung to the glossy cover. A blonde chewed on a silk pillow. Bright yellow lettering went Bi-Chicks Tongue in Slammin' Smokin' Muff-Banging Climax! The magazine stank of vinyl. Rick held it up and inhaled deeply. He began to page his way through the garden of frantic video stills. The magazine was a marketing tool aimed at introducing its audience to current and newly re-leased adult videos. Each movie was represented by action stills, a black spot hovering where a penis, tongue, or finger penetrated. The copy was pseudo-critical, with great attention to alliteration and monosyllabic compound euphemisms like *jug patch*, *tail gate*, and *Karnel Kellie's Hot Slot in Lapping Labia Lez Action.*

Rick flipped through a pictorial for *Little Oral Annie*, flipped past a review for *Pol-tergash II.* Paragraphs on the opposite page explained that a young starlet named Sasha Ferrari had accepted her role in *Nazi Sluts in the Sleaze Slammer* because, even though she had been out of the business for a year, she needed cocks. Big ones, fat ones, skinny ones, small ones. The pull-quote over the photograph of Sasha—looking down at a penis in each of her hands— "Sasha loads up on pork in *Lilith's Revenge.*" Rick flipped to the title "Hunting Chocolate Pussy." The series of photographs showed a groaning black woman sandwiched between two white men in Ku Klux Klan hoods. Another photograph showed a black woman in a camisole licking a piece of fried chicken and cutting her eyes ingenuously at a white police officer. There were also photographs of . . . yes, Ginger Quail. Ginger on all fours. A beautiful brunette with droopy plastic ruby earrings, long legs, and red pumps squirmed around beneath her. A black man watched them from outside a window. Rick flipped through the reviews for *Plumber Girls III: Shower Tales, A Night at the Office, True Confessions of Savannah Blue*, and *Ginger's Raunchy Roost.* The last was his favorite. Then before he knew it, he was at the back of the magazine, staring at advertisements for penis enlargement pumps and cum machines and Oriental hard-core comix and fetish party lines and free life-size solid-action partner dolls and chicks with dicks videos and Spanish Fly Formula packets and pages of smiling women with frosted hair holding telephones above numbers like 1-900-WET-ANJL or 1-900-GET-SUKD.

The smell of vinyl reminded Rick of that smell that blasted your face when you went to stick a good hard-core album on the turntable. Yeah, it was the sweet aroma of the SST label. Black Flag. The Minutemen. Bad Brains. Hüsker Dü. New hard-core porn and old hard-core tuneage. It reminded him of Ginger. Taste of her skin, shininess of her eyes. Reminded him of the thrill of loud raw music and loud raw sex. Noise like wet pussy.

Rick touched the magazine with his tongue. He could still smell the burned hair on his forearm. The flaming rags. The cigar smoke. The hot afternoon sky.

He leaned back and kicked his feet up on the bed. Scattered gunfire drifted from the TV.

The desert outside like religion, like faith. Ginger's body pink as watermelon candy.

► ► ► 56

It was moving toward midnight. Click, click, click went the clock. Rick was trying to estimate whether or not he'd need to make a final beer run. Click, click, click.

His other favorite video preview was a costumed number about three Elizabethan women on a picnic. *Sonnets for Joanna V.* Rick wasn't sure, but he decided that they must be the neighbors that gave the magazine its title. Whatever. Pornography wasn't really about consistency. Pornography was about something else. And, neighbors or not, the women were total wayhone nectar. Their bodies balanced against the blue sky, complete with wispy bikini tan lines courtesy of some place like Santa Monica or Huntington or Redondo.

Rick tossed his empty against the wall. *Clack.* One of the women reminded him of Tamara. Nice, long legs. Beautiful dark hair. Her eyelashes static on the page.

He closed the magazine and returned his attention to the TV. Flipped the remote control. A group of cheerleaders crowded into the cab of a dump truck. They were cheering.

The dump truck pulled forward as a bunch of muscular dudes in jockstraps scrambled to climb out of a cement swimming pool filled with Jell-O.

Rick dumped a thick paperback from the damp paper sack. The paperback had a blonde on the cover. She wore a yellow sundress that came to the top of her thighs. She had her hand on the rusted handle of a water pump. The paperback was entitled *Rapture with Eve & Maid of Lust—Two Novels in One*. The paperback had been published by the Honeypot Press.

Rick flipped open and began to read . . .

. . . if Lana could only wait until they reached the bedroom before she threw herself upon him!

``Come on,'' He forced, grabbing her hand. They ran up the stairs to her room, the door swinging open after them. Then fell on the bed together, arms and legs interlocking, lips pressed, his firm young dick parting her cuntal joy spot. ``Uhhhhhmmmmmm. Hhhhhhmmmmmm,'' she gurgled contentedly. ``Right up my snatch, all the way,'' she panted, the walls of her pussy collapsing around his fancy fuck-rod. ``Come on and let me have your jizz!'' Lana howled, fucking the vigorous pink prong, feeling the immense bulb raking the never-to-end fireworks display inside her loins.

``Lord, I can't take any more!'' she screamed as his pulsating tumescence withdrew, his hot white sauce exploding across her bouncing titties. ``Oh! This is good sex-fun!'' she yelped, the still-hard fuck-pole slamming back inside her and filling her with spiraling strings of fun-sap. But before she knew it she was being rolled over! Lana looked back, numbly realizing that it was Billy! Tommy's best friend! He was straddling her upraised ass! ``Oh, no,'' she whispered, frightened that her firm cheeks were about to finally taste that pearly stew Darlene had been bragging about all day by the pool. The heat of his spit-wet cock prodding the pink pucker of her anus.

``I knew it!'' She laughed as it occurred to her with great feverish amazement. She *looked around to find Darlene squatting beside her, still wearing the cute red undies that barely concealed her moist slot.*

Lana breathed huskily as Darlene reached over and cupped Lana's pendulous love-pillows. ``So you had to have it all, didn't you, Lanny?'' Darlene whispered with brazen relish. ``I knew you'd like to get your pretty nympho ass some real high school prick, so I arranged this little thank-you for the tongue-lashing you gave me the other evening. Come on!'' she ordered louder, gripping Billy by his cum-filled balls. ``Let's see if this hot little redhead bitch can handle a two-cock lunch!''

Darlene patted the young teacher on the butt and crawled up, stretching her perfect body against her friend and the two eager boys. ``Oh, Lanny,'' she whimpered, ``You'll never be able to thank me for this!''

Rick put down the book. The cheerleaders were slapping hands and doing a victory jig around the pit of trapped, cherry-flavored football players. "Hey!" Rick elbowed Jules. "Wake up. This is hilarious."

In spontaneous glee the girls were stripping and hurdling into the Jell-O. Their breasts cleaved through the gelatin dessert. Rick nudged Jules with greater force. The blonde leader clinging to some skinny guy who looked more like the team manager than part of the defensive line. She was teasingly forgiving him for some previous trespass, her fingers running Jell-O through his thin, pale blond hair. His glasses floated beside his hip.

Jules lifted his head and blinked at the screen.

"Look, dude. Dig it. *You're* getting the wayhone."

Jules turned uncomprehendingly to Rick. "Excuse me?"

"*You!* Check it out. That guy'd probably dreamed about Grace Kelly, too . . . and there he is grabbing the goods with his little bird-shop hands!"

Jules watched as the blonde gave the team manager an exuberant kiss, the credits crawling up the TV. The team manager's glasses sinking in instant dessert goo. "Rick," Jules said, skin translucent. "I don't wear glasses. Besides, that's not Grace Kelly."

"I *know* it's not Grace Kelly, squid! That's the point. *It's a bimbo!* A big healthy slice of America. Grace Kelly's gone. History. She married some stupid king type, prince whatever, and paid for it. She *left* the land of the free and the brave. Traded it. And for what?" Rick motioned to the screen. "*This* is your princess! This! And she's fucking real, get it?"

Jules stared at the screen, then looked back at Rick. "Prince Rainier. Of Monaco. And it just doesn't do much for me . . . I find it disconcerting . . ." His voice trailed away. "You consume this like a hummingbird consumes nectar."

"Copious nectar." Rick put his finger in his mouth and sucked on it. "So what?"

Rick ripped open the cover of *X-Rated Neighbors* and shoved it under Jules's nose. "Here. This is real life, squid. Don't you get it? It's not out *there,* it's right *here.* It's not on some fairy-tale island . . . it's *here.* Right here in Los Angeles. In the freeways, the noise, the red sky. The naked women."

Jules let out a small sigh and closed his eyes.

Rick stared down at the open page. Three men with bad skin and beer guts encircled a skinny girl on her knees. She cradled her large breasts in her hands, face upturned. Rick squinched his eyes.

"So what's the problem?"

He twisted the magazine slightly. "No one ever looks at the dudes anyway . . ."

"But what is the attraction?" asked Jules, wiping at his forehead. "Why do you prefer to keep yourself in a constant state of—"

"What?" asked Rick, still looking at the photographs.

"I was wondering," asked Jules sharply. "Why you find *that* so interesting?"

Rick looked up. " 'Cause pornography's hilarious. It's like America. You know, like *freedom.* Malt liquor, drive-thrus, whatever. You name it. You work. You relax."

"Freedom?" asked Jules. "*America?* I think it's all simply reducible to Homo sapiens' ability to mate with little regard for environmental contingencies or biological calendars. Like whales, only whales don't eliminate other species, don't destroy their environment. Now, take the short-tailed shearwater, a Southern Hemisphere species that winters off the coast of North America—"

"Shut up," snapped Rick, clicking the TV control. He settled on *The Twilight Zone.*

"Don't you listen when you're part of a conversation?"

"Yeah, yeah. We're all like birds that want to fuck all the time. Big deal. I like being that kind of bird. A monster bird of prey. A pterodactyl of bliss!" He turned and gave Jules the full gaze. "Everyone didn't grow up in a castle, squid. And, besides, we're not talking snuff films or kiddie games . . . we're just talking normal people, citizens of the dude and wayhone persuasion. Bumping uglies on camera. Getting sweaty. Maybe burning some batteries. Strapping on toys. I don't see the problem."

"I don't really believe," Jules started. "That you would condone—"

"*Condoning* is shit. I'm just saying that watching people fuck is like going to any movie. The difference is that you don't have to listen to people try to *pretend* they believe all that stupid-ass dialogue. At least in pornography everyone *knows* the gig is to get *crucial.* Get fierce. Yeah and okay, there are no killer special effects. But whatever. Instead of blowing up helicopters, the girls just moan. Same deal. Everyone out of control. Like you've got the technology? Provide the service."

"But the law—"

"Fuck the law. Being cool's the law. Having fun's the law. Not getting *bored* is the law. That's why we had to deal with those losers' truck. We had to exact retribution. It was *crucial.* They fucked with us and our wrath was righteous."

Jules stared at his hands. "Well, if forced . . . I'd say that I don't think that *that* magazine is *righteous.* I don't think it's *cool.* I think it tricks people into believing a lie.

I think it's false and I think anyone who feeds on it all day will starve."

Rick stared down. The scent of vinyl drifted up from the open page. Stay calm. The squid deserved it. This subject deserved it. "Squid, I don't think you *understand.* We're not talking about the way things *should* be. We're talking about the way things *are* inside of us. Like what's your favorite thing? Working with birds? Bowling? Princess stuff, like weddings and coronations?"

"And I like long walks," Jules added pleasantly.

"Great. Birds, bowling, walking. But *I* like drinking, driving, and fucking. So why are *you* right and why am *I* wrong?"

Jules shifted uneasily. "Because you threaten other people with your behavior."

"*Threaten people with my behavior?* How? 'Cause I get revenge on evil squareheads who try to kill me? Is that *threatening people?*"

Jules's mouth went tight. "You could have hurt someone innocent when that truck exploded. What if you had injured someone . . . a child, for example? You live a lie, Rick. You react to your environment and you call it *freedom.*"

Rick glared. It was really stupid to be arguing with this retarded bird junkie. He waited for a good answer. He couldn't think of one yet, but he would. *Fucking squid.* Fucking born-to-serve squid. "Eat some sunflower seeds." He threw the bag at Jules.

"Do you know"—Jules watched him—"that some gulls will observe their predators? Will actually travel out of their way to *watch* their predators . . . specifically if the predator has killed one of their own?"

"Yeah? And?" Rick listened to the clock go click, click, click.

"They learn from observing what threatens them. Maybe that is your attraction to . . ."

Rick stared at him. "To pornography? No, but maybe *you've* got it backward, squid. Maybe that's why *you're* hanging out with me. 'Cause if there's a predator, dude. . . it's me."

Rick turned to the TV. A jolly rotund man with a white beard smiled at a guy in a threadbare blazer.

The man in the threadbare blazer stepped into a lavish apartment of white, running his hands across the polished counters, cabinets, and walls. He paused. There was a framed painting on the wall of a statuesque woman with platinum-blonde hair and an elongated Rita Hayworth figure, shrink-wrapped in a white gown that flared at the ankles. The man in the threadbare blazer touched the ankles, turned back around to the rotund man in the white coat and white beard. "*Fats,*" he said, with hungry eyes. "*This'll do fine, just fine . . .*"

"I know this one. This is that one where the guy thinks he's in heaven."

Jules watched the TV. "What do you mean?"

"Oh, it's *Twilight Zone.* And this guy's up for the classic Twilight Zone burn. Yeah . . . his name's Valentine and he's this lame jewel thief who just got himself shot dead by a cop as he was trying to make it away from a heist. 'Cept he wakes up and now he's going to get everything he ever thought he wanted, you know, wayhones, *beaucoup* cash. All the goods. Never lose at the roulette wheel, etc. But he can't figure it out when he starts to get bored, starts to lose it. At the end, he asks the fat dude to *send him to the other place.* Figuring hell is going to be better, you know? *Comprende?*"

Jules stared at the TV. The rotund man with the white jacket and white beard pointed to a drawer. Valentine pulled it open and began laughing, throwing packets of crisp green money in the air.

"See?" continued Rick. "He's clueless."

"You mean?"

"Yeah. He's already *in* the other place. By the way, squid . . . how's that fever? Still sizzling?"

Jules put his hand to his forehead and shrugged. Rick reached over. Jules was hot. Rick went into the bathroom and stripped the sanitary wrapping from one of the motel glasses.

He ordered Jules to drink. Repeated this until Jules had drunk his fill of coldish tap water. "Now. Keep those blankets on and make yourself sweat. That's an order."

Jules looked at him. "I'm sorry. Illness makes me a rather unsavory road companion."

"*Unsavory?* I'm unsavory. You're something else." He patted Jules on the shoulder. "Stay casual, squid. I'm going outside to catch some fresh air."

Jules nodded and shifted so he could watch the two figures in the white room.

"It's only a matter of time for that hombre," added Rick. He pulled open the door and hovered against the purple night sky. "Only a matter of time."

Rick sparked a Tiparillo and leaned on the hood of the Buick Skylark. What was Ginger's problem? All he'd done was fuck her. Okay, so maybe he'd entertained the thought of taking her to a Laker game or something. Whatever. And here she was getting all tense? He couldn't figure it out.

The black summit of San Jacinto rose above the desert, reminding Rick of a giant circus tent. The white smoke of his cigar dissolved against the sky. Maybe Ginger would want to ride the aerial tram?

Ginger.

Yeah, she'd probably just been a toy for too long. A little love-toy. Wayhone on constant remote control. Getting it fierce from every direction and doing too much of everything. Structural breakdown imminent. Coked-out nectar. Slut Central.

He closed his eyes and wove the cigar under his chin. Tobacco sizzled the back of his throat.

So why was she so groovy?

Was he just a fool for bad girls? First Angela. Now Ginger? 'Cause he *had* to see her again. No doubt.

And . . . he couldn't *even* figure out what was really going on inside. He figured like most women, she just didn't trust men. And why should she? But there was something else going on . . . 'cause she was definitely tense about not wanting to see him again.

Yeah, it was probably *trust.*

Whatever. Trust was just an excuse for people too chickenshit to deal with standing alone. It had been another one of Tamara's favorite words. Trust. Trust. Trust. It had driven Rick up the wall. If you had to talk about it . . . it wasn't there. And you weren't going to get it by talking. Rick didn't think love or trust worked that way. Those words didn't work at all. They were bogus. Totally misused by the masses. If true love existed . . . well, it'd be pride and courage that'd make it hum. Pride. Not chickenshit trust. Trust like boredom. Trust like rules meant to be broken. Like good behavior. Like probation.

Yeah, the fat man in the white coat and white beard was definitely waiting. Had always been waiting. "*But, Mr. Jeffers, this is the other place!*" No doubt. Everyone knew that. 'Cause you were fucked as soon as you made a choice. You either hurt the people you cared for, betrayed their expectations, or you walked. Either way the jewels spilled from the sack and the *screw* caught you halfway over the fence with a bullet in your back. Either way, you woke up staring into the fat face with the white beard. Trapped. Laughter clawing at your head. The door to the penthouse locked from the *inside.* Forever.

But so what? Just change the channel. One story was as good as another. Why was he getting all bent out of shape? And what had that whole business with Ginger and the video camera been about? Did she just dig seeing guys jerk off? No, you'd figure she'd had a lifetime of that noise. And what was that thing about *not* thinking about her? Maybe she just didn't want to be the love-toy anymore. The fantasy. No, 'cause she wouldn't let him think about other women either. Weird. He didn't get it.

He closed his eyes, warm from the beer and the desert night. The empty parking lot, coyotes, pennyroyal, the corolla-lipped ghost flowers, steak houses, and dew-draped fairways. Palm

Springs: a subdivider's oasis of electric gates, white walls, and oleander. Jeffrey and sugar pine scattered along the ridges and clefts of sepia-tinted skyline. Windmill farms sparring. The whir of neon signs. And Ginger. Ginger running her fingers through the tiny umbrella of light between her thighs. Rick figured that the fantasy, the carpet space between Ginger at the camera and Rick in the chair, caught him in his own *thing*. Whatever that was. The dreaming image of Rick liberated and relaxed her. Relaxed her as it had relaxed him to watch her squirm and moan on a movie screen. Lust without consequence. Without the connectedness of pussy farts, premature ejaculation, postcoital depression. Menstrual pain. Days of stuff to get done before or after work, before or after paying your bills. Marriage. Babies. Sleepless nights. Arguing. But on the screen? No expectations. None of that business where the other one wants stuff. None of that business that makes you responsible for being around. Like with duties. Pleasure at its whitest heat when you can stand and watch the isolation burn in the eyes of a thing you can't touch. Lost in some private cave of light. Protecting you. A waterfall of light, but you never get wet. Yeah. Just calm and delicious in that fast waterfall of light.

Ginger was like one of Jules's silly princesses. 'Cept this meant nothing. Everything moved too fast. 'Cause it all was going to crash down on you in the end. And then you were just dead. Cold. Worm meat. And everything you believed was just another page of history. Pretending the door to the penthouse would open one day and you'd be standing in Evolution Meadow. A black bear climbing a diamond of scree. The sun in your face.

Backpacking and camping. It was the desert and luminous sky, the scent of sage that reminded Rick of those times. Like when he was a little kid playing Parker Brothers Mille Bornes. The card game where you tried to accrue the most mileage and avoid road disasters like running out of gas, speeding tickets, and terrible bone-crunching accidents. The cards printed in French and decorated with dynamic industrial illustrations of tow trucks, hazard signs, and punctured tires. The mileage cards decorated with animals corresponding to the speed attributed to each card. Turtle—25 mph. Sparrow—200 mph. Rick and his parents by the glow of the Coleman lantern at the Meeks Bay campground. Lake Tahoe. Eating graham cracker, marshmallow, and Hershey sandwiches. S'mores.

But no, thought Rick. You weren't playing Mille Bornes with the folks anymore and there was no reason to save those cards in your hand. *Panne D'Essence* is what you got for dreaming about being a kid. You might as well take that other one, that card with the turquoise gasoline truck, *Citerne D'Essence* and just drop it, dude. 'Cause all your cards are worth nothing and they'll fall from your fingers. Just flutter to the scarred picnic table. *200 mph . . . 100 mph . . . 75 mph . . . Roulez! . . . Roulez! . . . Roue De Secours . . . Creve!* Yeah. Even his favorite card. *As Du Volant.* Driving Ace. Those tense red hands that grip the steering wheel, slashes of kelly-green sharp as shadows from the safety wall at the edge of the track. Checkered flags snapping in the breeze. But there won't be anymore *Coup Fourré.* (The card that gave you free pass and let you drive forever.) No, 'cause you'd be done racing the clock. And all the revelations in the world would be shit. Tamara's needs. Jules's fears. Angela's loss. Jack's betrayal. Ginger's motivation. His own salvation. Sorry, dude. The Big Squid in the Sky has called. Time for the long sleep.

Later.

Rick checked his pockets for the Buick keys. Dug around in the backseat and dragged out a worn white T-shirt. The Wild Goose, Inglewood, Ca. on the chest pocket. A naked woman silk-screened on the back. She rode through the clouds on a swan. Splotches of red paint on the shoulder. He pulled off the *guayabera.*

Rick climbed into the car. He was thirsty. He wasn't into the idea of watching Jules sweat. No, thinking about mortality had perked him up. He wanted a cold one. He wanted to drive. He wanted something that didn't remind him of Death. He tossed the T-shirt on the front seat.

The V-8 rumbled.

The traffic lights were timed in his favor.

Coup Fourré! Coup Fourré!

57 ◄ ◄ ◄

Rick sat in the Buick and nursed a can of Ballantine XXX ale. The parking lot splattered with moonlight. An occasional set of headlights burrowed in from the blur of the boulevard back across the dunes.

He felt good about the way the evening was turning. Buzzed. And he still had four more cans of XXX ale.

He took a sip and stared past the blue ice plant and pits of pearly amaryllis. The lighted sections of Ginger's motel complex honeycombed with amethyst, purples laced in alexandrines of gold and rose. Pools of buttery night spilled over the clumps of bird of paradise.

Rick contemplated the chemical abuse he'd been heaping upon his body. Yeah, he deserved these increments of beauty. No one else had paid the price. No one else was Rick B. Jeffers. And he felt sorry for the losers. The squids. He wondered what it'd be like to be one of them for a day.

Probably dull.

He took another long sip and hazarded a guess at the time. Two-thirty? Close to that. But which one of the tile-spangled quadrilateral bungalows was Ginger's friend's place? The Eurydice pad? It hadn't been very close to the pool. He remembered that much. Remembered from earlier that morning, or night, or whatever it'd been when he'd watched Ginger click down the tiles with her angry little ass.

Rick opened the car door and got out, string of beers in his hand, his reflection on the windshield.

He raised the green Ballantine can in a silent toast. *Road trip.*

He was totally *there.* Pumped that someone'd been cool enough to invent cars. Pumped

L.A. had seen the future and jumped on it back in the early days. Dusting that bad public transit habit and getting down to figuring out freeways. Crucial freeways. Otherwise, where'd we be? Fucking carless. Carless and trapped. Piled on each other like a bunch of New Yorkers. Like Europeans.

He drained the can and tossed it over his shoulder.

So what if it was tough to breathe? At least L.A. knew how to party. And when we go down . . . we'll go down big. And not fucking whine about it like a bunch of San Francisco hippies. No, we'll just lift our brew and say *Sure!*

Rick popped another.

Yeah, just lift that cold one to eternity!

He swigged, then wiped his lips with the back of his hand. He loved getting drunk in the moonlight.

He loved when nothing mattered.

 **58**

Jack was in front of Tamara, her flannel shirt unbuttoned. A crystal champagne glass pressed lightly against her breast. Jack's fingers trembled. "Now the other." Tamara moved him by the wrist, parting her shirt so it slipped off her shoulders. "They're not quite the same size." It was late at night. Outside, heavy cars rolled down the street.

Her nipple disappeared into a smudged crocus of flesh and glass. Jack watched as a red bead of wine trickled down her ribs.

Tamara eyed him. "Well? Do I pass the test?"

Jack placed his palm flat against her stomach. Tamara began to breathe more consciously.

"Hey . . ." she whispered.

Jack moved his hand to the soft parable of her hip, running his finger across the pink serration beneath the elastic of her black skirt. Her skin pale above the rim of the champagne glass. She answered herself, "I *guess* they pass." Then guided his wrist up and touched it to her lips. "Let's get back to it." She motioned toward the Game of Life game board and paper money that lay beside an open silver box, a lily of white wrapping paper blossomed beside a bottle of Clos du Bois merlot. Two copies of *The Taming of the Shrew* were spread belly-down on the carpet. "I'm going to *nail* this audition."

Jack slipped his hand into Tamara's, noticing the vein that ran along her forearm. He bent and kissed her neck. "What's this?" sniffing audibly.

Tamara's voice blurred in his ear.

"Uh-huh, I *do*. What's it called?"

"Justine," she answered, pressing her chin against his sunburned scalp. She sniffed his neck. "And yours?"

"Ivory. And sweat. Like it?"

Tamara nodded. "Thanks for the champagne glasses," she added. "But don't you think we should be drinking champagne?"

"I don't like champagne." Jack pulled away and settled back on the floor.

Tamara looked at him.

"It's this thing with my dad. He drinks champagne."

Jack refilled both of their glasses. He motioned to the two copies of *The Taming of the Shrew* on the carpet. "You want to work some more? Or play?"

Tamara sat down beside him and began to realign her play money, organizing it into neat piles of $5, $10, $20, $50, $100, and $500 bills. "Let's finish the game and then we'll work some more." Tamara was trying to keep herself from overpreparing. She didn't want to get *too* tense. "What do you want, Jack?"

"Out of life? Or just right now?" Jack pulled at one of the belt loops on his chinos. "Not that I can really answer either one . . ."

"I'm sorry about your dad. I'm pretty close to my parents. It must be tough to . . ." Tamara didn't know how to say it. "If you just feel they're not there."

"It's not *they.* It's *him.* My mother is gone. *She* had no choice. And he doesn't even get it. He's talking all this advice at me. After fourteen years? Like nothing ever happened?"

Tamara looked at Jack. She could see how lonely it was for him. She reached over and rubbed his shoulder.

"I like you, Jack. But I don't know if I really trust myself. I mean, look at the men I've dated . . ." She smiled. "Like your best friend."

"Don't worry. No one's trying to tell you what to do."

"Will you be hurt if I . . . if we . . . if *this* just stops?"

Jack took a sip of wine. "Maybe. But I'm okay, Tamara. I don't want sympathy. I can hack it. However it goes."

"I want something, something different from what was going on before, but—"
"Rick?"

"I don't think so. I did, but I'm not sure now." She noticed his gaze stray to the drapery of her unbuttoned shirt. Her face clouded. She rebuttoned. "I should probably learn to spend more time alone," she finished. She stared at the top button as if it held the answer.

Jack didn't know what to say. The Game of Life. It had been his favorite when he was a kid. Now it depressed him. "Rick buy this for you?"

"No, it was mine. Mom brought it over here one day when I was baby-sitting my niece. Comprehension was a problem for a three-year-old . . ." Tamara shook her head. "You know my mom. Sweet, but not always there."

The idea behind the game was that you moved little cars along a winding black road of colored spaces, each space revealed another *event* in your life. The game ended when you had traveled the length of the board, tapping over the molded-plastic hills and down the molded-plastic valleys, arriving at a plastic antebellum mansion. Millionaire Acres. The object of the game was to get rich. If you didn't make it into Millionaire Acres, you had to go to the Poor Farm. This was bad. This meant you had lost the game. The game reminded Jack of the good days before his dad's disappearance. Before this hollow thing he was sick of carrying inside himself. Had been carrying. For fourteen years. Dad just popping back up last Easter and asking Jack to go play a few rounds of golf. Fucking golf. After fourteen years.

Jack didn't even know how to play golf.

But what hurt most were the memories of how things had been before. When he and his sister would find themselves bundled up in parkas to go deep-sea fishing on the charter boats that left from Redondo Beach. Heater on in the station wagon. Saturdays spent chopping through the black Pacific. Jack's head cloudy from Dramamine and the fumes that spilled up over the transom. Returning with a few sour bonitas that they'd end up feeding the cats before driving down to the Wild Lariat Grill for sirloins and baked potatoes and chocolate sundaes.

But his dad had just walked away. And none of them could ever have that time back. It was just buried there inside the past. Inside *history.* For the rest of their lives. And Jack had to carry that look on his mother's face. His mother alone with her death, while his father played golf.

The Game of Life. If you ended up broke, one space from the Poor Farm, a space marked Day of Reckoning, you still had a chance. You were allowed to put all your money on one of the numbers on the plastic roulette wheel set within the cusp of a green plastic mountain range on the middle of the board. You were allowed one spin. If your number came up, you became a Millionaire Tycoon. You won instantly.

Jack couldn't remember anyone ever becoming a Millionaire Tycoon.

He surveyed the board. Tamara had been collecting an annual Doctor's salary as well as collecting a small pile of five-thousand-dollar bills from various fortuitous events that had occurred as she had moved around her *life.* Jack had only managed to collect five little pink and blue pegs which snuggled right into the tiny holes bored into his plastic playing piece car. These pegs were children. They just cost money. Jack's salary was the lowest salary possible. Bachelor's degree. Also, he had to do a number of expensive things, like pay ten thousand dollars to get rid of his aunt's hundred angry poodles. He had also contracted a bad case of poison oak.

Jack wondered if the game was still being produced, and if so, how much money a bachelor's degree salary would be worth now.

"Do you think he ran off with her?"

"What?"

"I'm sorry, Jack. I was just thinking about Rick. I mean, Rick always joked about going to Vegas and getting married . . . what if he ran off with that *girl?*"

Jack crinkled the last couple of five-hundred-dollar bills and let them flutter down on his pink and blue plastic family.

"Wouldn't he call? I can't believe he hasn't called . . . He knows we'll worry about him . . ."

Jack stared at the crimson Stop! Day of Reckoning!

"What are you thinking about?"

"Nothing. Well . . . I guess I was just . . . I'll try my luck on number seven. I was number seventy-seven at Oakdale. *Football.*" The whole thing depended on Jack. He knew that much. It was up to him to deal with his dad. Up to him to deal with Tamara. With what happened between them. He was Wolverine. A psychotic loner who wanted to change into a man.

Jack knew Tamara was unsure. Had her reasons. Worried about hurting him. About getting stuck with him. Was trying to figure out what she wanted. Even in the way she listened to him read the lines from that play, *The Taming of the Shrew*. Asking him to explain them to her. Testing him.

But Jack didn't care. He liked being with her. At least with Tamara things really mattered.

Tamara looked Jack in the eyes. "I really want to quit cigarettes." She knew Jack smoked too much marijuana. She had a feeling he would understand. "It's silly, Jack. But I'd like it if you'd go with me to a meeting. I need someone to kind of, well, *watch* me. A Smokers Anonymous meeting. Keep an eye on me."

Jack laughed. "My track record isn't too good at those kind of things."

Tamara watched him.

Jack shrugged. "Sure, Tamara. Anything you want." He gave the Wheel of Fate a strong twist. The sound was someone dumping open a bag of bones.

Tamara listened. His voice was soft where it wouldn't be if he didn't care.

He's such a boy. His socks wadded at his ankles. A boy with this beautiful body. This thing with his dad hanging over him. Tamara remembered something. "How many—"

"What?" Jack looked up with disappointment as he slid his little pink and blue family into the Poor Farm.

"I was thinking," started Tamara, "I was wondering, first, can I trust you to be honest with me? You know, about the big things? I don't know what's going to happen. How I feel about Rick. How I feel about you. How I feel about anything. Except I want honesty. I want us to be able to talk about *anything.* That's all I want right now, Jack."

Jack shrugged yes, but his eyes were serious.

"And second . . . I was wondering . . . do you know how many shots the Rifleman shoots at the beginning of that show?"

"The Rifleman," Jack said. "The show was called *The Rifleman.*"

"Okay. So answer the question. Answer and I'll give you anything."

Jack looked at her. "Anything?"

"Anything. Comic books. My body. Whatever your little lonely heart desires."

"There's only one thing my heart desires." Jack looked down at the Wheel of Fate.

"Well then," she said. "Guess the lucky number." She touched his wrist. She could feel her eyes get soft. "It's like a game show, Jack." Tamara reached over and ran her finger around the lip of his champagne glass. Then gave him an easy smile. "Maybe you'll win."

▶ ▶ ▶ **59**

It was still Tuesday night. Sort of Wednesday morning. Rick stared up into the high-octane icefall of galaxies. He was shirtless. He waved his arms. He cackled. The cackle transformed into a dry *gack.* The back of his throat all scratchy from some tiny, winged thing.

A bug.

He fell to his knees and coughed at the grass.

He rained Ballantine XXX down his throat. Gold ale washed over his chin, slipping past the waist of his Levi's. He belched and crushed the green can, tossing it into the cement lagoon that swayed under the heavy Chinese evergreen and narcissus. The shiny lime canister filled, tipped down, sunk toward the tiled mosaic of a blonde riding on the back of a dolphin. Strands of kelp trailed behind her like a green bridal train. Rick watched the can hover above the swirled nest of yellow hair. He was glad he'd thought to drink. It'd probably been the only thing between him and insect asphyxiation. A horrible fate. Death by bug. Ancient Asian execution technique. The bug insidiously placed at the critical juncture in the victim's throat.

The screams, the silent screams at the edge of perpetual darkness. Yeah, heinous.

Rick looked up and began to count the stars. "One . . . two . . . three . . . four . . ." Then was on his back again. Blinking. Tears in his eyes. Laughing at the uproarious fun of impaired motor control. He opened his arms to the celestial chorus and whooped. Reached up and patted his head. What'd happened to his Laker cap? Lost it back in Old San Berdoo? He couldn't remember. Had he been wearing it when he'd sent those losers' truck to kingdom come? Boy, *that* was one hilarious sight. And fuck Jules. Jules *Squid* Langdon. Having the tiny balls to hassle *him,* Rick. Our hero. Hassle him about the coolest, most awesome moment of their whole road trip. Just 'cause he thought it was *threatening.* Like a baseball bat wasn't *threatening?*

Rick tried to stand. Tripped on nothing. Faceplant. He could smell the rich soil underneath the lawn. The dry desert air that moved up into the stars like black sherbet. The bugs. They were down there, crawling around in tunnels. And the plants. And their hungry roots. The plants would have caught him if only their hearts weren't stunned. An ice machine mumbled over in the hallway by a black door, a glimmering yellow porch light, a pattern of fronds hanging over the eaves.

You could have hurt someone innocent . . . a child, for example.

"Fuck you!" he snapped at the river of dry sky. "Fuck your bird-shop whining . . ."

He took a deep breath and tried to stand again, weaving. Whew, he was seriously wrecked! And what was he still doing hanging around by the swimming pool? It had to be almost morning 'cause hadn't he sat there for at least a couple of hours talking to that cool dude from TV. What was his name? Chuck Something? Chuck Steak? Good dude. Wanted to help Rick meet some wayhones. Do a nectar gig. Yeah, said he'd boast Rick the serious TV pussy. Major scruffage. Rick liked that idea. 'Cause Angela was in Kona or Manila or Bangkok. And Iona was in Barstow. And Tamara was gone. Off with his best friend. And Ginger was a bitch. But the Chuck dude had been holding spliff. Water lapping against the concrete as he and Chuck watched their telescopic blue feet in the pool water. Chuck handing him a card. Something about the wayhones. The scruffage. TV pussy.

Rick fumbled in his pocket and extracted a pink business card inscribed with a crimson heart, a single bronze arrow tearing beneath *Chuck Venison,* Cupid's Arrow, *Hollywood, California.* Rick squinted at the address and phone number, the minute gold print lost in predawn.

He tucked the card back in his pocket and started across the grass. Would Ginger still be angry? He hoped not. He also kind of hoped she'd figured out picking up some beers. He had a serious hankering for more beer. Cold beer. Heavenly beer. Beer of goodness. Beer of light. But she must've, right? She had money. She had a refrigerator.

She had the wicked, blonde vaginal wrench.

Rick stumbled in the direction of a bay window that glowed cyanotic. Curtains washed aquamarine. Charcoal forms grazing.

Who was with her? That guy? The dress-purchasing dude?

He attempted to step over a row of African violets, fell, grabbed the sill, and just averted crashing through the window.

Rick steadied himself, shouldered the wall. Peered through a crack in the curtains.

The room was a blue stain, Ginger on all fours, harnessed in a shiny black leather corset, wrists and ankles bound with white rope. A pink cat's-eye mask flashed with prickly bits of green as her head swung gently from side to side. Her mouth filled with a plastic object that looked like a lemon. A steel bar ran from a leather clasp around her neck to a chain threaded through silver O-rings at the base of her corset. A silver bar straight from her neck between her breasts to her waist held her head down. Her black garters *thwipped* against her naked thighs. A girl, who looked about twelve years old, lazily slapped Ginger's upraised butt with a cat-o'-nine-tails. A pair of stiletto heels kicked off near Ginger's naked feet. The girl had a dispassionate expression and seemed ignorant of the smoldering red alphabet that Rick traced, fingers against the glass, eyes on the lash as it struck.

The girl had the slender hips of a boy and breasts like tiny puddles of cream. She was wearing a plaid skirt high on her bare waist. She was also wearing white knee socks and patent leather saddle shoes. Rick watched as the girl turned from her ministrations toward three men playing cards around the glass table. Their voices drowned out by the stereo. Sinatra.

Except for the blue light, and the guests, *and* the visible bottles of liquor, the room was the same as when Rick had left it earlier that evening.

The whip snapped. The cat's-eye mask shimmered.

Then the bathroom door was a white bouquet. A weathered man in a stretch-knit Jack LaLanne–style jumpsuit rubbing his nose. He held a bottle of Chivas Regal. He watched the girl, then said something to the men at the table.

One of the men nodded, placed his cards facedown, stood. He had a handsome cleft chin. He took the whip from the girl and began to demonstrate the proper stroke on Ginger's ass, his spare hand rested upon the back of the girl's neck.

Meanwhile, the man in the jumpsuit put down the bottle and walked to the TV. He flicked his hand around in the blue air. A desolate glow darkened the screen.

Rick watched as the screen brightened, the dispassionate girl bending to her knees and unzipping the man's slacks, her small hands tickling into the man's unzipped fly. Then her head covered her hands and her head began to bob. The man in the jumpsuit must be rewinding the VCR.

The man with the cleft chin tapped the whip absently on the girl's back. Rick cursed. *He* was on the screen! *Rick B. Jeffers!* Naked on the chair with a swollen face, Levi's clumped on the carpet. Ropers at the end of his long naked legs. Masturbating.

Rick watched his own mouth move as he spoke to Ginger off-camera.

The man in the jumpsuit watched Rick on the TV, then turned down to Ginger on the carpet. He bent and whispered something to her, stood and took the whip. He began to whip

Ginger steadily and without pause, making sure to bring the whip down into the soft part of Ginger's inner thigh.

The man with the cleft chin watched, seeming to not even notice the small head doggedly bouncing at his waist. He turned as one of the poker players gained his attention and pointed to Rick on the TV screen. Then he gripped the bouncing head and shuddered.

Rick watched the whip with sick fascination. The man with the cleft chin shook his hips and milked himself into the girl's mouth. One of the men at the table pulled his tie over his head and swung it on the edge of the table in a parody of the man in the stretch-knit jumpsuit.

Jumpsuit stopped and walked over to one of the boxes marked Eurydice Productions, where he removed an amphora that glinted white like porcelain. He handed the jar to the little dispassionate girl and pointed toward Ginger. The girl bent and began to apply the ointment to the patches of bare skin not covered by the corset. Taking extra care to run the ointment up where the whip had kissed Ginger's thighs. The metal O-rings jingled blue as Ginger bucked silently, her back bent, stomach curved against the tiny hands.

Cleft Chin zipped up, sat back beside his fluted columns of poker chips, lifted his highball. The ashtray filled with cigarettes. Rick on the screen jerking off. The pink cat's-eye mask. The poetry of Ginger's new green eyes as they flickered.

Rick watched as the dispassionate girl began to rub the ointment on her own stomach. She cringed and shivered. Rick braced himself against the sill. Ginger. The female six-pack. She strained against the bar that ran the length of her leather black corset and pink body.

A man in suspenders, with white hair that soaked up the blue light and a blue, pocked face, handed a credit card to Jumpsuit. The other two men watched with interest as Blue Hair/ Pock Face began to explain himself. Jumpsuit looked back up on the video monitor, watching Ginger enter the picture and guide herself onto Rick, mussing his hair, arms around his neck. Rick watched himself peer over her shoulder and grin stupidly on the face of the TV screen.

The four men watched as the young girl took an ice cube from one of the glasses and slipped it across her neck. Jumpsuit whispered something in Ginger's ear, then patted her on the rump. Ginger's blonde hair shook as she tried to tilt her face upward, restrained by the silver bar.

All the men put down their cards, listening as Blue Hair/Pock Face began to explain something, Jumpsuit processing the credit card through a triplicate register that sat on the bar.

The young girl walked into the bathroom, and returned, arms laden with soaps, shaving cream cans, and tonsorial tools: disposable razors, long-handled scissors, a pink electric shaver.

The young girl filled her hands with shaving cream. The man in the jumpsuit turned and looked out the window directly into Rick's eyes. Rick froze. His breath clogged in his throat.

He pressed himself farther against the siding, peering back. Had they seen him? No, it didn't look like it. He could just make out the back of Jumpsuit, now blocking the TV screen. The man stepped out of Rick's line of vision. Rick was staring at Ginger's image on the screen, not prerecorded Ginger of early that night, but Ginger the Bound. Ginger the Tied-up. Ginger the Six-Pack. Ginger faced the camera on her knees. Her image stared back from the screen, acetylene flecks in the cat mask.

The young girl began to spread the shaving cream over Ginger's head, flattening Ginger's hair with her palms while massaging more gel into foam and smearing it down Ginger's neck. Jumpsuit gestured, sipping contemplatively at his drink.

They were going to shave her head?

The man in the suspenders bent across the screen, the can of shaving cream hovered in his hands, floating above Ginger. Oodles of gel spilled out. Suspenders rubbed the gel into foam and smeared the foam between Ginger's legs.

Her head jounced as she moved against the hand. The young girl tugged the sopping braids and chopped at them with the scissors.

Rick couldn't believe it! Her hair'd grow back. But *whatever.* Why cut it off just 'cause some yuppie-gangster-corporate losers wanted to get their rocks off?

Rick stared at Jumpsuit. He hated the motherfucker. Hated the *complacent* mother-fucker. The big man. The hot shit.

Rick stepped back. Okay, so maybe Jumpsuit'd bought her some dresses. And maybe he'd taken those photos back in Northridge. Maybe he'd done lots of *whatever* for Ginger, 'cause he was clearly in charge of the whole Eurydice scene, but did that give him the right to beat her up and scalp her?

Rick stared across the lawn. The sky a silver and orange line that made the mountains black.

Ginger.

He kicked at the African violets.

Then headed for the front of the bungalow, headed into the glow of the yellow bug light, a hexagon tile implanted in the plaster section beside the orange doorbell. The tile designed with the same swirling-haired blonde on a dolphin that had been at the bottom of the swimming pool. Condominium logo. Rick kicked the door.

Shuffling inside. The music lowered. The sound of the bathroom door closing with a *slap.*

More shuffling. Then he was staring down at a handgun over a foot long, the color of turpentine. Jumpsuit had a face wasted by sunshine and booze. Boyish features. Mean in the eyes.

The eyes recognized Rick.

"I need to talk to Ginger." Rick hunched back, legs spread.

Jumpsuit had a milky voice. "Go sleep it off." He pointed the point of the gun at Rick's crotch. "It's a little late for guests."

"I don't think so. I want to talk to Ginger. I have to talk with her . . . or do you want to shoot?" he added, slurred. He watched the gun. He hoped he looked tough, not scared shitless.

Jumpsuit lowered the gun. "Lot of crime around here," he explained thoughtfully. He smiled at Rick. "This thing will gut you, baby. Lungs, intestines. Name the organ. You'd be nothing but Campbell's soup and air."

"Sure," said Rick. "Just get me Ginger. She's a friend."

Jumpsuit's lips pulled tight. He stepped onto the porch and tugged the door behind him, squinting off at the orange dust skyline, the purple mountain ridge. Streaks of metal sky. "I'll tell you what, I'll get you some paper and you can write down your number. I'll make sure she gets it. She'll give you a call tomorrow."

"No, that's no good. I want to see her now . . . otherwise I'm . . ." Rick held his arm out and steadied himself against the wall. Otherwise he was doing what? "Causing trouble. Don't fuck with me." Rick let Jumpsuit see his ugly, bloodshot good eye. "I'm fucking *serious.*"

"Haven't seen her enough lately?" The man lifted the point of the gun back toward Rick's crotch.

"I don't want to fuck her," Rick said. "I just want to talk to her."

Jumpsuit laughed. "Guess you haven't known her very long." When he walked back inside, the door swept the blue light in with him.

Rick waited.

He heard voices behind the door. Ginger's voice sharp, then fragile. Jumpsuit's milky gurgle.

After a few minutes, the door opened and Ginger stepped out, wrapped in a silk bathrobe. Her hair hidden in a towel, Rick spotted traces of shaving cream on her neck and collarbone. She pulled the door closed behind her. Dark stains spread from beneath the silk bathrobe.

Mascara down her cheek in hairline fractures.

She was indignant. "What are you doing here?" she whispered, eyes narrowed. "I thought I told you . . ." Her whisper spilled off into silence.

Rick put his hands in his pockets. "Been in the shower?" He eyed the towel.

Ginger reached up. Her fingers glanced around. "Yeah," she said slowly. "I had to be up early . . ."

Rick ran his finger through a patch of shaving cream. Then held it up in the yellow air.

Ginger watched it like a knife. Her eyes were green slits. "Get out of here. I'm busy."

"No doubt."

Ginger took a deep breath and folded her arms across her chest. *Clink.*

Rick's gaze went soft. He gave Ginger's robe a pat. Palm flat on the hidden leather corset and empty O-rings.

Ginger knocked his hand away.

Rick tried to smile, but his lips merely crawled.

"What do you want?" she demanded.

Rick looked down at his green boots. "Let's go." He motioned to the closed door. "You don't need that—"

"Go?" Ginger asked.

"Yeah. *Leave.* With me."

Ginger looked back over her shoulder. Her weight shifted to her other foot. She nodded out into the open desert. "I'm not going anywhere. But *you* better."

"You don't need that," he repeated. "And don't let those fuckers shave—"

Ginger's jaw tightened. *"What?"*

"I said, let's *bail.* You and me. And forget those losers in there. I like your hair."

Ginger laughed. Her arms fell tight against her sides. "You stuck-up prick! Peeped in and didn't like the show, *huh? Tiger?* Didn't like my *acting?*" She jerked her thumb over her shoulder. "Maybe you're just jealous, huh, *Rick?*" She bit off his name. "Jealous of a little *coked-up slut?"* Wiped her hands against her robe. "But maybe you *need* a little coked-up slut! A poor, little baby *Ginger* to save? Well, dream on."

Rick started to say something, but Ginger cut him off by opening her robe and letting it fall. She shook the towel from her head and tossed it into his naked chest. A creamy smear slid into his hands.

"Get out of here. Get way out of here, *Rick.*" She turned away. "I've got work to do." She looked back. "Time to be someone's *toy.*" She winked. "Later, *dude.*"

Rick reached out and slapped her hard on the side of the face. Her eyes teared from the blow, hands still at her sides. "Ginger, let's *both* get out of here. Together." His voice was tense. *"Now."* He ran his fingers around her ear. "Now."

Ginger's new green eyes were shiny. "You were a nice fuck, Rick. But that's it. If Robby thought I was mixed up serious with someone, he'd just . . . well, I don't know what you saw in there, but if he gets mad—" She shrugged.

"Robby?"

"My husband," Ginger said, and motioned toward the door. "And you've got me in enough trouble already. I won't be able to sit down for a week."

"That burned-out loser is your husband? That guy with the gun?"

Ginger nodded.

"But I thought your husband was some dude in the Navy . . . in the Philippines."

"I lied." Ginger bent and picked up her robe. "Some guys get weird if they think my husband's in the industry. You know, and hanging around."

A car engine revved in a distant parking lot.

"But he's just whoring you out! He's not a husband, he's a pimp."

A trace of resignation like a smile on Ginger's lips. "Lots of actresses pull a little on the side. It's just another way to make ends meet."

"Ends? What fucking ends? Fancy clothes, champagne, and cocaine?" He thought of

the photograph on Ginger's refrigerator, the photograph of the naked man with the white bikini butt and the tan. He shook his head. He'd slept in that man's bed. The closeness of it made him sick.

"He thinks I can be a great actress . . . that I could get into straight stuff. Movies," explained Ginger softly. She leaned back and looked past Rick. "Do what I've always wanted to do."

"That's horseshit. You're his meal ticket. He'll tell you whatever he thinks you want to hear."

"Yeah?" asked Ginger. "And *you* wouldn't?"

"I'll lie to you everyday, if that's what you want. I'm serious, Ginger. *Serious.* Whatever you want. Let's just bail. Together."

Ginger's eyes flickered. When she touched his arm, her fingers were moist.

Rick looked down at the cleft of her breasts, then back into her emerald contact lenses. The green was *too* green. He tried to imagine her brown eyes. He took her wrist and began to run his fingers over the dust of gold hairs on her forearm, his fingers moved to her rib cage. She was sweating. The air fragrant with mentholated body lotion. "C'mon . . ." he whispered. *"C'mon."*

Ginger went calm. There was a clipped wave of her hand as she tried to reach for the doorknob. Rick held her. Twisted her back sharp at him.

His whisper was harsh, very low. *"Fine, Ginger. Go suck on the plastic lemon. Whatever. Who cares? Who's going to fucking care?"*

Ginger looked over her shoulder. The mascara beaded beneath her eyelashes. The hairline web of mascara toward her lips.

Rick brushed his hair back with his hand.

"You." Her dilated pupils measured him up. "You care, Rick." She turned back to the door. "I've got to go."

Rick stumbled, then squared his legs. "I don't think you should."

"I don't care what you think."

"Yeah . . . well, you *should.*"

"I don't though. I really don't, Rick." She opened the door, the music inside dim.

Robinson's voice, "Time's up. Let's go, Ginger."

Rick stared at the wedge of blue light. "Fuck you, *squid*!"

Ginger swung around and threw her fist at the white square of bandage on his jaw. The punch curled him to his knees. Rick couldn't believe it! Nice going, Ginger. Rick trying to stand when a hard kick took him out. Stopped him. Stole his wind. Robinson, black in the porch light. Then the maudlin *thump* that spilled down Rick's throat. Spilled through the blue doorway. The weird silver-orange sky collapsing. A hole of pain swinging from his neck like a head.

Rick rolled onto his hip, grabbing at the side of his face. His jaw! Something soft pushed against his side. He tasted his own tears, his own blood. His face a flag of pain in the wind. Ginger straddled him, tugged at his Levi's.

Rick against the weight of her. Confused. Robinson jamming a thumb into Rick's larynx. Rick's head flickered. Raging against the lack of oxygen. Ginger on his hips, rubbing her pussy, her chilly skin above him. The O-rings jingled. Her face blue from the doorway.

"*Well?*" he heard Robinson gurgle.

"Robby, please . . ." That floating voice. Clacky. Fragile. Urgent.

"Slip it in, you cunt. If you like it so much, slip it in."

The thumb a final punctuation, point of the gun scraping his clenched teeth. Slicing his gums. Blood. A distant tingling sensation in his groin. Balloon of sunlight in his skull.

Male after-shave. Ginger stared toward the distant ridge. Robinson's breath. The gun in Rick's mouth. A terrible swelling in his head. The flutter of air snagged shut. After-shave.

Blood. After-shave. Stale gin. After-shave. Mentholated air. After-shave. Sweat. Coconutty dry ice. Cold dirt.

Rick snapped his mouth free of the gun and bit sharp to the right. He bit hard. Ripped with his teeth. His teeth a message from way back inside where things were dark and fluid. Something brittle as a songbird crunched in his mouth. *An ear. Robinson's ear.* Crunch. Crunch. The back of his eyes went blue. A rustle of wings in his hips.

Weightlessness.

▶ ▶ ▶ 60

Rick remembered Ginger's long cool fingers, remembered their dance on his Levi's. A woodpecker tapping. The mumble of a lawn mower. Then an almost imperceptible *click* and it began to rain.

He crawled up on his knees. Sprinklers. He peered around at the exquisite cyclamens of sequined water.

The sun-god low in the sky. Hot. Shiny. Evil.

He reached up and wiped his mouth. His hand covered with blood. He spit out a stringy string of skin. His mouth trembled from his lacerated gums. There was a scarf of brown blood on his chest. He shaded his eyes. Palm Springs. A duffer with a metal detector strolled the edge of the distant parking lot.

His eyes were crusty and his head thumped above his neck. The skin sort of *tingly.*

Rick stood in the sprinkler rain, looking over at the entrance to the bungalow. The curtains black.

He felt uneasy, hollow when he tried to breathe, his hand at his jaw.

He must have crawled or something. Somehow he got to this hedge of ferns. Had that been Ginger screaming? He remembered something . . . was it *screaming?* But the nice thing was that for some reason he wasn't dead. For some reason he wasn't Campbell's soup and air.

Had Ginger saved him?

Had he saved *her* from the scalping session?

Rick's green boots were covered with dirt. Drops of spit and blood spotted them as he watched.

His shadow bent in front of him on the lawn. He straightened and stared up at the bright sky. Felt the red light dance on his eyelids.

Wait a second . . .

Rick moved his hand toward his eyes and wiped away the crust. It flaked. Blood. Yeah, of course. Then he figured it out. His hands ran up over his smooth, shaved skull.

Those motherfuckers!

He walked over and kicked the door of the bungalow.

No answer. Rick held his head sideways, the corner of his eye crusty from pus and dried blood. His face was an ugly thing. Way ugly. The shaved head didn't help. Fuck . . . the shaved *eyebrows!* He looked at his reflection in the window. Like a big cock with a mouth and a six-day stubble. Like a bruised worm. Like something that had been buried in a hole.

His eyes adjusted slowly to the dark interior.

The room was empty. The boxes marked Eurydice Productions were gone.

Part Four

The Castle of Birds

61 ◄ ◄ ◄

"Last chance!" Rick motioned out the window to the sign that went Hadley's Fruit Orchards. "Date shakes? Banana chips? Almonds? Desert eats for the stout of heart. Shotgun calls," he added. "That's road trip lingo."

Rick was chewing on a cigar. Jules was in the passenger's seat again, riding shotgun. Like a Western. On the stagecoach. Bandits behind every clump of oak trees, an ambush in every canyon. Jules's fever had broken, his pale hair a rooster crown in the speeding Buick. They had wrapped the Bronze Eagle in the coveralls and flight suit and slid it under the front seat. Jules with his bush hat and jungle boots and a pair of Rick's cutoff sweatpants and a Black Flag T-shirt. Jules's eye animate within the frame of the Ray•Bans. Jules knew something had happened back in Palm Springs. Something more than just another fight, as Rick had claimed. The shaved head was a tough one. Even under the Laker cap. Found in the backseat, thank you. Soaked in melted ice cubes. Spattered with red paint. As usual, Jules was talking about birds. Doing the bird gig full-on. Something about various species and their relative strengths: ornamentation, skill. Then launched into this thing about free-ways and providing a more *amenable* habitat. Like something other than ice plant. Something offering perches, cover. Proactive environmental planning policies. Pollutants. Wintering grounds. Rick was rubbing his tongue over the great painful wound that was his mouth. Handgun as toothbrush. Bad news. Very *uncrucial*. Ginger's fragrance all over him. Aerial displays. Courtship feeding. Not even the shower at the Twin Daughters Hideaway had killed her smell. The soft electric hum that stuck to every place her naked skin had rubbed. Damaging freshwater habitats. Acid precipitation. Male preference for colorful females in certain species. Female preference for males with desirable territorial authority. O-rings gently clinking as the oxygen leaked right out of his skull. As her breasts bobbed in the gentle predawn moonlight. The flank of the red Corvette Stingray. As her black panties fell in a shimmering crushed W. The industrial cleanser smell and starlight behind the Vesuvius. Her fingers lost in the white umbrella of light. The black eye of the video camera. Osprey nest poles dropped into coastal marshes. Poison moving up the food chain. Artificial tail extensions involving some birds on a plateau in Kenya. Grassland nesting sites. Mate selection. It never ended. The bird noise.

Rick was wearing his freshly bogarted mirrored cop shades. Cutoff Levi's. A dashiki. His green ropers. The Lynyrd Skynyrd cassette whined away on the dashboard. The monospeaker rig just spitting music against the hot windshield. Rick looked over at Jules and bared his teeth. Made some random coyote howls. It felt good to be cruising back to Los Angeles. Going out a longhair. Coming back a skinhead. Typical road trip noise. Taking the fun back toward the sea. "Man," he said. "I wish we had some drugs. *Real drugs.*"

Jules looked at Rick with apprehension. He was holding the blue-black record album. The white flames going X. The red letters *Los Angeles.* "Drugs?" Jules looked scared.

"Jesus." Rick laughed, shaking his head at Jules. "Same as it ever was, squid."

They were tailing a white Volkswagen Rabbit. The license plate LORIUSC. Three guys in the car.

Rick grinned, pulled the Buick up as close as possible, and stuffed his hand into the heart of the steering wheel. The horn was gold with volume. Rick watched as the driver's eyes glanced up into the rearview.

Rick waved.

The guy in the backseat was wearing a pink tank top. He had big shoulders and a tiny heart-shaped head.

Rick turned to Jules. "Which one d'you think's Lori?"

Jules slouched down in the seat. "I doubt *any* of them happen to be Lori."

"*Oh no?* You mean to tell me they *stole* Lori's car? That's an outrage!" Rick grinned, then hissed, "*Those motherfuckers!*"

Jules looked at the white Volkswagen, then back at Rick. "Maybe she's a friend or a relative. Wouldn't that make sense?"

"Sense," snapped Rick. "These losers *steal* Lori's favorite set of wheels . . . and *you're* talking to me about *sense?* Jules, I'm flabbergasted! That seem's kind of self-centered . . . maybe you should think about Lori for a change. And anyway, if it's not their car . . . then they shouldn't be driving it, right? Hell, I bet Lori doesn't even *know!*"

Jules braced himself against the skeleton of the car door. "We're almost home."

Rick glared at Jules. "*Home?* Now, how does *that* matter? Unless, maybe you just stop caring about people like if it's not convenient. Is that it, squid? Like we're almost *home,* so who cares? Who cares if these squareheads bogarted Lori's car? The car she worked for all through high school, probably selling corn dogs and cotton candy down at the Galleria." Rick worked his hand deeper into the horn. Facing Jules, the wind whipped them as they raced behind the Rabbit. "*Yeeee haaaw . . . yippie-yippie-kiyaaa!*"

Jules nodded sadly.

"Look at these twisted wimps." Rick laughed, hating the white Volkswagen and its occupants. Amazing. This hatred gig. He tried to pull backward into the next lane but a burgundy Mercedes blocked his path, a woman in a tam-o-shanter behind the wheel. A tawny braid looped over her shoulder. She had the smooth skin of a Tibetan monk. Grateful Dead sticker on the rear window. The woman reminded Rick of an older Angela. But sort of in a burnt-out, passive kind of way. A smooth and easy nostalgia rushed through him.

Dissolved.

"Lean back." He steered the Buick close to the sedan. "Lean back, Jules."

Jules stared ahead. "Rick . . . must you always *display?*"

The woman turned, noticed the Buick.

Rick waved, talking to Jules. "Own the *lek*, dude."

The woman smiled, waved back.

Rick sidled up to the Mercedes. *"Out of the fucking lane!"*

The woman cupped her hand against her ear.

Rick started slashing his hand into the air. *"Out! Out of the lane! That's my lane!"*

The woman nodded, then looked back for an opportunity to merge.

Rick grinned at Jules. "Jerry's kids," he explained. "Yuppie hippies." Rick watched the Mercedes. Yeah, he'd like to take them all on a one-way helicopter ride.

He pulled over and accelerated up to the side of the Rabbit. The three faces in the car stared out like bugs from a jar.

"How's Lori?"

The faces watched him.

Rick's hand twitched on the molded steering wheel. Had Robinson loathed him with the same suddenness, the same fierce sense of *right? "How's Lori?"*

The guy with the tiny heart-shaped head tapped the driver and said something. The driver smiled and nodded toward Rick.

Rick smiled back, giving them the peace sign.

He could toy with these losers just the way Robinson had toyed with him. Meanness. He owned more of it. He leaned out the window, his right arm on the wheel. *"She's a dick-sucking machine!"*

The guy's eyebrows twisted down. He leaned back inside and began to gesture at the guy behind the wheel.

Rick steered the Buick so the tires tapped the safety reflectors. *Bap. Bap. Bap.* He moved his fist in front of his mouth and sucked at the air to make his point. *"Deep-throat Fox!"*

The guy with the tiny heart-shaped head pressed up against the window, his face puffed. The guy in the passenger's seat leaned out and gave Rick the finger. The driver bobbed in the black harness of his safety belt.

Rick laughed. It was fun to attack people at random. He could see why drive-by killing had become so popular.

He brought the Buick up to the flank of the Rabbit. He was so close he could've reached and touched the gleaming enamel.

The guy in the passenger's seat stared at Rick, his face rimmed with the angry, irritated puffiness of steroid juice. He was very muscular, very quiet.

Rick guided the Buick with one hand, scrabbling around underneath the seat with the other. "Jules, the bow! Get the bow!" Jules complied, unwrapping the camouflaged weapon. The tires were a drumroll over the safety reflectors. Rick shrugged off his Laker cap and raised the bow like a Hollywood Indian and began to shriek, slamming it against the ceiling of the Buick. It probably wasn't historically correct, but he stuck his tongue out like he had seen these Fijians do on a TV documentary. He made his tongue wiggle like an evil snake.

Steroid Boy and Tiny Head paled like two spots of dough.

Delicately, the Rabbit decelerated, leaving Rick and Jules racing into the fast lane.

Jules shook his head and sat up straight as the Rabbit dissolved behind them.

Rick grinned. "What'd you say we start drinking?"

"I think—" started Jules.

"Of course you do. That's what I love about you. So, that settles it. Drinking it is."

It *was* a road trip. Why be cautious this late in the game? For all they knew, the real fun lay just down the road. Besides, he'd been *faced* by Ginger. Dissed as the homeboys would say, and there was only one thing to do once you'd been dissed. Drive to the hoop and go up strong. Give the crowd your beauty move and wait for the ball to nestle through the net. Then hustle butt back and play some D for a point or two. Knee the dude in the balls if he thought he was going to come back with some monster tomahawk school yard jam . . .

Rick sighed, raw in his stomach from Ginger. The thought that Ginger was *owned* by that loser Robinson. The thought that all Rick got was a gun in his mouth. Yeah, thanks. He had sucked the gun of love.

The Buick unerring. Combustion singing its gorgeous song. Everything cool. 'Cept they could probably use another quart of 30-weight. Maybe some new tires. New windows. Rick winced. Maybe complete bionic reconstruction.

The red needle wilted toward the big white E.

Well, that cinched it. Besides, thought Rick, Redlands was moving up on them fast.

Camouflaged transport planes lifted against the blue sky.

Rick looked over. Jules gazed past him.

"I'd like to learn how to use that hunting bow, would that be possible?"

Rick did a double take.

"I've decided to restructure my priorities a little bit. I think it would be beneficial if I could learn something from . . . well . . . from your *exuberance.* I think I could benefit from adapting."

Rick chuckled. "No doubt, dude. Adapting is *crucial.*"

"I'm a vulnerable person," added Jules. "I need to experience life more. Strengthen myself."

"Shit," answered Rick.

"Tell me what happened back there . . . in Palm Springs. Weren't you visiting a girl?"

"Yeah, but she got tense and she and this guy I didn't know was her husband sort of messed me up."

Raped is the word. Raped. Scalped.

And now here he was with the squid. The Road Squid. But what if Ginger had taken his offer? They could be hightailing it down to Tijuana City. Gone south and done the dog races, drunk Hornitos in clay shot glasses. Got some goofy tattoo. Or maybe the Skylark reupholstered. Something crucial. Definitely got a motel room for a couple long days and nights of R and R. One of those Mex hotel units with a balcony and a shower nozzle that just stuck out of the bathroom wall. No shower curtain, no bathtub. Just one big stall. Nozzle, toilet, sink. And Rick could've sat on the toilet, drunk a Tecate and more Hornitos, and let the water spray all over him like he used to do when he and Jack'd go on their Mexican road trips. Yeah. Ginger on the poplin mattress, naked. Ceiling fan going slowly, slowly, slowly. Shadow blades across the plaster. Spotlights from the helicopters over the plaza.

He'd always liked an excuse to disappear across the border.

'Cept he'd asked and almost got killed for his trouble. Yeah, otherwise it was just like love.

Rick spit out the window, tasting Robinson's ear. Robinson's skin.

Ginger.

He pulled off the freeway and headed for a Union 76 service station.

62 ◄ ◄ ◄

"Well?" He watched Jules bring the mug of beer down from his lips. The jungle hat hung around his neck on its green strap.

Jules smacked. "It's certainly different. How much do I have to drink?"

"Lots." Rick grinned.

"Lots?" repeated Jules. He stared back at the full glass. "Even if I'm not accustomed to it?"

Rick smiled. "Yeah, dude. *Lots.*"

Jules's eyes flashed. "It seems I haven't had a true friend in quite a while."

Rick looked at him. "We've been owning the fun. No doubt about it."

They were sitting in a dark bar in Redlands. Antler racks draped with strands of unlit Christmas bulbs. Hamm's sign quietly transforming on the wall. Turquoise stream of snowmelt twisting past a smoking campfire. Twin snowcapped peaks on the horizon. The image melting into itself. Stream wending its way under the green pine. Hamm's. Hamm's. Hamm's.

Beneath the sign was a jukebox. An ellipsoidal swathe of red, green, and blue.

"You like jukes?" Rick guessed, turning back to face Jules.

Jules had that expression Rick associated with birds and royalty. "They were my favorite part of our family bowling excursions. My father was very fond of country music."

"Uh-huh," said Rick. "Here." He dug into his pockets and withdrew a handful of quarters. Jules walked over to the jukebox, face illuminated from below.

Rick shook his head and took a long draw from his mug.

The bartender wiped aimlessly at the top of the counter. She was wearing a denim shirt that had faded at the elbows, along the ridge of her shoulders. Her hair was pulled back in a silvering ponytail. The rest was the color of walnuts.

There were scarred benches. Sawdust scattered on the floor. Behind him the jukebox engaged and a twangy drawl spread through the room.

Jules sat down.

"Who's this?"

Jules wiped at his eyes. "Is it smoky in here? Something's bothering me . . ."

"You've probably got anemic eyes, squid. Place seems cool." Jules nodded with resignation. "I only recognized the Hank Williams, the Buck Owens, and the Hoyt Axton, Tanya Tucker, Ms. Cline . . . and of course Mr. Cash." Jules looked around the bar conspiratorially. "I was torn between that and the Goodman, the Herman, the Ellington. The big bands."

"*Big bands?*" Rick whispered loudly. *"Big bands suck."*

He drained his beer for emphasis and got up to grab another. He watched as the bartender filled his mug. She never looked at him as she slid the mug and returned to wiping the bar.

Rick went to pull out some loose bills from his pocket and found himself staring at the card that Chuck Venison handed him back in Palm Springs. He read the address, realizing that it had sounded familiar before because the show was filmed in the studio across from his old favorite bar, the Firefly. Yeah, he remembered now. This was that show Jack was always yapping about, *Cupid's Arrow.*

Rick put some bills on the counter and held out the card. "Need a date?"

The cloth spiraled in her hand like draining dishwater.

"Really," added Rick. "All you got a do is call this dude and you're in there."

Her blue eyes watched him.

"Uh-huh . . . well . . . okay." Rick knocked his knuckles on the edge of the bar. "Not in the mood for chatting, are we?"

The woman looked at him.

Rick slipped the card back in his pocket.

"I've got my hands full," she said. "Why don't you use it?"

Rick laughed. "I've got my hands full, too. Besides—" He pointed to his bruised face, lifted the Lakers cap from his shaved, blood-specked skull. "I'm not really TV material."

"You're not getting any prettier, that's for certain."

Rick started to ask her name, but stopped himself. It felt fine to just stand and drink his beer. Felt fine. Felt fine. Felt fine. He could use a break from himself and everything.

Jules was dipping his fingers into his beer and licking them.

Jules saw Rick. He lifted the glass and took a brave gulp, then another. Hank Williams's *Your Cheating Heart.* A clip-clopping base, a fiddle, a twang like breaking glass.

Rick sipped at his beer. Alcohol doing that thing that only alcohol could do. He was exhausted with wonder.

He decided to call Tamara.

The quarters fell into the pay phone like falling rain.

Jack answered.

"Hey," said Rick flatly. "How you been?"

"Tamara's not here. What's the story, Rick? She was worried about you."

"Redlands. Just hanging out in white-trash, no-count Redlands."

"Oh."

"I know what's going on," Rick said. "About you and Tamara."

"Yeah." It sounded to Rick like there might be an apology. Jack was silent. Rick was wrong.

"Last Friday . . . at Tamara's. I saw you, Logan. Outside. Sort of sucking face with my girlfriend. I figured it out."

"Fuck you, Rick. *Ex-girlfriend.* You blew it. That's the story."

"Yeah," said Rick. "Okay, boss. Make the rules."

"Tell me I'm wrong. Tell me I'm out of line."

Rick was silent.

"This is the way it goes, Rick." Jack's voice was edgy, very pumped up. "You don't get *everything.* And you don't get to hurt Tamara. Not at all."

Silence.

"You just blew it," Jack repeated.

Rick stared across the empty bar. The room had that lifting-twisting feeling. It wasn't an earthquake.

"You don't love her," Jack added.

"Anything else?"

"Yeah," said Jack. "I do. I want her, Rick. So think over your next move." Jack paused. "You've fucked up enough. It's stopping right now."

"Thanks for the threat, Jack." Rick watched his wavy face reflect off the metal phone plate. Rick dropped the phone in the cradle and stared at the phone numbers carved in the wood paneling.

He looked at the phone.

Walked back and sat down as Jules finished his second beer, wiped his mouth with a napkin. Hiccupped.

"Pretty macho," said Rick.

Jules nodded. Belched.

"So I don't get it. You lost your home, right? But what about the Castle? Doesn't everyone get bummed when you're not around to throw hawks into the air conditioners?"

Jules pushed his empty glass along the top of the table, watching the trail of moisture.

"Like aren't the birds all lonesome?"

"My family passed away. My mother and father died. She died of lung cancer . . . he began to drink . . . soon after. Died from a broken heart." Jules lifted his glass, lowered it back to the table. "He just forgot everything when she died. He *changed.* Started blaming me. Then fell and hit his head one night."

"And the Castle?"

Jules's voice was tight. "I sold the Castle of Birds."

"Yeah? But that's no biggie, right? I mean the folks probably left it—"

"I *had* to sell it," Jules argued. "I wasn't prepared . . ."

"Want another beer?" Rick suggested.

Jules looked at him strangely. Rick stood up.

"I don't see what the problem is," he said, returning.

"No, you wouldn't."

"Hey, fuck you, too, squid."

Jules stared back.

"Everyone dies," Rick suggested.

"Yes, but *everyone* doesn't decide to sell their parents' life endeavor for thirty pieces of silver. *Everyone* doesn't end up by betraying the final wishes of the people they held most dear in this world . . ."

"Stop it. *Jesus,*" snapped Rick. "So you fucked up and sold the farm. Who cares? Your folks are dead. Worm meat. *You're* the one who's got to deal. Besides, if you sold it . . . then where's the coinage? How come you're roaming around spare-changing for chiliburgers?"

Jules's face in disarray.

"Do we need to blow something up?" Rick teased.

"Yes! That's what we *could* do. Blow them up! Decimate the whole terrible place!" Jules gulped another mouthful.

Rick nodded. "Sure, let's blow something up if it'll make you feel better."

But Jules was lost. He leaned his chin into his palm and looked up, voice miserable. "No . . . we'd only succeed in making martyrs out of them. Only succeed in their inevitable victory."

"Squid? I was just sort of kidding, dude. I'm burnt on mayhem and destruction. At least for this week."

"So you won't help me?"

Rick finished his beer. "I'll help you . . . but you don't want to blow them up anyway. You just said so."

"I don't know what I want to do," Jules admitted. "It's really . . . I just wish I could blame it all on someone else."

"Who are *they* anyway?"

"Casa de Pets."

"What?" asked Rick. "*Casa de Pets?*"

"Exactly. They're one of the new subsidiaries of Pilatech. I assume you've heard of Pilatech? The pharmaceutical company?"

Rick shrugged.

"Of course not," Jules responded with a new sarcasm. "Why would you have? They're *just* the company recently under investigation for illegally attempting to influence a number of federal officials in policy related to biomedical and biotechnical markets. Testing for pharmacological action. Toxicological effects of new drug compounds. They have set some shocking standards."

"Bribery?" interrupted Rick.

"Partially. More precisely, administrative *obfuscation.* Encouraging data manipulation. But it's difficult to trace. They're very diversified. Very discrete. One division was shuffling government funds allocated for *alternative* agriculture research and using these monies to develop certain new surgical instruments. Like a new staple gun of the type that has replaced traditional stitches. The victims, of course, were the hundreds of innocent animals sliced up and stapled. Who knows how many of them lost to much more terminal forms of torture. Injected cancer and the like. I realize we need diagnostic and therapeutic research, but there must be guidelines. Someone must be accountable for decisions. Beyond this, Pilatech was procuring the deregulation of the laws governing such research. You know," Jules added, "there are a number of organizations that are attempting to fight the present state of affairs, the present state of cruelty. There has to be some *humane* approach . . . effective regulation. Corporate responsibility. Animals are not *animal products."*

"Don't these people have anything better to do? I mean, research makes us live, right? Saves lives?"

Jules looked down at his beer. "Like my mother? My father? My sister?"

"Whatever. What the fuck do *I* know about cancer *or* broken hearts? Maybe the next mother, maybe the next father, or sister, you know? But why'd you sell the Castle to Pilate-head? If you hate 'em so much?"

Jules watched the scars on his wrist, traced the scars with his finger. "*Pilatech.* I was lost.

My father left me as executor of his will. His estate was to be divided between myself, my aunt and uncle on my father's side, and my mother's father, who was in a nursing home in Duarte. My aunt and uncle were in no particular hurry, but my grandfather was in his nineties. He needed financial support. It was all so intimidating . . . *so* intimidating that when the lawyer representing Casa de Pets approached me, I accepted. It was only shortly afterward . . . after I saw the disreputable changes . . . the sloppy sanitation . . . it was only *then* that I fully understood my act. More research revealed the connection that Casa de Pets *was* Pilatech. In addition, there is some suspicion that Pilatech has obstructed the development of natural pesticides based on pyrethrum and has been encouraging the development of DDT-based products, dumping what they can't sell inside this country outside in tropical areas with less-stringent policies. The effects in the food sequence are irreparable. *Everywhere.* Shells dissolve. Eagles find liquid eggs in their nests. It's horrible. Our global legacy." Jules stared at Rick. "Well, the money came through . . . cash on the barrel as the Casa de Pets representative said. I couldn't live with it. My share . . . it was blood money. Within weeks their lack of management ethics was obvious. And—"

"Sure," said Rick. "Major betrayal. Sad moment at bird central. But maybe . . . like *people* will benefit? You know, like *us?* Medical advances? More food?"

Jules looked unconvinced. "There are serious business responsibility issues. My father and mother based all of their efforts on that presumption. But I betrayed them, so I signed the money from the sale over to the National Audubon Society. One lump sum."

"And the house? You haven't been able to make the mortgage or something?"

Jules nodded.

"Why? Didn't you have some life insurance coming to you? or *something?*"

Jules nodded again. "Except," he started. "I don't deserve that money . . . since my father and mother . . . and the sale. Well, I've been rather ineffectual. I've chosen to live off my limited savings and I've shied away from the telephone. Everything terrifies me. I guess you could call me a hermit. It's just that the thought of that blood money. Those thirty pieces of silver. I should have immediately fought to get the Castle *back*! But the lawyers and contracts. I can't face it."

"So you just wander around?"

"Not up until last week. But people were coming around the house and I was forced to make myself scarce." Jules chest rose and fell under the Black Flag.

"So like you've just been doing a Howard Hughes gig? Growing your toenails and eating ice cream?"

Jules nodded. "I prefer Squirt."

"First you sold the family business and then you gave away the money and just . . . *hid out*?"

Jules nodded, then swallowed some beer. "Yes. I just *hid out.* I sat in the house and un-plugged the phone. There was a small market that I could walk to . . . but I couldn't face the bank. No, the bank horrifies me. So I just wrote checks on my savings and sat inside . . . I even avoided resisting when they processed out our inventory at the Castle of Birds. I just allowed everything . . . all the residents . . . to meet their fate. Some stayed. Some were sold. Some were shipped to the other divisions as part of their *product line.* Casa de Pets decided to concentrate on *tropical* retail. Parrots. Thanks to me, no longer would the Castle be at the forefront of global avifauna research."

"You took care of your grandfather."

Jules snorted. "Yes, but that doesn't justify it. Even *he* didn't want me to sell. I should have *arranged* for financial support some other way."

"Yeah, but you didn't know that," argued Rick. "You just did what you thought had to be done. So now you think you fucked up, so what?"

"I could even buy fresh bags of birdseed at that little market. Ten-pound bags that I kept in this metal can on the porch of the house . . ." Jules looked off. "It's important that you keep the seed fresh. Mold is bad for—"

"I'm lost. Birdseed?"

Jules nodded and finished his beer.

"Oh," guessed Rick. "You would've had birds at home, right?"

Jules turned the glass upside down and stared at it. "Cockatoos. White—or umbrella—cockatoos to be exact. It was a captive-bred project . . . Father developed the pilot at home." They were beautiful . . ."

"Right."

"I unhinged the cages after my father had gone and they all flew free while I watched the television. I followed the soaps regularly. *Days of Our Lives. General Hospital. The Young and the Restless.* I was an aficionado. My favorite was *General Hospital.* I remember the time Scorpio—"

"Right," interjected Rick. "But for over a year? Hiding in a house with a bunch of birds? I mean, are they at least like parrots? Do they talk?"

"Cockatoos screech. It's rather unnerving if you're not used to it."

"Sounds fun. It must be nice when they shit on everything. Didn't you have any *people* friends?"

"Yes," said Jules softly. "Except they died.

"I was so scared," Jules continued. "Scared and lonely. This has been a difficult period of adjustment."

"I guess," said Rick clinically. "That's sort of what you get for spending your whole life stuck around the same folk."

"I wasn't stuck. I *chose* to stay with them. There's a difference. But I don't think you'd understand that, would you?"

"What? I wouldn't understand *what*? Hiding in apartments? Or working in bird stores?"

"Choosing to stay with someone. Choosing to care."

Rick laughed. "Fine, squid. Make *me* the villain. 'Cept if it wasn't for me you'd still be hitching to Arcadia. And anyway, so what if I just think it's sort of stupid being sensitive and full of love twenty-four and seven, and three sixty-five?"

Jules shook his head. "It's so easy for you. It's so easy that you won't let yourself understand. You accept these things, this place . . ." Jules swept his hand through the air as if to suggest, not only the bar and Redlands, but the whole grand field of neon red, yellow curtains, freeway greenbelts, and cement infrastructure that crawled between the ocean, the desert, the mountains. "You're *too* adapted."

"Yeah?" said Rick. "So?"

"Well, I hate it," spat Jules. Tears crawled around his eyes. "I just simply *hate* it!"

"Then shoot yourself." Rick grinned. "Or hang yourself or move up to Oregon or something."

"I've thought of taking my life. But I wouldn't have the courage."

Rick snorted. "Then stop whining. And give me a break about your family. So you devoted your life to them and they croaked. Big deal. What did you expect? *And* you became a hermit . . . so what? I bet you drank a lot of Squirt and probably had yourself a high old time. Am I right?"

"I did enjoy certain days," Jules started. "Mornings were the most difficult . . . but a few of the afternoons. This one frail January afternoon . . . the light was so serene. The cockatoos were quiet. *Mogambo* was on the television. Yes, Grace Kelly, Clark Gable, *and* Ava Gardner. Rick, they were on a safari—"

"Yeah, whatever. Everyone has to brawl onward, Jules. That's what it's all about. We're all on safari."

Jules dipped his forehead. "I guess."

"Besides, you should give yourself credit for dealing with the whole scene. At least you didn't start wasting people at a McDonald's or something rude like that. At least you *dealt*."

"And what," Jules interrupted, "have you ever *dealt* with?"

"What do you mean? My folks are still living . . . at least the last I heard. Moved back

East. Promotion. Opportunity. Dad took the bait. Bailed on Angel City. Mom followed."

Jules shook his head. "That's not what I was referring to. I was curious as to whether there was a particular situation where you were hurt . . . emotionally." Jules gave Rick the same leading look.

"Like?" asked Rick.

"I don't know," Jules proposed. "What about back in Palm Springs? Something happened with regards to someone you cared about?"

Yeah, thought Rick, sarcastically. *Me.* "I don't care about shit," he explained. "I mean, not like the way you're talking. I *care* about driving and having some road kicks. I care about what's crucial. But other than that. I mean, there's no single *person* . . ."

Jules watched him. Rick looked down at his empty beer mug. Maybe he should slam back another.

No.

"Look, Jules. We're talking about getting *you* better, not me. I'm cool. I mean, yeah . . . obviously I care about some people." He paused, not wanting to get into explaining about Tamara and Jack. Not sure he really could. The whole thing was his fault . . . or, if not *his* fault exactly, then at least not *their* fault. 'Cause there he'd been . . . turning his back to Tamara for a girl so far gone into drugs and whoring . . . well, he probably'd always known he was leading her into a world of hurt. Always known he'd go too far 'cause he *always* went too far. Waiting for a woman to steal him away from himself. Tamara couldn't do it. But so what? Ginger and her husband hadn't broken him. And Jack and Tamara were a good idea. At least, he wasn't going to worry about her. 'Cause that's what had been driving him crazy. Knowing that he'd let her down. Fucked it up.

Rick thought of Ginger. Wondered if he wanted her just 'cause she was out of reach. Wanted her just 'cause she didn't care at all. Wanted her 'cause she was on her way down. Fast.

Jules was carving at the table with his Swiss Army knife. "Did that girl cut your hair off and your eyebrows?"

"Girl?"

Jules nodded.

"Nah . . . I mean, sort of. Yeah. Hey, why don't you go play with the juke again. Here . . ." He slid some quarters over at Jules. "I think this is our last number now, right?"

Both he and Jules listened.

It was "Ring of Fire" by Johnny Cash.

The sad chords trickled away.

"Pick something faster this time. Like we've had enough Skynyrd, but maybe they've got some Molly Hatchet or some Zep or *something*. Some fierce Seventies gig. They ought to have at least one tune on there that's not Charlie Daniels or rebuilt disco shit. Something fast. Unhinged."

Jules looked down at the quarters. "You'd rather be alone?"

Rick glared back.

Jules reached out and patted his shoulder.

Rick knocked the hand away. . . .

Had Jack really been sweating Tamara? Yeah, Rick *knew* Jack had always wanted her. You could smell it. But Jack wouldn't fuck Rick over.

No, Rick was the one off causing trouble. *He* started it. Whatever happened. However. It was his own fault. There were no victims in this gig. And he knew why Ginger punched him. 'Cause he broke the rules. He wanted to be something more than a good fuck. And being a good fuck was just the name of the game. There wasn't any other currency. No credit cards accepted. I mean, who was he kidding? Expecting her to disappear into his Mexican dream? What a joke. And why? Just 'cause the air was fuzzy around her? Just 'cause of that? Shit, he *really* was no different than Jules with his bird castle and his princess hunger. 'Cept *now*

Jules wanted a hunting bow. Jules was ready to get it in *gear*. Rick wasn't so sure about himself. *Too adapted?* Jules said Rick was too adapted. Sure, he'd acted tough at that Eurydice pad. Been cool with a gun pointed at his balls. Tough, drunk, and *lucky*. But if Ginger hadn't been there . . . who knows what would have been cut off. He motioned to Jules. "C'mon, squid. Let's get out of this one-horse town. Get back to Burbank. Homesville."

"But we haven't heard the next songs," Jules argued, his face flushed from alcohol. "Our quarters? The jukebox?"

"Forget 'em. Tunes are cheap. Drink up. Let's bail."

Jules folded his knife, tilted back his glass, and gulped. "Look." He pointed to the table.

J + G

"Grace," explained Jules.

Rick laughed. "You got princess on the brain, squid. When we get back home, you'll have to hang with me . . . you know, we'll figure out your hermit scene. Who knows, maybe we'll even get you laid."

"I couldn't allow any hospitality on your part . . . that is, my affairs are my own and I should straighten them out myself . . ."

"Whatever," said Rick, a little relieved.

Jules watched him as they walked to the door, waiting for Rick to insist.

Rick waved to the bartender. She smiled and shook her bar cloth. How long had they been sitting in there? He was buzzed. But shit, it'd been a fierce week. A *major* road trip. And here he was, riding high on another Wednesday. Rick shaded his eyes, looking off to where a belt of smog lay strapped across the jagged San Bernardino Mountains.

His eyes stung.

"Can I drive?" Jules asked as they walked to the Buick.

"*Huh?* You? I thought you didn't?"

"I haven't," admitted Jules. "But it seems simple. I step on that pedal and turn the wheel? Besides, I wouldn't mind trying if you will direct me." Jules looked at him.

"Step on the pedal and turn the wheel. Yeah, that about covers it. Maybe hit a blinker now and then. Shit. Why the fuck not?" Rick made a grandiose flick of his hand. "Can we see the Castle from the freeway?"

Jules shook his head.

"Well, what do you say we go check it out. Maybe park in front and hassle the customers?" Rick looked at Jules with his one good bloodshot eye.

Jules laughed, reached up, and covered his mouth. He really had an ugly face. His teeth still shiny. His mouth like some new kind of wet genital.

They exchanged places.

Rick fit himself in behind the frayed bungee cord, windshield a paisley of dirt and bug drippings. "Try the wipers," Rick suggested, pointing to the knob.

Jules pulled it and they both watched as the wipers smeared their way across the glass. The pale sky turned ashen, mustard. "Great," said Rick. "I'm a genius."

"What now?" asked Jules.

"Pull on that thing there that says Brake. Now here, move this gearshift . . . like this to get it into Reverse."

Rick continued to explain the basics. They both watched, holding their breath as the Buick yawned back, parting from the twin white parking lines.

Rick shifted into Drive for Jules and the car lurched forward. Jules tried to compensate and the car swerved.

"Isn't this killer?" asked Rick, laughing.

Jules concentrated, his face serene from the effort.

"Shit, you just needed to learn to drive, squid! You can't live in the City of Angels and never get behind the wheel! You're a cowboy now, dude!" Rick slapped him on the shoulder. "We need to smoke a cigar." He grabbed the tape player. He punched Play. More twangy Southern white-trash Seventies guitar noise. "Man, like *faster . . . faster . . . faster!*" He fumbled around in the glove compartment for a cigar. Found the box. Lit them both a Tiparillo. He looked up as Jules headed straight for the entrance of a glass building. Straight for the pink neon Gail's Nail Saloon. Rick grabbed the wheel, directed Jules around the parking lot in big circles and then out and down the boulevard, the Buick weaving. "We'll be at the Castle in no time, Jules. We'll storm the ramparts! We'll get ourselves a mess of arrows and get you a crossbow. It'll be *shitstorm* time!" Rick whooped, enchanted by the concentration on Jules's face. Enchanted at the thought of laying siege to a refurbished supermarket bird castle in Arcadia.

They went up the on ramp and merged into the westbound traffic, Jules's foot steady on the pedal.

Squares of sunlight revolved across Jules's unshaven cheek, his forehead flashed.

Rick yelled above the roar of the wind. "*Keep an eye out for the cops. Johnny Law, dude. Johnny Law is not our friend.*" Man, definitely stay *away* from the cops . . .

Jules looked over and winked clumsily through the frame of his Ray•Bans.

Road squid, thought Rick. Clueless bird saint. But Rick felt okay. Trashed-out tired. His mouth a bruised cunt. Riding that just-raped-at-gunpoint rush. That just-scalped buzz.

Something black, worn-out, private sitting high up in that tree.

Jules clung to the slow lane. There was a white line twitch to the lone eye that snapped in the broken Ray•Ban lens. Taking in the environment. It flickered at the fast river of metal that flew past them on the left. Jules looked at Rick and showed his wet, shiny teeth. His face had a lit-up warmth. His voice took on a burned-out tone. "*Whatever,*" he drawled like he was staring up from the bottom of a coma. "It's a road trip, *dude.*"

Rick peered over the top of his cop shades.

Jules explained, "Just a natural capacity for *acquiring* language. Much like . . ." He suddenly lost his grip on the wheel and the Buick waggled. "Oops!" Jules laughed a big laugh. "This is a real test of learned behavior." He shook his head. Then looked over his left shoulder. "Let's go *faster*."

Rick checked the oncoming. "Okay, squid. It's your lane. Jump on it."

The Black Flag T-shirt flapped as Jules's smooth hands turned the molded steering wheel, decelerating when his foot loosened on the gas pedal. The Buick Skylark hung for a moment between lanes. Jules stepped down hard and the V-8 tossed them headlong into the next lane. They came up quick on the back of a Chevrolet Impala. Rick reached over and tugged at the wheel. They bamped into the fast lane.

"Faster," said Jules, talking to himself. "Faster." The air tore around inside the Buick Skylark. The ceiling upholstery flapped. The door rattled. Bits of safety glass jingled their way down into the window slots. The rim of Jules's bush hat rippled. Rick closed his eyes and let it all rush all over him. All of it. Fast and fucked-up in this big trashed motel room of a vehicle. The tape player spitting and jambling on the dashboard. Piano noise. Guitar noise. Drum noise. All jangly and goofy and Seventies. The sun right up there at the top of everything, making it white and bitchen. Making it hot. This freeway. This *fucking* freeway. Rick wanted to sing. Rick wanted to fly. And this bird will never change. Oh no. Will never change.

Rick handled the air guitar. Jules handled the steering wheel. Lord, I can't change. Won't you fly high, free bird. The fast lane. All that dry hot air in your face. That bench seat, desert-gold American-car leather-vinyl whatever-the-fuck-it-was smell. That wicked guitar stuff all over your skin, inside your head. Jules's eye staring straight down the highway. Fly high. Free bird. Yeah!

The Buick Skylark rolled slowly up the suburban cement. Jules bumped them to the sidewalk and looked over at a little stone pathway, a Craftsman house. The yard unkempt. Leaves spilled over a dry flower bed of tiny black stalks. The ivy was a paisley of green and brown. Metal sprinkler heads poked out of the dirt at the border of a lawn of crabgrass. The house was a deep ivory. The window frames alabaster. Shaded by willow. Elderberry. The effect of something fragrant and hidden. The door was bolted with an industrial plate device. An objective municipal decision had been made during Jules's absence. Warning signs strip-peeled and pasted on the door. The windows had metal bar braces bolted with L-clips into the frames from the outside.

"Home?" asked Rick.

Jules watched everything in front of him. The curtains were drawn. Nothing moved. He got out of the Buick. His hands at his sides. "Let's go," said Jules.

"Where?" Rick was tired. It'd been fierce. It'd been fun. But there was this thing called rest. He could feel it out there like some annexed, residential community. And now they were just homeless. Living in a Buick.

Running low on cash.

"The Castle of Birds," said Jules. "I want to show it to you."

The batteries were winding down. Ronnie Van Zant's voice crawled through "That Smell." Rick punched Off. "Careful," he said as Jules steered past a strip of cosmetic landscaping and into the large parking lot of a planned multiple-store retail plaza. A U-section of linked buildings. Each outlet had the same large valentine-red backlit signs. What did you need? Pharmacy? Liquor? Sporting? Flowers? Hardware? Spanish-Moorish influence. Red-tile ledges and mock iron-railed balconies. Cute trees. A waterfall fountain spilled over an ornamental brick wall.

Younger dudes in Stussy hats and baggy shorts worked around on their boards. The rear-truck whine drifted as Jules killed the engine. A shirtless kid in a knit cap skidded down a handrail as another styled nose grinds on a concrete meridian planter. A white kid with dreadlocks in a Ministry T-shirt scraped through a fakie wallride. Water gurgled. The kid in the Ministry T-shirt ollied up onto the meridian planter, then fell back, clapping his hands.

Jules pointed to the far end of the U. Twin red-tiled turrets glowed above a blockish building with huge plate glass supermarket windows. The sign was in florid red script. THE CASTLE OF BIRDS. The sky above the building was empty.

"Let's dump the evidence," said Rick. They got out of the Buick as he rewrapped the bow. "This ride is way too obvious. And the cops are *unhinged*. Nothing better to do but eat donuts and hassle good citizens like us."

Jules was walking slowly toward the entrance.

Rick followed him.

The plate glass was pasted with white butcher's paper. CHEEP! CHEEP! PARROTS! EXOTIC BIRDS! TAKE ONE HOME! HUMMINGBIRD FEEDERS! SALE! SALE!

"Doesn't look so heinous." Rick followed Jules inside.

The air conditioner was supermarket cold. A few parents milled around with their children staring into the glass cages. There was a strange quiet. Rick looked up the walls at stacks of glassed cubicles filled with a gazillion birds. The cubicles were long and filled with various fauna. Most of it dry and dead. Metal walkways went up in tiers toward the ceiling. So many cages. So many birds. But they almost all looked like parrots. Brilliant color everywhere. Rick noticed a habitat cage with an empty cement pool and skeleton perches. In some of the cubicles, darkly feathered birds stared out at him. He recognized some sort of buzzard. A big fucking buzzard. Another intense bird nested in a large cage. It looked like a hawk. A sign went VISITOR, ON LOAN TO THE PILATECH CORPORATION. The floor space was segmented into areas demarcated by color. Yellow arrows moved along the floor with instructions. *Feeding.*

Reference. Residents—Domestic. Residents—Nondomestic. There was even an arrow that said *Children's Aviary.* This arrow led toward the back, where Rick saw a large green net that led from the ceiling down to a green wire-screened area filled with dead plants. There was no movement. A temporary stand-up sign said PARDON OUR APPEARANCE. A plastic plate glassed in by the front register served as an arrow directory. A floor plan guide. Each arrow led to a different area of colored floor. Primary colors were then subdivided. Blue floor meant *Domestic.* There was a lighter shade of blue within this section. The arrow said *Passerine.* The red floor meant *Nondomestic.* An arrow leading into a pink section said *Passerine.*

Passerine? Rick was going to ask, but Jules was ahead of him.

And everything looked like parrots.

Rick stood in his cutoff Levi's and dashiki and stared up at the glass cubicles leading up to the high ceiling. His finger trailed the crowded aisles. *Golden-capped conure. Indonesian Palm Cockatoos. Australian Crimson Rosella.* Bags of seed were piled around randomly. *Mexican red-headed amazon. Lesser sulfur-crested cockatoo. Fischer's lovebird.* There was much bird-type merchandise. *Chattering lory. Goffin's cockatoo. Red-vented cockatoo. Gray-checked parakeet.* He was being watched by a gazillion eyes.

Jules stood at the register. "Who's in charge?" He stared at the girl behind the register. She had on an apron that went Casa de Pets Welcomes You. Her name tag went Hi, My Name Is Tiffany.

"Sir? Can I help you? It's tropical bird month."

"No, it's not," said Jules. "And I'm *sure* these are not all sustainably harvested birds. Now who's in charge?"

Tiffany moved professionally to the microphone. A man in a white shirt and floral tie walked up.

Before the man could speak, Jules held up a backyard feeder. The box said Nectar

Delight. Hummingbirds hovered on the box design and nursed on pink water. "I would like to purchase this."

The man was confused. He looked at Tiffany. "Could you help the gentleman?"

"He wants you." Tiffany shrugged and looked at Jules.

Jules looked at the man in the white shirt and floral tie.

The man took the box and stepped to the register. "Always ready to help a customer. Casa de Pets cares about you."

Jules watched as the man handed back the bagged box of Nectar Delight. Jules took the bag. "There's nothing worse than doing the wrong thing well. To paraphrase Drucker."

The man in the white shirt and floral tie looked at Jules, bag in hand. The Black Flag T-shirt. The cutoff sweatpants. The broken sunglasses. The lone pale blue eye that glared out.

"Who?"

Rick watched this strange tableau.

"Peter Drucker." Jules held up the bag. "My father was familiar with some of his arguments. As with W. Edwards Deming and his work in Total Quality Management. Drucker is concerned with rethinking business *practices*. Rethinking our direction."

The man was lost.

"See." Jules dumped the Nectar Delight box out onto the counter. "Within a couple of days this sugar water will probably ferment. Hummingbirds will drink it and it will lead to enlarged livers. This will cause serious health problems. Did you think to *warn* me?"

The man looked at Tiffany. Tiffany looked at the man. The man looked at Rick. Rick gave them a flat sunglassed stare.

"If it's dangerous, it probably says so on the box. I just sell it." The man looked comfortable with this defense. "In the *instructions*. Why don't you look and see?"

"You are selling me a product that is potentially *faulty*. And you are doing it politely and efficiently, however you are not doing the *right* thing. Not acting accountable. I could *kill* the birds. And"—Jules pointed over to some bags of seed—"would you have warned me that damp seed can lead to poisonous mold? Or that irregular feeding can disrupt habitual breeding patterns?"

"I'm going to have to ask you to leave." The man looked at Tiffany and nodded. "Unless there's something we can *help* you with."

"*Leave?*" Jules moved up close to the man in the white shirt and floral tie. "This *store* was my life! And *you've* destroyed it!" Jules spun, waving his hands at the glass cubicles. "*Who* is your supplier? These guests are *illegals.* I'm sure of it. How many others had to die in transport? What price must our fragile ecosystem pay for your *profit?*"

The man turned around and reached behind the counter.

"*Watch it,*" whispered Rick to Jules.

Jules stared Rick hard in the eyes. Then grabbed the wrapped hunting bow from Rick and unfurled it.

"Oh shit." Rick stepped back.

Tiffany screamed. The man the white shirt and floral tie whipped around. Jules had an arrow in and was gritting back the bowstring.

"Oh fuck," said Rick. The squid has lost it.

"Okay, sir." Jules's voice was soft. "I want that red-tailed hawk. The one over there in the flight cage. Next to those yellow-headed amazons. Have Tiffany fit him with a hood. Crop him up with some dead mice. Then bring him over here. *Now!*"

The man laughed a nervous laugh. "That hawk? What do you want with that bird?" The arrow pointed straight at his chest.

"I don't know *how* to do that." Tiffany looked at Jules. She was terrified. "I just do *this.*" She pointed at the register.

Jules stared at Tiffany from behind the bow. "I would take *that* up with the management tomorrow." Jules stepped back toward Rick. "I'm handing you the bow. If he moves, kill him."

"What the *fuck?* Jules! No . . ." And suddenly Jules was jabbing and they were kind of both waltzing with the bow and then Rick had it and the man in the white shirt and floral tie was sort of just shaking and Tiffany was holding her hands up squeezing the air and Jules was off moving around and people were watching them and Rick yelled, "Don't anyone try to *leave* this *fucking* store. Or no one gets out alive! We're taking the *hawk!* Anyone who tries to stop us is *history!*" Rick thought, *Jesus.* Then he heard Jules's voice soft again, behind him. "Back up, Rick. Back up, slowly." Rick moved backward. People were looking at him strangely. A gazillion bird eyes blinked. Three steps four steps, five steps, six steps, a whole bunch of steps and they were standing on the rubber mat for the automatic door. Then Rick felt hot air and heard Jules snap, "Run!" And they were moving across the parking lot. That's when Rick saw the big fat hawk. Hooded. Jules sort of trying to run and walk at the same time. A glove with a leash and swivel on his left hand. "Give me the keys!" yelled Rick. "The keys!"

The naked legs went all smoothly up from the metallic gold pumps. The woman was wearing a gold pair of hot pants which she peeled as she gyrated. "Sweet Child O' Mine" blasting from back where the topless barmaids walked out, trays filled with drinks. The stripper pulled the hot pants up at the sides like a bikini. She swung her head around and let her blonde hair whip in the pink light. Then stretched down, squatted, and pretended to caress herself. She was beautiful and Rick thought of nothing but the darker trail of faint soft hair that traced down from her belly button. He was so glad she hadn't shaved it. Behind them someone whooped. Rick handed Jules a dollar bill. "Here. We're about rock-bottom, squid. Live it up." Jules looked at Rick. Rick said, "Take the dollar and hand it to the girl, squid. That's how it works. You know, *capitalism.*"

Jules drank a hearty gulp from his glass of beer and then stood. A mirror-fragment disco ceiling ball splattered white speckles across the stage. The woman's skin was pink. The stripper gave him a smile and arched her back. Her hands trailed down her stomach and over the rolled gold fabric. Jules handed over the dollar quickly and sat down. The stripper turned, and bent, looking at Jules through her legs. Her fingers crawled out between her legs and fluttered in a wave.

Jules blushed and lowered his eyes.

Then they had finished their drinks. Rick stared into his wallet. He needed to know what to do. He had basically *no* cash and they had a stolen hawk sitting in the backseat of his incredibly identifiable car that had just been used during one week to escape from two very bizarre crimes. The stripper shimmered. She pouted and wiggled her hips in ecstatic spasms. She plumped up her breasts with her hands and leaned down, eyeing Jules.

Later, they were listening to Led Zeppelin's "Going to California" and Rick was staring at a glass of melted ice and cheap tequila. Jules was still next to him. Except now the stripper had her hand on Jules's leg. Her name was April. She was a graduate student in earth sciences at a local university. Divorced with a kid, she said. She and Jules were in an animated discussion about fault lines, the Richter Scale, and the potential for The Big One. Rick listened. Some other stripper was up on the stage doing a veil dance. Two big-screen TVs had on a Laker game. The Lakers up. Finishing off some squid team. The Omaha Cougars, something like that. Some nowhereville expansion team, still looking for a good draw in the lottery. Rick watched as A. C. Green jammed at the end of a fast break. Magic dished off another nice no-look pass. Then muscled through the middle and dropped in a little reverse, drawing the foul. Three points. Rick sipped his tequila. *Magic.* Then April was buying *them* a drink. And then two more. Rick stared at his bottomless glass of tequila. He did not want get busted for this thing at the Castle of Birds. He looked over at Jules. The broken Ray•Bans folded over the neckline of the Black Flag T-shirt. Rick *did* have to give the squid credit. He was *adapting.*

Adapting fierce. Major adaptage. He was an adapting machine . . .

Jules leaned over. "April is nice. Isn't she?"

Rick nodded, "Kind of Grace Kelly like."

Jules smiled.

April leaned in. "Hey, you guys want to come over for a swim?" She ran her fingers along the back of Jules's neck. "I stay at this condo place with a pool and everything. Like a hot tub. And I'm out of here in an hour. I'll let you see my real life." At this, she looked at Jules.

Jules turned expectantly to Rick.

Rick to April. "Do you have a garage?"

"A garage? Yeah, but there're no *extra* spaces. I mean, you know, they're numbered. Can't you just park on the street?"

"We're heading back *East*," said Rick. "Northeast."

Jules looked at him.

"But," continued Rick, "give the dude your number and he'll call you later. In a couple of days. It's just, you know, we're in a big hurry to get back *home.* Get back to *Vegas.*"

"You're from Vegas?" She looked at Jules. "I thought you said your family used to own the Castle of Birds?"

Jules looked at Rick. "We did," he said proudly. "My name is Jules Langdon."

Rick sighed. Fine. Give the wayhone our *names.* Welcome to County Jail.

It was that time when the sun's red got purple. Then bled back to black. The Buick Skylark in the oily shadows at the rear of the parking lot behind the strip bar. Jules and April and Rick stood looking in at the hooded hawk, regal and violent. Mute on the backseat. What was left of Rick's clothes were up in the front, along with the plastic Twister sheet.

April placed her fingers on Jules's arm. "Beautiful, isn't it?"

Jules nodded.

Rick had to admit it was pretty damn cool. This *raptor* gig. The fierceness. The talons. The beak. The bird just sitting there like *fuck you*. Rick could imagine the bird just thinking *fuck all of you.*

April was wearing Wrangler jeans and a white cotton T-shirt and an unzipped purple-pile vest. She looked very comfortable. She had on a yellow digital sports watch. Work boots, laced half-way. "I used to love to go to the Castle of Birds when I was younger." She smiled at Jules. "The aviary was my favorite place. I took my little girl there though, the other day, and it was shut down. They said they didn't know if they were going to open it. The aviary, I mean . . ."

Jules nodded. "I sold it to the wrong people." Jules looked at April. "It's my fault it's not the way it used to be."

April said nothing.

They watched the hawk.

April said, "You can always start *another* Castle of Birds. You sold *that* castle. You didn't sell your knowledge, your skill."

Jules nodded. He looked at April and said, "We have to head out. We're *wanted men.*"

April gave Jules a soft kiss. "Thanks for the dollar." She handed him a slip of paper. Phone number?

Rick shook her hand.

They watched her walk away, Rick smoothing his hand over his shaved head. "Better ass than Grace Kelly. Not bad for someone kind of real and three-dimensional."

Jules turned, fit on the glove, leash, the jesses that fit to the almeris around the hawk's legs. Brought the hawk out of the Buick. Rick stepped back and watched as Jules unlaced the hood and held the hawk up, pointing it toward the sky. Removed the hood, the almaris. "The cage was large enough . . . I don't think the muscles will have degenerated."

Jules lifted his arm and uttered a sharp command. The hawk lifted up. Rick was stunned at the way it shot up and dissolved in the bloody black sky above the roof of the strip bar. Into the colors of sunset. Rick strained to follow the hawk's sharp flight.

Jules turned his face from the sky. "Let's go, Rick. I'll drive." He gazed off.

The booze was hitting Rick hard. Yeah, living on tequila. And *no one* could do *that* forever. Not without a little holiday in the city of sleep. But the squid was on a roll . . . let *him* handle the wheel. Yeah, and Rick could think.

Sure. Cool. Think.

Crucial.

Jules behind the wheel, Rick shotgun. What should they do? Bail to the freeway? Or sneak through the spooky back streets? Dragged from stop sign to stop sign? Fuck no. Maybe up into the mountains and then loop around somehow? Race up into Burbank through the back door? No, cops everywhere and we'd just plummet off a cliff, anyway. Maybe find a garage and park? *Oh no sir,* we're not *that* paint-spattered Buick Skylark GS, Officer, sir. Shit. Rick was up the creek. And kind of lit. Wrecked. The sky in flames. The back streets fucked. Too many cops out cruising around and looking into windows. The mountains fucked. One long road. Cops everywhere. Flashing their flashlights in parked cars. Looking for mutilated corpses. No, the freeway was the best gig 'cause you could maybe lose yourself in the traffic. Maybe see the cops coming and exit. I don't know. Confusion Central. And the Road Squid at the wheel? And now I've got to find a place to hang and the squid is cool, but whatever. Where do we go? Just get to Burbank and dump this ride. Scam some food. Maybe do that *crucial* sleep gig. Full-on. Yeah, something will click. Just got to close my eyes and stop for a second. I mean, no work, no clothes, no money, no apartment. Kind of really homeless. Out here alone . . . a Kwai Chang Caine gig. Nothing but half a tank of gas and a hunting bow. Except maybe for Tamara and Jack. The thing with Tamara and Jack is cool. Everything's cool. Even the *squid* is cool. Way cool. The squid is an *adapting* warrior. The Road Warrior. The *fucking* Road Warrior. No, we're going to make it. No one's alone. Not in this city. Angel City. The City of Angels. Just a cowboy heading home. Our hero. Riding shotgun. Driving under the big Los Angeles sky.

○○

The road trip ending when the car suddenly curtsied, metal wailing as Jules must have swung hard to the left, away from the skid in his ignorance. Blowout. The big back end of the Buick Skylark swooping around. Because later, after the Highway Patrol found the compound bow, Rick tried to supply the missing pieces. Tried, but all he could remember was the traffic headlights flashing on Jules's forehead; Buick lifting, coming down into a hard glide that ended in the flapping of torches; EMTs cutting through the wedge of car body with the jaws of life. Someone talking to him. *Remain calm.* The flutter of yellow barricade tape. Rick not wanting to die with a whine. Network of rope lifting him; swaying in a hammock of black rope. Silver spilling from his lips. Silver all over him. Wet silver. Blue torch-flame slapping against metal. Blue, black, silver. Then the EMT injected him with something. And it was much later and they asked him if he could move his toes and he remembered he could. Feeling delicious with warmth, a satellite slipping steadily across the night sky. A single moving star. Except he smelled tar, smelled something sour and used-up. The paramedic asking him questions about the tire, irritating baby talk that didn't really make sense. But fuck that, he dreamed. Fuck them all. He didn't need to answer any of their stupid questions. Not yet. Who cared about tires and what they did? He was a hawk alone in the sky. Asleep. Everything was thin and blue and cold. Just him, afloat. No one could tell him what to do. He could think about anything. Whatever. Think about Tamara. Think about Jack. Think about Ginger. But *not* about Jules. No, 'cause he'd seen the Twister sheet. Seen what it'd blown up against. Yeah, his gurney was rolling right past the Twister sheet and the plastic body bag. The long white body bag zipper smeared with red handprints. The garbage of Jules's death.

And Rick knew what was left after the choice was gone.

He kept thinking of Tamara. Of Jack. Of Ginger. Ginger. Corvette window lowering before her closed eyes, wind rustling her bleached hair. Ginger. Almost as if she were sleeping. Her robe falling in the porch light. Her black corset. Her smooth body. Her emerald, emerald eyes. Ginger. The motel spilling with lilacs. And he comforted himself with the idea of finding her. The idea that finding her would somehow matter. If only to talk for a moment. Two shadows under the sun. Yeah, two shadows under the dangerous sun. In this Western movie.

Acknowledgments

BobXLizforthechance&Janet&Nani,Mygrandmothers:Connie&inmemoryof
Margaret.TheSamoan&thedudes&wayhoneatWilliamMorrow,notscaredto
crankitup.Betsy.Campbell.ReadCapitalism.ReadAmericanNoise.HelloChitown&
Longpig.MikeLforthecomix.HowardG,Jill/MikeD,CathyB,Kim(Richard/baby
Max)&everyoneatBIGWEDNESDAYwhospunthewheelwithJenniferBlowdryer.
LikeHolman&NuyoricanPoet'sCafedowninAlphabetCity.Also,thankstoMAD/
Phil,DonSchneider&allofExecutivePrograms&thefolkatArden.Lars/Lisaforthepoetry
blasts&RonforPrague.InmemoryofMac.thankstoVoytek,TheVoyagers,TheAustinCravens,JerryH.
Lowlifeforever.Interstate5at120mph,Pete.Beatonthebratwith
abaseballbat,WHAT . . . IS . . . THE . . . DECIBEL . . . LEVEL/DoreforClubPenn
&buyingthatusedtypewriterintheVirginIslandswhenIwasbroke.Yeah,
Ginny,Reed/Maureen/Bronwyn,Stoever/Kris/Caroline,Marc,Matt/Mary
&babydudes.ToMimi&Lil'JoeDurham.(T.A.forthebracelet.)GregM:Rocky
RoadskateboardbumperpoolPing-PongCactusCoolermotorcycleTijuana
swimmingpoolwristrocketBobMarleyhistory&Kris/babySummer.&thanks
totheone&onlyJulieV:inkpalroseprincesswayhone.BobVessellsat
Shamrock.Lizzie&babySamWhitmanMcGrath.Thecoolnoise,words&shade
thatgotitstarted:X,GunClub,TheHüskers,Motörhead,R.H.C.P.,P.E.,HankR.,HankW.,TheFleshEatersfor
thefreshtuneage&oldvinyl.Bukowski.DenisJohnson,TheFirefly.TheRed
Room,TheNightCafe,TheFrolic.IvanforVegas&DerStuca.Debbieforthewhiskey.
CandyB1.JessicaatBilly'sTopless.MarvelComicsdudes.Hey,Nicole/
Jacob.Thanks:doctors&accountantsofstresslikeYaffe,Ruben,Friedman.Janet
LithicumbatRaptorCentral.Extravisualthanks:Robertwilliams.Extra
visualnoise:HouseofDreams.Crucialwordnoise:TheBirder'sHandbook,
RobertStoller,LindaWilliams.AlltheblissthatevercrankedcauseofSantaCruz:
KAOS,L.E.S.3,PedroQueso,RickyZ,Ouzel,VanNessHouse,TheDelusions,
McMillanStreet,Al&Philforthemicrowaveburritos&liar'sdice.(ForAnnieGintheMexicansun)
WiththankstoN.Mackey,J.Schaar,G.Amis,L.Clifton&College5.ThewayhoneatKingfisher.Howdy
&waytoDianeV,KieraCoffee,Amina,KiethBeatandallslanggods.Kaboom!Graffiti.Themosaic:
McKinley,G.Xmas,Maurice(fortheP),JunnoDean,Timoneyfor4.40&theMermaidFestival,ConeyIsland.
Christina&VW.AttheSchooloftheArts:Quincy,DanH,Lini,At666:JohnE,Rich,Andy&allwhodrank
OldeEnglishintheNothing'sShockinghaze.ToTom&Annie,forphoto&MaltaAussiefullonroadkicks.And
SvenjafortheExenecassette&600days:Hardcore,tequilaonice,paintingmyroom.Loud,loudmerengue.
SueD:AngelesCrest&comixcritique.KimBfortheredsun.MikeG(hairdown).Cleo,Cleo,Cleo.Rockin'good
news.O,what'sthatringaroundyourhotwaxangel?Earlyvinylbliss:SST,Tentacle,Slash,Metal
Blade.Toroadtrips.ToMelissafortheHotelManzanillo&Hornitos&toothbrushes
&HenryMiller&thetastydays&sexyhellpast(&Maury&Watsonville).AgaintoDave
&Paul&Mark.ToPhaedra.ToGingerLynnAllen(whosnotGingerQuail).Toevery
onewhomadethissofaburn!Goodluck,angels.Allofus.
And like, tojustgoingFAST!